THE OLD WOLVES

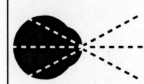

A RUSTY SPURR NOVEL

The Old Wolves

Peter Brandvold

WHEELER PUBLISHING
A part of Gale, Cengage Learning

GALE
CENGAGE Learning·

Farmington Hills, Mich • San Francisco • New York • Waterville, Maine
Meriden, Conn • Mason, Ohio • Chicago

GALE
CENGAGE Learning

Wheeler Publishing Large Print Cozy Mystery.
The text of this Large Print edition is unabridged.
Other aspects of the book may vary from the original edition.
Set in 16 pt. Plantin.

LIBRARY OF CONGRESS CATALOGING-IN-PUBLICATION DATA

Brandvold, Peter.
   The old wolves : a Rusty Spurr novel / by Peter Brandvold. — Large print edition.
      pages ; cm. — (Wheeler Publishing large print western)
   ISBN 978-1-4104-6508-5 (softcover) — ISBN 1-4104-6508-X (softcover)
   1. Prisoners—Fiction. 2. United States marshals—Fiction. 3. Large type books. I. Title.
PS3552.R3236O44 2014
813'.54—dc23   2014010697

Published in 2014 by arrangement with The Berkley Publishing Group, a member of Penguin Group (USA) LLC, a Penguin Random House Company

Printed in the United States of America
   1 2 3 4 5   18 17 16 15 14

For my old wolves,
Stella and Thor

ONE

Spurr was old. He'd give his detractors that much. And his ticker was chugging to a slow stop. It would soon leave him in a cold grave, bedding down with angleworms and diamondbacks.

He'd give them that much, too.

But by god, his eyes and his ears were as keen as ever.

So was his sniffer. And if that wasn't man sweat he'd just sniffed on the wet wind blowing at him just now in this Indian Nations hollow, on a cold, damp, early autumn night, then by god, he'd toss in his badge like his boss, Chief Marshal Henry Brackett, was urging him to do, and he'd retire to his drafty two-room cabin on the slopes of Mount Rosalie.

(He could not, would not call that grand peak west of Denver, the crown jewel of the northern Front Range of the Rocky Mountains, Mount Evans. No, sir. He'd first

7

known it as Mount Rosalie when he'd come west several years before the Little Misunderstanding Between the States, and that's how he'd know it until he stopped knowing *anything* — the politicians be damned!)

He reined his big roan, Cochise, to a sudden halt along the soggy trail he'd been following in the outlaw-infested Nations. The sour-smelling sweat — the stench of a man who'd been drinking liberally and hadn't bathed in a month of Sundays — drifted past his nose once more. A light flashed in the tangle of woods off the trail's right side. A quarter second later, a bullet buzzed past Spurr's right ear and pinged ominously off the shale embankment behind and to his left.

As the rifle's flat, menacing crack reached Spurr's ears, the old marshal yelled angrily and leapt down off of Cochise's back, ramming the butt of his rifle against the horse's hindquarters, sending him buck-kicking on up the night-dark trail and out of another possible bullet's path.

Spurr crouched in the middle of the rutted, weedy two-track, pumping a fresh cartridge into the rifle's breech, and squeezed off three quick rounds toward where he'd seen the orange flash of the dry gulcher's gun. He lowered the old 1866

First Model Winchester repeater — his detractors could shove their newer weapons where the sun don't shine! — and ran into the brush and burr oaks and flaming sumacs dripping from the recent rain, in the direction he'd seen the shooter's gun flash, and hunkered down behind the bole of a stout maple.

Lightning flashed erratically in the north, to his left, briefly illuminating the woods around him. He could see no sign of the shooter, only the weblike branches and boles of the deciduous forest lining this river bottom.

Moving forward, he held his cocked Winchester up high across his chest, glancing down only to make sure he wasn't about to trip over a deadfall. He ducked under low branches and heard the rain start again, ticking softly against the brim of his battered brown Stetson.

A crackling peal of thunder hammered the woods. Spurr felt the reverberation through his boots. Lightning flashed, turning the sky into a vast white candle. It revealed a man-shaped shadow in the corner of his right eye.

Spurr wheeled.

A sharp-nosed young man in a denim jacket and wet felt hat screamed savagely and bolted toward the old lawman, raising a large knife in his left hand while his other arm hung slack at his side.

As the sky turned dark again, Spurr's rifle roared, orange flames stabbing into the darkness. Spurr racked another round but held fire as he probed the darkness that appeared twice as dark after the lightning flash than it had before.

Nothing moved. He stepped forward, holding the rifle like a bayonet out in front of him.

Lightning flashed again, briefer than before. But in that half second, Spurr saw the sharp-nosed kid lying back in a tangle of branches, half standing, both arms now hanging slack at his sides. During another flash, Spurr saw that the kid was who he'd thought he was — young Brine Gatling. Spurr's first shots from the trail had nearly blown off the young brigand's wrist while the last spate had bibbed his chest with blood and nearly blown off his lower jaw.

It hung at a slant, blood bubbling down the corner of the kid's sagging lower lip.

Spurr wheeled and dropped to a knee, raising the rifle against his cheek, frowning into the darkness relieved by the intermittent flashes. If young Brine was here, the others in Brine's gang — which included his two brothers, a cousin, an uncle, a sister, and his stout, wild-assed mother, LaMona Gatling — could be, as well.

No, that was unlikely. The others had probably gone back to their hideout on up the trail. They'd likely sent Brine, the youngest of the ragtag bunch, each as deadly as he was crazy, back to scout the trail. They'd probably sensed that Spurr and three other deputy United States marshals had been shadowing them since their last army payroll holdup on the Deadwood-Yankton Freight Road up in Dakota two weeks ago.

During another lightning flash, Spurr leaned over young Brine once more. The kid's eyes, mean and owly even in death, were half open as they regarded Spurr with a perpetual scowl.

"Joke's on you, you son of a bitch," Spurr said as he started to make his way back through the trees, ducking under and winding around branches, deadfalls snapping wetly under his high-topped Indian moccasins, which were easier on an old man's feet than cowhide.

As he began tramping up the muddy trail after Cochise, the drizzle pelting his hat and his yellow india rubber poncho, he couldn't help feeling a smug satisfaction. The three other lawmen he'd been riding with — all young enough to be his sons, even his *grand-sons* — had ridden on down Henry's Hollow toward Red Creek, because that's the trail that ole LaMona Gatling had led them to believe she'd taken.

Spurr had known better, though he'd had to admit that the old outlaw queen and distant cousin to Jesse James had done a good job of making it *look* like Red Creek was where she'd headed, taking the right tine where the trail had forked about three miles back. But Spurr's sixth sense, honed by nearly twenty years of hunting owlhoots for Uncle Sam and fighting in the Little Misunderstanding and the Indian Wars before that, had told him that the trail she'd wanted him and the others to follow was just too obvious.

Shit, she'd been doing a damn good job of covering her tracks all the way down from Dakota. Why would she suddenly get sloppy so close to her home territory?

Spurr had insisted, albeit with slight reservation, that she'd led her gang up the fork's left tine, to the northeast as opposed to the southeast.

The other three lawmen had chuckled at him, however. They'd rolled their eyes and glanced at each other the way the younger folks do when they think the older folks have bats in their belfry. Deputy Windom Mitchell — nephew of the governor of Dakota Territory — had suggested that Spurr follow the trail he thought LaMona had taken.

"Go on up and check it out, Spurr. We'll say hidy to LaMona for you at Red Creek!"

Mitchell had grinned sneeringly. He'd cut his brash young eyes to the others, and they'd all laughed and shook their heads at how far the old, once-respected lawdog, Spurr Morgan, had tumbled in his old age. And they'd whipped their horses up the trail angling off through the creek bottom to the south, their horses' hooves kicking up gouts of mud behind them.

So Spurr had followed the northeast trail. And somewhere ahead of him lay La-Mona's hideout — one of many that peppered the Nations between the Platte and Red Rivers. That was an even safer bet now that he'd run into young Brine acting as scout. No reason for the young killer to scout a cold trail.

It took him a while to find Cochise. The horse had run a hundred yards up trail and found a little hollow off the north side, and a patch of thick, green bromegrass and a pool of fresh rainwater.

Spurr, whose ticker was a colicky iron crab

in his chest, was out of breath and footsore by the time he caught up with the horse, and slid his Winchester into his beaded elk-hide saddle boot. He didn't remember the long gun feeling as heavy as it was starting to feel these days. Over the past couple of years, actually. He was in his early sixties, after all, pushing on nigh to the end, he supposed.

If he was going to die, he'd just as soon die out here on the owlhoot trail. Lord knew the law still needed him, with his boss, Chief Marshal Henry Brackett, hiring men like the governor's nephew and the other two wet-behind-the-ears city boys — Wagner and Pritchett.

Spurr heaved his tired old bones into the saddle and rode ahead slowly, Cochise's hooves splashing through puddles and making squishing sounds in the mud. He kept a careful eye out for more scouts and La-Mona's cabin. He didn't want to ride unwittingly into her lair. LaMona was part Comanche, part Cherokee, with some Irish and Norwegian thrown in to make one crazy roaring bitch, and she was known to have slow-roasted a few federal boys in clay pots over small fires while she and her kin danced jigs to her screeching fiddle around the dying lawmen.

Spurr felt his oysters crawl up tight against his crotch as he considered such a miserable end.

When he'd ridden another fifteen minutes, a dull, red light shone in the darkness ahead. It was so faint that it could have been the glowing coal of a cigarette, but it was a steady umber light. Not a firelight, either. It was most likely a window light.

As Spurr continued riding, he reached forward of his right thigh and slid his old repeater from its beaded sheath, and held the barrel across his saddlebows. The light grew slowly until he could see the silhouette of a small cabin through the inky black forest.

When he spied a path rising from the trail and along the shoulder of a bluff on his left, he put Cochise up the slope, hoping the trace would take him to a spot above the cabin where he could reconnoiter the situation from a safe distance.

It did.

In scattered oaks and cottonwoods, he dismounted, led Cochise down the far side of the slope from the cabin, whose lights shone down off the bluff's southern side, and tied the horse to some wild plum branches. He removed his spurs and dropped them into a saddlebag pouch, so

15

he wouldn't rattle when he walked.

Returning to the crest of the slope, he hunkered down behind a low limestone shelf. He grunted and cursed his age as he tried to position himself on the cold, damp ground in such a way that he didn't feel he was pushing railroad spikes through his hips, knees, and shoulders, and he didn't feel as though his ribs were poking through his guts.

Christ, he was old.

He was beginning to wonder, along with Chief Marshal Brackett and the young deputies he'd outsmarted and everyone else in his sphere, why in hell he didn't retire. He knew some full-hipped old gals he could marry and haul back to his cabin in the shadow of Mount Rosalie. They would no doubt keep his natural male cravings properly satisfied, his feet warm on cold winter nights, bring him summer-night toddies out on the stoop, and even tend a kitchen garden to keep him in canned vegetables through the snowy Colorado winter.

The idle thoughts of a trail-weary old man . . .

When he'd found a relatively comfortable position, he lifted the field glasses to stare down through the brush and tree toward the cabin. He couldn't see much because of

16

the darkness — only what appeared a hollow with a hovel of some kind in it. There were five lighted windows in the place, all obscured by curtains.

Occasional shadows slid around behind those gauzy red or blue curtains.

Spurr lowered the field glasses, ran a hand down his warty face, scrubbed his gray-brown patch beard with gloved fingers, and considered the situation.

When those lights went out, he'd make his move.

And the devil take the hindmost . . .

He closed his eyes. His chin felt suddenly as heavy as an anvil. He lifted it, blinked, and chastised himself.

You can't sleep now, old man. You got a job of work to do before you turn in.

But then suddenly he felt the warm sun on his cheek, and as he lifted his chin from his gloved hands splayed on the ground before him, he realized it was morning and that what had awakened him was a woman's throaty voice singing off-key the old funeral hymn, "Bringing in the Sheaves."

Two

Someone had died.

As Spurr blinked and got his bearings, he wondered if he himself had expired.

No. He could feel his old heart chugging like an ancient locomotive in his chest. His hat had tumbled off his head during the night. A breeze had skidded it several feet off to his left and downslope slightly. He heaved up on his hands and knees, so stiff from sleeping on the cold, damp ground that he felt as though he'd been stoned overnight, and crawled out to fetch his hat.

All the while he heard the woman's off-key voice singing in the yard below:

Bringing in the sheaves, bringing in the
    sheaves,
We shall come rejoicing, bringing in the
    sheaves,
Bringing in the sheaves, bringing in the
    sheaves,

We shall come rejoicing, bringing in the sheaves.

As he scuttled back to the side of the limestone shelf, he cast a look down the slope. A blue smoke fog hung over the hollow. The smoke was rising from the broad stone chimney of the log-and-sod shack sitting behind a screen of trees about fifty yards from the slope's base.

The air was fresh from the previous night's rain. It was rife with the smell of green growing things and the mushroom smell of loam and of the wood smoke that hung over the hollow like a lid. The hollow itself was all blue shadows, for the sun had not yet risen over the southeastern hill, so Spurr couldn't see much but figures milling about in the dooryard below.

Then he hunkered lower, doffed his hat again, and pulled it down close to his chest as he squinted his eyes down the slope. A woman was moving toward him through the gnarled cottonwoods at the edge of the yard, heading toward a thin, tan footpath that Spurr could now see angling up the face of the bluff, a little to his right.

He could also see that the woman — stout as a well house and clad in a long, plaid shirt over blue denim coveralls — was La-

Mona Gatling. She was the one singing. She wore a tattered straw sombrero and black gumshoe boots. There were four others behind her, walking single file, following her over to where the path started up the slope.

LaMona sang:

Sowing in the sunshine, sowing in the
  shadows,
Fearing neither clouds nor winter's chilling
  breeze;
By and by the harvest, and the labor
  ended,
We shall come rejoicing, bringing in the
  sheaves.

Spurr gritted his teeth. If the woman was going to sing that loud, she ought to learn to carry a tune. LaMona's voice sounded like a whipsaw trying to cut a plow blade.

As she mounted the slope, walking slowly, her voice trilled and was laced with the grunts of her exertion. Behind her walked her daughter, Missy May — a slender girl with long, blond hair and tricked out in much the same fashion as her stout mother. Missy May wore no hat; a blue ribbon trimmed her hair.

Behind Missy May were two boys, Preston and James, most likely, LaMona's two boys. Spurr recognized them all from their sketched likenesses on wanted dodgers. Preston was a big, beefy lad with a baby-soft face framed by bushy ginger sideburns. James was built like his sister — tall and lanky, and he was blond like Missy May, too. The two boys were carrying a coffin on their shoulders, heads titled away from the pale pine box. Bringing up the rear was the cousin, Darrold Gatling, a short, fat young man carrying an old, Civil War-model Spencer rifle on one shoulder.

The others were armed, as well — Preston and James with pistols holstered on their hips, and Missy May with a pistol butt poking from her right coverall pocket. Following her mother up the path that slanted off to Spurr's right, toward some mossy oaks and stunt cedars around which several stone markers rose, fronting mounded graves, the girl moved her lips, singing softly and watching the ground while keeping her right hand wrapped around the grips of the pistol in her pocket.

LaMona walked around a large boulder humping up out of the ground, singing:

Going forth with weeping, sowing for the
    Master,
Though the loss sustained our spirit often

grieves;
When our weeping's over, He will bid us
  welcome,
We shall come rejoicing, bringing in the
  sheaves.

Keeping his head down, his rifle tight by side, Spurr figured it must have been La-Mona's idiot brother, Hyram "Frog" Andrews, in the box. Frog was fat Darrold's father. Spurr had heard that Frog had been wounded by a cavalry soldier when they'd robbed the army payroll south of Deadwood. He'd either died on the trail and they'd hauled him home or died last night. Whatever had happened, Frog was dead now, and LaMona's bunch was about to plant him in the boneyard that occupied a small, relatively flat area fifty yards to Spurr's right and about halfway up from the bottom of the slope.

LaMona continued to sing as the group moved up the bluff, her voice growing reedy now as the stout woman became more and more breathless from the climb.

Spurr quickly considered the situation. Then, dragging his rifle and his hat, he scuttled several feet down the backside of the slope. He straightened his sinewy old body with effort, gritting his teeth as his brittle bones creaked and popped like an ancient chair, and cast his glance down the slope behind him.

Cochise was lounging in high bromegrass, his legs folded beneath him, casting his rider a skeptical, faintly indignant look. The horse wanted food, preferably oats though parched corn would suffice, and water. He wanted breakfast.

Spurr thrust a palm-out hand toward the big roan, silently ordering the horse to stay where he was and to keep quiet. Over the long years he'd hauled Spurr around the wooly frontier, Cochise had grown accustomed to such signals. He could read them well. Now he just turned his head forward and twitched his ears, peevishly waiting.

Like Spurr, the horse didn't like to stay in one place very long. And he preferred his meals on time.

Spurr walked as quickly as his old legs and sore feet would carry him along the backside of the bluff, staying a good ten feet down from the crest so he wouldn't be seen from the other side. When he figured he'd walked fifty or so yards, he doffed his hat, got down on hands and knees, and crabbed to the crest of the bluff.

He was nearly straight above where La-

Mona Gatling's crew had stopped in the little cemetery. Between him and the gang were several gnarled, mossy oaks, cedars, and cottonwood saplings. There were several small, mossy boulders, as well. Preston and James had set the coffin down beside a freshly dug grave. Spurr scowled at the hole.

They must have dug the grave last night, before the rain had begun. If they'd dug it this morning, Spurr surely would have heard them.

At least, he hoped he would have heard them. He wasn't sure anymore. Hell, he'd slept all night without stirring at an owl's hoot!

LaMona had stopped singing. She and Missy May stood by the grave, and she was gesturing and speaking in annoyed tones to Preston and James, both of whom were bent forward, hands on their knees by the pine box, catching their breath. Short, fat Darrold was chuckling at the two younger men's misery while he rolled a cigarette, standing off to the left of the women, near Preston and James.

LaMona turned her head toward her brother's son and said shrilly, "Put that tobaccy down, you fool! We're plantin' your daddy here this mornin'!"

Darrold looked indignant. He said something to LaMona too softly for Spurr to hear.

"Put it down, now, you damn fool, and show a little respect. Your daddy was a helluva lot better to you than you deserved, and I'll be goddamned if I'll let you smoke at his funeral!"

"Pappy liked tobaccy just fine, Anty Mon!" Darrold returned, jutting his sharp chin at the stout woman. "And he wouldn't mind one bit if I smoked at his plantin'!"

Seeing his opening, Spurr pressed his cheek against his Winchester's stock and aimed the barrel down the slope. He had a good view of the gang between two oaks, and it wasn't going to get any better.

He loudly pumped a cartridge into the chamber and shouted, "Turn to stone, La-Mona Gatling, or I'll drill you where you stand! That goes for all you worthless Gatlings!"

LaMona jerked her head toward Spurr. "What the *hell*? Who's *there*?"

"Spurr Morgan, deputy U.S. marshal from Denver! Throw your guns down or join Frog!"

They all froze and scowled up the slope toward Spurr, who slid his Winchester from left to right and back again, keeping the entire bunch in his sights. Darrold dropped

25

his cigarette and nervously rubbed his big hands against his greasy elk-skin poncho.

LaMona shouted, "This is a family matter, lawman. We're in the midst of sendin' my dear brother to his reward. Now, you get the hell out of here. We'll deal with you *later!*"

Keeping his Winchester aimed at the group, Spurr rose with a groan and walked in his stiff, bandy-legged fashion down the hill, keeping the group in sight between the two oaks. "You don't understand, Mrs. Gatling. You're under arrest for murder and robbery. I'm takin' you in."

"*You're* takin' us in?" LaMona gave a caustic, raking laugh. "Why, you're older'n Methuselah!"

The others laughed. Missy May tittered. She still had her hand on the butt of the pistol poking out of her right coverall pocket. She would have been a pretty girl if her two front teeth hadn't been sticking nearly straight out of her upper jaw and one blue eye didn't wander.

Spurr stopped near one of the oaks whose main trunk trailed along the ground for several feet before rising at an angle and shaking its leaves in the fresh morning breeze. He set his right boot atop the trunk and pressed the Winchester's stock taut

26

against his shoulder, aiming at the deep valley between LaMona Gatling's enormous breasts pushing out her grimy plaid work shirt.

He nodded. "I have seen better days. But you five are wanted in three territories for armed robbery of federal monies, the murder of citizens as well as soldiers, and the raping of three female and one male bank teller whom you kidnapped from a bank in Norman, Oklahoma."

Spurr made a bitter face, shook his head in revulsion. "In other words, you're five of the slimiest damn sacks of burning dog shit I do believe I've seen in a month of Sundays, and I've seen a whole lot of Sunday months during my time in the U.S. Marshals Service. And right now, I'm feelin' pretty good about my job. Bringing you in or leaving you right here in your own little boneyard will be the capstone of my career."

They all just stared at him, as though they were having trouble digesting all that.

Finally, Preston Gatling said, "You sure do talk a lot!"

"I'm alone a lot." Spurr narrowed a menacing eye. "Now, throw down those weapons or I'll leave you right here in little hillbilly puddles of grease."

LaMona looked as though something had

just dawned on her. "Where's Brine?"

"Dead."

"Dead?" LaMona's fleshy lower jaw sagged, making a small round hole of her thin-lipped, little mouth. "I . . . I thought he musta got bored last night and went over to see that Beamer girl in Sandy Flat."

"Nope. He bushwhacked me last night. You'd have been proud of him. Only, he took about four rounds for his efforts. Nope, he's dead, all right. Now, I ain't gonna ask you people again. Throw down them irons or you're gonna be meetin' ole Frog and ole Brine in hell in about two jerks of a whore's bell!"

"My cousin, Jesse James, will hunt you down and kill you for this!" LaMona said, extending her arm and a pudgy index finger at Spurr.

Just then Missy May started issuing a strange sound. The girl stood stiffly, glaring up the slope at Spurr, her mouth opening wider and wider and the sound growing louder and louder until she was bouncing on the balls of her gum boots and fairly screaming.

She looked like a diamondback coiled to strike. Her eyes flashed fire. The others looked at her as though she'd suddenly been possessed by a demon. But they must have

28

heard the sound before, and taken it as a signal, because they all whipped their heads back toward Spurr, eyes as wide and bright as Missy May's.

Spurr had never heard a sound so haunting in all his days. It rocked him almost literally back on his heels. "You just simmer down, now, young lady!"

The last two words hadn't left his lips before Missy May dragged the popper out of her coverall pocket, and Spurr shot her.

THREE

Missy May dropped the gun as Spurr's .44 round punched her two steps back, snapping her head back sharply.

LaMona and the rest of Missy May's gang jerked shocked gazes at the girl, who looked down at the blood spurting out the hole in her baggy shirt, between the small pert lumps of her breasts, and then at Spurr. The light was already dying in her blue eyes as she lifted her right arm and pointed a finger at the old lawdog, as though to indicate the man who'd shot her. She moved her lips but no words came out.

She fell hard on her back, hair fanning out behind her on the grassy ground.

Spurr ejected the spent cartridge casing from the Winchester's breech, seated a fresh one, and pressed the stock against his shoulder once more. At the same time, La-Mona reached under her shirttails, squalling, *"You'll pay for killin' my baby, you old bastard!"*

But James was already jerking up his own two pistols, so Spurr shot him next. He slid his rifle back to the left and punched a hole in LaMona's fat hide just as the woman triggered one of her two Smith & Wessons at Spurr though both slugs screeched wild into the ground about three feet in front of the oak. As James went down, howling like a coyote, Preston and fat Darrold jerked up their own weapons and, crouching, cut loose at Spurr.

The old lawman was fleet of foot when he had to be, and as bullets wheezed and buzzed around him, punching into the ground before and behind him, he ran to the next tree to his right, and pressed his back against the trunk. When there was a relative lull in the shooting, he snaked his Winchester around the oak's right side and triggered three quick rounds at Preston, who'd hunkered down behind a pitted gravestone, and Darrold, who was using his father's casket for a shield, triggering his old Spencer repeater over the top.

Two of Spurr's slugs hammered the side of Frog's casket, but the third one drilled Preston a new eye — this one about two inches above the bridge of his nose. It punched him straight back until he was sitting upright against a gravestone directly behind the one he'd been using for cover. As Preston kicked his boots as though trying to dislodge fire ants crawling up his pants, Darrold punched a round into the tree about four inches right of Spurr's right eye.

The fat man's next round tore Spurr's hat off his head.

Spurr cursed and triggered his Winchester from his shoulder.

Darrold bellowed raucously as Spurr's slug plunked into his collarbone. As the fat man threw his empty Spencer aside and heaved himself awkwardly to his feet, he reached around to pull a huge bowie knife from a sheath belted behind his back.

"I'm gonna cut your black heart out of your miserable old hide for that!" he screeched and, stepping around his father's casket, lunged into a heavy, thumping run toward Spurr.

Spurr saw no reason to spare Darrold. Darrold was a dead man running, albeit one running with a big, savage-looking, antler-handled knife in his hand.

Bang!

The Winchester bullet took Darrold under his right eye, snapped his head back with a sharp cracking noise made by his splintering neck. Darrold's feet kept running for two more steps, but then he stopped, looked at Spurr with a confused expression, blinking once slowly, and then dropped to his knees.

He continued to stare at Spurr for several more seconds, blood bubbling darkly from the hole in his cheek, before he made a gurgling sound, dropped his knife in the grass, and fell forward on his face and big, round belly.

Spurr walked around to the front of the oak and dropped to one knee. He always knew without counting when he'd emptied his Winchester, which held nine rounds counting one in the chamber, and he quickly began thumbing fresh shells from his cartridge belt, looking around at the bodies strewn before him.

LaMona lay to the left of the pine box housing her brother Frog. She lay belly up, head toward the downslope, her shirttails ruffling in the chill morning breeze.

Missy May lay beyond her. Several yards to her right, Preston still sat against the headstone, his eyes open though one was filling with the blood dribbling from the hole above the bridge of his nose. Aside from the blood, he could have taken a seat there to gather some morning wool or plot his next nasty job of robbing and killing.

Darrold lay about ten feet in front of Spurr, facedown, arms and legs spread wide. Blood pooled on the ground beneath his chest and face.

Spurr had punched three fresh rounds through the Winchester's breech, when he froze suddenly, one round halfway through the receiver's loading gate. LaMona had stirred. Now she stirred again, rolling her head around and then, all at once, rising to her hands and knees.

She sighed and grunted as she hauled herself to her feet.

"Hold it there, now, LaMona!" Spurr warned, lowering his Winchester and pulling his Starr .44 from the soft, brown leather holster positioned for the cross draw on his left hip.

As though she hadn't heard him, LaMona looked around and then walked several feet to her right, leaned down with another, louder grunt, and plucked one of her pistols off the ground near the mounded soil of her brother's grave. LaMona swung heavily toward Spurr, ratcheting the Smith & Wesson's hammer back and hardening her jaws. Her eyes looked no larger than black pellets in her pale, fleshy face sagging to triple jowls that swelled and wobbled above her enormous, sagging breasts.

Her shirt just beneath her right breast had a pumpkin-sized bloodstain on it. Spurr didn't doubt that the woman's ample flesh might have absorbed the bullet he'd drilled into it, stopping it before it could strike anything vital. He wondered if he could ever hit anything vital in a woman ensconced in so much tallow.

Spurr cocked the Starr .44 and extended the revolver straight out from his shoulder. "Drop it, LaMona!"

The woman snarled and pinched her eyes and wrinkled her nose as she swung the pistol up with effort.

"LaMona!" Spurr bellowed.

But as she leveled her Smithy on him, Spurr's pistol roared. The bullet punched into LaMona's fleshy chest, causing her shirt to billow and her gun hand to waver. The Smithy barked, and the bullet spanged off a rock to Spurr's left.

LaMona staggered slightly but kept coming, swinging the Smith & Wesson up again. Spurr shot her again in the chest. She was moving around too much to try a head shot. Her big body was his best bet — if he could drill a bullet deep enough into her, that was.

"LaMona, goddamnit!" Spurr shouted as he shot her again as she triggered the Smith

& Wesson into the ground to his right this time.

The bullet took her in her left shoulder and she swung sideways. That knee buckled and for a moment Spurr thought she'd go down but instead she got her feet beneath her once more, and, mewling like a wounded she-bear, kept staggering toward him, cocking the Smithy again with a grating click.

Again, Spurr shot the woman, causing her next bullet to scream over his head and to ricochet loudly off a rock higher on the slope. He shot her once more, and then she was standing three feet in front of him, and he pressed the Starr's barrel against her forehead, yelling, "LaMona, for cryin' in the beer, won't you please just *die*?"

She stared at a spot somewhere on Spurr's chin as he squeezed the Starr's trigger.

Ping!

The hammer had landed on an empty chamber.

LaMona spread a dull grin, showing her small, tobacco-grimed teeth between her thin turkey lips. She gave another grunt as she tried to lift the Smithy, but the gun would not rise. Instead, she triggered it into the ground several yards to her left.

The bullet screeched wickedly. LaMona's

head jerked sharply to her right.

When it straightened again on her shoulders, Spurr saw blood gushing from the hole the ricochet had punched through the left side of her head, just above her ear.

The woman stared at Spurr, staggered from side to side, and then her eyes rolled up into her head until all Spurr could see was eggshell white, and LaMona fell straight back to hit the ground with a heavy thump.

Spurr lowered the Starr to his side. He stared down at the big, dead woman before him and shook his head. "That's troubling to me, LaMona. I never took you for a suicide." He gave a droll chuckle and drew a heavy breath, throwing his shoulders back.

Hooves drummed in the distance. He turned to stare down the hill. In the yard beyond the screen of trees, horseback riders jostled and wavered. Dust rose and the morning sunlight shone golden in it.

Spurr holstered the empty Starr and picked up his rifle from where he'd leaned it against the oak behind him. He continued loading the long gun, but as he watched the riders gallop through the trees and gain the slope, following the path toward the boneyard, he stopped.

Resting the Winchester's barrel on his shoulders, he glowered down at the three men riding toward him, their deputy U.S. marshal badges flashing on their coats.

Windom Mitchell was in the lead followed by Bruce Wagner and Calvin Pritchett. The young federal lawmen scowled beneath the brims of their Stetsons as they turned their heads this way and that, staring down in shock at the dead men and women strewn around the freshly dug grave and the pine casket.

Mitchell — tall and dark with a prissy, mustached face peeling from sunburn — slowed his horse just beyond the cemetery. The others did likewise, Wagner and Pritchett riding out to either side of the young lawman decked out in a tailor-made three-piece suit and crisp black Stetson with a jewel pinned to its crown.

The three stopped their horses on the other side of the carnage, shuttling their incredulous gazes from the dead Gatlings to Spurr, who stood in front of the oak tree, his rifle resting on his shoulder. His grim gaze belied his satisfaction at having proven the three younkers wrong in their snootily held opinions that the outlaws had taken the southeast path as opposed to the *northeast* path.

"Fancy meetin' you fellas here," Spurr said without inflection. "I figured you was still waitin' on me over to Red Creek. Well, since you're here, you might as well find some shovels and start buryin' the dead. Me? I'm gonna head on down to the cabin an' see what ole LaMona's cookin' fer breakfast. Been one hell of a long night, as you can tell. No rest for the experienced lawdog, ya might say."

He turned, picked up his hat, casually inspected the bullet hole in its crown, and set it on his head. He walked away from the silent young lawmen, grinning in mute delight.

FOUR

"Spur-urrrr," a girl's pretty voice said into the tranquil darkness at the edges of the old lawman's slumber.

Spurr grunted, smacked his lips, ground his head into the pillow, and let himself drift deeper into the warm tar of sleep she'd started to summon him from.

The girl's voice called him back toward the fringes once more. "Spurr, hon . . . wakey, wakey."

"Ah, hell," he said, still mostly asleep. "Le' me, le' me . . ."

"Spur-urrrr."

The voice was softer but it came from nearer this time. He could hear the girl's soft breathing, feel the warmth of her mouth up close to his left ear. Suddenly he felt the warm, wet softness of her tongue inside his ear, felt her small, pliant hand wrap around his manhood down beneath the sheets and autumn quilts, and give him a gentle squeeze.

"Come on, hon — you said you was gonna take Kansas City Jane to breakfast this morning. Don't you" — she swirled her tongue around in his ear once more and squeezed him a little harder — "re . . . *mem . . .* berrr?"

Spurr opened his eyes and groaned at the girl's manipulating hand that was causing the proverbial worm at the bottom of the tequila bottle to wag its tail. Spurr chuckled at the notion though the image of a tequila bottle caused lightning to strike his brain and make his ears ring. He'd had far too much of the ole tangleleg these past few days.

Tangleleg, tobacco, and women.

"Take a few days off, Spurr," Chief Marshal Henry Brackett had told Spurr after he'd gotten back with Mitchell, Wagner, and Pritchett from the Indian Nations and filed his report.

He reached up and sandwiched Kansas City Jane's face between his hands and planted a warm kiss on the tip of her nose. "You keep doin' what you're doin' with that nasty little hand of yourn, Janey my darlin', and I might have you on your back again. I don't think I got money enough for another poke *and* breakfast fer two. Been goin' through it mighty fast of late."

"That's all right," Jane said, stretching her lips back from her teeth — nearly a full set, with only one gap behind her right eyetooth. That was pretty much a full set for a whore in these parts. "I'll give you a free one . . . since you're celebratin' an' all, after taking down that nasty Gatling bunch over in the Nations. The way they were carryin' on for so many years, like a bunch of bloodthirsty wolves, why, I reckon every girl on the frontier owes you a poke, Marshal Spurr."

She leaned closer to him, raked her breasts across his shoulder, causing Spurr's old loins to tingle.

Spurr chuckled. He rolled the girl over on her back and buried his face between her firm, pale breasts, snorting and licking her and gently raking her with his beard stubble. She laughed and shivered, lifting her knees and writhing around, placing her hands on the back of Spurr's head and grinding his face tight against her.

"Oooo, that tickles, Spurr!"

Spurr lifted his head. He kissed each of the girl's pebbled pink nipples in turn, and then rolled over to the edge of the bed and dropped his feet to the floor. "Come on, Jane. If we do it again, I'll need a nap before we light out. I ain't as young as I used to be. Let's go out and see what Mr. Wong is servin' up for breakfast these days. Last time I was there, he was cookin' some right fine huevos rancheros." He glanced over his shoulder at Jane, who was sitting up and luxuriously smoothing her curly golden hair back behind her pink shoulders. "Don't that beat all — a Chinaman cookin' Mescin food?"

"What do Chinamen normally eat, Spurr?"

"Hell, I don't know. When I was scoutin' for the railroad a few years ago — hell, about twenty years ago now! — I saw 'em boilin' a lot of cabbage with rice and the like. They drank tea, too. Lots of tea." He glanced back at Jane again — if he remembered right, her real name was Nellie — and admired her firm, pink round ass facing him as she crawled over to the far side of the bed. "Their supper meals smelled — I hate to say it, Miss Jane — but a little like Indian stew."

"What do you suppose was in it?" The girl climbed down off the bed, turning to Spurr and pulling her hair back behind her head with both hands in that sweetly feminine way of hers. As she thrust her shoulders back, her tender breasts jutted forward, still a little red from Spurr's beard stubble.

"Do you know what's in Indian stew, darlin'?" Spurr rose, chuckling, and began stumbling around, gathering his clothes.

"No, Spurr," the girl said. "What's in Indian stew?"

"Uh . . . well, let's just say that when a farmer's missin' one of his hounds for more than a day, and there's some Injuns camped out nearby, he might as well figure he's seen the last of ole Rover."

"Oh, Spurr — please!" the girl intoned, making a face and cupping her hands to her breasts, drawing one knee toward the other one. "You shouldn't say somethin' like that when we're about to light out for Mr. Wong's!"

Spurr roared as he sat down on the edge of the bed with his clothes in his lap. "You asked, darlin'! You asked!"

She threw a pillow at him, and he laughed harder.

They continued to jaw at each other as they both dressed, the girl stumbling around the room, pulling one article of clothing on at a time, and Spurr trying his best at dressing without having to move around overmuch. His head felt as though several brawny tracklayers had shoved railroad spikes through his ears and poured wood tar down his throat.

When he'd gotten back from the Nations, a commendation from the governor of Colorado had been waiting for him, on Chief Marshal Henry Brackett's desk, as well as a fifty-dollar bonus. Spurr had to admit that, while he was normally a relatively humble man, the commendation from the governor as well as the chagrinned smile on the old Chief Marshal's face had gone to his head.

And why shouldn't it have?

A month ago he had gone out to breakfast with the venerable old marshal, and over omelettes and hash browns, Henry Brackett had once again suggested Spurr retire.

"Why don't you head on down to Mexico, like you've been threatening to do for the past ten years, Spurr? Leave this lawdogging business up to the younger men. You've made your mark. Hell, even old bull buffalos know when their breedin' days are over. They take it with a stiff upper lip and just wander away from the herd."

"Wander away from the herd, huh, Henry? Sounds a helluva lot like what the Injuns do. Look for some cave up in the hills they can die in alone, so the young folks don't have to bother with 'em."

"Oh, that's not what I'm sayin' at all, Spurr. A bad choice of words." Marshal

Brackett had nudged his small, rectangular spectacles up his nose, laced his hands together on the table behind his plate, and leaned forward. His eyes behind the glasses were somber, frank. "I'm saying the marshals service has gotten . . . well, it's gotten more complicated in these more modern times, Spurr. Colorado turned from frontier territory to a bona fide state almost five years ago now. The laws have gotten more complicated. Outlaws have gotten more complicated, too. More sophisticated."

When Spurr was about to interject, Brackett had lifted a hand to forestall him and said, "All that aside . . . well, you know as well as I do, Spurr, that with that old ticker of yours, you could go at any time. Face it, Spurr. Your best days are behind you. Leave it to the young folks to bring law and order to the *new* frontier."

Spurr had to admit, he'd considered it, just as he'd told Henry Brackett he'd do. He'd consider it over one more assignment — tracking the LaMona Gatling bunch from the spot of their last bloody robbery, though Brackett had insisted he ride "with three much younger but still very capable men, the new breed of deputy United States marshal.

"When you've ridden with these young

46

professionals, Spurr, I think you'll be able to turn in your badge with confidence that civilization is in good hands."

"Young professionals, my ass," Spurr said now, setting his hat on his head in Jane's warped mirror. He laughed, still boiling over with glee, despite the bottle flu, at his having turned the tables on the three snooty lawmen — the *young professionals* as the Chief Marshal had called them — and taken down the entire Gatling gang single-handed.

"What's that, hon?" Jane said, fully dressed and ready to go, sidling up to him in the mirror and wrapping an arm around his waist.

Spurr turned to her, hesitating. Then he laughed again. "Oh, I was just sayin' I think it's time you and this ole lawdog headed out for some o' the Chinaman's chow, and then we head on back here and I give you one hell of a professional ash-haulin'. How'd that be, Sweet Jane?" He reached into a pocket of his corduroy trousers hanging off his lean hips. "I think I got one more silver dollar rollin' around in here too lonely for words!"

Jane chuckled, and then she frowned. "Spurr, is that all you got left from the money the governor gave you?"

"Jane, my dear beautiful gal — a pine box

47

is a damn lonely place. You're there a long time, and there ain't one purty girl anywhere near for that whole long eternal time to spend it on." Spurr winked, pecked the girl's cheek. "Now, I'm so hungry my belly thinks my throat's been cut!"

Laughing, they left the girl's room together and strolled down the wide, carpeted stairs of George Cranston's Saloon, which everybody in Denver city proper and most of the county knew was a whorehouse — one of the best in Denver. Spurr didn't usually have the money for such a place — he often swore that his store-bought pants came with holes in the pockets — but after the governor himself had oiled his palms a little, he saw no reason not to splurge.

And he'd found this little blonde, who called herself Kansas City Jane, just a delight to make an old man's weak ticker feel almost young and strong again.

Spurr's spurs rattled as he led Jane on down the stairs, her arm hooked through his. It was still early by saloon and whorehouse standards, so there were only about five men in the large, dark, cavernous room that housed a long polished mahogany horseshoe bar and vast, gaudy mirror on the left. There were about twenty or so stout tables on the right, amidst the square-hewn ceiling posts and a couple of potbellied stoves, both of which ticked and smoked with morning fires. It was late August, still summer, but there'd been a pronounced chill in the air for days.

A gambling parlor lay through a curtained doorway, with blackjack tables, a roulette wheel, and a craps table, at the rear of Cranston's, but Spurr tried his best to stay out of the place lest those holes in his pockets should grow even larger.

"Where in the hell you goin' with my girl, Spurr?" This from the barman who also owned the place — Leonard Cranston, brother of George who'd been hit by a hansom cab a few years back, dying and leaving the business to his big, burly, blond-bearded brother, Lenny, who hired some of the prettiest doxies in Colorado.

"We're off to get married!" As Spurr led the girl, who wore a much more sensible dress and shoes than she normally wore about Cranston's, toward the front door that looked out on Arapaho Street, he lifted his hat high above his head. "Wish this ole duck good luck, will ya, fellers?"

FIVE

"Wish Miss Jane luck, more like!" called one of Cranston's regulars, Pearl Isaakson, who came in most mornings to partake of a sudsy beer to start the day, and anything remaining of last night's free lunch platter. He stood at the bar, grinning, one elbow on the bar top, a beer schooner in his fist.

The others in the saloon this early week-day morning, including Cranston, laughed as Spurr led the girl through the heavy, glass-paned door and out onto Arapaho Street. Traffic was light on this narrow, gravel-paved side street, about three blocks from the Mint and the Federal Building.

A beer dray was just now passing with two big mule skinners at the reins, both of whom waved to Spurr and lifted their battered felt hats to Miss Jane. The driver's shaggy dog was following the dray, tongue hanging and tail wagging, making the rounds with its master though giving chase to the occasional stray cat now and then.

Spurr had resided in or around Denver long enough to know well over half the faces — including the animals' faces — in the fast-growing old cow town once known as Denver City.

Spurr and the girl waited for a coal wagon to pass and then headed off across the street to angle toward an alley mouth, which would take them via the quickest route possible to the Chinaman's café which, if Spurr remembered correctly, was called merely Good Food — Cheap.

"You ever been married, Spurr?" Jane asked as they stepped up onto the boardwalk on the street's opposite side, passing the tonsorial parlor out front of which the barber, Roy Overhill, was sweeping horse and mule dung from his stoop.

"Me? Hell, no!" Spurr laughed. "Oh, I lived with a few women too stupid to know no better, but no, I never been hitched."

"I bet you'd have made a good husband."

"Really? Why's that, honey?"

"Oh, I don't know. 'Cause you're good. You're kind. You're sweet as all git-out in bed, and you got a nice laugh. Your eyes twinkle, too, and I like that in a man. Most men are so serious."

"Well, I'm old enough to know you can't

take life too damn serious. Why would you? It's too damn short!"

Jane laughed and rubbed her head against his arm as they walked. "Spurr, I hope you come back an' see me sometime."

"Ah, hell — you must be tired o' my stringy hide by now."

"You're a good man, Spurr. Sure, you got a few years on you, but . . ."

Spurr stopped and looked at her. "What is it, Miss Jane?"

She gazed up at him concernedly. "Don't take this the wrong way, okay, hon?"

"What is it?" he urged, patting her hand.

"Spurr, ain't you just a tad old to be doin' what you're doin'?"

"Ah, hell," Spurr said, twisting his leathery, patch-bearded, wart-stippled face like he'd just sucked a lemon. "Not you, too, Miss Jane."

"Last night, Spurr," the girl said, "I woke up and you . . . you didn't sound too good."

"Didn't sound too good? Hell, I was probably snorin'!"

"Well, between the snores your breath seemed to flutter a lot, like you were working at catching air."

"Ah, hell," Spurr said, patting her hand reassuringly this time. "I was just tired. Drunk and tired. You 'bout wore me out, girl! But that's all right. Gettin' his ashes hauled good, by a real pro like yourself, adds year to an old man's li. . . ."

Spurr let his voice trail off and beetled his grizzled brows as he stared across the street, toward four horses standing at the tie rack in front of the old Territorial Bank of Denver — a small, wood-and-brick structure sandwiched between a furniture shop and Petersen's Fine Watches & Watch Repair store.

"What is it?" the girl asked, following his gaze toward where a man in rough-hewn trail gear leaned against the hitchrack, his back to Spurr and Jane. Spurr could see him between a piebald gelding and a black-legged steeldust stallion. The man wore a long, coarsely woven coat, and he had his head down as though scrutinizing something on the ground around his boots, which were casually crossed at the ankles.

The horses were not tied. Spurr could see that the man leaning against the hitchrack was holding all four sets of reins in his hands.

Spurr looked at the bank. The shades were drawn over the front windows and doors. That wasn't unusual for this early in the day, but the horses standing out front of the place were damned unusual. As was the man standing a little too casually against the hitchrack, holding their reins.

Just then the bank door opened. Faintly, Spurr heard the bell over the door jangle. The shade in the door's window jostled. The door jerked as it stopped abruptly, as though running up against a boot, and then a man stumbled out — a hombre dressed in rough trail gear similar to that worn by the gent at the hitchrack. He was holding a pistol straight up in one hand, and the two men who followed him out of the bank were also holding pistols.

Spurr released Jane's arm and unsnapped the keeper thong over the hammer of the Starr .44 jutting butt forward on his left hip. Keeping his eyes on the three men hurrying out of the bank, he said quietly, with measured calm, "Jane, I want you to crouch down behind that rain barrel over there. Can you do that for me, please?"

"But, Spurr, what . . . ?"

"Now, Jane — *hurry!*"

As Spurr turned back toward the bank, he saw a shadow move in the corner of his right eye. He jerked his head in that direction. A man was moving quickly out from a store front a half a block away, extending a pistol straight out in front of him. The pistol exploded as the man shouted, "Trouble, boys!"

Jane, who had just started running up the street toward the rain barrel outside of a small grocery shop, had stepped between Spurr and the man with the gun at the same time that the gun roared. She gave a shrill scream as she jerked backward, got her shoe caught in a crack between the boards, and hit the walk with a heavy thud.

"*Jane!*" Spurr yelled, extending his Starr straight out from his right shoulder. He hastily aimed at the man running toward him, yelling and shooting, smoke and flames lapping from the barrel of his six-shooter.

Two slugs screamed around Spurr as the old lawman drew his left foot back, turning sideways to make himself a smaller target, and triggered the Starr twice quickly.

Bam! Bam!

He watched the man running toward him jerk his head back as his body flew to Spurr's left where it ran into an awning support post. The shooter slid down against the post, clapping one hand to his chest and triggering his pistol into the boardwalk.

"Jane!"

Spurr started running toward where the girl lay faceup on the boardwalk six feet away from him. But when the men on the far side of the street began opening up on him, the roar of the revolvers echoing loudly off the buildings lining the narrow, shadowy street, Spurr wheeled and returned fire.

The men were each taking their own horse's reins and trying to get mounted. But the horses were screaming and fidgeting as the men triggered their pistols at Spurr. Their wild shots broke glass and thumped into building facades or awning support posts around the old lawman, who, down on one knee, quickly emptied the Starr.

He pinked one of the bank robbers as the man was climbing onto his horse. The man yowled and clutched his right buttock and fell backward out of the saddle to hit the cinder-paved street, mewling.

But Spurr did not see the man hit the street, because just then an invisible mule kicked him in the chest and threw him backward into a slight break between two business buildings.

He lay flat on his back, gasping, his left arm feeling heavy and dead, the mule that kicked him now sitting on his chest. Time slowed down, as did his mind, and he fought to stay conscious and aware of what was going on across the street. As if from far away, he heard several more gun pops, and then he felt the reverberation of galloping hooves through his back.

He felt naked, lying there, that invisible mule sitting on his chest, keeping him from dragging a full draught of air into his lungs. His vision blurred, dimmed, and his tongue grew thick and dry. Nausea caused his belly to contract, and he managed to roll onto his side as sour bile exploded up from his chest and splattered onto the spur-scarred, sun-silvered boardwalk.

Then the morning light dimmed. He wasn't sure, but he must have passed out for a time.

He was drawn back to full consciousness by the sounds of men shouting and horses galloping. He lifted his head to see two Denver policemen approached the bank at a hard gallop, the city badge toters shouting and gesturing. As they pulled to skidding halts in front of the bank, the one nearest Spurr leapt out of the saddle of his long-legged bay, while the other ground the heels of his high, brown boots into his own bay's flanks and continued south along Arapaho.

The other policeman, attired in a blue, cavalry-like tunic with gold buttons, corduroy trousers, and a copper badge on his left breast, dropped his horse's reins and, holding a Winchester carbine in one gloved hand, ran up on the boardwalk. His boots tattooed a frenetic rhythm as he hurried over to where Jane lay unmoving, her blond head nearest Spurr, her hair having fallen from the neat coronet she'd started the morning with.

The cop knelt beside the girl, touched a finger to her neck.

Spurr was grunting against the pain in his arm, shoulder, and chest as he lay on his side and looked at the cop. "She . . . ?"

"Dead," said the policeman, whose granitelike face and walrus mustache marked him as Mark Trumbo, ex-cavalryman and lieutenant on Denver's sixteen-man police force. The man's pewter brows beetled as he walked over to Spurr and stared down, incredulous.

"Spurr?"

Spurr stared at the girl in shock, unable to wrap his mind around all that had just happened so quickly, so out of the blue.

"Where you hit, Spurr?" Trumbo asked, dropping to one knee beside the old lawman.

Spurr shook his head. He rolled onto his back. "Reach into my pocket . . . shirt pocket. Little bag in there."

Trumbo reached inside Spurr's thigh-length elk-skin vest and hauled the small hide sack from the pocket of his hickory shirt. "This?"

Spurr swallowed, licked his lips. "Take one o' them pills out, stick it under my tongue."

"Heart?"

Spurr nodded.

Trumbo's big fingers were awkward, but he managed to get the little bag open and shake one of the small, gelatin tablets into the palm of his hand. With his thumb and index finger, he plucked the pill out of his palm and, as Spurr opened his mouth and lifted his tongue, Trumbo set it inside the old lawman's mouth.

Spurr let the nitroglycerin tablet, prescribed by his doctor as the latest "heart-starting medicine," dissolve under his tongue. As the nitro gently exploded in his chest, nudging his tucker and making it begin to beat more regularly, the mule eased itself up off Spurr's sternum. The policeman was speaking to him, but Spurr wasn't listening.

His thoughts were with the girl, who'd taken a bullet meant for him.

He heaved himself up onto all fours, crawled over to Jane, who lay staring through wide-open eyes at the sky while her tussled hair blew in the breeze around her pretty head.

Her lips were spread, revealing her teeth, so that she almost appeared to be smiling.

Blood puddled the simple, light brown dress she'd donned that morning to have breakfast at the Chinaman's with the ragged old lawman.

"Oh, darlin'," Spurr said, sorrow racking him, as he gently took the girl's young face in his hands, brushing his thumbs across her eyes, closing them. "Oh, my dear sweet, beautiful darlin'!"

Six

Two weeks later, Spurr splashed whiskey into a tin cup and threw it back.

He sighed, smacked his lips, and set the cup on the crude table he'd fashioned from a pine stump beside the bed in his two-room cabin on the slopes of Mount Rosalie. He lay his head back against his pillow and stared toward the front of the shack filled with brown shadows.

It had been a warm day, and he'd propped his plank door open with a rock. Now the air was stitched with an autumnal chill. The light angling through it and through the low, sashed windows on each side of it, was touched with late-afternoon gold and speckled with dust motes.

Night would be here soon. Spurr had gotten out of bed once to scrounge up a sandwich to go with the whiskey he'd been sipping since dawn, and once more to prop the door open with the rock.

Outside, the dog who hung around the place started barking angrily. The sounds were harsh after an entire day filled with the peace and quiet of the bluffs and foothills rising toward the Front Range of the Rocky Mountains, and the vaulting, cobalt-blue, high-altitude sky. A long, quiet day now interrupted near its end by the barking of that damn dog whom Spurr called simply Dawg and who'd come out of nowhere and stayed around the place even when Spurr wasn't here, which was damn near all the time, though that would likely change now.

If they were going to cohabitate indefinitely, Spurr and Dawg needed to come to terms.

"Goddamnit, Dawg, shut your consarned mouth and go rustle up a porky-pine!"

The dog's barks did not dwindle in the least. In fact, they grew even more frantic. And then Spurr realized why as his sharp ears picked up the ominous ratcheting hiss of a rattlesnake.

"Ah, shit."

Spurr flung his single sheet back and dropped his stocking-clad feet to the floor. He rose with a heavy groan, feeling his ticker lurch in his chest, and then, clad in only the socks and his threadbare long-handles, shuffled over to his cluttered eating table. His Starr .44 sat on the table, beside a tin plate from which Dawg had earlier removed Spurr's steak bone from last night and chewed it, growling and whining his satisfaction, on the front stoop.

Spurr grabbed the .44, spun the cylinder, and shuffled out onto the stoop and stood over the grease spot that was all that remained of the bone.

The dog was running in circles about thirty feet out from the stoop, in the yard that was large patches of clay-colored dirt between yucca and mountain sage plants. In the middle of the dog's rotation, and the focus of its attention, was a coiled diamondback that was striking repeatedly while the dog, well accustomed to the perils of the wild, leapt back just out of the serpent's reach.

The dog — a black-and-brown shepherd mongrel with one shredded ear — had its hackles raised and was showing its teeth from which dripped the stringy foam of its wrath.

"Get the hell out of the way, and I'll shoot the son of a bitch!" Spurr shouted, stepping forward, blinking and pinching sleep out of his eyes. "Been needin' meat for the stew-pot anyways, and that damn viper nearly bit me two days ago when I was fetchin' firewood. Get out of the way, you fool cur!"

Spurr clicked the Starr's hammer back. He waited for the snake to strike at Dawg once more, and to draw its head back to its coil, and fired.

Dawg yelped and twisted around to look back at Spurr as the lawman's slug plumed dust about six feet beyond the snake. The report took the starch out of the cur's tail; it slunk about four feet back away from the snake. Not yet ready to let the serpent go despite the fool on the porch with the pistol, the dog lay belly down as it stared in dark frustration at the snake, whining deep in its shaggy chest.

The snake lifted its flat, diamond-shaped head, slithering its forked tongue. Its copper eyes, with all the expression of steel pellets, turned toward the cur hunkered before it. Spurr's Starr roared, and the head disappeared, leaving only a red, ragged end where the .44-caliber round had cleaved it from the body, thick as Spurr's bony wrist.

Even with its head gone, the snake tried to strike. The dog, horrified, leapt back with a yip and then, as the snake continued to writhe and whip its button tail, the dog stood about six feet away from it, shuttling its skeptical eyes from the viper to Spurr and back again.

Spurr stared at the snake in wide-eyed surprise at the shot he'd just made. "Shit," he said, looking at the smoking gun in his hand. "Did you see that, Dawg? That was one dog-gone good shot, wouldn't you say, boy?"

The dog mewled deep in its chest, regarded Spurr with one ear down, the shredded one half raised, tipped its head to one side, and then turned and slunk off for a pile of boulders sheathed in high, blond weeds and cedars, where it usually hunted for cottontails.

Spurr chuckled, still amazed — "I haven't made a shot like that in years!" — and walked down off the porch steps and into the yard. He ambled over to the snake that was still writhing wildly though its movements were gradually diminishing, and held the beast down with one of his stocking feet. He grabbed the viper just down from the ragged neck and held it up for inspection.

"That's a hog there!" he said, estimating the length to be around five and a half feet. "Throw him in a stew pot with some onions and pinto beans, and I'm gonna have me a meal!"

He'd started walking back toward the cabin, the snake still slowly coiling and uncoiling in his hand, when a clattering rose behind him.

He turned toward the west, where he could see, between a haystack butte and a rocky dike, the town of Denver spread out across the eastern plain about ten miles away. It didn't look so big from here and this high vantage — just a rather motley collection of red and black or brown buildings and stock pens surrounding a business section a little larger and more sprawling than Dodge City's or Wichita's, with the English castle–like Union Station standing watch over the silver rails of the Union Pacific, formerly the Denver Pacific, and a few other lines that were converging now on Denver and making it a right smart hub.

Heading from the direction of town, now just visible as it climbed the incline from the plains and was turning around a rocky-topped butte, was a spiffy-looking two-seater buggy upholstered in black leather and appointed with high, red wheels.

"Well, I'll be damned," Spurr said, narrowing his eyes speculatively, as he watched the buggy come along the shaggy, two-track trail angling like a long, flour-white snake through the pinyons and junipers and shin-high brome and needle grass spotted with the soft pinks and velvet blues of autumn wildflowers.

One man was driving the one-horse rig while another lounged in the seat behind him, to the buggy's far right side, holding a newspaper open before him. Spurr couldn't see much of the buggy's passenger except for a pearl-gray derby hat, but he recognized the driver, and that alone — as well as the fancy buggy — told him who was on his way for a visit. The driver was Chief Marshal Henry Brackett's first assistant, Leonard Foghorn, a graduate of Yale University and a member of some moneyed clan from the same rolling, green Maryland hills that the chief marshal himself hailed from.

When a fellow saw Leonard Foghorn — a well set-up lad in his early twenties and always dressed to the nines in a crisp, carefully tailored seersucker suit — you knew the Chief Marshal wasn't far behind. Henry Brackett wasn't now, either — only about three feet away from his blond, pink-cheeked assistant, reading the *Rocky Mountain News* while the buggy jostled him along the uneven two-track.

"Well, this has got to be bad — real bad," Spurr said after young Leonard had turned a broad circle in the yard and pulled the buggy sideways in front of Spurr, dust wafting in the salmon light. "I think in all the years we've worked together, Henry, you've been out here only once. On a huntin' trip."

Long ago, Spurr and the chief marshal had dispensed with formalities. They each addressed the other by his first name. Brackett was only two years older than Spurr, after all, and they'd worked together as deputies before Henry had been promoted to the chief marshal position about fifteen years before, when he was still a relatively young man. At least, younger than the old man he was now.

"Good Lord, man," Brackett said, scowling as his watery blue eyes raked Spurr up and down, grimacing as he gave the same scrutiny to the still-writhing snake in Spurr's hand. "You look as though you're just getting up!"

"Officially, I'm still in bed. *Un*officially I got out of bed to see what Dawg was barkin' about and just sort of *accidentally* filled the stewpot. You should have seen me, Henry. Cleaved this serpent's head clean off with my second shot!"

"Looks delicious," said Leonard Foghorn, who looked a little like a rawboned, clear-eyed farmboy from the Midwest, but one with prissy habits, like flicking his kid gloves held in one hand at blackflies buzzing around his yellow-blond curls.

"I'd invite you for supper, Leonard,"

68

Spurr said, "but I haven't tidied up around the place in a month of Sundays. The last woman who lived out here left . . . oh, nigh on fifteen, sixteen years ago, now. Just me an' Dawg and a skunk that lives under the porch out here, now."

Leonard turned toward the cabin's sagging front stoop and worked his nostrils, sniffing. "Is that what that smell is?"

"Either that or the coyote bitch that comes around to play with Dawg now an' then. I think she's smitten with him."

"Spurr, are you going to invite me to step down?" Brackett asked, setting his folded newspaper aside and folding the bows on his silver-framed, pince-nez reading glasses, "or are you just going to keep jawing with that writhing viper in your hand?"

"All right, all right, Henry," Spurr said, turning and ambling toward the cabin. "Come on in and get it over with. I know why you're here."

Spurr went in and tossed the snake on his cutting table that was still bloody from the steak he'd carved last night from the side of beef hanging in his keeper shed. He grabbed an uncorked bottle and filled one of his several dirty tin cups on his four-by-four-foot eating table.

Brackett tramped up the porch steps.

Leonard Foghorn remained in the buggy, leaning back in the leather seat and scowling down at Dawg, who was skinning a rabbit in the dirt near the buggy's front wheel.

Brackett stopped in the cabin's open doorway and doffed his pearl-gray derby that complemented his matching vest, white silk shirt, and black split-tail frock coat and trousers with gray pinstripes. A natty dresser, Henry was, though Spurr had always thought he'd looked more at home in the rugged, smoke- and sweat-stained trail gear that Spurr had always felt most comfortable in himself. Brackett's pince-nez glasses dangled from his coat lapel to which they were attached by a black celluloid rosette and a length of black ribbon.

He was a small, wiry man with a craggy, ruddy, handsome face, the skin drawn taut against the fine, almost delicate bones. His close-cropped hair was snow white, though his brows remained dark brown. He watched, slightly stoop-shouldered, as Spurr filled the tin cup clear to its brim with whiskey.

"That won't bring her back, you know," Henry said and hooked his derby hat over the back of the chair at the end of the table nearest the door.

Spurr looked into the cup as he raised it

to his lips, gave a little, caustic chuff, and took a swig. When he pulled the cup back down with a sigh, he felt a soothing flush rise in his cheeks and leach up into his brain. "Any sign of those killers, Henry?"

"No. We think they rode out of town a ways and then circled back later that night. They might have hopped an eastbound train for Kansas. I have my two of my best men on it."

"Why, thank you, Henry," Spurr said ironically though he knew the insult hadn't been intentional.

"Ah, shit." Brackett pulled out a chair and sat down, his back facing the wall and the front window left of the open door.

When he'd eased his wiry, compact frame into the chair, Spurr slid the bottle toward him. "Drink?"

"Will I go blind?"

"I make no promises," Spurr said as he retrieved a relatively clean cup from a shelf over his grease-splattered range. He set the cup on the table. As Brackett splashed a conservative measure of the busthead into it, Spurr sagged down in a chair across from him.

Neither said anything for a time. As if in acknowledgment of the gravity of the situation, Brackett hauled an old, soiled canvas makings sack out of his coat pocket and began to slowly, methodically build a quirley.

Spurr had to smile at that. Brackett had made it to the rank of chief marshal, probably hauled in six or seven thousand dollars a year, lived in a nice, tight brick and gingerbread house near Cherry Creek with a nice, smiling little gray-haired woman, and yet he still rolled his own cigarettes. No ready-made smokes for Henry Brackett.

When he'd deftly closed the cylinder and rolled it between his lips to seal it, he plucked a stove match off the table, scraped it to life on the base of Spurr's tarnished brass table lamp, and touched the flame to the quirley.

Squinting through the smoke billowing around his head, Henry cleared his throat and said, "Spurr, you're officially retired."

Spurr sat back in his chair and considered the words. They were no surprise. He'd been expecting them. Yet, they still rankled.

"The girl wasn't your fault," Henry added when he'd tossed back nearly his entire shot of whiskey and set the cup back down on the table. "She was in the wrong place at the wrong time. No one blames you for that."

"Well, thank you, Henry, but the bullet

she took *was* meant for me. And she was a hell of a nice girl though I admit I'm partial to doxies."

"I just wanted you to know that that in no way has this figured into your . . . uh . . . mandatory retirement."

"Good to know, but that won't bring her back, neither," Spurr said, splashing more whiskey into his old friend's cup.

Brackett waved a veiny, brown hand in halfhearted reproach, but he lifted the cup and took another sip. He set the cup down and took a pull from his quirley as he once again squinted through the smoke at Spurr.

The chief marshal's eyes were a little rheumy, and Spurr idly wondered if it was from the whiskey or emotion, or, possibly, both. They'd come a long way together, and in a way both men were staring out from atop the same steep precipice.

"If you yourself don't know when it's time to hang up the shootin' irons," Henry said, his ruddy cheeks reddening, "then it's come down to me to do it for you, thank you very much, you mule-headed son of a bitch!"

"Henry?"

"What?"

"One more."

Brackett scowled at him. He took another drag from his quirley. "One more what?"

"One more job." Spurr leaned forward on his elbows, staring at his old friend gravely. "Don't make me go out like this, with a dead innocent girl the last thing I got to remember before they nail the lid down on top of me. After all these long years of good service. I want to go out on a better note than that. I want to go out doing something right — however small the job. When I head for Mexico, I want to take that with me to mull over for the time I have left." He sat back in his chair. "Hell, it's all I'm gonna have to live on."

"You haven't saved anything?"

Spurr shook his head. "I always figured I'd die in some ravine somewhere down in Arizona or out Utah way, and it wouldn't matter."

Brackett snored, chuckled without humor. "After all these years, you have nothing to live on. It all went for whiskey and whores."

"Well, shit, I always believed in livin' till you're dead."

"And now you're gonna starve down in Mexico in your old age."

"With my head propped on a senorita's tender breast, Henry," Spurr said, grinning over the rim of his whiskey cup.

Brackett snorted, shook his head.

"One more," Spurr said, his voice thickly

serious again. "Just one more. Anything. But not courtroom duty, fer chrissakes. I wanna finish up on the trail — me an' Cochise."

Brackett drew a ragged breath. He studied Spurr for a time, and then he turned his head toward the door and yelled, "Leonard, bring my valise!"

Seven

Aboard the Union Pacific flyer headed north toward Cheyenne, Spurr closed the file on his lap, sat back in the green plush seat, and reached inside his elk-skin vest for a long, black cigar.

He bit the twist off the panatela and scraped his thumbnail over a stove match, lighting up. When he had the slender cheroot drawing properly, sucking the sweet-peppery smoke deep into his lungs, he lowered the cigar and absently studied its coal though it was not the panatela he was thinking about but the assignment he'd just read in the file Henry had given him.

The chief marshal had sent one old man after another one. An old man waiting in a constable's jail in some remote mountain village called Diamond Fire.

Well, that was fitting. The prisoner written about in the file was only two years younger than Spurr. George Blackleg was wanted on an old federal warrant for robbing a mail train six years ago in Kansas. A bounty hunter had picked up the old gent in a whorehouse up in a little mining town in the Medicine Bow Mountains and run him into the local lockup to claim his reward.

Whether the bounty hunter just had a good memory or had recently seen one of the old federal wanted dodgers — they often hung in post offices, barbershops, and Wells Fargo offices for years — Henry didn't know. All he did know was that he had an old man to pick up in the Medicine Bow Mountains, a hundred miles as the crow flies from Denver, and he didn't want to waste his younger, busier deputy marshals on such a tedious, routine assignment.

Henry hadn't put it just that way to Spurr, of course. He'd much less crassly told his senior-most deputy that he might have one more job for him though it included more horsebacking in the mountains west of Camp Collins, in northern Colorado, than actual lawdogging. Which made it appropriate for Spurr's last assignment, given the old deputy's bad health. So if Spurr wanted it, Henry supposed he could take it.

Spurr had taken it, pleased to have one last job beyond the one in which he'd gotten a pretty girl killed.

One last slow, easy job with which to ride off into eternity . . .

Spurr chuckled now as he looked out the train window at the Front Range of the Rockies sliding past, beyond the rolling blond prairie under the vast, cerulean, high-altitude sky. For some reason it had just dawned on him that Henry had ridden out to his cabin with every intention of giving Spurr the easy job of hauling old George Blackleg back to the federal courthouse in Denver. Henry hadn't let on, and he'd done a good job of fooling Spurr into believing he'd handed the job over reluctantly.

The truth of it was, Spurr now realized, Henry had packed that file in his valise with every intention of allowing his old friend to go out on a better note than he otherwise would have, so that the dead girl wouldn't be Spurr's last memory after twenty years of more or less exemplary service.

"I'll be damned," Spurr said as he blew a long plume of aromatic tobacco smoke at the soot-streaked window.

"Sir, I'm going to have to ask you to watch your tongue — there is a young lady present!"

Spurr jerked with a start, and turned to see a stout woman in a gaudy traveling frock and feathered picture hat scowling down at him. She was a tall, blond woman with double jowls and angry little eyes, clutching a pink leather grip in one hand, a parasol in the other. She waved the parasol and made a face. "And would you mind opening a window and blowing that wretched smoke *out it* instead of merely *against it* and right back *into* our *faces!*"

Spurr frowned up at the big woman, who appeared in her late thirties, early forties. As far as he could tell, she was alone. Was *she herself* the "young lady" she'd been referring to? Spurr found himself grinning devilishly and asking wryly, "I'm sorry, ma'am, but I only see . . ."

A young girl's face rose up from behind the woman's right shoulder. Spurr's tired ticker lurched in his chest. The girl was pretty and brown-eyed, her thick, wavy, wheat-blond hair pulled back behind her head in a loose French braid — and for a moment Spurr saw Kansas City Jane staring at him from over the big woman's shoulder. For another moment, he thought that Jane was about to say something to him from the misty otherworld beyond this one.

But then the girl slid her curious, vaguely impatient eyes from Spurr to the big woman in front of her, and said in a needling voice totally unlike Jane's, "Can I have the window seat, Aunt Alice? You know how awful sick I get if I can't see out!"

"Only if you think you can stomach the smoke, dear?" The old woman glowered at Spurr. "We left the last car because of the cacophony kicked up by three drunkards. Here, we have to tolerate the smoke from your cigar!"

"Here, here — I'm opening the damn window, so get your frillies out of a twist!" Spurr said.

The woman gasped.

Spurr glanced over his shoulder, sheepish. The girl was scowling over her aunt's shoulder. "Uh . . . do pardon my French, ladies," he said, lowering the window half-way and then stepping back against his own seat, remaining standing and giving a gentle-manly bow to the ladies.

The young girl, dressed in a plaid dress with a delicate little bow tie and bullet-brimmed straw hat with a brown silk band, wriggled her way around her portly aunt and sagged into the chair directly across from Spurr. The big woman then sort of half-tumbled and half-folded herself down into the seat beside her niece, and Spurr slacked back down into his own seat.

He took another drag from the cigar and made a point of blowing the smoke out the window. Still, both the girl and the big woman scowled at him, the big woman making a face and waving her hand though Spurr couldn't see any smoke blowing at her.

"I do apologize," Spurr growled and, knowing he could no longer enjoy the panatela, carefully raked the coal off the end and onto the floor and stuffed the remaining cigar back into his shirt pocket for later.

He ground the coal beneath his moccasin boot. Both the girl and the big woman regarded him like an unsightly something a cur had left on the parlor rug. Spurr smiled at them and, since they were all sitting here together in the rocking, rattling parlor car, heading north across the vast, lonely plain, he tried to make conversation.

"You ladies headed far?"

The girl turned to the woman and arched a brow. The woman touched the girl's wrist, wagged her head not to speak to the unwashed stranger, and snootily directed her gaze out the window. The girl shuttled her own gaze past Spurr and out the window, and Spurr gave a snort, wishing he'd gone ahead and kept his panatela lit.

Uppity bitches.

He sighed, sagged down in his seat, and pulled his hat brim down low on his forehead. Might as well catch a catnap or two before detraining at the little station east of Camp Collins. His mind stayed with the women, however. He couldn't help feeling a little injured by their rude dismissal.

He opened one eye, furtively looking out from beneath his down-canted hat brim at the girl sitting across from him, her head turned toward the blond prairie sliding by, beyond the smoke lacing back from the locomotive. A pretty, young thing, this girl. Prettier than young Jane if you only took surface features into account, but Jane was far more lovely because of the tenderness in her eyes. Jane had had a hard life, and it had softened her heart, whereas this girl had lived a pampered life, and she had little time for anyone but herself.

Spurr tried to shunt his mind onto a different track than the one Jane was on. She was dead, and there was no bringing her back. As he turned his mind to other pursuits, he opened one eye again to regard the pretty girl sitting across from him once more.

He found himself remembering a time — years ago, of course — when he'd raised a flush in the cheeks of such a girl as the one sitting across from him. When such a girl would respond to him shyly, maybe bat an eyelash or two, and indulge him in demure conversation.

He remembered taking walks along country creeks with such a girl as this one, walks down country lanes, of picnicking with such a girl in the hills above his father's farm in Kansas, before he'd lit out west to make a new, wild life for himself.

Well, he'd had that life. Used it all up. He'd burned the fuse from both ends, and here he was in warty old age, sitting across from a pretty girl who wouldn't even look at him let alone indulge his conversation.

He was old enough to be the girl's grandfather, of course. The unkind fat woman sitting beside her was young enough to be Spurr's daughter. And neither one had the time of day for such a man as the one he'd become — old and used up and ugly and now only fit to transport one prisoner nearly as old as he himself was down the mountains to Denver for trial.

And then that was it.

His job was over. And since his job had been his life, what could possibly be left?

The girl turned to him. Her eyes met his. A pink flush rose in her cheeks.

Well, he'd be damned . . .

And then she turned to the older woman and rolled her eyes at Spurr. Spurr, deep in thought, had forgotten he'd been staring at the girl from beneath his hat brim. He'd apparently offended the girl.

The woman turned to him, beetling her blond brows over her deep-set eyes, and said, "Sir, please — a gentleman would not stare!"

"One," Spurr said, straightening in his seat, "I ain't no gentleman. And two, neither one of you is anything like no lady should be." He heaved his creaky bones to his feet and adjusted his cartridge belt and holstered .44 on his lean hips. "So there. Stick that in your pipe an' smoke it. Me . . ." He reached into the overhead rack for his saddlebags and his Winchester. "I'm gonna go out to the vestibule and smoke my friggin' cigar. I hope you *ladies* don't get too lonely without me."

"Well, I never!" said the older, fat woman.

"Don't doubt it a bit," Spurr said as, his saddlebags draped over his left shoulder, the Winchester in his right hand, he pinched his hat brim to the pair and headed on out the coach's rear door.

In the vestibule between the cars, he sat down with his back to the wall of the car he'd left, his saddlebags on one side of him, his rifle resting across his thighs, and relit the cheroot.

The air whooshed past him on both sides of the gap between the cars, dragging smoke from the locomotive along with it. Spurr stared out across the prairie to the purple mountains, smoking and thinking over the long years behind him — long years that had rushed past faster than the prairie sliding past him toward Denver now — and he was glad when the train came to a jerking halt at the water stop and the little station hut on the open prairie east of Camp Collins.

While the locomotive took on water and the conductor and one of the brakemen smoked and talked with the old black man who ran the depot hut in the shade of the hut's little brush arbor, Spurr led Cochise down the wooden ramp from the stable car and tightened the roan's saddle cinch.

"Where you off to this time, Spurr?"

The old lawman turned to see the old black man, Sebastian Polly, walk toward him from the station hut, puffing the quirley he held between his lips with a gnarled, arthritic right hand. The sideburns running down from the blue uniform cap were steel-colored, as was Polly's thick mustache, with only a few threads of black showing through the gray.

"You mean, for the *last* time, Sebastian,"

Spurr said. For as long as Spurr had been a federal badge toter, Sebastian Polly had been living out here on this backside of nowhere east of Camp Collins, sixty miles south of Cheyenne.

Polly lived in the station hut, and Spurr couldn't remember ever stopping at this point and not seeing the black man here, tending the hut that saw business only when the train stopped to take on water or to let a passenger off. There had been a stage line through here, years ago, and Polly had run the relay station, but of course the stage line had closed when the Union Pacific connected Denver with the Northern Pacific line at Cheyenne. That's when Polly went to work for the railroad and moved into the depot hut.

Over the years, the black man's hair had gradually turned grayer, and he'd grown a little thinner, his molasses eyes a little rheumier, his shoulders clad in the age-coppered blue uniform coat a little more stooped.

"What you talkin' about, Spurr?" Polly said, blowing out a plume of cigarette smoke and knitting his grizzled brows together.

"This is it for me." Spurr slipped Cochise's bridle bit through the horse's teeth and then grabbed his rifle from where it leaned against the wooden loading ramp slanting down from the stable car. "Last job. I done been retired."

"You don't say!"

"I said it."

Spurr slid his rifle into his beaded elk-hide scabbard and then tossed his saddle-bags over Cochise's back, tucking them under his bedroll around which his heavy buckskin mackinaw was tied, to hold the bags in place. He'd soon be climbing into high, cold, rough country.

"You don't look too happy about it, Spurr," said Sebastian Polly, scowling, flicking ashes from his cigarette onto the cinder bed and rubbing the sparks out with his boot so as not to start any wild prairie fires.

"Who could be happy about retirement, Sebastian?"

"Well, shit, I will be . . . when my time comes. I reckon I got another year to go, and then I'll have me a stake big enough to go live down in Denver and watch all them pretty girls walk by."

"Watch 'em all walk by, huh?" Holding Cochise's reins in one gloved hand, Spurr turned to the old man. "Is that good enough for you? Just sittin' out on some rooming house porch and watchin' 'em all walk by?"

Polly tipped his head to one side, his dark eyes curious. "Spurr, how old are you?"

"I'm sixty-three, give or take a year. Record keeping wasn't valued much over where they hatched me out."

"Well, shit, that's five years older'n me. You ask me, you done pretty well. You should be stompin' with your tail up in celebration of all them good years you put in, huntin' bad men. Lawd knows there's damn few lawmen been workin' as long as you have without they ended up, long time ago, in a boot hill somewhere, worms in their mouth, pushin' up crocuses every spring!"

The station agent laughed at that.

"Well, you're just an optimistic man, aren't you, Sebastian?"

"Yes, sir, I am! Spurr, you got no cause to go 'round lookin' like some dog headin' back to the farm after getting' hisself sprayed by a damn skunk! Time for you to move out of that old shack of yours and move into a nice roomin' house in Denver."

Spurr turned a stirrup out and grunted as he poked his left foot through it. He heaved himself up onto Cochise's back, the leather squawking beneath him. He said with a snort, "And sit out on the porch and just watch them purty girls stroll by, eh, Sebastian!"

"Sho 'nuff, Mister Spurr. You try to whip them girls with your trouser snake, your old ticker'd plum go out on you!"

"That's what you think. Whippin' girls with my trouser snake is what's been keepin' me so young."

"Then how come you're so old?"

Spurr leaned out from his horse and said as though conferring a deep secret, "Looks can be deceiving, Sebastian."

He grinned and straightened in his saddle, ignoring the tightness in his chest he was still feeling occasionally after the seizure on Arapaho Street in Denver that awful day.

"I'll be seein' you once more, Sebastian. On my way back through. That'll be the last you see of me. I'll be headin' on down to Mexico to whip the senoritas with my ole trouser snake while I dig for gold!"

He neck-reined Cochise around and ground his heels into the big roan's flanks, loping off along the old army trail to the west.

"Spurr, somethin' tells me you think you're gonna live forever," Sebastian said behind him, blowing smoke out his long, mahogany nostrils. "You ain't got the word, have you? *We all gonna dahhh!*"

89

Spurr scowled over his shoulder at the old gent who was way too pleased with himself. Sebastian poked a gnarled finger at him, jeering, and he showed his old, yellow teeth under his gray mustache, raising one thigh to slap it, his guffaws staying with Spurr as the old lawman galloped on down the trail to the west, toward the purple and lime-green mountains humping tall above the horizon.

Spurr snarled, cursed under his breath, and spat to one side.

"You just keep laughin' like a mule with a mouthful of cockleburs, Sebastian!"

He was so angry that he did not look back again. If he had, he would have seen three men leading their horses down the stock car's loading ramp and staring after him.

EIGHT

"That's him, all right," Collie Bone said, staring after the old man who'd just ridden off on the rangy roan stallion, heading toward the mountains.

"You sure, Bone?" This from a Wyoming outlaw named Quinn McCall, who was leading his bay Arab down the ramp alongside Bone.

Both men gained the ground alongside the gravel bed of the railroad tracks, both staring off into the dust kicked up by the old man and the handsome roan. Behind Bone and McCall, the outlaw known only as Tatum to anyone who'd known him in the past ten years came down off the ramp at a trot, holding the headstall of his frisky ex-cavalry sorrel, who'd had one ear half chewed off.

"That's ole Spurr, all right," Tatum said. "I recognized him when he looked right at me, when he boarded the flyer at Union

Station."

"He looked right at you?"

"Looked right at me," Tatum said, "but I could tell he didn't recognize me. My god, has he gotten old! Looks like a side of coyote-chewed mule deer buck behind that scraggly beard and them old duds that hang off his ancient bones. Got more age spots and warts than freckles."

Tatum threw a stirrup up over his saddle to tighten the sorrel's cinch.

"Spurr Morgan — well, I'll be damned," said McCall, lifting his funnel-brimmed Stetson to run a hand through his thick, close-cropped, copper-red hair. He wore a thick beard of the same color. "I hope he remembers us. You think he remembers us, Collie?"

"Hope so. Don't matter." Collie Bone was setting his saddlebags over his horse, behind his saddle cantle and bedroll, and staring after Spurr. "He cost all three of us six years in Yuma pen. I woulda hunted that old man down, but, shit, I thought for sure he'd be dead by now. Ain't that what we heard, Tatum? Didn't we hear he bought a bullet in Nueces?"

"I can't vouch for what you heard, Collie, but that's what I heard, all right. I remember cryin' real tears, that night, too. Right in front of a rather expensive Abilene whore, too. Very embarrassing. I'm gonna give him one bullet for that when we run him down, in addition to all the others for Yuma."

"One bullet for every month," McCall said, gritting his teeth as he stared after the small, brown, jostling blur that was the old lawman and his handsome roan. "Or until he dies howlin'. How'd that be?"

He grunted angrily as he shucked his double-action Cooper Pocket Revolver, an old cap-and-ball weapon, but one that McCall still always carried with two other more modern weapons because it was a double-action piece and had sentimental value in that it had seen him through his early days on the frontier just after the Civil War.

He quickly checked the loads in the Cooper and was about to check the loads in one of his matched Remingtons when a deep, resonate voice said, "Where you fellas headin' off to in such a hurry?"

Tatum, Bone, and McCall turned toward the station agent — a gray-haired, gray-mustached black man who'd been smoking in the shade of a large, dusty cottonwood slouched just west of the stopped train. He was strolling toward them slowly, rolling a quirley in his long, arthritic fingers.

Beyond him, several young children played

along the rails, running after each other and yelling — two boys and a younger girl, while a young woman in a Mother Hubbard dress and matching bonnet stood nearby, cradling an infant in her arms. Several men stood beyond the woman, smoking and conversing, just waiting for the order to reboard.

Tatum hefted the Remington in his right hand and said, "Ain't no one ever told you not to ask questions, you dark-skinned old son of a bitch?"

The old man stopped and scowled at the three men standing by their horses. "I reckon I'm old enough to ask any questions I want."

"That a fact?" Tatum held his pistol in the flat of his hand as he walked slowly toward the old station agent, holding the gun up menacingly.

"That's enough, Tatum. Take that hump out of your neck." Collie Bone, the unofficial leader of the outlaw trio, swung up onto his buckskin, and gave Tatum a commanding look. "We got other fish to fry, my friend."

"Any o' them fish named Marshal Spurr Morgan?" the black man asked darkly.

"What's that to you?" asked McCall, stepping up onto his bay Arab. "What if it is about Spurr?"

94

The station agent slowly, thoughtfully licked the cylinder he'd just pressed closed. "Spurr's old and feeble," he said, shaking is head gravely. "Why, he hardly recognized me, an' we been friends for years. Bad ticker, too. He's on his last job now, an' then he's headin' for Mexico."

"That right?" Tatum chuckled. "Well, he should've headed for Mexico last week. 'Cause it as it turns out this here is the last week of his . . ."

"Tatum!" Collie Bone jerked his chin toward the sorrel. "Fork leather an' let's ride!"

Grinning shrewdly, Tatum did as Bone had bid, while Bone jutted his spade-shaped chin carpeted in a thick black goatee at the old station agent. "And you, old man, best keep your mouth shut from now on — understand? Otherwise, you're gonna wake up some night in that shed yonder screamin' and just so damn surprised to see your tongue hangin' off the blade o' my bowie knife!"

The black man lowered his hands to his sides and shook his head. "Please, leave him be. Leave Spurr be. He ain't half the man he once was."

"Smoke your cigarette, you old darkie!" McCall snarled as he booted his Arab after

Bone, who'd put his buckskin into a ground-eating gallop up the wagon trail toward Camp Collins.

"Oh, please, leave that feeble old man alone," beseeched the station agent, staring after them, his eyes wide with concern.

As the three obvious long-coulee riders dwindled to blurs kicking up a single dust trail, Sebastian Polly lit his freshly rolled quirley and grinned through the smoke.

"That old goat keeps a steady pace — I'll give him that," Bone said as he and the others followed a northward bend in the trail.

"Probably too senile to know what he's doin' to his horse." Tatum was checking the loads in one of his Remingtons again, which he did obsessively.

"Maybe he just has a good horse," said Bone, glancing toward Camp Collins, which lay to the north, off the trail's right side — a shabby collection of mud-brick, brush-roofed dwellings languishing in the prairie sun. Since the Indian trouble had become almost nonexistent, the stockade-less encampment was now garrisoned by twenty to thirty soldiers at a time. These days, Bone had heard that desertion was the outpost's biggest problem. That, prairie fires, drunkenness, and syphilis.

The camp's flag looked washed out and dirty in the bright sun, buffeting in the cool, dry breeze of the barren parade ground a half a mile from the main trail.

"Maybe he ain't worth it, fellas." McCall leaned forward to light a cigar while holding his Arab to a spanking trot just behind the others. "If his mind is gone, like the darkie said it was, what's the damn point? We'd best head on to Cheyenne, maybe. Bill and the others is gonna wonder what's keepin' us."

"Bill can wait," Tatum said. "You know how many times I was bit by sewer roaches in the ole Hell Hole? One mornin' I even woke to one sitting on my chest trying to chew out the food between my teeth!" He gave a shudder, shook his head. "No, sir — that ole bastard is gonna pay for that. I'm gonna pop a .44 pill into both his knees for that."

"Tatum's right," Bone said. "I couldn't sleep a wink from now on if I knew I had a chance to kill ole Spurr Morgan and didn't take it. You know how many men have wanted to do that over the years?"

"Well, it would have been more satisfyin' a few years ago," McCall said. "When he coulda remembered what he was gettin' turned under slow for, but what the hell. I reckon you boys are right."

He tipped his hat brim low and held the bay at a steady pace beside Bone, who kept his gaze straight ahead along the trail. He didn't like it that, aside from the fresh prints in the trail left on the wagon track, he could not see the old lawman riding ahead of them. Spurr had a wily reputation. He was liable to pull a bushwhack. At least, a younger Spurr would have done that. The old man he and Tatum and McCall had seen aboard the train was a used-up old shell of his former self.

Hell, he probably didn't even remember where he was heading most of the time but merely left it up to his horse to get him there.

Bone, Tatum, and McCall held up once when, smelling a coffee fire on the wind, they suspected that Spurr had taken a break probably to rest himself as well as his horse. When they saw the man ride out from a copse of willows along the Cache la Poudre River, they mounted their own rested horses and rode on.

They followed Spurr's trail north along the Poudre and into the mouth of Poudre Canyon — a wide gap between limestone and sandstone peaks cut by the river tumbling down from ten-thousand-foot Cameron Pass eons ago.

Bone knew that the canyon was one of the few routes from the eastern plains to both the Never Summer Mountains south of the pass and the Medicine Bow Mountains to the north of it. Spurr must be heading into one of those ranges, though why the marshals service would send a man as old as Spurr into that rugged country was anyone's guess.

Why in the hell was he still wearing a badge, anyway? He must have caught the governor with his pants down in the company of some other mucky-muck's young wife.

Bone smiled at that as he and the others rode up into the cooler climbs of the canyon, the river rippling through its rocky bed on the trail's left side — a slow-moving stream this time of year though Bone, who'd once ridden the pass preying on stagecoach lines, knew that in the spring, when the snowmelt plunged down from the pass fifty miles west, it could be one hell of a mighty torrent.

Bone and the other two men rode up the canyon until well after sunset, stopping when they spied the glow of a campfire off the trail's right side, in some trees along the river. They picketed their horses well off the trail, shucked their rifles from their saddle scabbards, quietly pumped fresh rounds into the breeches, and slowly made their way toward the fire's glow.

The glow dwindled gradually as they approached the bivouac.

Bone looked around carefully, wary of a bushwhack. As he and the others drew within forty yards of the camp in a small clearing amongst pines and aspens, Bone started hearing something. Low, regular snores.

Bone couldn't help smiling at that. He cut his eyes to the other two men — McCall moving slowly about ten yards to his left, Tatum moving about fifty yards straight out on his right.

They glanced back at him. By the wan glow of the slowly dying fire, Bone could see Tatum curl his upper lip. The light danced in McCall's narrowed eyes, beneath his down-canted hat brim. Bone's heart quickened. He thought of the Hell Hole again, and he almost slavered like a wolf with the scent of an imminent kill in his nose.

He looked around for Spurr's horse but saw no sign of the mount. It must have been picketed near the river — probably hobbled so it could drink and forage at will. The mount would be a nice appropriation. Bone and his two partners would draw straws for it. A second mount — especially one as fine as the roan — would come in handy.

At the edge of the fire's glow, Bone stopped. McCall and Tatum stopped, as well. The fire was about fifteen feet away. The hump that was Spurr Morgan — Bone recognized the hat tipped down beside the saddle that the old lawman was using for a pillow — lay on the fire's far side. He lay abutting a stout pine, high-topped moccasins standing neatly beside Spurr's form humped beneath the blankets.

It was almost dark in the clearing. Occasionally the fire popped and sparked and there was some fleeting light. But mostly there were only shadows. The only sounds were Spurr's regular snoring, the soft crackling of the fire, and the ceaseless chugging and rippling of the river in the bank about fifty yards to Bone's right.

Bone looked at the others. They were both watching him, taking his lead. He nodded and started forward, raising his Winchester in both hands across his chest, gently drawing the hammer back to full cock.

He set each boot down carefully in the fine dust and pine needles around the fire. He skirted the fire's left side and approached Spurr, who lay before him in the velvety darkness. The old lawman continued to send up his loud, slow, regular snores.

To Bone's left, McCall gave a soft whistle. Bone looked at the man, who jerked his head to indicate something above Bone. Bone lifted his gaze to see, in the dense shadows and flickers of umber light from the fire's coals, what appeared to be a rope.

The rope was hanging from a branch of the pine. Bone glowered up at the rope, and cool, dry fingers of apprehension raked across the back of his neck.

The rope had been fashioned into a hangman's knot. It hung about four feet over Bone's head. He could feel the tension in the other two men as they, too, studied the knot.

Spurr continued to snore.

The snoring stopped.

Bone, McCall, and Tatum all jerked their heads down to look at the humped shape before them. Bone began to bring his Winchester down, aim the barrel at a spot in the blankets just beneath the down-canted hat.

A shadow slid out from behind the tree. Two eyes glowed red in the fire's dim umber glow. A raspy voice shouted, "Bone, McCall, Tatum — you're all under arrest!

Gonna come peaceful?"

Bone heard himself scream as he lurched back a step and aimed his rifle at the vague, red-eyed silhouette of a hatless head poking out from behind the stout pine. He only saw a gun flash, which fleetingly showed the devilish grin on the wizened old lawman's haggard face, before he stopped hearing anything at all.

Spurr's pistol roared three times and then once more as if in afterthought, the flames stabbing from the barrel lighting up his little encampment in the trees along the river. The man to Spurr's left was the only one of the three who'd gotten off a shot, the slug plunking harmlessly into the pine bole.

Then all three figures were humped on the ground to either side of the fire, groaning and mewling, boots raking the dirt as the dying outlaws kicked and flopped spasmodically.

It took only a few seconds before they stopped moving, ceased making sounds of any kind.

Spurr stepped around the tree in his longhandles, the Starr .44 aimed straight out from his right hip. Gray smoke curled from the barrel. He walked around to each dead man, making sure that each had, in fact, given up the ghost.

Spurr gave a satisfied chuff and returned the Starr to the holster coiled beside his saddle, near where the Winchester leaned against the pine. He threw his blankets back, tossed away the small pine branches he'd heaped there, and crawled back into the roll.

He looked up at the noose he'd thrown over the pine branch, shook his head, and chuckled at his own joke.

He tipped his hat down over his eyes, smacked his lips, and yawned. "Now, maybe a washed-up old lawman can finally get some shut-eye!"

NINE

Four days later, in the winding, narrow little canyon that housed the town calling itself Diamond Fire in the Medicine Bow Mountains, Spurr stared down at the man with his head hanging over the creek, and said, "Sir, if that creek comes up another inch, or you lower your head same, you will drown."

The man did not move. He was hanging half off the bank of the creek that tumbled down the canyon, splitting the town in two. The man's shaggy, light blond hair sagged toward the water that bubbled over the rocks, barely an inch beneath his nose. One arm also hung over the bank while the other arm was thrown out beside him. He wore a shabby wool coat, dungarees, and the hobnailed boots of a miner.

"Sir!" Spurr intoned, staring down from Cochise's back. He'd just ridden into the shabby outskirts of the town. It was late afternoon, but the sun had already dropped behind the steep, rocky western pass, and piano and fiddle music could be heard all up and down the canyon, the players seemingly competing for raucousness.

Still, the man hanging over the water did not move. Sound asleep. Passed out, more like, from the snake piss sold in such camps as this one and calling itself whiskey.

With an angry grunt, Spurr hauled himself out of the saddle. He dropped to a knee, rolled the sleeping man over onto his back, and saw that he had been sleeping, all right. Asleep for all eternity. The ragged hole in his forehead, just left of center, told the story. Blood had oozed out of the hole and into his hairline and coagulated there in a thick, dark brown crust.

"Want a poke, mister?"

Spurr lifted his head. A girl stood on the second-story balcony of the broad, three-story building behind him. Called Reymont & Chaney's Dovetail Frolic House, it was an unpainted structure built of vertical whipsawed pine planks, with unpeeled pine logs framing the sprawling first-floor veranda. The girl, a willowy blonde, wore a sheer wrap that Spurr could see through, and she opened the unbuttoned garment wider to give him an unobstructed look at her breasts.

She smiled. "I'm free with a bottle until seven o'clock this evening." She hefted her breasts in her hands, and winked. "We're in competition with the Chinaman on Denver Avenue, so Reymont and Chaney got us all marked down for a time."

"A purty girl like you for the price of a *bottle*?" Spurr said, scowling with incredulity as he straightened. "Well, that's an insult and a cryin' shame to boot!"

The girl smiled and waggled a bare knee, charmed.

"Say, this man appears to be dead," Spurr said, pointing at the dead man.

"I had a feelin'," the girl said, releasing her breasts. "He hasn't moved in a long time."

"How long's he been here?"

The girl shrugged. "Since I woke up this mornin', around eleven or so. I got a feelin' he's been there since last night. Heard a spate of gunfire out here around mignight, men shoutin' an' carryin' on like they do." She turned the corners of her pretty mouth down and shook her head. She did nothing to cover her well-rounded breasts, the pink nipples pointing slightly outward.

"The constable ain't been summoned?" Spurr said, as incredulous as before.

"What constable?" the girl said. "Owen

107

Wiley's dead as last year's Christmas goose."

"When did this happen?"

"Two nights ago. His woman found him sittin' in his privy with his throat cut."

"Holy shit," Spurr said. "Has someone taken over for him?"

The girl nodded. "The mayor's fillin' in, though he ain't spreadin' it around over much, seein' as how the town constable ain't a very popular line of work here in Diamond Fire."

"Could you direct me to the mayor, then, honey?"

She smiled down at him, leaned forward on the balcony rail. "Say, you're sweet. You talk sweet and you got a sweet face."

"My face has been called a lot of things, honey," Spurr said, chuckling, "but sweet ain't one of 'em."

The girl laughed. It sounded a little like Kansas City Jane's laugh. The girl was blond like Jane, too, though her heart-shaped, blue-eyed face was prettier.

Just the same, being reminded of the dead whore made Spurr's heart heavy.

"Say, you ain't headin' east soon, are ya?"

Spurr regarded her curiously. She glanced behind her and then over the railing to see if anyone else was within earshot, and then cupped a hand to her mouth as she said, "If you were, I was wonderin' if I could tag along. I'd like to get out of this perdition before the snow flies." She shook her head darkly. "This is one crazy place, mister, and I'd just as soon not spend the whole winter here with these crazy miners."

"I'd like to help you out, honey, but I'm here on business."

The girl turned her mouth corners down and nodded in understanding. "You'll find him up the canyon and on the other side of the creek. Just follow the screams to the tonsorial parlor. Burke does tooth extractions, in addition to barberin', for a good bottle of whiskey or fifty cents."

Spurr pinched his hat brim to the girl. "Much obliged, sweetheart. You'd best get inside. Sun's goin down fast and a chill's a-buildin'!"

"I like you, mister," the girl said. "If you're out lookin' for a poke later, look for Greta. That's me. I'll curl your toes for ya!"

"Maybe I'll just do that," Spurr said, feeling a knot in his groin tug tight as he looked at the girl's nicely rounded mounds once more.

He turned away and led Cochise on up the canyon lined with buildings of every size and color and constructed of about any material available, including white canvas stretched across a pine log frame. They were painted all colors of the rainbow. Wood smoke sat over the canyon like a gauzy kettle lid, but Spurr also smelled the spicy tang of opium and the fresh-cut-hay smell of marijuana.

All that was second only to the aromas of every brand of perfume concocted, and wafting up and down the canyon on invisible wings. The gaudy fragrances connoted all things female, and, despite a heavy feeling in his heart for Kansas City Jane, Spurr felt his old sap run.

First things first, he told himself as he led Cochise across a halved-log bridge spanning the narrow creek that dug deeper into the canyon the higher it climbed the floor's steep incline.

When he'd led the horse past one of the louder saloons spewing ribald female laughter and the din of off-key piano music, he did indeed begin to hear a man screaming.

"Oh! Oh! Oh, Christ!" the man shouted as though around a mouthful of rocks. "Just pull the damn thing an' get it over with, you devil!"

"I will if you'll keep your damn mouth open, you damn fool!" returned another man.

"Ah, the music of a high-mountain gold

camp!" Spurr said. "Just wraps a feller's heart in warm wool — don't it, Cochise?"

The horse didn't look nearly as comfortable as Spurr did in such a boisterous place, with noise emanating from nearly every shop and saloon lining both sides of the streambed and the street. Even a Chinese laundry on the other side of the canyon was loud; a little Chinese woman was giving holy hell to some fancy Dan in a three-piece suit holding a stack of freshly folded clothes in his arms and wagging his head, as though he wasn't satisfied with the woman's service.

Spurr tied Cochise at the hitchrack fronting Burke's Tonsorial Parlor — a little, unpainted frame shop with large glass windows on either side of the door propped open with a small stool. Inside, the barber/dentist was working on a big, burly gent tipped back in the barber chair while three other burly men stood around watching the proceedings in terrified fascination.

And bloody proceedings they were. The towel draped down the patient's chest was scarlet with the stuff. And just now, as the man whom Spurr assumed was Burke jerked his right arm back, more blood spurted from the patient's howling mouth.

"There you go, McCloud," the dentist bellowed down at the man, angrily, holding the bloody tooth in his pliers. "And it would have gone a whole lot easier if you'd shown a little backbone and kept your friggin' mouth open!"

The dentist was as big as his patient and the other men standing around. A tumbleweed of thick, curly red hair ensconced his head around a palm-sized bald spot at the crown. His Irish brogue was thick enough to float a clipper ship.

When his patient, continuing to howl and bellow around the cotton the dentist had stuffed in his mouth, had paid for the misery he'd endured, and left with the three men following him and looking owly, the dentist turned to Spurr and said, "Next!"

"Hold on, ya damn butcher!" Spurr intoned, laughing and holding his hands up, palm out. "The few teeth I got left in my head you ain't comin' anywhere near. I'm here for your prisoner. Deputy U.S. Marshal Spurr Morgan at your service. A pretty little doxie named Greta said you was the mayor and the temporary turnkey till the camp could find another man stupid enough to take the deceased one's place."

"Thank Christ," the man said, tossing his bloody pliers in a tin pan and wiping his bloody hands on a towel. "I didn't think anyone was ever gonna come for that demon. A wretched one, that! And dangerous, I hear, too!"

"Dangerous? I heard he was damn near as old as I am."

Burke tossed the towel onto the leather-padded barber chair and began rolling his white shirtsleeves down his freckled arms. He was big, but he had large, intelligent brown eyes and a somewhat nonplussed air — likely a learned man for whom the violent climate of a deep-mountain gold camp did not set well.

"Oh, he's old," Burke said, shaking his head ominously. "But I understand he is not who he said he was when the constable sent that telegram to Denver. Since then his true identity has come to light, and he is the member of a somewhat notorious gang. One that is headed in this direction — so he claims, and I don't doubt it — to spring him from our rat-infested little icehouse."

"Who is he if not this George Blackleg fella?"

"I can't remember the name, now. You can ask him yourself."

Spurr said, "Did you telegraph that news to Henry Brackett? He might like to hear about it."

"I'd have had to ride clear down to Wet Fork to send it, as we have no telegraph here. Even if we did, I wouldn't have known who to send the telegraph *to*. Not my area of expertise. I'm surprised Arney Haverlick did. He was the constable who got his throat cut while he was trying to take a nice, leisurely constitutional last week."

Burke shook his head again and grabbed a brown derby off a hat tree by the door. "Imagine having your own privy invaded by some knife-wielding ruffian? Haverlick's poor wife found him sitting there with his trousers around his ankles, covered in blood."

"Any idea who wielded the blade?"

"Hell, take your pick!" Burke said in exasperation as he headed out the door, shrugging into his wool suit coat and beckoning for Spurr to follow.

Outside, he locked the door, pocketed the key, and then started walking on up the canyon. Spurr followed, trailing Cochise by the roan's bridle reins and weaving through the foot traffic. The smoke from chimney pipes and outside cooking and heating fires was so thick as it wafted on canyon downdrafts that it made Spurr's eyes water.

The jailhouse — aptly identified by JAILHOUSE lettered on a wooden sign jutting on poles into the nearly dark street — sat only a few buildings up from the barbershop, between a surveyor's office and an assayer's office, both closed and dark. In the break between the jailhouse and the assayer's office, two beefy men in animal skins were arguing over a painted girl clad in pantaloons, black shoes, and a ratty wolf coat. She was yawning, looking bored as she waited for the men to settle their dispute.

The jailhouse was a flat-roofed stone block behind a small, weathered-gray veranda trimmed in bleached deer and elk heads, a covered water barrel sitting by the front door. Spurr had seen whores' cribs larger. The place was dark but a man's voice emanated through the Z-frame door, singing an Irish ballad in a Texas twang and changing the words to make the ballad even bawdier than in its original form. The man's voice was accompanied by the tooth gnashing raking of what sounded like a tin cup across a barred door.

Both the singing and the banging stopped when Burke tripped the leather-and-steel latch and threw the door open.

"Fire's out," a deep voice croaked from the jailhouse's cold, dark shadows. "Been out for a couple hours now, Tooth Fairy."

Spurr frowned as he followed Burke inside. The voice had sounded vaguely familiar to the old lawman, as did the man's

115

wry tone.

"Busy day," said the dentist, walking toward the desk that abutted the front wall. "I brought you a visitor."

"She better have big tits," came the voice from one of the dark cells lining the back of the small, earthen-floored office.

"They're big but they got hair growin' between 'em," Spurr said, chuckling.

He stared into the shadows at the back of the room. He could see the prisoner's muddy silhouette standing behind the door of the center cell. The man did not say anything. Spurr felt the man's gaze probing him, as though the prisoner had sensed something as familiar in Spurr's voice as Spurr had sensed in the prisoner's voice.

Burke scratched a match and lit the table lamp on the previous constable's desk, which was merely three boards spanning stacked packing crates. The dentist/barber held up the light, pulled two keys and a small ring from his coat pocket, and walked over to the cell.

Light from the flickering lamp slid across the uneven earthen floor. It reflected dully off the iron bars of the cell, shone in the eye of the man standing behind the door, staring out from between two strap-iron bars, his large, brown hands wrapped around a bar to either side of his head.

The prisoner had a large, bearded face the color and texture of ancient sandstone. He wore a thick, black beard stitched with less gray than one would expect for his age — early sixties, Henry had said, around Spurr's same age. The rest of the man's face looked every day of his age, or older, with many, deep, crosshatched lines and dime-sized liver spots on skin stretched taut across high, severely tapering cheekbones. Both cheek nubs were especially wrinkled and leathery from overexposure to the elements and extreme temperatures.

The prisoner wore a patch over his right eye. The lone eye, devilishly slanted, was chocolate-brown, the iris runny at the edges. It was as shrewd and piercing as a hawk's dark eye set deep in the leathery hollow of the socket. On the man's head was a black felt bowler hat, the badly frayed brim showing the cream cording beneath the felt.

"Well, I'll be damned," the man said, his chapped, pink lips moving inside his beard. The pupil in his lone eye appeared to expand and contract as it bored into Spurr, the man's lips remaining slightly open in shock.

Spurr stared back at the man with a similar expression. The visage before him had aged considerably, making him only a shadow of the man Spurr remembered. But there was enough of the man Spurr had known — mainly, the expression and the cunning, shrewd, mocking light in the lone, slanted eye — to cause Spurr to say with an incredulous grunt, "That you, Boomer?" He stepped forward, his right hand automatically sliding across his belly to close around the handle of the Starr .44. "Boomer *Drago?*"

TEN

The man in the cell said, "That you . . . Spurr? Well, I'll be *damned.*"

At the same time, both Spurr and the prisoner said, "I thought you was dead."

Spurr pulled the Starr from its holster, raked back the hammer, and held the gun out in front of his chest. "But you're as good as dead, you son of a bitch. You know how many years I was after you? And then, when I lost your trail, I still kept lookin' — everywhere I went. Every saloon or whorehouse I walked into. Always lookin' for your face — the one with *two* snakey eyes in it, 'stead of just one. Finally gave up — what? — maybe ten years ago, now?" He shook his head slowly. "Thought for sure you was shovelin' coal in hell."

The man staring at him through the cell bars grinned jeeringly, showing large, chipped, cracked teeth grimed with coffee and tobacco stains.

Burke sidled tentatively up to Spurr, staring at the prisoner with a cautious air, and cleared his throat. "So . . . this is Drago, then? Boomer Drago? Just like he said . . . ?"

"That's Boomer Drago, all right."

"How do you know this man, Deputy?"

"We rode together a couple times, nigh on thirty years ago, now. Just after the war. Even joined up with the marshals service together. But then ole Boomer split with the good and decent, right under our noses, and joined up with a bunch of train robbers. Turned to stealin' and killin' for his livin'."

"Better money," Boomer Drago said, grinning at Burke.

"Ain't nothin' worse than a lawman going bad. Joinin' up with the curly wolves — becomin' one o' the worst ones himself."

"I never heard of Boomer Drago," Burke said.

"Back before your time," Drago said.

"And then he let Drago die, switched his name, must have switched his area of operations."

"The proliferation of the Iron Horse out on the frontier has been a boon to all us curly wolves. Was able to move on from Kansas, Oklahoma, Colorado. Plenty of trains in Nevada, California, even Arizona, if you can stand all them dirty little 'Paches . . . not to mention the rattlesnakes and the heat."

Drago shook his one-eyed head. "Spurr, you ever spend a whole summer in Sonora? There ain't enough beer and tequila in all the world to take the edge off that blastin' kind of hellish heat!"

"Changed his name to George Blackleg," Spurr said, staring at his old nemesis, the man who'd managed to stay two trails ahead of him, frustrating him no end back when he was a younger man and trying to make a name for himself as a federal badge toter. "When did you do that, Boomer?"

"Do what?"

"Change your name. What the hell you think I'm talkin' about?"

Drago stared with his one wide eye at the pistol in the old lawman's tight's fist. "Hey, you best let down the hammer on that ole Starr, Spurr! Slow-like, I'm sayin'!"

"How 'bout if I let it down fast-like, Boomer? Make up for years of bitter frustration. Damn your worthless, murderin' hide. I thought you was dead! Only changed your damn name!"

"Spurr . . . now . . . you're gettin' all worked up. Ain't good for an old man's health. Ain't good for *my* health." Drago chuckled nervously, his one eye on the Starr.

"When'd you change your name?"

"Hell, if I know! Lemme think." Drago scratched his ratty beard. "Must be about ten years ago, moved on up to Montana, robbed a few trains, then lit down to Mexico for a coupla winters, movin' on up in Arizona and California to rob a few more. Then me an' the boys headed back down to a little three-goat village down in the Sierra Madre. Nice girls down there. All brown and plump. Good cooks, too — if you like your grub spicy hot!"

"What'd you come back here for?"

"I got my reasons."

Burke interjected with a dubious air, "The point is he's here. And whoever he is — George Blackleg or Boomer Drago — I'd just as soon get him out of here. I'm tired of feeding him as well as keeping a fire burning in that stove."

"What fire you been keepin' burnin' in that stove, Mr. Tooth Fairy?" Drago said, his voice low with menace. "Haven't you noticed a definite chill in the air? My pecker done froze to my thigh several hours ago. Gonna have to fetch me a warm whore to thaw it out!"

"Oh, it hasn't been that long!" the dentist said in disgust, turning toward the bullet-shaped stove in the corner.

As Burke opened the stove door and started laying a fresh fire, he said with his back to Spurr and Drago, "My point being, Deputy Morgan, that I hope to hell you intend to take this man out of here first thing tomorrow. Get him down the mountains, for godsakes, before the first snow flies! We've had enough of him here."

"Yeah, he's had enough of me here," Drago told Spurr with a mocking light in his lone, dark eye. "Especially since he learned my old gang is headin' this way — fast as high-country lightning bolts — to bail me out of this cell with a whole passel of lead."

"Yes, especially because of that," Burke said as, kneeling, he shoved shredded bits of newsprint through the open stove door.

"He's jerkin' your chain," Spurr said.

"Oh, it's the truth," Drago said, scratching his head as he pondered the cocked Starr remaining in the old lawman's fist. "And they ain't gonna like it one bit if, when they get here, they discover they rode here for nothin'. So why don't you just be a good man, Spurr, and very gently ease that hammer down against the firing pin there. After you aim the barrel away from my delicate person, if you wouldn't mind."

Boomer Drago grinned.

Spurr looked at the gun in his hand. He hadn't actually considered shooting the man. It was just old, bitter hatred and frustration at having been so badly hornswoggled by the outlaw that had caused his hand to close over the Starr of its own accord. He had never killed a man in cold blood, and while this was an exceptional situation, he supposed he shouldn't start now, this being his last job and all.

Spurr held the revolver's hammer back with his thumb, tripped the trigger, releasing the hammer, and then eased the hammer down to the firing pin with a click.

Drago drew a ragged breath at the sound of the click. "Now, can we talk like two civilized human beings, Spurr? Huh? Would that be all right with you? Damn, you're lookin' . . . *old*!" Drago laughed.

Spurr slid the Starr into its holster. "You ain't no spring chicken, you blackhearted son of a bitch!"

"*Black*hearted! Come on, now — that's harsh!"

"Gentlemen, *please*!" Burke stood facing the old lawman and the old outlaw, his back to the stove in which a fledgling fire danced. "I didn't bring you over here, Marshal Morgan . . ."

"Call me Spurr."

". . . Marshal Spurr . . . so that you could have a shouting match with my prisoner. Now that you are here, however, I was hoping you could tend to the man — feed him, empty his slop bucket, and keep the stove stoked — so that I can go back to the tonsorial parlor. Quite a few miners come into town at night and the first thing some want, before a poke, is a bath and a shave."

"And dental work," Spurr said with a wry snort, still staring at Boomer Drago, having a hard time believing that's who was really standing before him. It was like watching a ghost swimming up out of the ancient past.

"Joke if you want, but I get fifty cents a tooth. Well, then — do we have a deal? I take it you'll be riding out first thing in the morning. Perhaps you could stay right here and see to his . . . uh . . . *needs*?"

The jailhouse door opened abruptly. As it flew back against the wall, Spurr wheeled and slid his hand across his belly to the Starr over which he had not secured the keeper thong. A man stood in the doorway, clad in bearskin coat and a bearskin hat. The coat was open, the flaps shoved back behind two pistols.

He walked into the jailhouse followed by two more men dressed similarly, all with pistols prominently displayed.

Spurr said, "Now, who in the hell are you?"

The first man was short, with a full blond beard. The other two were taller. They were all in their late thirties, early forties, and they had a wild look. They smelled wild, too — like bears fresh from the den.

Prospectors. Spurr recognized the haunted looks in their eyes. Living too long alone in the mountains without women, with the frustration of knowing their mother lodes were right beneath their feet — if they could just dig it up . . .

"Step aside, old man," the first man said. "We're gonna take your prisoner off your hands."

"What in blazes?" said Boomer Drago, staring at the newcomers over Spurr's left shoulder. Burke stood in front of the crackling wood stove, looking constipated.

"That won't be necessary," Spurr said, keeping his voice mild. "But I do appreciate the offer. Now, kindly drag your raggedy asses back wherever in hell you dragged 'em in from."

"Louis said to step aside, old man!" said the last man into the room, waving an arm. "We heard you got Boomer Drago locked up in here — hell, it's all over these mountains now — and we come to kill him!"

"You're right popular, Drago," Spurr said, keeping his eyes on the three scraggly men facing him, standing about two feet apart in front of the door. "Now, why would you fellas want to come stormin' in here with blood on your mind? Not that I didn't have the same notion, but Drago here is property of the government of the United States of America, and since I am a deputy U.S. marshal, I reckon it's my place to ask."

"We rode with him, nigh on five years ago, now," the smaller of the three said. "Remember us, Vernon?"

"Vernon?" Spurr said.

"That was the alias he was ridin' under at the time."

"One of many," Drago said. "Well, hi, Louis. Dewey. Elwyn, is that you? Didn't recognize you under all that bearskin. Have you lost weight?"

"We was hopin' we'd run into you again, *Vernon*." This from the smallest newcomer, Louis, who had his thumbs tucked behind the waistband of his smoke-stained duck trousers. His mean eyes were pinched together. "Wasn't very nice, walkin' away with that strongbox. Wasn't much in there, but, hell . . ."

"Took our share of the gold, took my girl

127

Connie," said Elwyn. "She always was a double-dealin' little whore. It's the gold I missed. It's the gold you're gonna die for, *Vernon* . . . or Boomer Drago, or whoever in hell you are."

Louis jerked his head impatiently and closed a hand over his right-side pistol. "Step aside, old man. You don't wanna die here tonight. Not for him."

"Go out and get yourself a drink," said Dewey, curling his upper lip. "You look like you could use it."

"Ah, Jesus," Burke said, sidling away from the stove. "Marshal Spurr, just turn him loose. The old catamount is not worth all this. He is not worth the trouble!"

"Listen to him, Marshal Spurr," said Dewey. "You're old and used up and you don't wanna die this way. Three against one is long odds however you wanna stack 'em."

Spurr sighed, hooked his thumbs behind his cartridge belt. "This man is my prisoner. He will not be leaving his cell until tomorrow, at which time we will start our trek down the long trails back to the Union Pacific tracks east of Camp Collins. If you want to make a play for him, then go ahead and make it now, and stop wastin' my time."

"Ah, shit, Spurr," Boomer Drago said.

"Marshal, I don't think you should be

encouraging this," Burke said in his heavy accent. "What you want to do is *dis*courage it."

"I'm too old to fuck around like this," Spurr said.

Behind the old marshal, Boomer Drago stepped back away from his cell door. "Spurr, you think you can take these fellas? They don't look like they got much backdown in 'em."

"I don't, neither," Spurr said. "So I reckon we'll just have to see how well I do. Wish me luck, Boomer."

Spurr had to admit, if only to himself, that he was feeling less than confident about his ability to take down these three before him. One, they were younger. Two, he had once been fast, but over the years he'd slowed down, so he'd instinctively avoided such situations as these.

This one, however, was not going to be avoided. He could see that by the hard glints in the three pairs of eyes staring at him.

Drago said, "Good luck, Spurr. I never thought I'd say those words, but, shit, I'll go ahead and say 'em again. Good luck."

"Oh, bloody hell! Oh, Jesus!" Burke said, backing against the far wall. "Could I please be excused? I am merely the turnkey here. I have no authority to either hold this man or let him go, but if I did, I would certainly order Marshal Spurr to turn him bloody well loose! I, in fact, have no business here. So, lest I should be caught in the crossfire —"

"Shut up," Elwyn said out of the side of his mouth.

Then he drew. A half a wink later, the others drew their own weapons.

Spurr's old instincts had kicked in. He'd sensed it coming. It was almost as though he'd inadvertently been reading Elwyn's mind. Spurr's hand jerked across his belly of its own accord, unsheathed the Starr .44, and ratcheted the hammer back.

It belched smoke and fire in Spurr's knobby hand.

Bam! Bam! Bam! Bam-bam!

Two of the three hard cases were blown back out through the jailhouse's open door and into the street.

Louis was the fastest of the three, and he got off two shots. One kissed the nap of Spurr's left coat sleeve before ricocheting off the cell door with an ear-ringing clang. The other, fired just after Spurr's first bullet had torn a quarter-sized hole in his heart, was triggered into his own left ankle.

"Oh," Louis said as he flew back against the open door and stood there, his smoking pistol aimed at the floor.

The cutthroat stared down at the blood pumping out his chest, between the flaps of his bear coat, and he said, "Oh. Oh, shit." And then he looked at Spurr in disbelief, his head wobbling on his shoulders, his eyes rolling back in his head.

He staggered forward, pinwheeled, and hit the floor on his back.

Silence.

Spurr's gun smoke wafted in the lantern-lit room. The fledgling fire, whose weak flames were dwindled, softly cracked and popped.

Behind Spurr, Boomer Drago whistled. "You old coot. You still got a few left in the chamber."

Spurr himself was amazed. He looked down at the Starr and the old hand wrapped around it, as though they belonged to another person.

"Yeah, I got a few," he said.

He walked over to the door and stared out at the two in the street. Neither was moving. He turned back into the office. Boomer stood up near his cell door, amazement lighting his lone eye. Burke was squatting against the far wall, his hair rumpled. He held his hat in his hands and was staring, pale-featured, at the hole in its crown.

He slowly lifted his eyes to Spurr and said in a low, shocked voice, "Bleedin' ricochet. Might have taken my eyes out."

"Or your brains," Drago opined.

Burke looked down at his hat again, nodding gravely.

Spurr flicked the Starr's loading gate open and began plucking out his spent shell casings, tossing them into a small wastebasket near the desk.

"Spurr."

The old marshal looked at Drago.

"Them three were nothin' compared to the men in the gang comin' to fetch me. Come on. Let me out of here. You'll never make it against them. Hell, there's twenty, twenty-five of 'em. You did good here tonight, and I do appreciate it, but these three never were good with them hoglegs. Slow as molasses in January."

Spurr stared at the old outlaw as he plucked fresh cartridges from his shell belt and slid them into the Starr's wheel, rolling the cylinder between his thumb and index finger, listening to the soft clicks. Burke continued staring at his hat as though the hole were really bird shit and he was wondering how he was going to get the stain out.

Spurr's heart fluttered. He'd had too

much excitement for one day.

"I'm tired," he said, shoving the pistol down into its holster and fastening the keeper thong over the hammer. "I'm gonna go stable my beast and then stable myself for a long autumn night's nap. I'll see you in the mornin', Boomer. Sleep tight. Burke, make sure his horse is saddled and ready to go at first light."

Burke stared up at him, the barber/dentist's lower jaw hanging.

As Spurr turned and walked through the door and stepped over the dead men in the street, he heard Burke say behind him, "Jesus, Joseph, and Mary — that's just bloody wonderful!"

ELEVEN

Spurr stabled Cochise in a livery barn he'd
seen on his way into town, leaving his prized
roan in the hands of the black liveryman,
Mortimer Lang, who assured Spurr the
mount would get the best care in all the
Rocky Mountains. Lang smiled broadly and
held out his gloved hand for Spurr to drop
several coins into.

For grub, Lang recommended the tent
shack next door to the livery barn. For
sleep, Lang said the man who owned the
grub shack also had cribs behind the place,
with cots as comfortable as any bed in
Diamond Fire.

"The bedbugs there don't bite as hard as
elsewhere around here," Lang said, chuckling as he led Cochise into the barn's musky
shadows.

Spurr walked down the wooden ramp and
into the street. There were all brands of
commotion up and down the narrow canyon

housing the perdition of Diamond Fire, with bonfires burning here and there and shunting weird shadows of reveling men and women. The town reminded Spurr of a circus, as did most mining camps he'd visited. The raucous, darkly festive air about the place was that of a short-lived party. Soon, when the gold played out, the camp would go bust and all the revelers would be hitting the trail for other opportunities.

Spurr didn't recognize a man's anguished groan for what it was until he started walking into the small, log-frame tent shack just west of the livery barn. The groan got louder, echoing above the din, and Spurr turned to see a man walking out of a little gray cabin on the other side of the canyon.

By the light of a fire burning near the small stoop of the cabin, whose large shingle over the front door read simply BEER AND SANDWICHES, Spurr saw the man stumble out the front door, slamming the door back against the cabin's front wall. He was clamping his hands over his belly from which what appeared to be a knife protruded.

The flames shone on the knife's dark, silver-capped handle.

The man — hatless, wearing a striped blanket coat — dragged his boot toes out onto the stoop, spurs chinging on the floorboards. He stumbled down the stoop's three steps, dropped to his knees in the street, and fell face forward in the dirt and gravel. He lay jerking with death spasms.

The men and the few women in the area didn't pay much attention to the fast-dying gent. A big man and a copper-haired woman were fornicating against the wall of the next building over from the beer and sandwich place. The man held the woman up against the building, her bare legs wrapped around his waist, and he was hammering his bare hips against her, bobbing her up and down.

His pants were bunched around his ankles and tall miner's boots. His bare white ass jerked back and forth. The woman's dress was pulled up to her waist. A high-heeled shoe dangled off one of her feet grinding into his back. The other shoe lay on the ground near the miner's feet.

The big, fornicating miner merely glanced over his shoulder at the man and then continued diddling the grunting woman.

As Spurr watched, another man strode through the same door as the dying man. He was tall and lean, and he wore a wolf vest over a plaid shirt. He calmly descended the porch steps, kicked the now-still gent over onto his back, planted a boot on the man's right hip, and jerked the blade out of his belly.

The man wiped the blade off on the dead man's pants then held it up to inspect it, making sure he'd cleaned it thoroughly, and slipped the knife into the sheath on his left hip. The tall man looked around slowly.

If he saw Spurr staring at him from across the streambed, he didn't show it. He merely swung around, mounted the porch steps, and ducking his head under the low doorway, disappeared inside the beer and sandwich place.

Spurr looked at the dead man. He supposed he should do something about the killing, but he had no inclination. He was tired, and when you got down to brass tacks, the murder was not in his jurisdiction. True, there was no lawman here in Diamond Fire at the moment, so that officially made the killing his business, but he was dead-dog tired.

His heart felt heavy and sore in his chest.

He should look into it, but this was his last assignment, and he just wasn't going to do it. He was going to pad out his belly with grub and whiskey-laced coffee and roll up in a mattress sack. He needed a good night's rest before lighting out on the western trail toward Cameron Pass again tomorrow.

He ducked through the tent shack's flap. There were three long tables and benches, not enough lanterns hanging from low beams to keep a man from tripping as he walked to a table.

Only one of the tables was occupied by two old, long-bearded salts hunkered over their plates and eating in silence. As Spurr sat down at a table right of the graybeards, a black man looked through a curtained doorway at the back.

"Supper?" he called to Spurr.

"That's why I'm here. Coffee. Whiskey, too, if you got it."

The black man said, "Fifty cents a shot for the good stuff. Twenty-five for the bad." He was a little older and heavier than the black man in the livery barn, but they otherwise owned similar features.

Spurr chuckled at the family operation and wagged his head at the cost of the tangleleg. But this far up in the high and rocky, beggars couldn't be choosers.

"Bring me the bad stuff," he said, allowing for his soon-to-be dwindling income.

A minute later, the black man — round faced, early thirties — brought out a plate of pork roast, potatoes and gravy, boiled greens, and a hot cross bun, and set it on the table before Spurr. He set a bottle and tin cup on the table.

"You look like an honest man," said the black man. "I'll trust you to count your shots."

He rolled a sharpened stove match from one side of his mouth to the other and pinned Spurr with a stern look.

"Bad luck to cheat a trusting man," Spurr said and popped the cork on the half-full bottle. "Your brother said you got some cots out back."

"Cousin."

"All right." Spurr poured whiskey into the cup. "Which leg you want for a good night's sleep?"

"Keep your leg, mister. Cots are fifty cents."

"Well, that's reasonable."

When the man went away, Spurr ate the good food hungrily. He imbibed four shots, hoping like hell he'd still have some money to get him down to Mexico. He didn't want to get hung up anywhere in between and die in some snowy mountain range, wolves gnawing at his old, withered limbs.

Damnit, he deserved to go out better than that.

"But now you're just feeling sorry for yourself, you miserable cuss," Spurr said under his breath as, his plate cleaned, he looked into the remaining whiskey at the bottom of the cup. "You have not lived well. You've trifled away your years. You could be in Mexico by now, with a good woman who almost loved you, if you hadn't been so damn afraid of death that you clung to your job as though it were life itself. Damn fool!"

He was thinking of a particular woman, a pretty, aging percentage gal who called herself Abilene. Spurr had called her "Texas" for kicks and giggles. He'd known her down in Texas and then he'd seen her again in Wyoming. They'd talked half seriously, half drunkenly of running away together, but Spurr had lit out after outlaws and never got around to returning for her.

The last time he'd seen her, she'd been married to an old rancher from the southern Big Horns.

"Damn fool!"

"What the hell's the matter with you, mister?"

Spurr looked at the two graybeards sitting on the far side of the long table to his left. They were both scowling at him. The one who'd spoken to him squinted his washed-out eyes inside his beard and said, "Which one of us you callin' a fool?"

The other one pounded the end of his fist on the table. "You're the damn fool!"

"That's right — I am a damn fool."

"Then what you're callin' us fools for?" asked the man who'd first taken umbrage.

"I wasn't. I was . . . ah, hell." Spurr threw his whiskey back and slammed the cup back down on the table. "Go to hell, both of ya!"

He rose from his table, feeling low-down mean and angry though the two graybeards had nothing to do with it. If he were twenty years younger, he'd go looking for a fight. But his chest ached and he was tired from the ride and from killing, and he was downright frightened, too. He'd ridden into a job up here he hadn't been expecting — one that was much larger than either Henry Brackett or even he, himself, thought he was capable of seeing to a satisfactory conclusion.

This job that was supposed to be routine. His last job that was supposed to have given him something else to think about besides the girl who'd taken a bullet meant for him.

"What the hell's going on here?" the black man said, stepping out from behind the rear curtain, wiping his hands on a towel. "Can't you three get along? Look how old you all are!"

Spurr laughed at that. He'd thought the graybeards were older than he, but now, upon closer scrutiny, he saw that they were probably around his age. They returned his look with owly, indignant looks of their own. If he and they were about thirty years younger, they'd likely be throwing chairs and fists about now, none of them knowing why.

Spurr laughed at that notion, too. He was just drunk on the whiskey and altitude and the general nonsense of life. He was needing a bed bad.

"What do I owe you?" Spurr asked the black man.

The black man figured the charge for the meal and the whiskey and then he added on the fifty cents for the cot. Spurr paid him, gathered his gear and his rifle, and left through the rear kitchen where a black woman was scrubbing pans, her hair in her eyes.

Another tent lay directly behind the rear one, a little black boy perched on a stool beside the pucker. He wore a wool watch cap, a thick gray scarf around his neck, and a man's ragged wool dress coat that sagged on his shoulders. He clutched a lidded wooden box in his lap.

The boy held out his wool-gloved hand. Two of the fingers were worn so that his fingers showed through. "That'll be one dollar, mister."

Spurr scowled. "What's that?"

"Cots are one dollar."

"Oh, are they? Well, I heard they were fifty cents. In fact, that's just what I paid your pa in yonder!"

The kid jerked his hand impatiently. "Fifty cents in there, fifty cents out here. And he's my uncle."

Spurr laughed and shook his head. He was too tired to argue even if he'd had the gumption to argue with a shaver with holes in his gloves. He slapped two coins into the kid's hand and pulled the cloth cap down over the kid's eyes.

The boy laughed. Spurr chuckled and pushed through the pucker and into the hotel tent. There were eight or so rickety cots along either side of a narrow alley. Only three cots were taken, it still being early. They'd no doubt fill up fast around midnight.

Spurr chose one farthest away from the snoring men as he could get, dumped his gear on the floor, and undressed as quickly as his popping bones would allow. Outside, a gun cracked.

Spurr jumped.

There were two more pops followed by another as though in afterthought. The shots had come from a long ways away.

They were followed by muffled shouting.

Spurr sighed and, clad in only his balbriggans and socks, sagged onto the edge of the cot. Such commotion likely went on all night. His heart fluttered. His nerves were shot. He was exhausted. He'd be glad to get back out on the trail tomorrow, even in the company of a notorious old outlaw trailed by the outlaw's savage gang.

He rolled up in the flea-bit blanket, turned onto his side. "Spurr, you retired one job too late, didn't you?" he rasped to himself.

He drew a long, deep breath, let his lids slide down over his eyes.

He was asleep before he realized it — long, deep, and dreamless. Only a couple of times did he rouse even slightly when other men came in to undress and to claim the empty cots around him.

When he woke fully, it was to the loud, ratcheting click of a gun hammer and the cold barrel of a pistol pressed against his forehead.

Twelve

Spurr opened his eyes and stared up past the cocked pistol pressed against his head to the rugged, bearded face glaring down at him. The man's own eyes widened as though in shock, and he stitched his black brows together.

"You ain't Albert."

"No, I ain't," Spurr said, his voice raspy from sleep. "If you don't remove that gun from my face in the next second, you best go ahead and use it."

The bearded man pulled the pistol back, tipped the barrel up, and depressed the hammer. "Sorry, amigo." He shook his head, chuckled wryly. "I almost shot the wrong man."

He straightened, turned away, dropped the hogleg back into its holster on his right hip, and walked away through the thick, purple morning shadows. Men snored around him, one grinding his teeth and wheezing.

Spurr rose to his elbows and stared at the man walking away from him until the man had ducked out through the tent's front pucker. Then the old lawman blinked for the first time that morning, smacked his lips, and ran a hand down his face, pinching the sleep from his eyes with thumbs and index fingers.

He shook his head, noted the gradual slowing of his heart that had commenced to beating a war drum in his chest when he'd awakened to the pistol and the glaring eyes. He chuckled, a little giddy. That had been close.

But then, this was a mining camp, really no woolier than most — he remembered hearing guns popping last night in his sleep — and mining camps didn't place much value on a man's life. There was damned little civility, which was refreshing in some ways, downright horrifying in others.

Well, time to hit the trail. The silence and solitude of the open mountains beckoned. He just hoped he could enjoy it with Boomer Drago in tow.

Spurr threw the wool blanket back and immediately noticed the steely chill in the air as he dropped his feet to the floor, which was bare ground with tufts of sage growing here and there amongst the prickly gravel. From somewhere nearby, beneath the snoring, he could hear the scratching of a rodent, probably a pocket mouse.

Spurr took his time dressing. Over the past several years, it had taken him longer and longer to wake up in the mornings and he never really came around until he'd had a mug of black coffee with a jigger or two of whiskey in it. When he'd gotten his boots on, and had donned his hat, he sat down on the cot, fished around in his saddlebags until he found his hide-covered traveling flask, and took a generous pull.

The prickly heat washed down inside him, and blossomed throughout his being, smoothing out the ratcheting in his feeble heart. He returned the flask to his saddlebags, strapped his Starr and his cartridge belt around his waist, pulling his hickory shirt tight across his slight paunch and stuffing it into his wash-worn canvas trousers.

His rifle in his right hand, saddlebags draped over his left shoulder, he made his way on out of the hotel tent to the restaurant tent, and indulged in a hearty breakfast of flapjacks, ham, and pinto beans, with a cup of coffee and a jigger of the proprietor's expensive, rotgut whiskey. He'd save his own for the trail back down to Denver.

He'd likely need it.

With his belly padded and his ticker ticking with a relative and pleasingly noticeable lack of discomfort, he dropped coins onto the table, gathered his gear, retrieved his horse from the liveryman, and rode on over to the jail. He was pleased to see a saddled horse — a stocky bay — tied to the hitchrack fronting the stoop.

Burke was inside, building another fire in the stove while Boomer Drago berated him for the chill. Drago's breath plumed through the bars of the cell door.

"Spurr, I protest my mistreatment here in Diamond Fire. I didn't sleep a damn wink last night. This son of a bitch, the friggin' *Tooth Fairy,* done banked the fire and left. Only, he must have banked it with green wood, because it went out an hour later without ever workin' up any heat!"

Spurr closed the jailhouse door behind him.

Burke stood, slapping his hands together, and closed the stove door with a metallic clang. He turned the squeaky latch handle, and favored Spurr with a pleading look.

"Please, get him out of here — I beg you."

"About that, Spurr," Drago said, directing his gaze to the old lawman standing in front of the plankboard door. "I hope you had time to think it over real good. My gang will be showin' up here any time now." He shook his one-eyed head darkly. "When they do, you sure don't wanna be here. There'll be hell to pave an' no hot pitch!"

Spurr looked at Burke. "Do you have any confirmation his gang really is headed this way, Mr. Mayor?"

Burke shook his head. "Just his word."

Spurr chuckled. "You know what I think, Boomer? I think you're just an old wolf that your gang done kicked out of the pack. I don't think they're comin' after you at all. I think you an' me are gonna have a nice, quiet, easy ride all the way down the mountains to the railroad and on into Union Station. Nice an' quiet. Maybe we can even do some catchin' up."

Spurr glanced at Burke. "Open the door. Let him out of there." He removed a pair of handcuffs from his coat pocket, and tossed them to the sitting mayor of Diamond Fire. "Throw those on him."

"Hold on, now!" Drago snarled. A red scarf was tied over the top of his ragged bowler, over his ears, knotted under his chin. "I ain't had breakfast yet. I ain't even had a cup of coffee. My old ticker don't get goin' until I've slurped down a cup o' mud!"

"Don't make me tear up, now, Boomer.

It's so cold in here my eyes'll likely freeze open!" Spurr gave the dentist another impatient nod. "Get him out of there, Burke. We're burnin' daylight."

"My pleasure!"

Burke walked over to the cell.

"Hold on!" Spurr said, unsheathing his .44 from beneath his buckskin mackinaw. He clicked the hammer back and wagged the piece at the prisoner. "Get back away from the door, Drago. Good Lord, Burke, how often you done this?"

The dentist looked sheepish as Drago grinned and, removing his hands from the strap-iron bars, backed away from the door.

While Spurr held his pistol on Drago, Burke shoved the key in the lock and swung the door wide on caterwauling hinges.

"Step out here, Drago. Let the Tooth Fairy cuff you. You make one false move, I'm gonna make this trip a whole lot easier for both of us."

Drago's eyes glinted angrily. "You're a bad one, Spurr. I always knew it. Heart like granite, makin' a man hit the cold trail without nary a bread crumb in his teeth. No coffee."

He shook his head as he walked slowly out through the cell's open door, holding his wrists out in front of him. He kept his

150

hard eyes on Spurr. "When my boys catch up to us, it ain't gonna go well for you. Not well at all!"

"It'll go well enough," Spurr said as the dentist clicked the cuffs closed around the prisoner's wrists.

Burke stepped back away from Drago. Spurr walked around behind the old outlaw and prodded him on outside with the barrel of his cocked Starr. When Spurr had Drago on his horse, Burke came out with a rifle and saddlebags.

"What about these?"

"Any weapons in the saddlebags?" Spurr asked.

"Just pots and pans." The dentist snorted. "A couple of wanted dodgers with his own likeness on them. Several different aliases."

Spurr glanced at Drago, who smiled and shrugged.

"You keep the rifle," Spurr said. "Toss those saddlebags over his horse."

"That's a prized Colt's repeating rifle, Spurr. I'd admire to have it with me till the end."

"You can kiss my ass."

Drago told Spurr to do something physically impossible to himself.

Spurr looked up and down the canyon. There were no humans out, just a couple of dogs sniffing around trash heaps. Smoke fluttered under the cold, gray sky, snagging on the false fronts of the buildings lining the canyon. The silence after the previous night's din was funereal.

Or did it just seem ominous to Spurr, whose nerves were drawn taut from the possibility that Drago's men might be on the lurk, possibly planting a bead on his back at this moment?

He honestly didn't know if Drago was lying about his gang being headed toward Diamond Fire. Something told him the old outlaw was not.

That would be the first non-lie for Boomer Drago.

When Burke had draped the saddlebags over Drago's horse and walked back up onto the porch, Spurr caught Drago grinning at him shrewdly. "Oh, they'll be along soon, partner. I'll guarantee you that."

"I'm not your partner," Spurr said with a grunt as he untied the reins of his and Drago's horses, and heaved himself into the leather. "I'm the lawman who is finally going to ride you to justice."

Drago laughed.

Spurr pinched his hat brim at Burke, who just stared back at him, and then Spurr put Cochise east along the canyon, avoiding a dead man lying in front of a pink-painted brothel with one boarded-up window. He ground his heels into Cochise's flanks, and jerked Boomer's bay along behind him, Boomer saying, "No such thing as justice, my friend. You'll find that out soon enough, partner!"

They'd been on the long trail down the mountains for three hours, when Spurr cast another in a series of suspicious looks behind him, over Drago's left shoulder. Boomer turned to follow Spurr's gaze.

"Let me ease your nerves, partner," Drago said. "If my boys was back there, you'd know it. They ain't the type to do any sneakin'." He chuckled devilishly, showing his yellow, crooked teeth inside his grizzled black beard, squinting his lone brown eye.

"How many are they?" Spurr asked. "Not that I believe they're behind me, but someone's been shadowin' us for the past hour or so."

"You sure?" Drago widened his eye in surprise and glanced behind him once more, holding his saddle horn with both his cuffed hands. "How do you know?"

"My lawman's sixth sense. How many?"

"Uh . . . let me see," Drago said, lifting his gaze and moving his lips, counting to himself. "There's Tommy and Leo and Quiet Ed and Tio Sanchez and Sam 'Coyote' Keneally, and . . . Oh, I'd say an even twenty, if you count Curly Ben Williamson. You ever meet Curly Ben, Spurr? He's a gunman out of Texas. One o' them new kind with cutdown holsters and steely eyes. Scaly skin that takes no color even when he's out in the sun all day every day, all year long!"

Drago chuckled, pleased with himself. "You ever hear of him, Spurr?"

Drago knew Spurr had heard of him. Curly Ben was a big name these days in Texas and Oklahoma. Most lawmen had heard of him. What Spurr had not known was that Drago had been riding with the likes of the cold-blooded killer out of Texas.

If Drago was telling the truth, that was — something Boomer hadn't been known for even when he'd been riding on the right side of the law.

"Never heard of him. But if I see him, I'll be sure to shoot the son of a bitch on sight. Any cork-headed prissy bastard goin' around callin' himself a Nancy-boy name like Curly Ben deserves a bullet drilled through both ears and his carcass sent home to his no-account family in pieces."

Drago guffawed. "Damn, Spurr — you got

a burr in your bonnet! Hey, where we goin'?"

Spurr had reined Cochise off the right side of the trail and was splashing across a shallow creek, jerking Drago's bay along behind him. "Time to build a fire and boil some coffee. I don't know about you, Boomer, but I'm hungry."

THIRTEEN

In truth, Spurr was tired.

The trail to Diamond Fire had taken more out of the old lawman than he'd expected. The trail hadn't gotten any easier when he'd reached Diamond Fire to discover that his prisoner was his old enemy, Boomer Drago, a man he'd been after for years and had finally given up on ever running to ground.

While he was pleased as punch to finally be bringing the man to trial, the truth was, he hadn't caught the old bastard himself. Some bounty hunter had. Spurr was just the delivery man. That took some pop out of his punch. Besides, the delivery wasn't going to be easy — not if Drago wasn't just stringing silver beads and his gang really was behind him.

Spurr was tired and his mood was sour. That seizure on the street out in front of the bank on Arapaho might have taken more out of him than he'd thought. The high altitude of the Medicine Bows wasn't doing him any good, either. His lungs felt tight. His head ached dully. He constantly felt hungry though food didn't seem to fill him up.

What he needed was some bacon, beans, biscuits, and coffee, all of which he'd lain in at a stage relay station the day before he'd reached Diamond Fire, figuring that game might run scarce near the settlement. Another couple of belts from his flask would ease the twinge in his ticker. He might even have to have one of his heart-starter pills. He'd gotten a fresh supply from his saw-bones in Denver though the man had told him to go easy and warned him that taking the pills with whiskey was liable to blow him sky-high.

Spurr didn't know if the old bone cutter was serious or not. He didn't think so. He'd been washing the nitro down with his whiskey for the past two years, and he'd be damned if it didn't always put a grin on his face and for a brief time cause naked girls to dance before his eyes.

"Get down," Spurr ordered Drago, when he'd stepped down from Cochise's back about a mile off the main trail, in a little ravine through which another creek gurgled, its water speckled with fallen autumn leaves.

Spurr couldn't see much of his back trail from here, but he kept his ears skinned for hoof thuds. He hadn't taken the time to cover his trail, but he didn't think the horses had left much of one over the country they'd traversed — mostly thin soil over shale and sandstone.

Drago hooked his cuffed hands around the saddle horn and gave a grunt as he swung his right leg over his bedroll and saddlebags. He dropped to the ground, stumbling slightly, wheezing. He fell back against the side of his bay, his cheeks red above his beard, his lone eye watery and red-rimmed.

He smiled weakly. "Christ, look at us, Spurr. A couple of old goats. We don't belong out here. We should be laid up with some fat whores and Kentucky bourbon."

"Hell, I oughta just lay you out with a bullet in your depraved old head." Spurr narrowed an angry eye over the barrel of his extended .44. "Make this job a whole lot easier. Why don't you make a play on me, give me the right excuse?"

"Ah, shit — what do you need an excuse for?" Drago's eye flashed fire. "It's just you an' me here, Spurr. Brackett's a long ways away. Just us and the crows. Go ahead and drill me, you cantankerous old bastard. Do it now and get it over with or finally shut the hell up about it!"

"Ah, hell."

Spurr felt cowed. He and Drago both knew Spurr wasn't going to shoot the old outlaw in cold blood. He'd never pulled such a stunt before — he'd always given men at least half a chance to be taken in — and he had no intention of starting now, on his last assignment.

Spurr jerked his head to a small, flat-topped boulder near a lightning-topped pine. "Get over there and sit down."

When Drago had done as he'd been told, Spurr hauled his own saddlebags off Cochise's back, dropped them near the base of the tree, fished out an old, rusty pair of ankle-irons, and slung them over to Drago. They landed at the outlaw's feet.

"Put 'em on."

"You don't need them, Spurr."

"Put 'em on, so I don't have to watch you like a hawk. You ain't goin' anywhere or doin' much of anything — at least, not very fast — with them ankle bracelets. Go on, they'll look purty on ye!"

Spurr chuckled.

When Drago had grudgingly closed the irons around his ankles, he sat down against the boulder, dug his makings out of a pocket of his shaggy gray wolf coat, and began rolling a smoke.

Meanwhile, Spurr unsaddled their horses, hobbling both mounts so they could drink and forage with limited freedom. Spurr gathered dry wood from the bottom of the ravine and built a small fire under the pine.

When the flames were popping and crackling, he started coffee boiling with water from the creek and got out his five-pound flitch of bacon wrapped in burlap. He sliced the pork into a cast-iron skillet, set the skillet on a rock near the flames, and then fished his burlap bag of baking powder biscuits from his saddlebags. He set those on a rock near the skillet then sat back against the pine with his whiskey flask.

"I'd take a pull from that," Drago said.

"Sure you would." Spurr popped the small cork on the flask, and took a pull. "Damn good stuff. But coffee will do for you."

Again, Drago told Spurr to do something physically impossible to himself. Spurr chuckled and took another conservative sip, sloshing the liquid around to judge how much he had left. Only about half. Somewhere, he'd have to get more. He hadn't been about to buy any tarantula juice in Diamond Fire, where it would have cost him two days' pay. He had to start keeping a watchful eye on his dinero from here on in, if he didn't want to starve or freeze to death.

Spurr returned the flask to his saddlebags and began forking the bacon around in the pan that had begun hissing and crackling, juice bleeding out from the meat to glisten in the pan that had been blackened from countless fires.

The white-speckled black coffeepot was beginning to chug, steam rising from the spout.

"Spurr, I got a confession to make."

Spurr chuckled.

"I ain't tryin' to hornswoggle you, now. I admit I was before, but not now, 'cause I see you're still tough as spikes and ornery as a Brahman bull down in the Brasada country."

"All right, go ahead," Spurr said, smiling indulgently as he dumped a handful of Arbuckles into the boiling coffeepot.

"My gang has no intention of turnin' me loose."

"No, shit? Well, damn, now you've gone and surprised me, Boomer!" Spurr had cast his words in irony, but the old outlaw's confession had buoyed his spirits some. He didn't know what or what not to believe when it came to Boomer Drago, but having his back trail clear would sure take a load off his mind.

He turned away from the steaming coffeepot and the sputtering sidepork and narrowed a skeptical eye at his prisoner. "But how can I take your word on anything?"

"You can take my word on this, partner. I got no reason to lie about it. In fact, I got every reason to finally tell you the truth, since it don't look like you'll listen to reason and turn me loose." Drago wagged his head sadly, and sighed. "Like I said, my boys ain't out to free me from you, Spurr. They're out to kill me."

"*Kill* you?"

"Hey, you're burnin' the belly wash!" Drago said, glancing at the roaring coffeepot that was spewing black coffee and copper bubbles from its spout and lid.

Spurr grabbed a burlap swatch and removed the pot from the fire. Letting the pot cool near the two cups he'd retrieved from his saddlebags, he kept scowling skeptically at his prisoner. "Why would they wanna kill you, Drago — you bein' such a likeable cuss an' all?"

"We got crossways."

"You don't say!"

"Yes, we did. And I have lived to regret it. I was on the run from that bunch when that bounty hunter, Kershaw, caught me with my pants down in that little whorehouse in Idaville."

"What'd you do to piss them boys off so bad, Boomer?"

"Ah, hell — the usual stuff. You know how it is with my kind, Spurr — we're always out to double-cross each other. Well, they tried to double-cross me by givin' me a smaller percentage of a recent haul on account of I was old and they'd started delegatin' me to holdin' the horses outside the banks we robbed. They said I was no longer worth a full share. So, damnit, I went and *took* my share and rode out on 'em."

"And that piss-burned 'em bad enough to make 'em wanna *track* you and *kill* you?"

Drago licked his lips as he stared at the coffeepot, gray smoke now curling from its spout. "Spurr, you wouldn't mind pourin' me up a cup o' that mud, would you? I swear, I've been thinkin' about a cup all mornin', and here it is after noon!"

Spurr filled both cups, handed one to Drago, who took it in both cuffed, gloved hands, staring at the smoking brew like he'd just been handed a pound of pure gold. He blew into the steam and closed his upper lip over the brim, sucking. "Damn, it's hot! But it sure tastes good. I remember you made good coffee, Spurr. One of the few things I liked about you."

Drago laughed.

Spurr lifted his own cup to his lips and looked at the horses that were grazing contentedly along the creek a ways down the ravine. Cochise had a good sniffer as well as keen ears, and he usually announced riders a good ten, sometimes fifteen minutes before Spurr could hear or see the company coming. He was happy to see the big roan hadn't spiked his ears or arched his tail.

He didn't know what to think about Boomer's new story. He wasn't sure if it made any difference from the previous one he'd told. Whether they wanted to free Drago or kill him, Spurr was pretty much in the same tight spot. All it could change was that the gang might strike with a little more venom if it wanted to kill Drago rather than free him. They could circle around Spurr and his prisoner and spring a bush-whack without warning.

If Boomer's gang really was trailing them, that was. Or everything Drago had told Spurr was in fact nothing more than smoke fog, trying to distract Spurr from his purpose, instilling fear, and possibly looking for the old lawman to make a mistake which Drago could take advantage of and use to shake himself loose.

Spurr sipped his coffee and leaned forward to fork the bacon around in the pan. Drago was staring at him over the brim of his own smoking cup.

"If they kill me, partner, they'll sure as hell kill you, too. Bet on it."

"I done told you to quit callin' me 'partner,' " Spurr groused. "We haven't been partners in damn near twenty years. And I don't know what you hope to gain from all this jawbonin'. You an' me is headin' for Denver. I hope to make the Union Pacific tracks east of Camp Collins by Wednesday, and that's that."

"You won't make it. *We* won't make it."

Spurr was peeling the biscuits open with his thumbs.

"We're old, Spurr. Both of us. Why don't you just turn me loose? I don't have much of a chance, because they'll follow me and I know they ain't far behind. Probably within a mile or two right now, followin' our sign. I seen a couple scoutin' ahead of the others near Idaville, so they're on my scent, all right. But you got a fair chance of making it out of this thing alive. They got no truck with you. You'll live long enough to retire and frolic with fat whores till the end of your days."

"I appreciate your concern for me, Boomer. Makes my old ticker feel warm." Spurr folded the bacon and shoved the chunks into the biscuits he'd opened. He set two on a plate and set the plate on the ground near Drago's chained ankles. "But you an' me are gonna be tight as Siamese twins all the way back to Denver, when I turn you over to the turnkeys in the basement prison of the Federal Building."

"Damn, that's good!" Drago said, chewing a mouthful of biscuit and sidepork. He looked up at Spurr as he chewed, narrowing a shrewd eye. "What I just told you is bond, Spurr. I just want you to know that. I ain't gonna say another word about the situation, because I can see I ain't gonna change your mind. You'll see soon enough how it lays out, and by then, I'm sorry to say, it's gonna be too late."

Boomer took another big bite and chewed, groaning and shaking his head. "I will say this, though — you make one hell of a breakfast sandwich, partner!"

FOURTEEN

Spurr sat back and ate his biscuits that he washed down with coffee strong enough to melt an andiron.

He kept an eye on both horses as he ate, not liking how the hair under his collars was pricking. That usually meant trouble, and it wasn't unlikely. He'd sensed someone on their back trail earlier.

Could be nerves, but he didn't think so. He'd never been one for bad nerves, unless old age had brought them on. But he was pretty sure that someone had been riding the trail out from Diamond Fire, maybe a mile, a mile and a half behind himself and Drago.

When he'd stretched a look back along the trail earlier, he thought he'd glimpsed the brown speck of a rider moving through an aspen-studded valley that he and his prisoner had crossed a half an hour before.

He'd thought it might have been a deer or

an elk. Maybe a mountain man looking for game. Drago's men would have been moving faster. And there would probably have been more than just one.

Spurr resisted the urge to roll a smoke and sit here with another cup of coffee. The temptation was old age speaking to him. He didn't have time to lounge around, not when Drago's men might or might not be after him. He answered Boomer's plea for more of the black brew by filling the old outlaw's cup with a caustic grunt.

Then he set the pot down and heaved himself to his feet. His ankle was sore for no good reason, and he limped over to where he'd leaned his rifle against a tree and racked a fresh round into the breech.

He worked the kink out of his ankle.

Holding the smoking cup in his hands, Drago watched Spurr darkly, a shrewd kind of fatefulness in the haggard outlaw's lone eye. The sun peeked out between high, fluffy clouds, offering a wan-golden mountain light, and it reflected dully off the old outlaw's battered bowler pancaked to his head by his red scarf, and caused the scarf to glow like fresh blood.

The chill wind blew the man's grizzled, coffee-colored beard.

"We ain't as young as we once was," he said.

"How'd you lose your eye?" Spurr asked him, kicking dirt on the fire, which they no longer needed.

"Got trapped in a bank in Whiskey Creek, California. We was shootin' it out with the town marshal and his deputies. Big shard from one of the windows cut into it." With one hand, he lifted the patch from over the bad eye. It was bad, all right — eggshell white and sort of shriveled in the scarred socket. "Funny how I can see just as good through just the one."

"I reckon we adapt."

"Adapt or die. That's the whole story, ain't it?" Drago sighed and glanced at Spurr's rifle. "Where you goin'?"

"Gonna take a look around. Settle back, have a nap. I catch you up to anything, I'll gut-shoot you."

Boomer's eye glinted behind the steam rising from his coffee cup. "But then you'll have to listen to my caterwaulin'!"

Spurr headed for the creek. He knew that, shackled and cuffed as he was, Drago wasn't going anywhere. He couldn't walk and he couldn't ride, and there were no weapons lying around. At least none that Spurr was worried about. He'd check the man later to

169

see if he'd squirreled away a fork or a butter knife with the intent of sticking it in Spurr's back.

The old lawman crossed the creek via a beaver dam. His moccasin slipped off the dam and soaked his ankle. Drago laughed jeeringly behind him. Spurr threw up an arm in salute and then angled his way up the gully's far slope.

He was winded by the time he reached the top. The slope wasn't that high, but his old ticker wasn't much good at this altitude. It beat fast and then slow and sputtered and hiccupped, and he felt it tighten up on him like a clenched fist in his chest.

When he finally got some wind, he walked through a stand of pines, squirrels chittering around him. At the edge of the trees he stopped, shouldered up against a fir, still breathing hard, and cast his gaze back along the long, gradual incline up which Spurr had come when he'd left the main trail.

It was a tan-and-green valley, the tan being broom grass and occasional clumps of chokecherry and wild mahogany. The green were pine copses fingering out from the slopes on both side of the valley. To the left jutted a low ridge capped with gray rock. More, taller ridges with pine-studded apron slopes lay far away to the north.

It was a big, forbidding country. Cold and windblown and swept by cloud shadows. The chill bespoke the coming winter when the snow would be ten feet deep, fifteen to thirty in ravines and the valley bottoms. Diamond Fire lay just over the next ridge straight out away from Spurr, a treeless, wind-scoured saddleback that dropped into another broad valley. It didn't look that far away from Spurr's vantage, but then nothing did in this lens-clear light.

It was so clear, in fact, that even his old eyes could make out the single rider wending slowly along the outside edge of a distant copse of mixed evergreens and autumn gold aspens. From this distance of a good mile, the rider was a mere light brown speck, but by the way it moved, it was a man on a horse, all right.

And since he was following the same route Spurr had taken right down to passing to the right of a small boulder field pushed out of the ground by the last glacier, he was shadowing Spurr and Drago.

One of Drago's men? Possibly a scout rider?

Spurr had to assume so.

Spurr continued to stare as the rider rode toward him, just walking his horse, in no big hurry, following the sign. A cloud shadow swept over the rider, hiding him for a few seconds, and then there he was again, riding out of the cloud shadow and into the salmon-gold sunlight.

The wind rushed off the slopes around Spurr, carrying the occasional crackling of a falling branch.

Spurr turned and made his way back through the trees. He descended the gully slope carefully, not wanting to twist or break an ankle out here. If he did, he was crow-bait. Drago would dance a jig over him.

He crossed the dam without slipping off this time. When he got to the other side, he saw that Boomer was asleep against the boulder, head thrown back and to one side. His empty cup was turned over by his right thigh. Drago's mouth was open, and beneath the wind's steady rush his snores sounded like a dull whipsaw.

Spurr started forward. Drago jerked awake with a start. He stared at Spurr, wide-eyed for about five seconds, and then recognition dawned in his lone eye, and he drew a long breath.

"I was dreamin' I forgot to feed the chickens."

"What chickens?" Spurr said.

"Chickens back home on our old Texas ranch, I guess. I dream about 'em from time to time, more lately. It was my job to make sure the chickens got fed and watered and to pen 'em up at night and to make sure no foxes got in the pen. Every once in a while I dream I left 'em out or I forgot to feed 'em or both and I got this feelin' my old man is gonna wale the holy hell out of me."

Spurr walked down to fetch the horses.

"They're back there, ain't they?" Drago asked him.

"Yep," Spurr said, bending down to remove Cochise's hobbles.

Drago drew another ragged breath. "Wish you woulda listened to me. Cause hell's sure enough gonna pop now, partner."

Later, after Spurr and Drago had stopped for the night, and Spurr had built a fire in the shelter of a mountain wall, the old lawman took his rifle and walked back in the direction from which they'd come.

They'd followed a deer trail up from the floor of a narrow, deep valley to the base of the stony cliff — high ground from where Spurr thought he could keep a better watch on his back trail below and from where he'd have a better chance against attackers. He followed the deer trail down the open slope and into aspens, holding his rifle up high across his chest in both hands, walking slowly, cautiously, alert for the sounds of stalkers.

The sun had gone down but there was still an hour's worth of wan green light left in the sky. The steely breeze sliced across Spurr's cheeks. The wind was out of the south, facing Spurr now, which was good because it blew the smoke of his and Drago's campfire back against the northern cliff face rather than into the valley, where Spurr had spied the flicker of a campfire after he had finished building his own.

He'd left Drago bound and gagged this time, in case the man got the notion to call out for his old gang. Spurr had left his prisoner in a spitting, grunting, red-faced rage. Spurr didn't trust the old outlaw any farther than he could throw him uphill against a stiff west wind.

Spurr descended the slope at a slant, which was easier on his old knees. Below lay the creek, its dark water splashing over rocks in its narrow, tree- and shrub-lined bed.

Spurr could smell the freshness of the water and the rocks and the green of the damp trees. As he approached the game trail that ran along the bottom of the slope, beside the stream, he cast his gaze downstream about fifty yards and into the woods on the creek's far side.

A campfire flickered orange in the dense shadows. The camp was likely butted up against the base of the cliff on that side of the canyon.

Spurr was only a few feet above the game trail when his left moccasin boot slipped out from beneath him. He gave a grunt as both feet flew out from beneath him, and he dropped his rifle as he lowered both hands to break his fall, which they hardly did at all.

"Shit!" he exclaimed under his breath as the ground came up to smack his butt and back hard, jarring his breath from his lungs. He rolled several times to his left and ended up on the damp game trail, belly down, raking air in and out of his lungs.

When the shock of the sudden tumble had passed, he jerked his head up and looked over his shoulder to see if anyone had heard and come running from the direction of the campfire. What a way to go out — falling on his ancient ass and lifting a silly din to alert a dozen or so hard cases to his presence. He imagined Drago's unwashed horde running out from the direction of the fire, pistols and rifles raised, whooping and hollering like coyotes.

He scanned the trees, lips stretched back

from his teeth, thin hair hanging in his eyes.

Nothing stirred but a squirrel peering over a branch on the other side of the chugging, gurgling stream and chitting raucously as though jeering at the clumsy human interloper.

"Shut up, ya pesky rodent!" Spurr snarled when he was satisfied he hadn't been heard. Drago's tough nuts might not have heard him but the squirrel's tirade could certainly be heard as far away as the fire.

If it *was* Drago's men over there. Spurr had no idea, but who else could it be? He had to find out, learn what he was up against.

The squirrel flicked its tail and, continuing to glare down at Spurr, stopped chittering.

"Thank you," the old lawman said, rolling onto his back to take stock.

He didn't think anything was broken. His ass was mighty sore. The back of his head throbbed dully. His left ankle ached. He'd twisted it slightly but he didn't think it was broken. As he lay there, he was glad to feel a gradual cessation of his miseries.

Finally, he hauled himself to his feet, walked back up the slope to where he'd dropped his rifle, and scooped it and his hat off the ground. He donned the hat and brushed the dirt from the Winchester's stock, vaguely noting a fresh scratch on the already well-scratched and scuffed walnut forestock. He'd have to rub bear grease into the wood when he got back to his cabin west of Denver.

He was just damn lucky the old popper hadn't gone off. He'd had an old lawman friend who'd dropped his rifle, and the damn thing had triggered, sounding like a detonated dynamite keg, alerting the cutthroats he'd been stalking.

Ben Ryan never stalked another cutthroat again. He'd been buried down along the Arkansas River, going on twelve years now. Nothing more than a few shovelfuls of dust . . .

Spurr set out once more, ambling downstream along the deer trail, wincing against the pain in his ankle as well as that in several other joints and his tailbone. *Should have known that grass would be wet down here along the creek, damn fool . . .*

The creek was shallow enough that he made it across the rocks without getting his boots wet. On the southern side of the stream he began moving through the forest in the direction of the flickering flames. He'd just pushed through some ferns when a man shouted loudly, angrily. The voice echoed around the canyon.

Spurr froze as a girl screamed.

A gun barked. It was the hollow pop of a small-caliber pistol.

Spurr crouched and scowled. "What in tarnation?"

FIFTEEN

A man bellowed as though the slug had struck its target.

The girl shouted again, and then another man shouted. There was the snap of a twig beneath a heavy foot.

Spurr dropped to a knee and stared through the dark foliage toward the fire's glow in the trees about sixty, seventy yards away and up the incline toward the base of the cliff. As the man continued shouting, Spurr heaved himself to his feet, and hoping the shouting covered his footsteps, he bulled through the brush and ducked under and around pine branches, the firelight growing in front of him.

He stopped behind a tree at the edge of the firelight, and heard a man yell, ". . . Told you what would happen if you ran out on me, you stubborn wench!"

Another man was groaning while the first man shouted.

Spurr doffed his hat and edged a look around the tree, the girl shouting, "You don't own me, you bastard!"

Her voice broke on that last and she sobbed as Spurr cast his gaze around the side of the tree and into the slight clearing amongst the tall pines and firs forming a horseshoe around the boulder-strewn base of the southern cliff. The girl was on the ground to Spurr's left, facing a tall man in a long, sheepskin coat with a wool collar. Another man was on one knee behind the tall man, holding a gloved hand to his bloody ear.

The tall man held a small, pearl-gripped over/under derringer butt forward, and shook it at the girl threateningly as he gritted his teeth and said, "I do own you, Greta. I paid good money for you from Giff Montgomery, and by god you're gonna earn back every penny, or I'm gonna — !"

He'd been walking toward the girl, swinging his hand holding the gun back behind his left shoulder as though he were going to lay the popper across her face. Now he stopped suddenly and turned toward Spurr as the old lawman stepped out from behind the pine. Spurr loudly racked a fresh cartridge into the Winchester's breech, aiming the long gun straight out from his right hip.

180

"Your momma never taught you it wasn't nice to hit girls, I reckon."

The girl turned to him, and even in the dark shadows that the dancing orange flames shunted around the camp he recognized her from the second-floor balcony of the brothel in Diamond Fire. Only now she was sporting a split lip from which blood trickled down over her chin. Her gray-blue eyes were bright with fear and anger.

The man hardened his jaws and furled his brows. "Who the hell are you?" His voice sort of trailed off when his eyes flicked down to the moon-and-star badge pinned to Spurr's buckskin mackinaw. He was a tall, handsome man in whipcord trousers and tall, black boots with silver spurs. His beard and mustache were impeccably trimmed. The high-crowned Stetson on his head appeared to never have been rained on.

"Spurr Morgan, Deputy United States Marshal. It ain't no federal offense, hittin' a woman, but just the same I'm gonna drill you another belly button if you don't drop that little popper in the dirt there, Steve. Then take three steps back to your friend with the ugly ear and tell me what the hell this is all about."

"He hit me!" the girl said in a pinched voice. "He thinks he owns me!"

"I *do* own her, lawman," the fancy Steve said as he angrily tossed the pearl-gripped derringer onto the ground to Spurr's right. "I paid good money for her from a saloon owner in Deadwood and brought her out here at my own expense."

"I didn't want to come out here!" the girl yelled at Fancy Steve.

"You agreed to the proposition that I pay Montgomery a flat fee and give you free room and board and two percent of all profits for *two full years*!"

"But you didn't share any of the profits!"

"That's because you hadn't yet earned back the flat fee I paid to Montgomery!" Fancy Steve shouted back at the girl, leaning forward on his long legs.

"Now, this doesn't sound like a very fair business venture for the girl, who does most of the work," Spurr interjected. He shifted his gaze to the man with the bloody ear — a short, dark-haired gent who was furtively dipping his right hand into the coat pocket on the far side of his person from Spurr. "And I'll thank you to go ahead and fish out of that pocket there whatever you're fishing for, friend. Do it real slow. I'm talking slow as a glacier. One fast move and you'll be sportin' a new ear hole."

The shorter man bunched up his large,

rawboned, thick-nosed face, and slowly lifted his right hand. He held a nickel-plated Bisley revolver between his thumb and index finger.

Scowling at Spurr, he tossed the pistol into the dirt near the tall man's derringer, which Spurr assumed had started out with the girl. In fact, it was probably a bullet from the little popper that had taken the lobe off the shorter gent's left ear.

"Any more pistols on either one of you?"

"No," Fancy Steve said.

"Liar!" the girl yelled at the tall man, jutting her pretty chin at him.

Spurr locked gazes with the tall man and grinned. When the Fancy Steve and the stocky gent had both produced two more pistols of varying calibers apiece, and tossed them down with the others near Spurr, Spurr said, "Well, now that we're all friendly . . . are you all right, young lady?"

"That bastard punched me," she said, spitting the words out at the short gent who slowly gained his feet while glaring at the girl and continuing to hold his hand against his bloody ear.

"I punched her because she called me a bastard," he said in an English accent that did not go with his crude looks. But he was well attired in a sleek bear coat and high-crowned martin hat. His head came up only to the Fancy Steve's shoulders. They were an odd-looking pair.

The girl standing beside Spurr, while not nearly as well dressed in a ragged wool coat and shabby green scarf, was beautiful.

"And then she shoots my damn ear off!" the fat bastard added.

She looked at Spurr, her blue eyes dancing in the firelight. "They said they were going to punch me where the bruises wouldn't show and then tie me over one of their horses and drag me back to Diamond Fire."

"We still are," Fancy Steve said to Spurr.

Spurr felt the burn of anger boil up inside him. Three kinds of men piss-burned him above all others — those who were cruel to children, women, and animals. He had a feeling these two had committed all three sins.

Slowly, he walked up to the Fancy Steve, who stood about two inches taller than Spurr. He was straighter and broader but only because gravity had been pulling on Spurr for twice as long as it had the Fancy Steve.

Spurr held the tall man's glare. The tall man's upper lip curled. His nostrils flared. Spurr rammed the barrel of his Winchester hard into the man's crotch. The man screamed and folded like a barlow knife, thrusting both hands over his crotch and closing his knees.

"Son of a *bitch*!"

The shorter man, who was built like a boxer, bolted toward Spurr. From somewhere, he'd produced a knife. It flashed in his right hand as he came in low with it, intending to disembowel the old lawdog.

Spurr had seen it coming in time, and he squeezed off a Winchester round, the rifle barking loudly. The stocky gent leapt straight up in the air, dropping the knife in the dirt and pine needles. He howled and hopped several times on one foot, holding his other foot off the ground. It sported a hole in the dead center of the man's brown boot.

"You old *bastard*!" he howled, finally dropping back against a pine bole, holding his wounded foot about ten inches above the ground, breathing hard, his face swollen and red, little eyes pinched to slits.

Spurr pumped a fresh cartridge into the Winchester's breech and looked at Fancy Steve, who'd dropped to both knees and was hanging his head as if in prayer though his shoulders bobbed as he breathed. "What about it — you two still think you're gonna manhandle this little lady back to Diamond Fire? I hope I've given you the opportunity to reconsider, because I honestly don't have any more time to waste on you."

Both men groaned and wheezed, the short gent now sitting down against the tree and holding his wounded, shaking foot in both hands.

"I asked you a question. That still your intention?"

Fancy Steve said something under his breath.

"What was that — I couldn't hear you?"

He jerked his handsome, red face with gritted teeth up at Spurr. "I said *no* — we've reconsidered, you crazy old coot. For *now*, yes, we've reconsidered."

"Oh, I see. For now." Spurr chuckled. "Well, for now then why don't you two haul freight? Go on, git your asses back out to wherever you left your horses and start foggin' the trail back to Diamond Fire. I see either one of you out here again tonight, I will kill you on sight and throw your carcasses to the wolves."

Fancy Steve looked at the short gent. The short gent looked back at him. The short gent's eyes were bright. Tears dribbled down his cheeks. If he ground his jaws any more

186

tightly together he'd turn his teeth to powder.

Slowly, as weak as a man three times his age, Fancy Steve rose to his feet. He said in a pinched voice, "Come on, Chaney," and began walking heavily out away from the fire, throwing his shoulders back and holding his hands straight down at his sides. He walked as though he'd just awakened after a week-long bender.

"Come on, Chaney — stop your caterwaulin'," Spurr said, waving his Winchester in the direction of Fancy Steve. "Limp on after your partner before I decide to shoot the whole damn foot off."

Chaney glared at Spurr and then at the girl and then back at Spurr again as, with great effort, he hauled himself to his feet. When he'd limped tenderly away on his bad foot, sending venomous glares over his shoulder at Spurr and the girl, Spurr glanced at her.

She was staring at him, the corners of her mouth quirked in a grin. Her gray-blue eyes were long and slightly slanted. Her skin was white as milk. Her hair was the gold-blond of ripe wheat. "You're my hero."

"Ah, hell," Spurr chuckled, his ears warming. "It wasn't nothin'."

"No, you spared me from a painful ride

back to Diamond Fire with those two varmints. They've been known to haul girls belly down across saddles for miles and miles. They'd have done the same to me and then whipped my ass raw with a rawhide quirt once we got back to town."

Spurr stared after them. He could see only their jostling shadows now as they high-tailed it out to their horses. "Who were they, anyhow?"

"The tall man is Boyd Reymont. He owns the Dovetail Frolic House in Diamond Fire with that baboon partner of his, Marcus Chaney."

"You must be purty important for 'em to both come after you."

"They don't have any tough nuts workin' for 'em. They're too cheap. They just hire girls and keep order themselves. Even serve the drinks and sweep up every night after closing."

"Well, I admire their entrepreneurial spirit."

"One girl gets away and then they all want to run. That's why they came after me."

"You stay here," Spurr said as he walked out into the darkness beyond the fire.

He stopped and pricked his ears. He could hear the two men yammering in pinched voices and grunting. Tack squawked. They were getting mounted. A horse nickered somewhere off ahead of Spurr and to his right.

After a time, hooves thudded slowly, dwindling off to the west, brush and branches snapping. When Spurr had heard the riders cross the creek, he turned back and walked back into the girl's camp. She was sitting on a rock by the fire, looking forlorn and miserable. The blood dribbling from her lip was beginning to dry.

"I do appreciate the help," she said, lifting her eyes to Spurr.

"How long you been shadowin' me, young lady?"

"Since you left town. I heard you were riding east with that old outlaw. I thought you looked kind the other night, so I figured I could do worse than follow you, stay near enough for your protection if I needed it. I didn't mean to be a burden, it's just that I don't have much of a sense of direction and I would have gotten lost in these mountains."

"Where you headed?"

She hiked a shoulder. The firelight played across her smooth cheeks and long, fine neck. "Cheyenne, Casper . . . I don't know. Anywhere but Diamond Fire, I reckon."

Spurr pitched his voice with paternal

admonishing. "These mountain trails are no place for a girl. Especially a purty girl. Besides . . ." He let his voice trail off. There was no point in adding that there was a good chance his heels were being dogged by well-armed human coyotes.

Now, however, he was beginning to doubt both of Drago's stories. He'd seen no sign of anyone following him — outside of the girl, that was. It was beginning to look more and more like old Boomer was tellin' a big windy, wanting only to try to frighten Spurr into turning him loose.

Spurr was now confronted with the problem of the girl, but she was far less of a problem — and even a pretty problem, at that — than a dozen or so armed killers would have been.

Spurr dropped to a knee beside the girl and dug a handkerchief out of his pants pocket. "Here, let me tend that for you. What's your name again? I'd forget my own if I didn't have it written down."

"Greta. Greta Ford, originally of Hayes, Kansas."

"Greta, I'm Spurr." He dabbed gently at the jelled blood on the girl's lip. "Hurt bad, does it, girl?"

"Nah." She smiled at him. Her long legs crossed sexily. "You're such a nice, good man," she said. "I just know you're gonna help me down out of these mountains, aren't you, Marshal Spurr?"

Spurr looked at her. Her smile seemed to grow, her pretty eyes twinkling.

"Ah, hell," Spurr said as he continued dabbing at her rich, red lip.

SIXTEEN

"Sorry for the long walk, girl." Spurr had rigged up her horse, which she'd tied a ways off from her camp, and he was leading the mount up the steep hill toward his own bivouac.

He was breathing hard with the effort. Walking along beside him rather than ride the horse over such treacherous ground at night, she was, too. He supposed her profession didn't allow her to get out for fresh air overmuch, to build up her lungs.

"Why on earth did you camp this high up, Marshal Spurr?"

"Please, Greta," Spurr said as they came out of the trees to see the faint glow of the dying campfire. "Just Spurr will do. I don't hold much with form. And I camped up here to hold the high ground . . . in case it needed holding."

"Why would it need holding?"

"Some mighty unsavory characters in

these parts. Mighty unsavory. I'm sharin' my camp with one."

Spurr nodded toward the dying fire's dim glow as he continued leading the girl's paint mare — he didn't even want to know if the horse was stolen, but it most likely was — up the slope and into the camp at the base of the cliff. Drago sat against the tree that Spurr had tied him to. He was a vague silhouette in the near darkness relieved only by the lambent glow off the chalky ridge wall and the kindling stars.

Drago was muttering through his gag. Spurr had heard enough men mutter through gags to be able to translate the muddy language, and he could tell that Drago was reading him and his entire family out to show his distaste at being bound and gagged and left by a dying campfire with the cold mountain night falling hard.

Spurr dropped the horse's reins and leaned his rifle against a tree. He walked over and pulled the bandanna down beneath Boomer's chin, and the outlaw instantly laid into Spurr, cursing like a sailor. When Spurr had tossed several dry deadfall branches on the fire, and the flames had leapt up to reveal the beautiful blonde standing by the fire, staring down skeptically at the raging outlaw, Drago cut himself off midsentence.

His lone eye flashed as it swallowed the girl like a giant, hungry mouth. It flicked up and down her willowy frame, the voluptuousness of which was poorly disguised by her cheap floral-pattered pink-and-white cotton dress showing beneath her waist-length, ragged wool coat. The hem of her white pantaloons shone beneath the dress, brushing across the tops of her rabbit-fur moccasins.

The outlaw's lower jaw hung to his chest. He stared unblinking at the girl for a good thirty seconds before he rolled his lone eye to Spurr, who was breaking branches to add to the pile by the fire, and said, "Spurr, I underestimated you. Truly, I did. I thought you done hoofed off like a lamb to the slaughter. But, no — you've returned, bearin' a blond-headed angel minus the wings."

Greta laughed as she stood warming herself by the fire. "This is your prisoner, I take it?"

"I don't normally truss up my friends like calves for the brandin', Miss Greta."

"I'm relieved to hear that, Spurr."

Voice pitched with unabashed awe, Drago said, "Holy moly — I like how she talks. There's nothin' like a woman's voice, especially when you've been incarcerated as long as I have, to sing like Lillie Langtry in an old man's ears."

"I'm standing right here, sir," said Greta. "As I'm not a mute, there's no need to speak as though I was out of hearin' range."

"Sassy one, too," said Boomer, lifting one cheek. "I like sassy women."

The old lawman shrugged at Greta, who arched a skeptical brow at the old outlaw and then walked around the fire toward her horse.

"You leave the mount to me," Spurr said. "Here, I'll take down your bedroll, and you can rest easy like, Miss —"

"Don't you worry about my horse, Spurr," Greta said. "And just so you don't think me a stock thief, I bought the lovely mare, Betsy, from a down-at-heel saddle tramp in Diamond Fire. She has all the cowboy's rigging. I can ride and tend her just fine. I don't want my tagging along with you boys to cost you any extra work. To earn my keep, I'll cook, and I make damn good coffee if you like it strong."

"Strong enough to singe a nun's habit," Boomer said.

She winked at the old outlaw and led the paint into the woods toward where Spurr had picketed his and Drago's mounts.

Spurr stared after her, smitten in spite of

himself. What was it about women that tied his tongue in nearly as many knots now in his old age as it had when he was twelve years old?

"Quit droolin', Spurr," Drago admonished him. "It ain't becomin' of that badge you're wearin'."

"Ah, shut up, you old burnin' sack of dog shi . . ." Spurr cast another quick, sheepish glance toward Greta, and let civility steer him to silence.

Drago chuckled. "Where did you find her, Spurr? If you got more stashed somewhere down there in the canyon, it would have been nice if you'd brought back an extry one for me. Or is *she* for me? She looks like she'd be a catamount in the mattress sack. With your ticker, you'd better swing shy!"

Drago laughed. "And, say, would you mind untying me? It's a mite embarrassin' to be all trussed up like this when I'm trying to lure a purty little lass into my bedroll."

"You ain't leadin' her anywhere, amigo."

Spurr had set the coffeepot and a kettle of beans and bacon on the fire, figuring that Greta might be hungry. He stirred the beans and glanced off to where he could see the girl's blond-headed shadow moving in the dark pines just west of the camp, where the horses were all snorting and nickering as they got to know one another.

"She's on the run from the varmints that had her imprisoned in some parlor house in Diamond Fire," he told Boomer. "She's gonna join us on the trail down the mountains. You best be on your best manners. She's been through a bucket o' buffalo dung."

"That's what the shootin' was about?"

"I don't normally shoot game after dark."

"You leave any of 'em alive?" Boomer asked with a snort.

"Alive but one with a sore foot."

"Trigger-happy's what you are."

"You didn't accuse me of that back in Diamond Fire."

Drago scowled and brushed a cuffed wrist across his nose. He didn't say anything for a time but only stared off across the open slope and into the dark trees that moved slightly every now and then when a breeze stole across the mountainside.

"Spurr," he said finally, as the old lawman lay back against his saddle, waiting for the coffee to boil.

"What is it?"

"You might've done that girl a great disservice."

"How's that?" Greta asked, moving up out

of the trees, grunting under the weight of her saddle, bedroll, and large, overstuffed carpetbag.

"Here, let me get that for you, girl." Spurr's bones popped as he heaved himself to his feet. "You shoulda whistled for me." Seeing a girl working under such a heavy load just went against his grain, even though she was young enough to be his grand-daughter, damn the friggin' fates, any-way . . .

Drago chuckled again jeeringly as Spurr hurried over and grabbed the girl's saddle and bedroll off her shoulder.

"Thanks!" she said, drawing a deep breath as Spurr set the gear down beside the fire. "I haven't hauled a saddle around in a while. They didn't used to seem so heavy. I reckon that's what I get for makin' my livin' on my back for the past two years."

Spurr's ears warmed at the girl's frank-ness, and he could see Drago's cheeks darken and his eye acquire a sharp, amused light.

Greta frowned as she cut her eyes from Drago to Spurr, who untied her blanket roll from her saddle and unrolled it on the ground for her, doting on her like an old woman. "How could letting me trail with you fellas be a disservice to me? If it wasn't for Marshal . . . if it wasn't for Spurr, I'd be heading back to Diamond Fire tied across my horse's saddle!"

Spurr said sharply, "Boomer, will you stop cuttin' with that old saw?" He glanced at Greta as he gave the beans another stir, making sure they didn't stick to the bottom of the pan. "Boomer there's been blowin' smoke up my . . . well . . . he's been spinnin' ragged yarns about his old gang gunnin' for him. First, they was just trailin' him to turn him loose and fill me full o' holes. Now they're trailin' us to fill us *both* full o' holes."

Spurr winked at the girl, who was now kneeling by her carpetbag by the fire. "Truth is, he's so old his gang likely turned him out. Sort of like the buffalo do with the old bulls. He was caught by a bounty hunter with his pants down in a bawdy house, and he just can't get over it. So he's tryin' everything he can to convince me I gotta cut his hobbles lest I should contract a bad case of lead poisonin'."

Drago said gravely, "I feel it's fair to warn you, my dear, that your life is in more danger now than before this old badge-toting reprobate hauled you up here. The truth is, I've piss-burned the members of my old gang, and they are most likely right now gathering from all points of the compass in Diamond Fire — in preparation for heading this way. They've been scouring these mountains for me."

He turned his dark, one-eyed stare at Spurr, who was spooning beans and bacon onto a plate and chuckling quietly. "Two or three of those boys could track a snake across the ocean, my aged amigo."

"Here you are, Greta. Supper beans warmed up special for you."

"Why, thank you, Spurr." The girl accepted the plate and then scuttled onto her bedroll and sank back against her saddle, lines of consternation cutting across her forehead as she poked a spoon at the beans.

"And don't listen to him," Spurr advised her. "The man's a gravel-crawed criminal. He'll do anything he can to get himself shed of those cuffs. Shut him from your mind, Miss Greta, and take heart that you're with one of the wiliest lawmen west of the Mississippi. I will make certain sure you trail down out of these mountains without one hair mussed on your purty head."

"Ah, Christ, Spurr — you're gonna make me air my paunch!"

"Shut up, Drago, or I'll take my cartridge belt to your rancid hide!"

"Unchain me, and we'll make a fair fight of it!"

"Boys, boys!" Greta intoned, cutting her wide, startled eyes between them. "Please, don't fight on my account!"

Spurr glared at his prisoner. Drago glared back at him.

Ashamed and embarrassed at his behavior in front of the pretty girl, realizing he was probably behaving like the men she was fleeing in Diamond Fire, Spurr sank back against his saddle. "I do apologize. I guess I just don't cotton to takin' much guff off a snake such as that."

Greta started eating her beans, continuing to cut her slightly skeptical gaze between the two men. "You two seem to know each other. You go back, do you?"

Drago said, "Too damn far, Miss Greta."

"We go back a ways, that's for sure," Spurr said, rummaging around in his saddlebags until he'd produced his small, flat brown bottle, which he held up. "I take it you don't disapprove of busthead . . ."

Greta's pretty, blue eyes flashed eagerly. "I should say I don't! And boy, do I have a surprise!" She set her plate aside and dipped into her carpetbag. She pulled out two bottles of Kentucky bourbon, grinning like the cat that ate the canary.

"Boys, how about a drink on Boyd Reymont and Mark Chaney?"

Spurr's heart lightened at the sight of those two, labeled brown bottles. He didn't think it was possible to find labeled bottles in this neck of the woods.

He and Drago whistled at the same time. "Lookee there," Spurr said. "And here I was already gettin' the fantods over the prospect of emptyin' this little medicine flask of mine."

"Not to worry," Greta said. "I took three bottles out from behind the bar before I left this mornin'. If we ration ourselves, we should make it down to the eastern plains with a sip or two to spare!"

"What're you doin' with so much liquor, Miss Greta?" Boomer asked as the girl spilled liberal portions into three tin coffee cups. "I didn't figure you of the swillin' type sort."

"I figured I'd have to pay my way down these mountains one way or another," Greta said. "And after all I been through, I'd just as soon pass around the liquor as pass around myself." She winked and handed one of the cups to Spurr.

"Hey, what about me?" Boomer scowled at the old lawman as Spurr took a deep pull from his cup.

"It's against federal regulations for prisoners to imbibe," Spurr said, though he'd heard no such regulation. "Don't worry, Boomer — I'll make sure yours don't go to waste!"

"Oh, Spurr, it's a cold night!" the girl said, her eyes making a plea for Drago's case.

Playing it to the hilt, Drago hung his head toward his upraised knees.

"That one-eyed old killer don't deserve no Kentucky who-hit-john!" Spurr said. But the girl kept her wide, pleading eyes on him. "Ah, hell," the old marshal relented, handing Drago's cup to the pretty girl. "I reckon it's your busthead, Miss Greta. Yours to waste on the likes of that ole curly wolf, if you're so inclined."

Spurr thought Drago's lone, shining eye would pop out of its socket as he watched the girl walk around the fire and hand him the cup. "Be careful," Spurr warned Greta. "That's a catamount, that one. Best not linger around him. Wouldn't doubt it a bit if he used you to get to me."

"Are you really a killer, Mr. Drago?" Greta asked when she'd settled back down with her whiskey, huddling low in her coat against the penetrating mountain chill. "You don't look like one."

"I only kill when someone needs killin'."

Drago spat the words at Spurr. "Mostly, I'm a train and bank robber. Oh, we'd hold up a stage now an' then when times was tough an' the girls expensive" — he chuckled devilishly — "but mostly we hit trains and Wells Fargo boxes loaded with gold or silver. Once we stole trinkets off a rich man from New York City, one o' them robber barons, and sold 'em down in Mexico. That dinero got me through two whole years down there, cavortin' along the coast of the Cortez Ocean with purty Mexican damsels."

"Sounds like you've had quite a life, Mr. Drago."

"Call me Boomer."

"That's just one of his names. He's had many, Miss Greta." Spurr finished the whiskey in his cup and smacked his lips together. If he'd tasted better tanglefoot, he couldn't remember when it had been, though being low on his own tarantula juice and this far out in the high and rocky probably had something to do with it.

Drago sipped the whiskey, sloshed the liquid around in his mouth, and shook his head as he let it slide down his throat. "Say, that's some good coffin varnish there. I do thank you, Miss Greta."

"The pleasure's mine, Boomer. I'm just glad to be here. I couldn't have spent another winter in Diamond Fire. Most of the good folks — if there is such a thing — leave before the first snow hits. That leaves the dregs . . . and we pleasure girls. I've been in some nasty camps, but Diamond Fire is in a bucket all its own."

"I'll vouch for that," Spurr said. "Say, where you headed for, Miss Greta? Cheyenne, did you say?"

"Oh, I don't know." The girl sipped from her cup and wrapped her arms around her knees, giving a little shiver against the chill. "Just out of the mountains for the winter. Out of the mining camps for good. I knew a man in Cheyenne, a few years ago. He was married, but he said he loved me. I heard recently that his wife died . . ."

She looked down, her eyes sheepish, sad. "Not too many options for a girl of my profession."

She sipped her whiskey.

Spurr felt sorry for her. He'd known many women who'd gone into "the trade," as it was called, because they'd run out of other options. Most were orphans or young widows without families to help ease their journey through life.

The frontier was a tough place for girls without families, for women without men. They'd whore for a while, but then they'd become pregnant or too early they'd lose their looks or their health. Most died before they hit thirty.

Greta threw the last of her drink back and set the cup on a rock by the fire. "Well, if you'll excuse me, gentlemen. I think I'll prepare for bed. I'm a mite on the sleepy side."

When Greta had risen on her long legs and walked away through the dark trees, Drago turned to Spurr, his eye sharp. "You an' me gotta talk, partner. We gotta talk before it's too late."

"I know, I know," Spurr said. "Your ole gang's comin' for you."

"They is." Drago blinked. "And you'll rue this night you didn't listen to me, old man."

Spurr gave a wry snort and threw the last of his whiskey back. Lowering the cup from his lips, he looked at Boomer once more. The old outlaw still had his lone eye aimed at him, dark as a pistol maw.

A cold finger of doubt pressed against Spurr's lower back. He considered it for a time, disregarded it.

He should know better than to listen to anything Boomer Drago told him. The man was a liar. Always had been, always would be.

"Well, Boomer, time to tend nature,"

Spurr said, rising with a grunt and tossing his cup down against his saddlebags. "Then we're gonna throw down for a good night's sleep, get an early jump on the morrow."

SEVENTEEN

Spurr woke with a start. It was dawn, the sky lightening, the trees relieved in shadow against it. Birds chirped in the branches.

The birds weren't what had awakened Spurr. He blinked as he rose on his elbows.

He looked toward where Greta lay on his right, and his weak ticker heaved and coughed when he saw a pair of legs standing between him and the girl. The man wore high-topped brown boots, blue denims stuffed down inside the wells. Copper spurs dully reflected the dawn light. Spurr trailed his eyes up the man's long legs and dirty cream duster just as the man turned his head to look at Spurr over his shoulder.

The man wore a week's growth of ginger beard. He stretched his lips back from large, white teeth, and his brown eyes flashed delightedly. As he half turned toward Spurr, the old lawman saw the smoking, long-barreled revolver in the man's hand. Beyond the end of the barrel, Greta was stretched out on her back, her head tipped to one side, mouth slack.

There was a quarter-sized hole in the girl's forehead. Blood dribbled out of it and trickled across the smooth skin toward her ear. Her half-open, accusing eyes stared past the gunman toward Spurr as if asking the old lawman why he hadn't done anything to save her.

Then Spurr saw that it was not Greta lying there in the mussed blankets with the bullet hole in her forehead. It was Kansas City Jane as she'd looked that morning she'd lain dead on the boardwalk across from the bank.

The gunman laughed as he swung quickly around toward Spurr. "Worthless old man!" he shouted, clicking the revolver's hammer back and bringing the big pistol to bear on Spurr.

"No!" Spurr shouted, reaching for the Starr .44 holstered beside him.

A girl screamed. Spurr froze, and then he was not staring at the unshaven gunman but at a willowy blonde in a pink cotton dress and fur moccasins standing beside the fire from which sparks were rising. Greta had one branch in her hand as she stumbled backward, a blanket draped across her slender shoulders, her wide eyes bright with fear.

"Spurr!"

Drago sat against the tree to the girl's right, glaring at Spurr, his blanket pulled up around his knees.

"Holster that hogleg, you old coot!" Boomer admonished him. "You're dreamin'!"

Spurr looked at the gun in his hand. It was cocked and aimed at Greta's chest.

Horrified, he tipped up the barrel and depressed the hammer, easing it down against the firing pin. He lowered the gun to his lap, looked to his right. Only Greta's saddle, canteen, and carpetbag were there, a whiskey bottle standing beside the bag.

Kansas City Jane was nowhere to be seen.

"Old and used up," carped Boomer. "And he's the ramrod. Lord help us all!"

Greta swallowed as she stared down at Spurr. Her eyes lost their fear. She glanced at the branch in her hand, tossed it into the fire she'd been building, and dropped to a knee beside Spurr. She placed a hand on his forearm resting with the gun across the blanket twisted on his lap.

"You all right, Spurr?"

Spurr looked back at her. Her eyes were genuinely concerned. It warmed him. It also made him feel worse about scaring her. Old and used up. Maybe both Boomer and Henry Brackett were right. His heart was heavy; his shoulders felt weighed down by a blacksmith anvil.

"I'm sorry, Greta." That's all he could think of to say. He looked again at the pistol in his lap. The gnarled, brown hand with knotted, bulging veins could not be his hand. Not Spurr Morgan's hand. But it was. And with that old claw he'd almost killed this girl. His second one this month.

"It's all right," Greta said with a tender smile, squeezing his forearm and then rising. "I'm gonna get coffee boiling and then I'll make breakfast. I brought some canned meat from town, and six pickled eggs."

"I got bacon in these bags here," Spurr said numbly.

"We'll have a feast then!"

Greta picked up the coffeepot and swung around to start down the slope toward the creek for water.

Spurr looked at Drago. Boomer cursed and gave a caustic shake of his head. "Doomed . . . that's what me an' that poor girl are."

Despite the dream, Spurr didn't feel doomed. Not any longer. The girl's presence had helped him shake the anvil from his shoulders. Greta didn't seem to believe they were doomed, either.

The autumn day was clear, the sky blue, the sun warm, the air cool. The breeze smelled like cinnamon and pine. In the canyons that the trio rode along, there was the added moist, loamy, green smell of the creeks.

Spurr kept a sharp eye on their back trail, and he kept his eyes and ears skinned on the land around them, his rifle resting across his saddlebows as he rode. But he saw no sign that his party was being stalked.

He hadn't felt any instinctual uneasiness since he'd sensed Greta on their trail out from Diamond Fire. He doubted very much that there was any truth to Boomer's story — to *either* of Boomer's stories — though the old outlaw continued to make a good show of looking worried as he cast frequent dark glances along their back trail and gave ominous sighs.

Boomer Drago was a shrewd nut, and a tireless one — Spurr would give him that.

Spurr enjoyed his time on the trail, knowing it would be his last as a federal lawman. Probably one of his last, period.

He found himself paying close attention to the familiar but somehow magical details

— the clomps of the horses' hooves, the mounts' snorts and nickers, the rattling of the bits in their teeth. The smell of the horses themselves and the leather of the tack. The chuckle of the creeks tumbling over their rocky beds in the deep, fir-studded canyons.

The smell of coffee and wood smoke. The crunch of pine needles under the soft soles of his moccasins.

The girl was an added bonus to this trip. While Kansas City Jane still haunted the old lawman, he found himself able to appreciate Greta's own, singular beauty. The way she smiled and the way the light danced in her long eyes, and how her eyes crossed slightly when she joked and teased, which was often.

She was a girl who'd lived a hard life, and it had taken its toll on her — Spurr could sense that in her frequent though short-lived, brooding silences. But she took full advantage of the buoyancy of happiness, stretching it out, savoring it, making it last.

Spurr figured it was a quality in women who'd had it rough. That's how his old friend, Abilene, had been, as well. She loved to joke and horse around, but her quiet times were quiet, indeed — and gloomy. Hell, he supposed that's how he himself was, though he certainly didn't claim to have had as harsh a life as a frontier percentage girl.

The three travelers camped that night along another canyon. Greta cooked beans and beef and boiled the coffee extra strong, adding several shots of bourbon to the pot. Even Drago lightened up after several cups of the spiced coffee, and Spurr felt good, bedding now near the girl with a full belly and a light head, after he'd taken a scout around the camp to make sure they were alone.

Nothing but the owls and coyotes and the little burrowing creatures that made faint scuttling sounds all night. Occasionally, Spurr heard the brief squeal of a rabbit likely being pulled out of its den by a stalking wildcat.

The next morning, after he'd taken another slow, careful scout around the canyon, Spurr was doubly sure that Drago had been spinning yarns about his old gang. There was no smell of campfire smoke on the air and no sign of movement anywhere along their back trail. What's more, there was a noticeable lack of hair-prickling tension beneath the collar of the old lawman's hickory shirt, under his mackinaw.

When Spurr returned to the camp, where

Drago and Greta were packing gear and rigging the horses, Drago with his hands and ankles still cuffed, Spurr saw and heard the old outlaw laughing and joking around with the girl. Drago had apparently decided to forget his ruse about his old gang. He was having too much fun trying to impress Greta with his lies about old outlaw escapades to continue to look dark and gloomy, as though he feared for his life.

In the afternoon, they followed a windy, twisting ridgeline down out of the Medicine Bow Mountains and set up camp at the base of Cameron Pass, which was a natural bridge between the Medicine Bows and the Mummy Range just south. They made camp early, as it was dark here between ridges, and now they only had about a three-day ride to the Union Pacific line.

When Spurr had tended the horses and staked them all to a long picket line, he rigged up a fishing line with string and a palming needle, using a steel-cut button from a woman's dress as a lure, and hauled in three nice-sized red-throated trout.

Greta fried the trout and made corncakes from Spurr's stores, and they ate and drank well that night, Spurr and Greta sitting up close to the fire, Boomer trussed up as usual and tied to a nearby aspen bole. Spurr wasn't taking any chances with the old outlaw, not only because he wanted to see Boomer brought to justice, but because he didn't want to bung up this last assignment and put an extra bee in Henry Brackett's bonnet.

That night, Spurr was skinning a buffalo in his sleep, as he and Boomer Drago had once done in the old days just before the war had broken out between the states and they'd both headed east to fight for the Union. (Spurr had seen no good reason for one man to own another, but he'd mostly joined the federals because as a native Kansan he'd wanted to help keep the Union intact.)

Working on the buffalo, flies buzzing around his head in the hot, humid Kansas air, Spurr cut the skin down the inside of each leg, grunting as he sawed the sharp blade of the skinning knife against the bull's tough hide. He was cutting a strip around the beast's thick neck, trying to work fast because the captain of the crew, pugnacious Old Billy Kramer, would be coming fast with the wagon, when someone rammed a boot toe into his ribs.

It was either Drago or Jack Crawford — probably Drago stumbling around Spurr as he ineptly worked on his own buff near his partner's. "Goddamnit, Boomer," Spurr snarled, "you couldn't hit the ground if you *fell!*"

He opened his eyes and found himself sitting straight up in his bedroll. Someone moved to his right, and he felt the hard point of another boot rammed into the same place in his ribs.

Spurr cursed and grabbed his rib cage as he flopped on his side and looked up.

A tall, round-faced, green-eyed man in a black opera hat and long leather duster stood in inky silhouette against the lilac dawn sky. The man's blond-bearded head and his shoulders were massive, making him appear short though he was at least six feet tall.

He stared down at Spurr, smiling with satisfaction. He had a big, stag-gripped Colt Navy in his right, black-gloved hand, and, half-turned away from Spurr, he was aiming the pistol at Spurr's face.

He spoke through his yellow, brown-crusted teeth. "Just lay there, old man, or I'll kill you now."

Spurr looked around the man's leg clad in patched broadcloth, and he heard himself wheeze a horrified gasp. Greta was sitting up in her own bedroll six feet away from Spurr. Two men were standing around her while another man in a battered bowler hat and red vest under an open, shaggy wolf coat, knelt behind her. He held one hand over her mouth. With his other hand he pressed a cocked pistol against Greta's left temple.

Greta stared wide-eyed at Spurr, her face smooth and floury pale above the man's brown hand. Her chest rose and fell sharply as she breathed, terrified.

"Ah, shit — oh, hell!" Boomer Drago yelled about ten feet to Spurr's left, sitting tied against the aspen. Two more men stood around Drago, and one was just then withdrawing the boot he'd slammed into the old outlaw's rib cage, waking him.

"Goddamnit, Spurr!" Drago shouted, leaning forward and sideways over his battered ribs. "What'd I tell ya?"

"Spurr," said the big man standing over the old marshal, narrowing his cunning green eyes. "Old Spurr Morgan. I thought you'd been turned under a long time ago."

Spurr cursed against the lingering agony in his side and stared at the man holding Greta. "You let her go, goddamn your worthless hide!"

He glanced to his right, where he'd coiled his pistol.

The big man standing over him said,

"Quiet Ed's got the Starr. Your Winchester, too."

Spurr followed his glance to the big man with Indian features standing a ways back in the trees, Spurr's Starr wedged behind the cartridge belt wrapped around the outside of his blanket coat.

The big Indian held two rifles on his shoulders. One was Spurr's Winchester. He was not looking at Spurr. He was staring down at Greta just as the man behind her removed his hand from her mouth, turned her head toward his, and kissed her.

Greta fought against him but he held her taut in his arms, kissing her.

"Let her go, goddamnit!" Spurr said as he bounded up and lunged forward off his stockingfeet, his blankets tumbling away. He'd intended on bulling into the big man before him, but he'd only taken his second step before the big man rammed his right knee up against Spurr's forehead.

Spurr stumbled backward and hit the ground hard on his back, lights flashing in his eyes.

"Goddamnit, Spurr!" Drago bellowed. "Why in the hell couldn't you listen to me? Now, here they are, and we're all dead!"

EIGHTEEN

The man in the gray bowler and red vest drew away from Greta, grinning, spittle stringing from his lower lip. He was missing his two front teeth. His face was like a raisin, eyes dark and nasty mean.

Greta bunched up her face and slapped him, the crack sounding like the report of a small-caliber pistol. The man's face jerked to one side. It hardened. He snapped his own hand up, laid the back of it against Greta's left cheek.

Greta screamed as the blow whipped her head to one side, blond hair dancing across her shoulders.

Spurr glared helplessly, his heart chugging heavily, at the man who'd slapped her. The man was laughing now. Vaguely, Spurr wondered if this was all just another savage dream. But he didn't think so. If it was, he hoped he'd wake up soon.

He sat up, wincing against the pain in his

ribs and his head, and heard the harrowing impotence in his own words as he said, pointing at the man with Greta, "I'm gonna kill you, you son of a bitch!"

"Oh, you think so, do you?"

The man with Greta started to rise, angry eyes on Spurr, who heaved himself to his feet, balling his fists. His chest felt tight. He prayed his heart wouldn't go out on him.

"Forget him," said the tall, blond-bearded man with the pistol aimed at Spurr. "He's old and dried up."

He walked around the fire to Drago. A man with pale skin and pale eyes and wearing cut-down holsters stood near Boomer, a cocked pistol aimed at the old outlaw's forehead. That had to be the Texas gunman, Curly Ben Williamson. His pale skin was scaly, like a lizard's.

There were a dozen dangerous-looking, unshaven men standing around the camp, most looking at Greta.

The man to Spurr's left kept a carbine aimed at Spurr's side as he rolled a sharpened stove match around in his mouth. The big Indian, Quiet Ed, was staring expressionlessly at Greta, who knelt on her blankets, chin down, hair obscuring her face.

The big Indian's eyes smoldered.

Spurr walked over to the girl, dropped to

221

a knee beside her, and wrapped his right arm around her. He could feel her shivering against him. Desperation was like a living thing within him.

Desperation and shame.

He'd let himself get hornswoggled. This pack must have been on his heels for at least the past couple of days. Just like Boomer had warned, they'd probably got on his trail in Diamond Fire. Spurr was outnumbered, outgunned by much younger men. All he could do was try to save Greta, somehow keep her out of the jaws of this savage pack.

The blond-bearded leader with the massive head and shoulders and wearing the black opera hat and leather duster was Sam Keneally, an Arizona outlaw with several bounties on his head. He stood in front of Drago, boots spread, sliding the flaps of his duster back as he planted his fists on his hips, just behind his gun-heavy holsters.

He stared down at the old outlaw. Drago grinned sheepishly, glancing from Keneally to Curly Ben Williamson. "Well, hello, Sam. Fancy meetin' you here. Curly Ben, you're lookin' fine though I would appreciate it if you'd stop aiming that hogleg at your old friend, Boomer."

Keneally stepped forward and slashed his right fist against Drago's face. There was a sharp smacking sound that made Spurr's own cheekbone ache.

The blow snapped Boomer's head to one side. Spurr saw blood leaking from the short gash across the old man's cheek. He didn't know why, but seeing Drago treated that way graveled him, though the old outlaw had certainly brought it on himself.

"Still got a good right hook, Sam — I'll give you that," Drago said. "It ain't nice to hit a man when he's all tied up like this, though. Didn't your ma teach you no better?"

"Where's the money?" was Keneally's only response.

Drago turned his mouth corners down and stared mutely up at the broad-shouldered man.

Keneally slid his Colt from its holster, thumbed the hammer back, and pressed the barrel against the center of Drago's head. "A dead man can't spend it. Might as well tell me. Besides, if you don't, me an' the boys are each gonna take a turn with that purty girl over here. Drag her out in the brush and give her a grand ole time. How'd you like to see that — you with such a tender heart toward womenfolk?"

Drago said, "You leave that girl alone, Sam. That ain't what we're about. We ain't *never* been about that!"

"Ain't no more 'we,' Boomer. Not since you killed Teagarden and White an' lit out on your own with the strongbox." Keneally swept his free arm out to indicate the other gang members standing around watching him and Drago, though Spurr could tell that the big Indian, Quiet Ed, was staring at Greta as though she were a hot meal. "You piss-burned us all real good."

Spurr wondered if there was any way he could kill Quiet Ed, who seemed both literally and figuratively the biggest threat toward Greta. If only he could get his hands on a gun . . .

Boomer swallowed, said with a nervous tremor in his voice, "She had nothin' to do with the strongbox, boys. That was just me. We ain't about hurtin' women. *Never* been about that."

"I'm the leader of the gang, now, Boomer, and I say we *are* about that." Keneally glanced over his shoulder to cast his cold, green-eyed gaze at Greta. "Right here an' now, this morning, we're gonna start to be about that. Might even give Quiet Ed there first crack at her, since he can't seem to take his Injun eyes off of her. Shit, Boomer, even after I drill a bullet through your head an' you're shovelin' coal in hell, you'll be hearin' this poor girl scream."

Drago said without further hesitation, "Martín's cabin. Two loose boards under the table. You'll find it there."

"Martín's cabin."

"That's right." Drago swallowed as he looked at the scaly-skinned gunman, Williamson, and then glanced around Keneally toward Spurr and Greta, his anxiety plain in his lone eye. "You boys best be hittin' the trail. You'll be burnin' daylight soon."

"We'll all be hittin' the trail together, Boomer," Curly Ben Williamson said. He was oddly soft-spoken, which somehow enhanced the menacing quality of his yellow-eyed, scaly-skinned countenance. "Just like old times. Only, this will be the last time for you. And you best hope that money's where you say it is, 'cause if it's not, dyin's gonna come slow and hard."

Keneally said, "You'll never believe how slow. But first . . ."

The outlaw leader turned to Greta. "First things first," he said, quirking up the corners of his mouth inside the thick, blond beard. "First, I do believe me an' the boys need a little rest and relaxation."

Greta turned to Spurr, her breasts rising and falling sharply behind the dress she'd worn to bed because of the high-mountain

225

chill. Her eyes begged the old lawman for help.

"No," Spurr said, shaking his head slowly. "You leave this girl alone. Drago gave you what you come here for. Now, take him and get the hell out of here!"

"She's got no part in it," Drago said. "Leave her be, goddamn your ugly hide, Keneally!"

Keneally seemed fueled by the old men's objections. "Sorry, Quiet Ed. But she's too purty. I'm gonna have to have her first. Hell, you're liable to kill her without even tryin' — big and wild as you are with the girls."

Curly Ben Williamson laughed softly.

Before Spurr knew what he was doing, he'd bolted off his heels and rammed his head and shoulders into Keneally's belly. Keneally must have been as surprised by the old lawman's fast, savage move as Spurr himself was. The outlaw gave a surprised yowl as Spurr drove him over backward, reaching for the big Colt still holstered on his left hip.

He closed his hand around the grips, jerked the gun up, tearing free the keeper thong, and rolled to one side off of the outlaw leader. He clicked the hammer back and aimed the gun at Quiet Ed just now lunging toward him, black eyes bulging in their sockets.

Before Spurr could get the popper leveled, he glimpsed Keneally's right hand slashing toward him, the man's fist filled with his other Colt. The fist and the revolver's butt slammed across the bridge of Spurr's nose.

Spurr heard the pistol in his hand bark, but only distantly, as though someone else had fired it from a long ways away. Because by then he was tumbling down, down into a well filled with cold tar.

Even more distantly, Greta screamed.

Spurr continued to hear her screams from the bottom of the tarry pit he'd fallen into. But they were muffled. Sometimes he couldn't hear them at all.

He could feel the reverberations of violent movement through the tar. He tried to swim up out of it, but he felt as though a boulder were sitting on top of him, keeping him pinned to the bottom of the pit filled with the thick, black substance as cold as spring snowmelt.

He was only vaguely aware of an eerie silence. He was more aware of the throbbing in his head, as though a spike had been driven through his ears, and the sensation of steel jaws clamped down hard on his logy heart.

A hot skillet pressed against the back of his neck.

Oh, Christ — now they were burning him!

He lifted his head with a start, opened his eyes.

He was amazed to see bright sunlight washing over him, threatening to blind him as it increased the hammering pain in his skull. He closed his eyes and then opened them but did not look straight up at the sun, which was hovering just over the twelve-o'clock position, beyond pine tops that were dark against it.

Blood stained the pine needles and gravel beneath him. His nose was so swollen that he could see it bulging like a ship's prow. Likely broken.

He climbed to his hands and feet, taking stock of his old body. His body, however, seemed fine except for the gnawing ache in his ribs and the customary tightness in his chest. He could live with that. It was the hammering between his ears that seemed nearly unbearable.

That pain was worse even than the dull thudding of his broken nose.

He looked around quickly as the brain fog cleared enough that he remembered all that had happened. Then he whipped a look behind him, over to where he'd left Greta. She wasn't there. The sun blazed down on the twisted blankets and saddlebags and tack and on the stone ring for the fire inside of which was mounded white ash.

Spurr hauled himself to his feet. His heart hiccupped as he stumbled forward in his stockingfeet and his longhandles, which was all he'd worn to bed. He dropped to his knees by the fire ring, dipped a hand in the ashes.

Cold.

"Greta?" he said, his voice sounding weirdly nasal and raspy, as though he'd left half of it in his chest.

The girl was nowhere in sight.

Spurr looked at the tree to which he'd bound Drago. Boomer was not here. Spurr hadn't expected him to be. Keneally and the rest of the gang had taken him off to Martín's cabin, wherever in hell that was, and to the money Drago had absconded with.

Keneally.

Curly Ben.

Quiet Ed . . .

Shame hammered Spurr's temples, pummeled his shoulders. He'd let them walk right into camp where he'd been sound asleep. They taken Drago and they'd most likely taken Greta, as well.

As he continued to look around, he found the girl's torn dress a ways down the slope to the west, among the gold medallions of sunlight filtering through the pines and the firs. A horse whickered to Spurr's right, and the old lawman turned to see Cochise standing at his picket line. The horse pawed the ground nervously while watching Spurr, aware that something bad had happened. Drago's horse was no longer with the roan, but Greta's paint mare was.

Maybe they hadn't taken her, after all.

If not . . .

Spurr's heart thudded weakly, erratically. He looked down the sun-dappled slope through the trees, toward where a waterfall filled a broad pool beneath it amidst scattered boulders at the base of the ridge wall.

If her dress was here, she was likely down here somewhere, as well. Likely dead, Spurr told himself as though consciously trying to absorb it, to take some of the bite out of finding her.

He continued down the slope but stopped after only a few more steps. White cloth lay twisted in the grass. As Spurr moved closer he saw that it was a chemise and a pair of white cotton pantaloons.

Both garments were torn and bloody.

Nearby, there were deep scuffs and scratches in the forest duff. Greta must have gotten away from the gang and run down here in an attempt to escape her attackers. It had been a futile attempt, for here they had taken her.

Spurr looked around closely at the trees and the short grass and prickly evergreen shrubs tufting amongst the bed of pine needles and cones. Dread ached in him nearly as keenly as his physical ailments, for he expected to find her naked, bloody body here anywhere.

But then he found a thin trail of blood that led him down the slope toward the falls. He stopped beside the pool at the bottom of the falls, which was a slender column of water rolling through a cleft in the ridge about thirty feet up on the rock wall.

He dropped to a knee, traced his finger around two circular indentations in the sand and gravel. Someone had knelt here. Not long ago. Water had been splashed over the sand, which was still damp.

Footprints shone in the sand where the girl had walked away after she'd finished bathing. Spurr followed the tracks with his eyes to the edge of the cliff, on the west side of the pool.

Clouds were moving in, casting gray shadows. The shadows made the girl's blond hair stand out from the sandstone cliff, where she lay, wrapped in a green blanket, in a small notch cave at the cliff's base. She lay curled in a ball, facing Spurr, the blanket drawn up to her throat.

"Leave me, Spurr," she said tonelessly.

Spurr straightened. "You can't stay out here, Greta." He glanced at the sky. The blue was being covered quickly by large, charcoal-bellied clouds, and a chill breeze had risen. "Gonna rain soon."

"Please leave. I want to be alone."

"Are you all right, girl?"

"Please leave me, Spurr." She'd spoken in the same dull voice as before, not looking at Spurr but staring blankly straight out from the notch cave.

"All right."

Spurr looked around. His heart ached. Everything in him ached. His knees felt like putty. Rage burned behind the pain. Rage and frustration because he did not know where the gang had gone. Even if he did know, there was little he could do against them.

They were a dozen fierce men much younger than he. He was one old man. Besides, he couldn't leave Greta.

232

So, his prisoner was gone. And the men who'd taken him and savaged Greta were gone as well, and there wasn't one damn thing Spurr could do about it.

"I'm gonna go up and build a fire. You come up when you feel well enough. All right, Greta?"

She didn't answer or even nod her head. She just stared.

Spurr limped back up the slope through the trees to the camp.

NINETEEN

Drago's men had taken the bottle that Greta had left sitting out, but they hadn't known about the other two inside her carpetbag, which they'd also left.

In fact, the only gear they'd taken was Drago's saddle and bedroll, which he'd need on the trek to Martín's cabin. They'd taken Spurr's Starr .44 and his Winchester, but when he'd taken a liberal pull from one of the two remaining bottles, easing only slightly the agony in his body though doing nothing to assuage that in his mind, he'd looked inside his saddlebags.

He was glad to see they hadn't found his spare Schofield and an old over-and-under, brass-chased derringer. The Schofield was also old — he'd taken it off a curly wolf he'd run down several years ago, for a spare — and he'd rarely had to use it.

He was glad he had it now, though. He pulled out one of his two boxes of .44 shells spotted with bacon grease and loaded the slightly rusty, black-handled weapon. He had four .41-caliber shells wrapped in a tattered scarf for the derringer, which he'd also rarely used. He breeched the handy little popper, slid a shell into each barrel, and snapped it closed.

He slid the Schofield into the holster still lying by his saddle. When he'd pulled on his baggy denim trousers, he donned the holster and cartridge belt, and slid the derringer into the back pocket of his pants. The wind was picking up, howling through the trees and tossing dead leaves and dust this way and that. It was cold. A front was moving in, which meant it would soon get colder.

He glanced down the slope toward the falls and considered Greta once more, worry jabbing at him. But there was little he could do for her except build a fire and hope that when she got cold enough she'd come to it.

Spurr dampened his neckerchief with water from his canteen, and used it to wipe the crusted blood from his face. He took another pull from the whiskey bottle, and then moved around the camp, gathering firewood.

When he had a pile by the fire ring heaped with gray ashes, he built a fire with effort, for the wind was sweeping up the westward slope, wreaking havoc with the fledgling flames. Finally, to keep it going, he held up one of his blankets until the flames were large enough to keep burning on their own.

He added more dry wood and then sat down against his saddle. He was breathing hard, worn out from all he'd been through this morning. When he felt somewhat rested, he cooked some beans and side pork, and made coffee. He wasn't hungry, but he knew that to start healing he'd have to eat something. Greta would need food, as well.

Thunder rumbled. He looked up to see dark clouds playing around the edges of the ridge crest a thousand feet above him and the jostling pine crowns. A cold rain began sifting down through the trees.

"Ah, shit," Spurr said, struggling into his mackinaw.

But only part of the storm bank slanted across the old lawman, the bulk of it heading northeast. There was not enough rain to douse his fire. He finished cooking the meal and the coffee but could eat only a little of it.

He wasn't hungry. He felt sick inside.

He leaned back against his saddle and when the wind died some, and the sun broke through the high, puffy clouds, he rolled a smoke. As he did, he cast frequent glances down the slope toward the falls that sent its sputtering, tinny murmur up the hill. Except for the water, there was no movement down there. Greta was staying huddled in the notch cave.

Spurr smoked his cigarette and then drifted down the slope to tend the horses. He released them from the picket line and hobbled them so they could range around the camp and draw water from the pool at the base of the falls. Then, worn out again, he sat down against his saddle, washed a nitroglycerin tablet down with whiskey, pulled his hat over his eyes, and settled back for a nap.

He woke to Cochise grazing around the edges of the camp. The horse gave Spurr a puzzled look as he casually nibbled the bluestem and needlegrass growing along the base of a large fir. The horse was puzzled as to why they were remaining here in the camp. The roan was used to moving through the day, camping only at night. Also, Spurr knew the horse well enough to see that Cochise was concerned about his rider.

Greta's mare stood nearby, sticking close to Cochise, also grazing. The paint had probably picked up on Cochise's worry. Horses were more sensitive than some folks gave them credit for.

Spurr looked around. The sun had fallen and gray shadows were tumbling down the ridges. The temperature was dropping. He'd let the fire go out.

He quickly rebuilt it and then looked down the slope once more. Still no movement from Greta. How long was she going to stay down there? He considered taking a cup of hot coffee down there to lure her out of the notch cave but decided to give her a little more time. If she didn't leave the cave in another hour, he'd have to do something. He wouldn't let her freeze to death.

No, you won't let her freeze. You'll let her be raped by seven savages, but you won't let her freeze. Good on you, old man . . .

He sat down against his saddle once more, took a pull from the bottle he kept by his side, and stared into the building flames. Soft footfalls rose behind him. Cochise snorted.

Spurr turned to see Greta moving up the slope, wrapped in the blanket. Her legs were bare beneath the blanket, and her blond hair blew in the breeze.

She did not look at Spurr as she came into the camp.

"Greta, I was worried about . . ."

He let his voice trail off as she stooped to

238

pick up the bottle from beside him. She took a healthy pull of the whiskey, wiped her mouth with the back of her wrist, and then slid her saddle up close to the fire. She let the blankets drop to her ankles.

Appearing to not care that she was naked, she squatted beside her carpetbag. She pulled out several articles of clothing — an undershirt, a sweater, a pair of faded denims, and heavy wool socks. She dressed beside the fire, staring gravely into the flames. Spurr could not help watching her though he kept his eyes on her face. It was as if her soul had retreated to a tiny place at the core of her.

When she was dressed, she lay down against her saddle and curled up in her blankets, turning away from the fire and raising her knees until the blankets hid her stockinged feet, pine needles clinging to the soles.

Spurr reached forward, grabbed the leather swatch, and filled a coffee cup. He added whiskey to the coffee and then sat back against his saddle, sipping the coffee and watching the light bleed slowly out of the canyon. As the darkness thickened, the sound of the falls and the breeze grew louder.

Stars kindled. Occasionally, the faint cry

239

of a coyote reached the old lawman's ears. An umber light in the southeast showed where the moon was rising from behind the ridge.

When he finished the coffee, Spurr rose to check on the horses and evacuate his bladder. He built up the fire, glanced at Greta, who seemed to be sleeping peacefully, hands sandwiched beneath her cheek against the saddle. But thin lines dug into the skin around her eyes and across her forehead. She groaned and whimpered, and her eyelids fluttered. Spurr knew that she was reliving the attack.

He wished there was something he could do for her. He wished he could reach into her sleep and soothe her somehow, take the teeth out of the memories, but he could do no more for her now than he'd been able to that morning.

He couldn't help going over the last couple of days and flagging every mistake he'd made. He should not have let her join him and Drago — not when there was even the faintest possibility that they were being followed by the old outlaw's gang.

Also, he should have taken Drago at his word despite his doubts. It was always safest to assume the worst. But Spurr had let the pretty girl fog his thinking. To him, it was almost as if Kansas City Jane had returned from the dead to set things right in his soul.

Only, Greta wasn't Jane. She was another pretty young blond woman altogether, and one whom Spurr had almost gotten killed. Maybe what had happened to Greta had even been worse.

But where he had made his biggest mistake was in not retiring two, maybe three years ago, back when his heart had started to go and, deep down, he'd known that his skills were fading. His thinking had not been as sharp as it once had been. Emotions had begun to count for more than reason, because he'd known in a vague, troubling way without really looking at it straight on that his wick had burned down and was about to go out.

And he was scared.

He realized that he had taken his life for granted. He'd fought against dying, as though such a thing were possible. But in reality all that he had done was become a foolish old man too stubborn to turn in his badge when he should have. Before he'd gotten anyone killed, or worse.

But that's what he had done, and now he had to live with it. That's what he would take back to his cabin and his old dog on the slopes of Mount Rosalie.

Ponder that out in your yard in the evenings, you old son of a bitch.

Spurr built up the fire and lay back against his saddle, drawing his blankets up to his chin. He stared up at the stars that faded gradually as the orange autumn moon kited above the ridge and began quartering across him to the northwest.

He pulled his hat brim down over his eyes and slept fitfully. He woke every fifteen or twenty minutes, all night long, starting at shadows and at all the little night sounds that haunted the canyon like witches and warlocks — like savage gang members out to beat him senseless and rape the girl in his charge.

He woke at dawn and quietly built up the fire again, letting Greta sleep. He hadn't heard her stir all night and she remained in the same position as the one she'd first assumed.

Deciding it was too early for coffee, he took a walk around the bivouac and checked on the horses. Cochise stood, knees locked, eyes closed, asleep, while the paint mare, Betsy, lay nearby, also asleep.

Spurr ambled back to the camp and rolled back into his blankets. He'd sleep until Greta woke, and then he'd make coffee and breakfast. He didn't even think about how he'd spend that day. One thing at a time, he told himself. He'd travel when Greta felt like traveling. There was no hurry. He had no more assignments waiting for him back in the Denver Federal Building.

He hadn't realized he'd fallen back asleep when he woke to the sounds of movement and the smell of frying bacon. He jerked with a start, reaching for the pistol beside the saddle but stayed the movement when he saw Greta crouched over the fire in front of him. She wore the heavy brown sweater and faded denims and the moccasins she'd worn before. While the sun was up and flashing golden on the pine boughs, the thin air was cool. She had a blanket draped around her shoulders.

"Shit," Spurr said, surprised.

She was forking the meat around in the pan. The coffeepot was gurgling on a rock near the sputtering, crackling flames. "You gonna sleep all day, old man?"

Spurr yawned and settled back against his saddle. "Why the hell not?"

" 'Cause we got a job to do, you an' me."

"Job to do?" Spurr cursed again. The poor girl was addled. He was glad to see her up and about — she'd even brushed her hair — but she was addlepated, just the same.

"We're goin' after those sons o' bitches," Greta said, hardening her jaws as she spooned beans from a pot into the pan of frying bacon. "You an' me."

Spurr stared at her, not quite believing he'd heard what he thought he'd heard. "You're talkin' crazy, now. We gotta get you to a settlement. There's one up the Poudre Canyon. There might be a doctor there. He'll —"

She cut him off with: "You got the pistol. I got money. We'll buy another gun or two off someone along the trail. And then we're gonna track those bastards." She looked at him, her jaws hard, eyes resolute and slightly crossed, as was their custom though there was no humor in them at all. Only a hard resoluteness. "You can track, can't you, Spurr?"

"I used to be able to track. Used to be able to do a lot of things."

"Oh, come on," she said. "I'm the one they stuck their dicks in. Not you. They just roughed you up a little."

Irritation raked Spurr. "Greta, you can't ride after the pack of savages who done ya like that. And neither can I. They're a whole day ahead of us and I have no idea what direction they're headed. I got no idea where Martín's cabin is. Shit, it could be up

244

in Wyoming or way over in Utah."

"Wherever it is, you'll track 'em to it."

"They're a dozen men, Greta. A whole passel of younger, meaner, crazier sons o' bitches. Now, I do appreciate your vote of confidence in my limited abilities, but the truth of it is, I'm old and stove up. I'm injured bad, with a logy heart, achy ribs, and a sore head, and in case you ain't noticed, my nose is swollen up like a door handle!"

Spurr shook his head. "I'm gonna take you to Manhattan — that's the settlement up the Poudre. I'm gonna drop you there to recover, and I'm gonna head on back to Denver and turn in my badge to my boss. And it's high time I did!"

Her eyes flashing angrily, Greta removed the pan from the coals and slammed it down on a flat rock beside the fire ring. Some of the beans and bacon leapt out. She tossed her fork into the dirt and strode over to Spurr. She stood over him, glaring down at him.

"Are you going to tell me you're going to head back to Denver with your tail between your legs just because you're old and you got your nose broken? They took your prisoner, for chrissakes!"

"Greta, because of me, those men ravaged

you. They could have killed you. I'm surprised they didn't!"

"They didn't kill me because they had no fear of me. They didn't kill you for the same reason. We weren't even worth a bullet to them, or the effort it would have taken to slit our throats. They didn't fear either of us. They even left our horses because they didn't figure either one of us was up to trailing them."

"And they were right."

"To them, you were just an old bag of bones. I was just a warm place to put their — !"

"Greta, for Lord sakes — that's enough of this! There is no way in hell I'm goin' after those firebrands, much less taking you with me to get what they done to you done all over again!"

Spurr shrunk beneath her harrowing gaze. He looked around sheepishly. Damn right he was scared. But what's more, he was smart. Finally, he knew when to call it quits.

But when he finally looked up at her again as she continued to stare down at him, he saw that her jaws were still hard, her face flushed with fury. But her eyes were filled with tears. The tears of humiliation and rage and a frustration as deep as the deepest hole anywhere on earth.

Her eyes spoke to him, reached in, and turned his heart.

Why shouldn't he go after them? Why shouldn't he take her along, if she could ride? True, he was old. But he might as well die out here on the trail of Greta's ravagers as back home on the slopes of Mount Rosalie.

She must have read the change of heart in his eyes.

Because suddenly she was smiling.

TWENTY

Something hard bounced off Boomer Drago's shoulder.

"Ouch, goddamnit!" the old outlaw intoned, lifting his head from his saddle and gritting his teeth.

"Rise an' shine, old man," Keneally called from across the ash-mounded fire ring. "Get your rickety ass up and start breakfast. Better be tastier than last night's supper, or I'm liable to take a quirt to your double-crossin' old hide."

Drago looked over his shoulder at the blond-bearded man sprawled beneath his blankets and lifting his head toward Drago, squinting his hard green eyes. The others, blanketed humps around Drago and the cold fire ring, were groaning or snarling at the rude awakening.

"That hurt, you bastard!" Drago lifted his cuffed hands to rub his shoulder.

"Get to work." Keneally lay his blond,

massive, lantern-jawed head back against his saddle.

"Pipe down, goddamnit — I was sound asleep!" This from Tio Sanchez, lying under an aspen on the south side of the fire, left of Sam Keneally.

Keneally picked up another rock and threw it at Sanchez. There was a dull thud. The rock must have hit its mark because Sanchez lifted his head, clapping a hand to his temple. "Ow! That hit me!"

"I meant it to." Rolling onto his back and sitting up, Drago saw the yellow-brown line of Keneally's teeth against his blond-bearded face framed by bushy blond side-burns.

Sanchez sat up, glaring at Keneally, but he knew well enough not to push the matter. He gave an indignant grunt, rolled onto his side, and lay back down, drawing his blankets up to his chin.

"How'm I supposed to cook all trussed up like a pig?" Drago wanted to know, sitting up and holding his cuffed hands out in front of him.

"Get over here," Keneally said and yawned.

Drago's heart thudded. Keneally had taken off his cuffs and his shackles last night, so he could tend the camp like a house slave. Drago had gone to bed hoping he'd be freed again in the morning, because he'd contrived a few things on the upslope side of falling asleep. He'd thought about it so hard, in fact, that his anticipation, not to mention anxiety, had kept him from getting the kind of rest an old man needed.

Oh, well — he'd sleep once he was free of these killers, who would surely kill him after they reached Martín's cabin and found out that he, Drago, had lied about stowing the money beneath the kitchen floor.

Feigning disgruntlement over having to play the kitchen help to this group, most of whom he'd once led, Boomer threw his blankets aside, rose with a heavy grunt, and dragged his shackled feet over to where Keneally lay against his saddle between Quiet Ed, who had not yet stirred, and the lizard-skinned, yellow-eyed Curly Ben Williamson, who lay belly up and grinning at the gang's disgraced leader.

The young wolves were thoroughly enjoying their downtrodden former alpha male's humiliation. However, they and Drago himself had known he'd mostly been a figurehead. He'd commanded respect because of his age and his reputation, but Keneally had for over a year been the gang's true leader before they'd all gotten together and relegated Drago to holding the horses' reins while the others pulled the holdups.

Drago had sensed that the green-eyed killer had been about to either kick him out of the group entirely or, more likely, kill him just before Drago had killed Rufus Teagarden and George White and ridden off with the loot they'd stolen from the bank in Stove Prairie.

Now Drago gave another snarl of feigned indignity and knelt down by the gang's new leader. Keneally smiled at the older man jeeringly as he dug the keys, which he'd taken from Spurr Morgan's coat pocket, out of his boot and removed Drago's handcuffs.

When he'd removed the clevis pin from the shackles, freeing Drago's ankles, Drago felt his heart quicken. Keneally narrowed an eye at him, as though reading his mind.

"Stay close, now. Don't try to run, old man. You know you can't get far, and I'd hate to have to drill such a notorious old outlaw between his shoulders."

Drago drew a ragged breath, scowling down at Keneally, and rose and stepped into his boots. His breath frosted in the chill air around his head as he pulled his wolf coat on and donned his hat. He glanced around at the lumpy shapes of the other gang members, most still snoring beneath their army blankets or ragged quilts.

Keneally lay against his saddle, hands behind his head, grinning, enjoying the older man's humiliation. He seemed the only one awake now, as Williamson had closed his eyes, his belly rising and falling slowly, regularly. Quiet Ed was only quiet when awake. Sleeping, he snored as loudly as a hibernating grizzly.

Drago spat and raked his eye across the blanketed mounds once more, feeling the fires of fury kindle in him as he remembered Greta. Saw her running, trying to get away from them while they pulled at her clothes, stripped her naked. Then she'd screamed more shrilly as, one by one, they'd taken the poor girl on the hillside west of the camp . . .

Boomer muttered angrily under his breath. He drew air into his lungs, and got himself settled down. He wanted to kill these men, or at least as many as he could before they killed him, but that would have to wait.

First, he had to get himself free . . .

He looked around the clearing along the side of the hill they'd camped on, above the Crow River that ran along the hill's base, in the lower slopes of the Mummy Range. There'd been a wildfire through here several years ago, so most of the trees were dead and black, and there was lots of down wood strewn around boulders.

Just beyond the trees west of the camp — forty or so yards away — a canyon dropped off sharply toward the river.

Drago gathered a couple of armloads of wood nearest the camp first, and piled the wood near the fire ring. He started away for one more load of wood, and his heart increased its pace even more. As he walked toward the trees up the slope beyond him, he stared through the shadowy aspens at the lip of the canyon. He couldn't see the river from here, of course, but he'd seen it last night when he'd been off gathering wood at the top of the slope.

The night-dark water, slick with the salmon light of the autumn moon, had slithered along the bottom of the canyon about thirty feet below the ridge.

Not such a hard drop into water. At least, it wouldn't have been a few years ago.

Still, at sixty years old, Drago could weather it. He still had some sinew and muscle holding his old bones together. And he could swim. The only thing he wasn't sure about was how deep the river was this time of year, and how many rocks might impede its — and his — path. He'd feel like a damn fool if he made his escape only to be brained by a river rock.

He glanced over his shoulder. He couldn't tell from this distance in the hazy, dawn light, but he thought Keneally might have fallen back asleep.

A hard, throbbing pulse drummed in the old outlaw's temples.

To make it look good, in case Keneally was watching from beneath his hat brim, he stopped to pick up a charred deadfall from where it leaned against a fallen fir. He cradled the two branches in his left arm. He continued walking at a slant up the slope, wending through the trees, his boots crunching the short grass and fallen leaves.

He stooped to pick up another branch. He added it to the two in his arm. And then he reached the crest of the hill. He looked over the lip and into the dark water below.

It swirled gently around a couple of barrel-sized rocks. It was dark and cold-looking. It would probably stop Drago's heart the moment his boots broke the surface. If not, he might hit bottom and snap his spine. But the darkness of the water told him it was deep enough that he wouldn't hit bottom.

His mouth was dry. His knees trembled slightly. His heart hammered in his ears.

He almost laughed at his trepidation. What the hell was he worried about? If he didn't die here on his own terms, he'd died tomorrow when he led the gang to Martín's cabin in the northern apron slopes of the Never Summers, in the shadow of Crow Mountain.

When they discovered that not only was the money not hidden beneath the floorboards but that there were not even any floorboards in the old outlaw Martín de Segura's ancient cabin, where they'd holed up once to cool their heels two years ago after robbing a payroll shipment outside Laramie, they'd probably gut-shoot Drago and toss his slow-dying carcass to the wolves in the nearest ravine.

He glanced a cautious look over his left shoulder. He drew a short, sharp breath through his nose, and hardened his jaws.

His heart hammered like a locomotive's pistons.

Curly Ben Williamson was strolling toward him, grinning. The yellow-eyed killer in a long, ratty, deerskin duster over a sheepskin vest was thirty yards away, just now entering the trees at the top of the slope, and closing slowly. He had his pale thumbs hooked behind his double cartridge belts. His cut-down holsters were thonged low on his slender thighs clad in black denim, the cuffs of which were stuffed into the tops of his black Cheyenne boots.

"You'll never make it, old-timer. You'll hit one o' them rocks. That'd be a bad way to go out, after all you been through." Williamson spoke in a soft, cold voice though he continued to smile, showing the even line of his teeth between his thin, pink lips.

"What the hell are you talking about?"

"I seen you pondering that stream last night. You didn't think I was watching, but I was." Williamson kept coming, pausing to nonchalantly kick a rock, as though he were taking a slow, dawn walk to gather his thoughts.

"Shit," Drago said, feeling water pool in his belly as Curly Ben stepped up beside him and dropped his chin to stare down into the shallow canyon. "Kid, you give me too much credit."

"Yeah, well, I gave you credit for not double-crossin' us, too. Killin' two of your loyal partners and makin' off with nearly fifty thousand in scrip and specie."

Williamson narrowed a yellow eye at the old man beneath the brim of his black hat. "I didn't think you'd do such a corkheaded thing as that, too. And then be stupid enough to get caught by some bounty hunter while you was throwin' the wood to some whore in Idaville."

He shook his head. "You're old and washed up. Too many miles in the saddle. Too many cases of clap. Too much whiskey and too much tobacco. Too many times you'd been throwed on your head. Ah, shit — just too many years, Boomer."

Williamson laughed softly, keeping his mouth closed. He didn't laugh long. When he saw the chunk of wood arcing toward his head, his eyes nearly popped out of their sockets. He opened his mouth and raised his arm to shield himself too late.

Thunk!

The branch Boomer was wielding smashed across Curly Ben's left temple, flattening his hat brim against his forehead.

Williamson screamed and flew backward, stumbling.

Gritting his teeth, hatred flaring in his lone eye, Drago walked after him. The old outlaw smashed the branch across Williamson's left cheek.

Curly Ben cursed and tried to grab one of his pistols from its holster but then he was sent stumbling back again when Drago hammered his right jaw on the backswing, cracking the branch in two, the half not in his hand winging off through the trees.

One of the other outlaws shouted. As Curly Ben rolled up against the base of an aspen, squalling, his face and head bloody, Drago cast a quick look toward the camp.

Three of the other men, including Keneally, were scrambling out of their bedrolls, yelling and reaching for their guns, one climbing into his boots and grabbing his Winchester. Drago turned to the lip of the canyon. He stared down at the water. It looked like oil, its skin dappled gray in the gradually strengthening light.

Drago stepped off the ridge into thin air, stretching his arms out to both sides. As his body dropped, his heart leapt into his throat. He drew a deep breath and stopped when his boots hit the water.

He broke through the surface and jetted toward the bottom as the current instantly grabbed him and swept him downstream. The water ensconced him like a frozen hand, squeezing. His heart was a hammering war drum. He could feel it pounding in his feet as well as his head.

A rock slammed into his left knee but then the sweeping current thrust him back to the surface, and his head broke through the frigid skin to cold air. He gasped, drawing a deep breath, but he sucked water into his lungs, too, and he started coughing while at the same time trying to breathe.

He wondered if Keneally's men were shooting at him from the ridge but he was too busy trying to keep his head above water to look upstream, though he doubted the current would even let him.

The canyon dropped quickly. The water moved faster, thrashing boulders jutting out from both canyon walls. Drago tried to give himself over to the water and not fight it — because it was one battle he could not win — though he knew he couldn't stay in the cold stream long without it jellying his blood and drowning him.

There wasn't must use in trying to swim. The fast-moving current kept his head above water. Drago held his arms above his head to cushion himself from the rocks the current dashed him against.

There was another, short drop. And then Drago stared ahead along the stream that was curving through dark pines and jagged pinnacles of rock. The stream widened slightly and became a flat sheet of dark ink. Fifty yards ahead lay what appeared a beaver dam — a low, jagged, black ridge across the stream.

The whiteness beyond the dam was the water splashing up from its base.

Shit, the old outlaw thought. *I hope it ain't*

a very steep drop because I'm almost done for the way it is.

He let the stream carry him however it wanted. There was no fighting it. Sometimes a man had to throw himself into the turmoil. He hardened his jaws and sort of dog-paddled, just keeping his head above the water that wasn't as cold as it had looked from the ridge. But it was cold enough.

The beaver dam swept toward him quickly. He felt the woven branches gouging him, the water pushing him relentlessly against them. They caught his clothes and ripped them and pinched and jabbed his skin.

He groaned and yelped and cursed.

Suddenly he was atop the ridge and about to roll on over when he glimpsed a long, black witch's finger poking out from the left bank. The tree that had been torn out of the bank lay four feet in front of him, just on the other side of the dam, two feet above his head.

Drago screamed as he ground his boots into the dam and threw himself straight up in the air. His chest rammed against the stout branch. He screamed again, cursed, lifted his chin, felt the cords stick out from his neck as he summoned every ounce of his strength to his arms and shoulders.

He wasn't sure if the cracking sound he

heard was the branch or his ribs, but by god, he held onto the branch just the same. He wasn't about to give himself back to the monster stream that would swallow him now for sure and spit him out dead.

"Too many years, huh?" he muttered against the hammering pain in his chest, laughing wildly, insanely, hearing his laughter echo off the near ridges. He remembered how he'd left the yellow-eyed, lizard-skinned killer from Texas battered and bloody atop the ridge.

"We'll see about that, Curly Ben!"

TWENTY-ONE

Spurr reined Cochise to a stop in a narrow canyon, scowling in befuddlement.

He stared ahead along the main trail he'd been following, which angled around a bend and out of sight behind a jutting stone belly of rock sheathed in crimson sumacs and chokecherry shrubs. Along the base of the rock, a freshet ran. It was littered with yellow aspen leaves and marked with deer, raccoon, and rabbit prints. But no horse prints.

Spurr swung his gaze left to stare up a narrow, steep trace that forked off the main trail to climb through aspens and scattered firs toward a hidden ridge. No prints along that trail, either. At least, none that he could see from his vantage.

"What is it?" Greta asked, sitting her paint directly behind Cochise.

"No tracks, Greta. The rain last night, this morning wiped 'em out."

"You said you were finding some."

"*Part* of some . . . a couple miles back. They done ran out and I don't even know if the gang came this way. They mighta swung south or they mighta swung north. At this point, we're ridin' blind."

Greta heeled her mare up beside Spurr. She wore her scarf over her ears. Her eyes were angry, accusing. "You just want to give up, don't you?"

"I don't see much point in —"

Spurr heard something on the trail that rose toward the ridge. Spurr shuttled his gaze up through the trees. It had sounded like a man's voice but he could no longer hear the sound above the breeze-rattling leaves and creaking branches.

"Someone's up there," Greta said, staring up the trail.

"I'm gonna check it out. You stay here."

"Be careful."

Spurr muttered a curse and put Cochise up the steep trail, the saddle squawking beneath him and sliding back toward the roan's broad rump. As the horse clomped along the muddy path, Spurr stared through the gray-purple shadows beneath the forest canopy, toward the sky capping the ridge about a hundred yards away.

What the hell was he going to do if he ran into Drago's old bunch? He had one old six-shooter and the two-shot derringer. He supposed he could spit on them.

He wagged his head, chuffed angrily, and held the reins up close to his chest as Cochise turned along the switchbacking trail. Beneath the rattling of the leaves and the thuds of his own horse's hooves, he heard the voice again.

A man's voice. It seemed to be growing slightly louder.

A mule brayed.

Cochise twitched his ears.

Spurr slid his Schofield from his holster and held the gun against his right thigh, gloved thumb on the hammer. As Cochise continued climbing toward a jutting pinnacle of gray rock as large as two small cabins, the voice continued to grow louder. It sounded like two men riding along, conversing.

As he approached the thumb of gray rock, Spurr realized he was hearing only one man. One man conversing with who . . . ?

". . . I says to her, what makes you think I'll continue to put up with such black-hearted, twisted doin's, Adelaide? You think I got no spine a-tall? You think I'm so soft on womenfolk I won't lift a boot to your backside, next time I see you with that no-account, Henry Philpot? Well, if you do, then you got another think . . ."

Thirty yards up the slope from Spurr, the man stopped the mule he was riding and widened his eyes in shock at seeing another rider on this lonely mountain trail.

"Tarnation!" he said, reaching back for the old rifle in his saddle boot.

"Keep it holstered, old-timer!" Spurr had stopped Cochise at one end of the large rock rising now on his right. "I ain't Henry Philpot."

He booted Cochise on up the trail. The mule brayed raucously, apparently not used to seeing strangers way out here. Spurr could feel Cochise tighten his muscles uneasily beneath the saddle. The man on the mule sat staring at Spurr slantways, as if one eye was better than the other.

He was a stocky old man with a curly, gray beard and washed-out blue eyes beneath the brim of his felt, bullet-crowned, black hat. His skin was weathered a deep tan, and it sagged on his cheekbones, like stained parchment. He wore a sheepskin poncho and patched canvas trousers.

"Spurr Morgan," the old lawman said when he'd stopped Cochise in front of the stranger's mule.

"Andrew Jackson Lowry," the old man said, keeping his gruff, skeptical glance on

Spurr, knitting his coarse gray brows over the bridge of his nose. "Spurr Morgan . . . where have I heard — ?"

"Never mind," Spurr said. "You ain't seen a gang runnin' off its leash out here, have you?"

"You're a U.S. marshal. Now I remember where I heard of you. Key-*rist* — you're still kickin'?"

"Will you just answer the consarned question?"

"I seen you once in Santa Fe. Why, your hair was all brown back then, an' so was your beard, and you was roarin' drunk carryin' one girl up the stairs over a shoulder with one more under your arm!" The old man guffawed.

Suddenly, he clouded up and looked about to rain. "Good Lord . . . you got old. And, say, what happened to your nose? Looks just miserable!"

"In case you didn't notice, old-timer, you got old your ownself. Now, you seen 'em or haven't you?"

"Say, she ridin' with you?"

Spurr followed the old man's glittery gaze to the trail behind him. Greta was riding up the hill, toward Spurr and Lowry, her head canted skeptically to one side.

"So what if she is?" Spurr asked the old-timer, his impatience with the old man growing.

"Kinda young, ain't she?" Lowry grinned. "She the one that broke your nose for ya?"

"Mister, you're gettin' on my nerves just awful."

"No, I never seen no gang. Can't say I regret not seein' 'em, either, if you're after 'em." Lowry's eyes grew large and he jerked his hand up as something dawned on him. "Say, a gent robbed me yesterday. Maybe he's one of the varmints you're lookin' for."

Spurr scowled. "Robbed you? Just one?"

As Greta reined her paint to a halt behind Spurr, Lowry said with an angry air, "Sure enough. I was takin' a dip in the creek and some gent slipped up out of the bushes. I didn't see him right away, but when I did it was too late. He was hot-footin' out of my camp with a pouch he took out of my saddlebags. He tried to take old Webster here, too" — he leaned forward to pat the mule's left wither — "but Webster gave him a good kick for his efforts, an' he run off."

"What'd he look like?"

"I didn't get a long gander at him, but he wore an eye patch and he was old. Old as us. Wore a wolf coat. No hat. Looked raggedy-heeled — you know, like he hadn't a good meal since the last blue moon.

Seemed to be limpin'."

Spurr glanced back at Greta, who parted her lips.

Spurr turned back to the old-timer. "What'd he take?"

"A little pouch of beans and deer jerky, and a tin box of stove matches. Took my pistol, too. Probably woulda taken my rifle, but he must not've see it under my gear, and he was all hepped up about my mule!"

"When was this, Lowry?"

"Like I jest told ya — yesterday around noon."

"Which creek did you say?"

"Injun." The old-timer hooked his thumb over his shoulder. "Two draws northwest. Luther St. Peter and his old squaw used to live in there, about a mile on. We used to have some shinin' times, me an' Luther — before he got him a squaw. We come out here from St. Louis together a hell of a long time ago, now. Let's see, we was trappin' for beaver up the Poudre . . ."

"Let's go," Spurr said, reining Cochise around the mule and pinching his hat brim to the old man. "Thanks for the information, Lowry. Have a good winter."

"Ha!" Lowery laughed caustically, hipping around to follow Spurr with his gaze. "You try to have a good winter in these mountains. If I could stand the smell and the commotion, I'd head for Cheyenne. No, I reckon I'll die up here. Crows'll pick my bones clean, but I reckon they gotta eat, too . . ."

The old mountain man let his voice trail off as Spurr rode on up the trail, Greta following and asking, "You think that was Drago? The man who stole the old-timer's pistol."

"Sound like him to me," Spurr said, touching heels to Cochise's flanks, pushing the horse on up the steep trail toward the brightening cobalt sky beyond the ridge. "One-eyed and raggedy-heeled and in need of a weapon and matches. Sounds like he must have given Keneally an' them the slip somehow."

He shook his head and nibbled at his scraggly mustache. "Wouldn't put it past him. Crafty son of a bitch — I'll give him that."

At the top of the ridge, he reined Cochise to a halt. Greta came up behind him and checked down her own mount a ways off Spurr's left stirrup. "You know where the creek is — the one the old man mentioned?" she asked Spurr.

Spurr nodded. "Been through there a time or two."

"Well, come on, then," she said, impatiently turning her horse south along the crest of the ridge.

"Hold on, girl! We just put these hosses up a steep climb. They need a blow, and we need to adjust our saddles less'n we wanna end up hangin' down one side!"

Greta checked the paint down again. Her eyes sparked angrily and she opened her mouth to speak but drew her lips together and let the sharp light fade from her eyes. She looked around, the wind blowing up from the treeless western slope to tussle her hair and the ends of her scarf, which was knotted beneath her chin.

As Spurr crawled off Cochise's back and started tightening the latigo beneath the horse's belly, Greta winced as though from a sudden pain inside her, and stiffened, leaning a little forward in her saddle. When the spasm appeared to have passed, she dipped her right hand into the carpetbag hanging from her saddle horn.

She pulled out one of the remaining bottles, popped the cork with a hand clad in a powder-blue knit glove, and took a sip. She closed her eyes as she brought the bottle down and stretched her lips back from her teeth. She swallowed hard and then took another swig from the bottle and swiped her wrist across her lips.

Spurr watched her grimly. "You all right, Greta?"

She glanced at him and smiled. "Sure. I only took a few more men than I'm used to in one night, that's all."

"Greta . . ."

"That Quiet Ed had a nasty backhand." She rubbed her purple cheek, touched the cut that ran down her upper and lower lip. "But you know what really burns me, Spurr, is the bastards didn't pay."

Spurr walked around behind Cochise and tightened her latigo in silence, staring sadly up at the girl and her pretty, battered face. A rage burned in him, but he kept the fire low lest it should burn right through him.

"I'm gonna make 'em pay, Spurr."

Greta looked around at the countless ridges bulging around them, at the high, rocky peaks in the north, and then she turned to Spurr once more. There was a haunted quality to her eyes now that disconcerted the old lawman. The ravaging and the beating she'd taken had done more than physical damage to her.

She was jumpy and impatient, probably not seeing things too clearly, and he hoped to hell he was strong enough to keep her from getting herself killed.

"That's all I want — I just want to make them pay."

Despite his growing doubt that they'd ever even see the gang again, Spurr said, "We'll make them pay, Greta."

"No, I don't mean revenge, Spurr," she said, shaking her head. She leaned into the fist she was pressing against her lower belly and shook her windblown hair from her eyes. "I mean I want them to pay me what I'm usually paid for my services. Three dollars and fifty cents." She chuckled. "Only this time, I get to keep it all, not just a lousy two percent like what Reymont and Chaney dole out to me."

A claw of uneasiness gripped Spurr's own belly. He wasn't sure if she was teasing him. He doubted she was.

He held her gaze, her blue eyes straight and level but opaque with some other, wild thing that he feared would put her life in grave danger. He wished now that he'd been more vehement about refusing to take her on this vengeance quest.

"That's not too much to ask — is it, Spurr? For the money they owe me for my services?" Quirking her mouth corners in a dubious smile, she held up the bottle. "Drink?"

Spurr took the bottle from the girl. He

took a deep pull, watching her around the side of the bottle as she stared southwestward, the direction in which Indian Creek lay. She continued to lean into her fist, blinking rapidly against the wind, that frozen half smile on her battered, red lips.

Spurr took another deep pull from the bottle and then handed it back to her. When she'd taken another couple of bracing sips herself, she returned the bourbon to her carpetbag and snapped the top closed.

Spurr touched his heels to Cochise's flanks, moving out along the crest of the ridge. An hour later, as he dropped down into the canyon bisected by Indian Creek — a silvery blue thread of water flashing between wind-brushed aspens in full autumn bloom — a rifle cracked.

The echo of the shot hadn't finished bouncing off the surrounding ridges before another rifle thundered, adding its own echoes to the dying ones of the first shot.

"Greta, you stay here!" Spurr shouted, and he booted Cochise along a deer path hugging the trees lining the steam.

As the shooting continued, the old lawman slipped his Schofield from its holster but wished like hell he had his Winchester.

Twenty-Two

As Spurr trotted Cochise up the trail, holding the Schofield against his right thigh, he glanced behind. Greta was staying put for now, curveting her horse in the trail and staring after him.

Good. Maybe she'd follow his orders and keep out of harm's way. He didn't think he could take another young lady dying on him.

Chances were the shots were fired by hunters laying in meat for the long mountain winter, but he had to tread carefully while he investigated.

As he rode, tension climbed his spine. The shots increased until he thought he could hear three rifles and at least one pistol. The shooters weren't hunters. Somewhere ahead men were swapping lead.

He followed the game trail along a southern bend in the trees and the stream, which hugged the base of the southern ridge. He reined up just before the stream straightened out and deadheaded south between tall, craggy peeks, and swung down from Cochise's back, moving heavily and tenderly, his ribs balking at every strain.

Judging from the loudness of the pistol pops and rifle cracks, the shooters were within a hundred yards, kicking up an angry din. Spurr led the big roan back into the forest and tied him to the up-jutting branch of a deadfall tree. Walking south through the aspens, he quartered back toward the clearing and the game trail.

The shots seemed to be coming from the far side of the trail and ahead maybe fifty, sixty yards.

Spurr could hear men yelling back and forth, the echoes of their angry voices joining the reverberations of their rifles and the sporadic pops of the pistol. He followed the din through the woods, staying out of sight of the far side of the trail. He'd just spied the cabin sitting in a little clearing to the east, tucked into the scattered aspens and firs, when a nearby horse whinnied shrilly.

He turned to see three horses tied to branches about thirty yards ahead. Startled by the gunfire, they sidestepped and jerked at their reins, their latigo straps dancing freely beneath their bellies.

Spurr moved slowly to the horses, gripping his pistol in his right hand, holding his left hand palm out, reassuringly. He whistled softly as he approached the nearest horse, a pinto, tied with its head away from Spurr. The horse sidestepped, looked at the stranger sidelong, and gave another ear-rattling whinny.

Spurr stopped, holding his left hand up higher and gritting his teeth as he looked through the trees on his left, toward the cabin around which smoke was puffing as the shooting continued. Spurr had spied a saddle ring pistol dangling from the pinto's saddle. He wanted that gun but he didn't want the horses giving his presence away to the shooters.

A voice in his ear told him these three horses belonged to Drago's former gang. And that the men now shooting at the cabin were Keneally's boys. Which meant Spurr could use another pistol if not a rifle. Hell, he could use a whole damn arsenal, but beggars couldn't be choosers.

He continued to ease up to the pinto, whistling soothingly. The horse's muscles were tensed, neck arched. It stared at Spurr with white-ringed eyes, but it let the old lawman sidle up to it. Quickly, Spurr slipped the knot on the leather cord tying the pistol to the saddle, and stepped back away from the dancing mounts. He looked at the gun in his hand — a .44 Colt Army Model in good condition and with six in the wheel. He spun the cylinder, shoved the popper down behind his cartridge belt, and moved to the edge of the trees.

He sidled up to a birch and dropped to a knee, staring across the game trail and into the clearing at the stout log cabin roofed with tightly woven, sun-bleached aspen saplings. There were a few dilapidated outbuildings and skinned log corrals behind the place, dwarfed by the granite mountain rising behind it.

Smoke issued from a tin chimney pipe. The cabin's shutters and halved-log door were closed.

A man was hunkered down behind a small boulder in the sage-stippled front yard, to the left of the path leading to the front door. His back faced Spurr.

The man lifted his carbine to his shoulder. The Winchester leapt and barked in the man's hands. The bullet hammered the front door with a loud *whap,* carving a dog-get out of the wood. The bullet did not appear to have penetrated the heavy door, which was probably constructed of sturdy timbers.

The shutter left of the door swung open quickly. A shadow moved in the window, a pistol was thrust through the opening. It belched smoke and flames twice quickly, and the man in the front yard ducked down behind his covering boulder as both slugs hammered the rock's far side.

The man behind the rock laughed loudly and slid his head around the boulder's right side as he shouted, "Close one, Drago — but you missed me! Hah! You can stay in there all day and all night. Hell, we don't care! We got plenty of ammo, and when you're all out, we're gonna come in there and drag you out and shoot you through both ears!"

Spurr's heart thudded heavily, anxiously. He'd recognized the voice of the Texas gunman, Curly Ben Williamson. That meant it was indeed Boomer Drago holed up inside the cabin.

At least three of Keneally's bunch had him trapped like a rat in a privy. Spurr could tell that there were two other shooters — one flinging lead from the woods on Spurr's right, and one shooting from a corral behind the cabin. From his vantage, Spurr could see the smoke plumes of both shooters' weapons.

As the shooters' horses continued to

nicker nervously in the woods behind him, Spurr slid his new Colt from behind his cartridge belt and looked around carefully.

Where were the other gang members? Obviously, they weren't here or they'd be on the cabin like a cat on a baby robin. But, having heard the fusillade, they could be headed this way.

Spurr took a minute to think over his options, deciding he really had only once course of action. To kill these three sons of bitches — back-shoot them if he had to, for they deserved no better — and pull Drago out of there. He no longer cared about hauling the old outlaw to justice. He now had bigger fish to fry — namely, the running to ground of the rest of his gang and delivering some vigilante justice for Greta, his badge be damned.

"Ah, shit," he said, hefting both pistols in his hands and returning his gaze to the cabin. "I'm startin' to sound as crazy as Greta!"

Spurr looked at the man straight out ahead of him — fifty yards away. He recognized the long deerskin duster and the black hat beneath which Curly Ben appeared to have a white bandage knotted around his forehead. The bandage glowed in the bright sun.

Spurr looked at the infrequent smoke plumes rising from the wood on his right. There wasn't much cover between Spurr and Williamson, so he'd have to move as quickly as he could, keeping low, lest the man in the woods should pink him before he could beef the dooryard shooter.

Spurr raised both pistols in his hands, scrubbed his right wrist across the tip of his sore nose, and started running, meandering through the gray-green mountain sage. He hadn't run ten yards before the man in the woods on his right shouted, "Curly Ben — behind ya!"

Spurr stopped, dropped to a knee, and extended his right-hand pistol as the man ahead of him turned to face him, pressing his back against his covering boulder. Spurr aimed carefully, squinting one eye, and fired his Schofield at the same time a slug tore up dirt and sod two feet right of his right boot.

Curly Ben screamed and lurched back against the boulder, clapping a gloved hand against his right shoulder. Spurr dropped to a knee and shot the man once more — this time through the dead center of his chest — and flinched as another bullet hurled out of the woods to curl the air in front of his nose.

Spurr dropped to a knee and started to

turn toward the woods on his right when hoof thuds brought him up short.

With a sick feeling, he glanced to his left. Greta was galloping her paint toward him along the deer trail that hugged the woods. She leaned forward over the gelding's outstretched neck, and she was ramming her heels against the mare's flanks, urging more speed.

"Oh, Christ," Spurr heard himself mutter as he turned toward the fool girl. "Greta, get back! Get back, damnit!"

But then she'd passed him and was flying down the trail toward the south. She wasn't heading directly toward the man in the woods south of the cabin, but she was making herself a clear target for him.

Spurr cursed and ran toward the cabin, shouting, "Drago, it's Spurr, damn your eyes! I'm here to help you, so you best not shoot me you ugly, one-eyed son of a bitch!"

"*Who's* that?" Drago shouted from inside.

"Spurr Morgan!"

"I can't hear fer shit — my ears is ringin'! Did you say *Spurr Morgan?*"

As Spurr pressed a shoulder against the front of the cabin and glanced first into the woods south and then toward the corral behind the place, he shouted, "Shut up and hold your fire!"

Smoke puffed in the woods south and in the corral behind the cabin. Spurr jerked his head back behind the front wall as one slug hammered into the cabin's south wall while the other one, triggered by the man in the corral, hammered the corner, spraying silver wood slivers in all directions.

Spurr dropped to a knee and triggered three rounds toward where he'd spied the smoke plume in the southern woods. When he turned toward the east, he saw the third shooter running toward him from the corral, a green neckerchief billowing down around his black vest and red-and-black calico shirt. As the man stopped and raised his rifle, Spurr triggered a wild shot at him.

The man's rifle lapped flames, and Spurr drew his head back behind the corner of the cabin just as the slug tore into the near logs with an angry *whump*.

Spurr jerked his head and his Schofield around the corner once more. The third shooter was running toward him again. Spurr triggered one shot at that man and then, as another slug came hurling out of the woods, he fired two more shots toward the second shooter, pleased to hear an agonized yelp amidst the frantic crackling of trampled brush.

Spurr glanced behind the cabin. The third

man was down on one knee, cursing, holding his rifle in one hand as he clutched the bloody knee of his outstretched leg with his other hand. He'd lost his hat and his long, brown hair hung in thin strands around his face and shoulders.

Tio Sanchez.

Spurr grinned. Sanchez gave a wild yell and, placing both hands on his rifle, raised the gun to his shoulder.

Both of Spurr's own pistols spoke, and Sanchez was thrown straight back, triggering his Winchester at the clear, blue sky a quarter second before he hit the ground on his back and lay rolling from side to side, howling.

Spurr glanced toward the southern woods as he pressed his back against the front of the cabin. He set down the smoking Colt, flicked the Schofield's loading gate open, and began reloading. He could see no movement in the trees or along the trail in the direction he'd last seen Greta.

The old lawman said, "Where in the hell . . . ?"

A man's scream rocketed out of the southern woods.

It was followed by a girl's scream.

Spurr slid the loaded Schofield into its holster, picked up the Colt, and glanced back toward where Tio Sanchez still lay shouting and mewling like a gut-shot puma. Spurr began reloading the Colt as he strode quickly toward the southern woods, stepping around sage shrubs and rocks.

An eerie silence had followed the girl's scream but now the silence was relieved by another scream from the man.

"You pay me, you bastard!" Greta shouted so shrilly that her voice was breaking and quivering.

Spurr increased his pace, staring into the pines peppered with aspens, now seeing a commotion in the trees about fifty feet in from the edge of the clearing. He popped the last pill into the Colt, spun the cylinder, and held the pistol straight down in his right hand as he jogged into the trees and stopped suddenly.

"You pay me, you bastard!" Greta screamed again, extending her hand to the burly man sitting on his butt before her. The man's bloody left arm hung slack. Blood was dribbling down from a nasty welt on his forehead, as well. Spurr saw the bloody rock in Greta's left hand, which she squeezed threateningly and shook in the man's face while extending her other hand, open-palmed.

"I don't give it away for free, you son of a

bitch!" Greta screamed at the tops of her lungs, bending forward.

"Get away from me, you crazy bitch!" shouted the outlaw Spurr now recognized as Bryce Hannibal, who was as bald as an egg though his ginger beard was as thick as wool. He cast his horrified eyes at Spurr. "Get her an' that damn rock away from me, lawman!"

"You pay me!" Greta screamed again, cocking her right hand and jerking it forward, hurling the rock at the man's head.

The rock hit its mark with a solid thunk and bounced down between Hannibal's spread thighs. The outlaw howled and cupped a hand to his left temple.

One of his two holsters was empty, but a revolver jutted from the second one. His rifle lay in the brush behind him. As Hannibal reached for the gun, Spurr leaned forward and grabbed the pistol out of its holster.

Greta lunged toward Spurr, took the gun out of his hand. Taking the long-barreled Smith & Wesson in both her hands, she thumbed the hammer back and aimed the pistol at Hannibal's head.

The outlaw cowered behind his arms, leaning back against a tree bole, screaming and kicking his legs. "She's crazy! Stop her!

She's loco!"

"Pay me!"

The pistol leapt and roared in Greta's hand, the kick rocking her back on her heels. When she got her feet under her again, she ratcheted the hammer back once more, and drilled another round through Hannibal's red-wool, black-buttoned coat.

She fired until the hammer pinged on an empty chamber. She glared at the dead man over the smoking barrel of the big pistol in her small, pale hands. Slowly, she lowered the weapon and glanced at Spurr, her eyes filled with tears.

"I just wanted him to pay me!" she screamed. "I don't do it for free with no one!"

She dropped to her knees and hung her head, sobbing. Spurr walked to her, knelt beside her, and wrapped his arm around her shoulders. He drew her tight against him and kissed the side of her head.

"You got him, Greta. You made him pay."

A gun blasted near the cabin. Spurr jerked with a start, slipping his Schofield from its holster and clicking the hammer back. "Ah, hell," he said, weary. "You stay here, girl."

TWENTY-THREE

Spurr wearily shoved off a knee, gaining his feet, and walked away from Greta, who remained kneeling near the dead man, sobbing. At the edge of the clearing, Spurr looked around, caressing his pistol's cocked hammer with his thumb.

When he'd shuttled his gaze east, he stopped caressing it. Boomer Drago stood over Tio Sanchez off the cabin's rear corner, a pistol hanging straight down by his denim clad right thigh. Boomer brought his right boot back and rammed it into Sanchez's side.

Sanchez yelped and used his heels to scuttle feebly away, screaming, "Stop it, you crazy old bastard! Leave me to die in peace!"

"Where's the others?" Drago shouted down at the bloody half Mexican.

"How the hell should I know?" Sanchez screamed. "We split up north of here to track you down!"

"How far north?"

"How the hell should I know?"

"How long since you split up?"

"Shit, we split up last night! Now leave me, damn you, Drago. Can't you see I'm dyin' here. And I'm too damn *young* to die!" He bawled.

"We all gotta go sometime," Drago said as Spurr walked toward him across the clearing. The old outlaw extended his pistol at Sanchez, who screamed again and tried to shield his face with his black-gloved hands.

Drago's pistol cracked. Smoke and flames stabbed slantwise down toward Sanchez. The bullet slammed through Sanchez's left hand, slapping that hand across the half Mexican's face as the slug continued on through the hand and into Sanchez's left cheek.

The young outlaw's head bounced off the ground. The outlaw glared up at his killer, gave a sigh, turned his head to one side, and expelled a long, raspy breath. Apparently, Drago hadn't heard Spurr approaching. He whipped his head at the old lawman now, widened his eyes, and then turned full around, raising his pistol.

The barrel was aimed at Spurr's belly.

Drago had a shrewd, steely cast to his eye,

a cunning smile on his lips inside the coarse black beard.

Spurr kept his own revolver hanging at his side as he flared his nostrils at the old outlaw. "If you think I'm here for you, you got your thinker box screwed on backward. You ain't worth a hill o' cow shit to me, Boomer."

Spurr glanced at the Winchester lying where Sanchez had thrown it when Spurr had shot him. "Grab that carbine. We're gonna need it. I'm gonna fetch us some horses."

Spurr swung around and started back toward where he'd left Greta. She stepped out of the woods, carrying a pistol in one hand, a rifle in the other. Her cheeks were tear-streaked but her eyes had reacquired that resolute hardness and frankness.

She looked around, her gaze glancing off Boomer, who was just now retrieving Sanchez's Winchester, and said, "Where're the others?"

"Maybe not far." Spurr canted his head toward the cabin. "Why don't you go on inside and rest a bit? I'll fetch the horses."

"I'm not tired."

Spurr turned back to her and gave a wan half smile. "Well, I am. We'll have some coffee and whiskey and then get the hell out of here before the others show up. We don't wanna be pinned down in that cabin like that damn fool Drago was."

Drago was walking toward them. He gestured angrily with the rifle as he told Spurr to diddle himself and then apologized to Greta.

Spurr gave a snort and walked out to retrieve Cochise. He rode Cochise through the trees to retrieve the dead men's three horses. As he rode into the clearing in which the cabin sat, he was glad to see Greta's mare trotting toward him, dragging its reins.

The horse gave an eager whinny, obviously relieved to be with others of its kind, and Cochise returned the greeting. The dead men's horses were still jumpy but they let Spurr lead them up to the cabin, in front of which Boomer was sitting, knees up, his back to the front wall.

The cabin's door was closed, as were the shutters. Smoke gushed from the tin chimney pipe. Drago must have built up the fire for Greta, resting inside.

Spurr eyed the old outlaw, who leveled a return stare at the old lawdog. When he'd stepped down from Cochise's back, Spurr loosened the saddle cinch of his own horse as well as Greta's and slipped their bits from their mouths so they could graze. Spurr spat to one side, glanced at Drago again, who sat with a rifle poking up from between his knees, and then walked over to the dead Curly Ben Williamson lying behind the boulder. Curly Ben was as dead as chopped liver. His face looked like raw hamburger beneath the bandage around the top of his head. Even in death, Curly Ben appeared to be grimacing up at Spurr.

The old lawman looked at Drago. "What the hell happened to him?"

"Took him to the woodshed, you might say." Drago chuckled. "Had me a grand ole time . . . for as long as it lasted."

Spurr picked up the dead man's carbine. He glanced down at Curly Ben again, looked away, and then looked back down, frowning.

"Well, I'll be damned."

Spurr reached down and pulled his own Starr .44 from behind the man's cartridge belt. He checked to make sure it was loaded, and then removed the Schofield from his cross-draw holster, and replaced it with his own beloved Starr.

He walked back over to the horses and dropped his two spare weapons into his saddlebags. He looked into the dead men's saddlebags, draped one pair over his shoulder, and then, also carrying a dead man's saddle-ring carbine, whose cracked fore-stock was wrapped with shrunken rawhide, and whose initials had been brass-riveted into the rear stock, walked over to Drago.

The old outlaw glared up at him, canted his head to indicate the cabin behind him. "What the hell are you doin', draggin' that poor girl all the way out here after what she's been through?"

"Ah, shut up, you old ringtail." Spurr sat down beside Drago with a grunt and leaned back against the log wall. "If it wasn't for her, I'd be draggin' my old ass back to my cabin and you'd be deader'n overcooked pot roast."

Drago turned his grizzled face toward Spurr and dipped his chin, narrowing his lone eye. "Chop that up a little finer for me, old man."

"It was her idea."

"Get on with ya!"

Spurr set the saddlebags on his lap and opened the flap on one of the pouches to peer inside. "How'd you get away from them fellas, Boomer? Don't tell me they kicked you out on account of how you smell like rancid porcupine!"

"I jumped into a river. Think my old ticker stopped tickin' for a full hour. When I was kickin' around in the water, I saw naked Injun girls all around me, and that kept me goin'. Crawled out, talked some old man out of a pistol and stove matches and a little grub —"

"I met the gent you robbed — that's how I found you," Spurr groused.

As though he hadn't heard the lawman, Drago continued with, "And run into this old cabin here. Believe I knew the gent who lived here once, years ago."

"Luther St. Peter."

"That's him! Right likeable fellow till he took up with a Ute squaw. Changed him. Wasn't sociable no more."

"A woman will do it. There we go. Just what the ole sawbones ordered!" Spurr's eyes lit up as he drew a bottle wrapped in wool out of the saddlebag pouch. He set the bottle down beside him and then hauled out a small burlap pouch. Opening the pouch, he discovered a dozen or so strips of what looked like deer jerky.

"Them boys was well provisioned."

"I taught 'em to do that," Drago said, plucking the cork from the whiskey bottle. "Never knew how long we'd be on the run, couldn't risk ridin' into town to stock up on whiskey an' grub. At least they learned something from me, though they were damned ungrateful about it."

Drago tipped the bottle back.

"I guess their tender feelin's sorta stalled when you stole that bank loot from 'em, Boomer."

Drago jerked the bottle down, spraying out a mouthful on a raucous laugh. Spurr gave a snort, then, too.

As Drago leaned back against the cabin, guffawing, Spurr started laughing nearly as hard. He hadn't meant what he'd said to be funny but suddenly he saw the humor in it through Boomer's eyes. It was probably just the nervous tension of the past several days, but laughter boiled up from deep inside him. He leaned back against the cabin wall, guffawing until he thought his ribs would splinter and poke through his skin.

They both sat there against the cabin wall, laughing like a couple of schoolboys.

Finally, when the mirth was boiled out of him, leaving him rib sore and washed out, Spurr lifted the bottle to his lips and took a pull. He handed the bottle to Drago, whose own laughter was dying slow, and Boomer shook his head, wiped tears from his eye with the back of his hand, and tipped the bottle back.

He handed the bottle to Spurr and said, "What's she doin' out here, Spurr? Greta."

He glanced toward the cabin's closed front door.

That sobered Spurr like a visit from the parson. He looked at the lip of the bottle he was holding up to his mouth and said with a skeptical cast to his voice, "She wants 'em to pay her for what they took from her, I reckon. Leastways, that's what she said."

"Ah, hell."

"Yeah."

"That's damn sad, what they done to her. You're lucky you was passed out and didn't have to hear it, see it . . ."

"Yes, I am." Spurr drew a deep breath as he felt the flames of fury well inside him with all the power of when he'd first spied her curled up in that notch cave near the falls.

Drago was about to say something else on the matter when the door squawked open to his and Spurr's left, and Greta stepped halfway out the door, bending a knee and resting her left heel in front of her right foot. "You guys got some grub you feel like sharin'?"

"Sorry, Greta," Spurr said, handing the sack up to her. "Thought you were sleeping."

"Not with you two out here chinning like a couple of church crones." Greta plucked a couple of pieces of jerky out of the bag and then handed the bag down to Drago. "I'd take a shot of that busthead, too."

Drago handed the bottle up to her, and she took a couple of hard pulls then returned the whiskey to the old outlaw. She came outside, stepped into the gap between Spurr and Drago, then sat down and gave Spurr a peck on the cheek.

She turned and did the same to Drago and then leaned her head back against the cabin and said, "I'm glad we're all three together again. I've missed our little group."

"Well, I didn't," Spurr grumbled, looking off.

"I'd as soon have drowned in that stream as had to look at his ugly face again." Drago rubbed his shoulder against Greta's. "But it's worth it to get to look on yours again, Miss Greta."

"Ah, quit makin' calf eyes at the girl," Spurr growled. "You're liable to give her nightmares."

They all chewed jerky and passed the bottle around. The horses plucked at the short, brown grass, occasionally swishing their tails at flies. They dragged their reins across the ground, latigos hanging free beneath their bellies.

Greta looked first to the north and then

to the south along the tree-lined stream running along the base of the western ridge. "Where do you suppose they are? The gunfire would have carried a long ways, echoing around this canyon."

Spurr bit off another chunk of jerky. "Maybe they figure Boomer ain't worth the trouble and they headed to Martín's cabin to pick up the money."

"Could be." Drago laughed and adjusted his eye patch, chewing jerky.

He kept on chuckling devilishly. It was more of a snicker that he couldn't contain.

Greta and Spurr shared a curious look. Spurr looked past the girl to the old outlaw. "You gonna spit it out or choke on it?"

"The loot ain't in Martín's cabin."

"Well, hell, that ain't no surprise. The day you start tellin' the truth about anything the devil's gonna be chippin' ice from his goat beard!"

Drago continued to chuckle and stare at the ground between his legs. Spurr and Greta shared another curious look.

Greta turned to the giggling outlaw, and asked, "Where is it, Boomer?"

"Somewhere safe and well cared for."

Greta shrugged and sat back against the cabin. She didn't care about the money. Spurr did, however. He continued to scowl at the old outlaw as he said, "Come on, spill it, Boomer. I'm just curious more than anything. All I really care about now is borin' .44-caliber holes in them friends of yours."

Drago cast Spurr a dubious look. "If I didn't tell them, I sure as hell ain't gonna tell you. Uh-uh. No, sir. Wild hosses couldn't drag that one out of me."

"Boys?" Greta sounded strange. She was staring at Spurr's roan, Cochise, who had turned to gaze north along the creek, toward a notch in the stony buttes. "I think we best pack up this picnic."

Cochise arched his tail and, staring toward the gap in the bluffs, loosed a warning whinny.

TWENTY-FOUR

Gaining his feet and shoving the cork down into the whiskey bottle, Spurr shuttled his glance between Cochise and the trail. "The girl's right, Boomer. That hoss don't start at forest sprites."

"Ah, shit, I was just gettin' comfortable," Drago said as Greta helped haul the old outlaw to his feet.

Spurr walked over to Cochise and draped the spare saddlebags over his own pair behind his bedroll. Quickly, he and the others tightened their latigos and shoved the bridle bits through their horses' teeth.

Spurr racked a round into the chamber of his "new" carbine, all the while staring nervously back along the creek.

While Greta and Drago continued to ready their own mounts, Spurr walked out toward the creek, leading Cochise by his reins. When he was halfway between the cabin and the trees, he stopped. His heart hiccupped when he saw a single rider trotting toward him along the game trail, holding a rifle across his saddlebows. The man's head was turned to his left. When he turned it forward, staring toward Spurr, he drew back on his horse's reins, stopping the mount in the trail.

Facing Spurr, he kept his rifle resting across his saddle.

Spurr said out of the side of his mouth, "Come on, Boomer. You rode a horse before — let's pull foot."

Drago said, "I just got one more stirrup to adjust. Leave it to me to pick out the hoss of the shortest rider of the three!"

"Pick out another one," Spurr said through his teeth as he continued to have a stare down with the rider, who sat his horse about seventy yards north along the creek.

"I like this one," Drago said, then lifted his chin to stare over the saddle of the speckled barb he'd picked out. He winced. "That's Avrial Farmer — no-account from Tennessee."

"I didn't know there was any accountin' for anyone in Tennessee," Spurr said as he wrapped his reins around his saddle horn and then poked his left boot through his right stirrup.

"Christ, you two oughta throw a tea

party!" Greta complained, already astraddle her mare.

"It's age," Spurr said. "We realize we soon ain't gonna have no one to talk to in our cold graves, so we gotta get it out now. Why don't you boot Betsy on up the trail, Greta? We're gonna have to find some high ground to fort up on . . . if this Avrial Farmer ain't alone, that is. If he is — shit, I might just go ahead and shoot him right now from here."

Spurr had just started to raise his carbine when Farmer snapped his own rifle to his shoulder. Farmer got off the first shot though Spurr's was only an eye blink behind.

His bullet plumed dust over Farmer's left shoulder while Farmer's plumed dust over Spurr's right shoulder. Spurr pumped a fresh bullet into the carbine's breech. His heart hiccupped again when two more riders galloped around a bend behind Farmer.

They were followed by two more. And then three more, as far as Spurr could tell, which meant the others were likely close, as well — just out of sight. He had to believe the whole gang was here . . .

Spurr and Farmer each exchanged another wild round apiece and then Drago was ramming his boots into his barb's flanks and shouting, "Come on, Spurr — stop playin' with yourself and lets kick up some dust! We can't make a stand out here in the open!"

Spurr snapped off one more shot, holding Farmer and the other riders back, and then turned Cochise south. Greta was galloping off ahead with Boomer not far behind her, riding crouched low in the saddle, his thin, dark brown hair blowing around the bald top of his head. Spurr kicked Cochise after them, casting another look back to see Farmer and the others now cutting out after him.

Shouts rose from behind. Then guns popped and cracked above the thudding of the outlaws' galloping horses.

Slugs plunked into the trail behind Spurr and to each side, one shaving a small branch from an aspen tree on his right. Spurr shoved his Winchester into its scabbard, slid his Starr from its holster, and snapped off a shot behind him. He snapped off another and then one more and was glad to see that his return fire slowed the trail wolves if only slightly.

He and Greta and Drago tore on up the trail, past where the creek curved to the right and into another canyon. Spurr looked around desperately for high ground they could reach and try to hold before they all

302

got perforated by the gang's screeching bullets.

Just ahead of Spurr, Boomer jerked back on his horse's reins and flung his right arm out. "Canyon this way — we might be able to lose 'em in there!"

Reining Cochise to a halt while Greta stopped her own mount just ahead of both men, Spurr said, "I don't think there's gonna be any losin' this bunch, but I got no better idea!"

"Ha-*yahhh!*" Boomer cried, ramming his heels into his barb's loins and shooting up the trail angling off to the right of the main one they were on.

Spurr waited until Greta had passed in front of him, and then he flung two more .44 rounds toward the outlaws just now galloping around a bend in the trail behind. Holstering the Starr, he booted Cochise into a gallop up the narrow canyon trace.

The trace was hemmed in on both sides by heavy shrubs. It twisted and turned and then rose and fell over a low divide, and then they were heading through a gorge dark and fragrant with spruces and balsams. They rose up and over another divide, and then the trail grew wider and the trees gave way to steep, weathered, rocky ridges rising on the right and left.

Suddenly, Drago reined his barb in so quickly that Greta nearly ran her paint into him. The old outlaw cursed shrilly. Spurr saw why.

The trail through here had been entombed under a rockslide. Boulders, rocks, and broken pines like giant matchsticks formed a hundred foot dam across the trail. Only a mountain lion could get across that ridge, and such a climb would take some doing even for a wildcat.

"Great idea, Boomer!" Spurr bellowed, as mad at the fates as at his old nemesis. "Got any others?"

He and Drago looked around. The ridge to their left was sheer rock for two thousand feet above the gorge. The one on their right was gentler but it rose to a line of trees and rock that appeared to have tumbled from the ridge crest above maybe at the same time the canyon trail had been blocked.

Beyond the trees was another broad boulder field rising more steeply to the high, gray ridge top.

Guns cracked on the trio's back trail. Spurr whipped a look behind. Keneally's men were hammering over the last saddle, galloping toward him, shooting and shouting, horse hooves clacking on the stony trail.

"Up there's our only choice!" Spurr

shouted. "Come on, Greta — let's go!"

Spurr put Cochise up the northern slope.

The first part was steep and the horse had to take lunging strides, almost unseating Spurr, who was trying to keep an eye on Keneally's men, who were now opening up on him, Greta, and Drago in earnest. Greta's paint leapt up the ridge to Spurr's left. Drago's barb leapt up on Spurr's right side, Boomer groaning and clamping his left hand to his upper right arm.

"Sons o' bitches!" he carped, jerking an angry look back at his old gang.

"Keep movin', Boomer!"

"What the hell you think I'm *doin'*?" Drago shouted back, grinding his heels into his barb's flanks.

They climbed the ridge around the rocks and stunt cedars, boulders, and the trees that the boulders had mowed over when the rocks had tumbled down from the ridge. Bullets sang and danced through the air around them, pluming dust and blowing doggets of rock shards from boulders and bark and wood slivers from the trees that slanted amongst the rubble.

Greta grunted and shook her head wildly as a bullet curled the air too close to her right ear, and then her horse gave a shrill cry and lunged forward and sideways, fall-

305

ing hard.

"Spurr!" the girl screamed as she tumbled out of her saddle.

"Greta!" Spurr jerked back on Cochise's reins and leapt out of his own saddle as three bullets kicked up dust and rocks around his boots and around Cochise's dancing hooves.

Spurr grabbed his canteen and his Winchester from the horse's scabbard before Cochise ran on up the slope, wending its way amongst the boulders and screaming at the shooters flinging lead at him from below.

Spurr glanced toward Greta, who had fallen beyond her horse that appeared to have taken a bullet through its lungs.

Spurr dropped to a knee and triggered several rounds at Keneally's men, who were leaping off their horses' backs and shooting from the canyon floor. Spurr's shots sent them all diving for cover. The old lawman lowered his rifle and ran toward where Greta was climbing heavily to her feet, the heels of her hands bloody, her denims dusty and torn.

"You all right?"

Before she could answer, Spurr grabbed her wrist and began jerking her along behind him as he headed on up the ridge through the boulders, some of which were as large as wagons. A few were larger than cabins, offering the best cover.

"You got her, Spurr?" Drago called as he triggered lead back down the slope at his old gang.

"I got her!" Spurr paused to drill a Winchester round through the head of Greta's wounded paint, putting the mare out of her misery.

Spurr then led the girl around one of the largest boulders and continued on behind it and up the slope. His old heart was chugging madly and his chest felt like someone had slammed a horseshoe against his breastbone. But he kept moving his legs, knowing they had to get higher on the ridge. They had to gain the highest ground possible. Outnumbered as badly as they were, with the whole gang back there, it was their only chance.

As he moved through the jumble of fallen and standing trees and smaller boulders, holding his Winchester in one hand, the girl's hand in the other, Spurr noted a sudden drop off in the shooting. That meant at least for now the gang below didn't have Spurr's party in its sights. They were back down behind the larger boulders.

Boomer came around a boulder to Spurr's right, wearing two pistols on his waist and holding Sanchez's rifle in his hands. His canteen was slung over his neck and shoulder. He, too, was breathing hard and sweating, his thin hair pasted to his forehead.

"We're gettin' too old for this shit, pardner," Drago said as they moved as quickly as they could up through the trees and the rocks.

Spurr swallowed hard, shook his head. "I told you we ain't partners."

"We sure been through a lot not to call each other partners!"

"I'm with Boomer," Greta said, breathless, walking on her own now and casting wary looks behind. "I think you'd best resign yourself to the fact that you two have thrown in together, Spurr."

"You two keep movin'," Spurr said, ignoring them both. "I'm gonna fetch my saddlebags."

Cochise was standing between the trees and the steep slope climbing to the gray ridge, eyeing its rider skeptically. Spurr ran up and grabbed his saddlebags off the horse's back and then wrapped his reins around the roan's saddle horn. "Hightail it, now, Cochise. Go find cover!"

Spurr slapped the horse's rump, and the horse lunged off to the right along the edge of the trees.

As Spurr caught up to Greta and Drago now climbing the steep slope hard, guns began cracking behind them once more. Bullets spanged off rocks with ear-rattling whines. Spurr dug his moccasins into the steep slope, keeping his tired legs moving, breathing so hard that he could taste copper in his mouth.

His feet were raw and sweat-soaked in his boots. His throat was tight and dry. His breaths sounded like unoiled door hinges.

As they continued climbing into the large boulders, both Spurr and Drago stopped occasionally to forestall the outlaws with a few wild shots. Keneally's men kept coming, however, weaving around boulders and triggering lead.

Ahead and above, the ridge crest was like a heavy brow. There was no way that Spurr's party could climb it.

It appeared to the old lawman that there was a cave at the base of that brow, however — one with plenty of clear, steeply sloping ground around it. If they could gain the cave, they could hold the outlaws off — at least until they themselves ran out of ammunition, which, at the rate they were snapping caps, probably wouldn't be long.

Twenty-Five

Spurr shouldered up to a wagon-sized boulder, turning to the downslope. Greta was ahead of him, climbing crouched forward and using her hands. Boomer was behind, face shiny with dripping sweat. He was breathing with his mouth open, his eye wide and sharp with agony. His lungs wheezed like a bellows.

"Keep goin', Boomer. Head to that cave yonder. I'll cover you."

Boomer staggered past him, lower jaw hanging, only nodding once in acknowledgment.

Spurr raised the carbine. The gun was unfamiliar, making him yearn harder for his own '66 Winchester, but he drew a bead on one of the outlaws just now coming around a boulder, crouched over the rifle in his hands.

The man was broad-shouldered, with a head like a big rock. He wore a full blond beard beneath a black opera hat, and his green eyes were pinched to enraged slits. The man stopped, crouched over his own rifle, and looked up the slope toward Spurr, his breath frosting the bright air around his head and the collar of his dark blue coat.

Spurr squeezed the carbine's trigger. The damn rifle strayed left or he would have drilled Keneally between his two green eyes. Instead, the bullet crashed into the boulder to the man's right, and the outlaw leader jerked back behind the boulder and out of sight.

Spurr took aim at two other outlaws, both of whom had seen him and were diving for cover, and triggered three quick shots. As he ejected a spent round, he stepped back behind a boulder and, seating a fresh round in the carbine's chamber, glanced up the slope toward the cave, which Greta had reached. She knelt on the lip outside the ragged-edged, black, egg-shaped opening that appeared about ten feet wide at the bottom and maybe six feet high at its apex, and was reaching down to help Drago up the last few steps.

Spurr edged a look out from behind his own covering boulder but jerked it back as he saw smoke plume from over the top of a rock about thirty yards downslope and left.

The slug hammered the boulder a few inches above his head and set his ears to ringing as he aimed and triggered the carbine, and blew the top of the shooter's head and hat off. The man was dead instantly, flying back down the slope, his hat bouncing along the ground ahead of him. It flew a half-dozen yards before the wind caught it and swept it even farther down toward the canyon floor.

Several of Keneally's men shouted.

Spurr grinned despite the hammering of his heart and the straining of his lungs. Behind him, guns popped and cracked, and Greta shouted, "Come on, Spurr — we got you covered!"

"What the hell you waitin' on — *Christmas?*" Boomer bellowed as, cheeked up against Sanchez's Winchester, he fired downslope at the angrily shouting renegades.

Spurr looked at the sharp rise of ground — a fifty-foot stretch — between him and the ledge. He felt as though he'd been beaten about the head and shoulders by a madman wielding an axe handle, but he drew a deep breath, pushed off the boulder, and lunged toward the cave.

He ground the heels of his moccasin boots

into the gravel and heaved himself up the slope.

His left boot slipped and he dropped to a knee but bounded off the opposite heel and continued moving. His lungs now felt like a locomotive chugging uphill too fast for its own good, and low on water, but a bullet crashing into the slope to his right kept him lunging and bounding, leaning forward and willing himself toward the cave.

"Take my hand!" Greta shouted, setting her own carbine down and reaching toward Spurr.

A bullet crashed into the lip of the ledge between her and Spurr. She screamed and jerked back, startled, and Boomer fired his Winchester, evoking a yelp from one of the outlaws.

The old outlaw guffawed loudly as he racked another shell into his Winchester's chamber. "Got him, Greta. Don't you worry, hon — Boomer Drago's here!"

Spurr scrambled up the slope unassisted, crawled over the lip, and collapsed on his belly, lower legs still hanging down over the ledge. "That's supposed to make her feel *good*, Boomer?" he raked out between breaths that sounded like the raucous squawks of a red-winged blackbird piss-burned by squirrels.

Greta was sitting back against the rock wall right of the cave's mouth, her knees up, head down, rubbing her face with the heels of her hands. Her rifle lay beside her.

"You all right?" Spurr crawled up to her, back and out of sight of the shooters on the downslope, as Drago continued firing every ten seconds or so.

"Just got sand in my eyes," Greta said. "I'm all right."

"Come on," Spurr said, taking the girl's hand and tugging gently.

He crawled into the cave and she followed.

As Spurr eased back against the cave's east wall, Greta rested against the west wall, a foot or so from the opening. Spurr let the saddlebags tumble down off his shoulder and stretched his legs straight out in front of him, drawing deep breaths in and out of his lungs that felt as though they'd been scoured inside and out with sandpaper.

"Christ," he said when he was able to speak, sweat dribbling down his forehead and cheeks, making his eyes sting. He shook his head. "Oh, Christ almighty — it ain't no fun gettin' old. Used to be I could make a climb like that in half the time it just took this old bag of crippled bones."

"Ah, quit braggin'," Boomer said, rising to all fours and crawling straight back away from the opening.

The outlaws continued to fire, but most of their slugs were merely ripping sand and gravel from the lip of the ledge or blasting the cave's ceiling at the edge of the opening.

Pressing a cheek against the cave floor, Boomer said, "I coulda made a run like that in a third the time and still had the strength to fight a wildcat with only a bowie knife."

Spurr snorted. Boomer relaxed there on the cave floor, keeping his cheek to the ground. Spurr looked at Greta, who sat with her knees up, forearms resting on them, head hanging. Her hair obscured her face.

Spurr reached into the saddlebags, hauled out the pouch of jerky and the whiskey bottle, and, keeping out of sight from the men on the downslope, who were still triggering occasional shots, crawled over to her.

He pressed his back against the cave wall beside her and popped the cork on the bottle.

"Have you a pull o' that, girl. Do you good."

She lifted her head, shook her hair back from her face. She looked drawn and pale behind the bruising. The cut on her lips had come open and was oozing a little blood.

"You okay?" Spurr asked. He didn't like

how she looked. She appeared as drained as the two oldsters around her.

"Just tired." She took the bottle, threw back a deep swallow, and handed the bottle back to him. "Thanks."

She drew a breath and stared wearily down at her moccasins. "I reckon this is it, ain't it? There's no way out of this."

Spurr looked around. The cave appeared deeper than he'd expected, but through the shadows he could see the rear wall at the base of which lay a pile of stone rubble. They were surrounded by three stone walls and seven or so outlaws no doubt packing plenty of ammunition.

Despite those steep odds, and as exhausted as he was, Spurr wasn't yet ready to give in to despair. He patted Greta's hand, and then crawled up beside Drago, who lay unmoving on the cave floor, and doffed his hat.

He brought his carbine up close against his chest as he edged a look over the lip of the ledge. He pulled his head back behind the lip when he saw a gunman bear down on him from behind the boulder Spurr himself had used for cover only a few minutes ago.

The slug tore into the lip of the ledge, spraying Spurr, Drago, and Greta with sand

and gravel.

Silence.

Dust sifted. Greta coughed and shook her head, her tangled blond hair jouncing on her shoulders.

"Might as well come on outta there, Spurr!" Keneally shouted from the down-slope. "You got nowhere to go! If Drago tells us where he hid the loot, we'll let you an' the whore go!"

Spurr kept his head low as he shouted, "Well, you're just a kindhearted feller, Keneally. The only problem is this: I ain't goin' anywhere until I kill every last one of you low-down, dirty, girl-abusin' sons o' bitches!"

He rose up on his knees and snapped a shot down the slope a half second after Keneally had pulled his big, blond head back behind a boulder. Spurr's slug tore into the side of the boulder where the killer's head had been a moment before.

Spurr ducked his head again and arched an appreciative brow at the carbine in his hands. "Damn, I'm startin' to get the hang of this little devil."

"Spurr?"

He turned to Greta. She was staring down at Drago, who lay as he had before, cheek turned to the floor of the cave. He lay flat on his belly, Sanchez's rifle by his side.

Greta glanced fearfully at Spurr before lowering her eyes again to Drago. The old man's fur coat ruffled in the cool breeze funneling up the slope and into the cave. Half of Drago was in the crisp autumn sunshine, the other half in the heavy purple shadows of the cave.

Spurr said, "Boomer?"

"He hasn't moved since he lay down there," Greta said, tonelessly.

Spurr nudged the old outlaw's shoulder with the back of his left hand. "Hey, Boomer, ain't no time for a nap."

Drago didn't move. Spurr stared at his back, which did not appear to be rising and falling as he breathed.

"Goddamnit, you old bastard — don't tell me you got us into this mess and slipped out the back door. If that wouldn't be just like you!" Spurr wrapped a hand around the man's shoulder and started to turn him over onto his back. *"Boomer!"*

Drago jerked his head up and snapped his eyes open.

"What is it?" he cried, bringing his rifle up and looking around wildly. "Where in hell are we? We best haul freight before that posse gets here!"

Greta sighed with relief.

"Hold on, hold on!" Spurr said. "You crazy old coot, the posse's already done got here!"

Boomer looked at Spurr as though he'd never seen him before. Then he looked at Greta, and he seemed to remember. A sheepish expression passed over his bearded face, and he blinked his lone eye.

"Ah, shit. Here I thought we was in the Nations headed for Kansas City." He cast a cautious glance down the slope and then scuttled back against the wall beside Greta, set his rifle across his knees, and picked up the whiskey bottle. "Had a girl there, years back. Her name was Maybelline." He popped the cork on the bottle. "Maybelline Walker."

"Percentage gal?" Greta asked.

"Preacher's daughter."

"Figures," Greta said. "What happened?"

Drago took a long pull on the bottle, some of the whiskey dribbling down around the bottle lip and into the patchy beard on his chin and neck. When he lowered the bottle, he stared at it for a time, and then turned his sad eye to Greta.

"We had a place we met up at whenever I was in the country. An old stage relay station, part of the old Weston and Nash Line out of St. Louis. Anyways, I went there to

319

take her away to marry me and give up my evil ways, and she'd been there only to leave a note. She'd done married up with the banker's boy, an' she was movin' to Denver where the boy was openin' up his own bank."

Drago's lone eye acquired a gold sheen. A tear oozed out of its corner to drop down his cheek and roll up in the dust caking his grizzled black beard. Greta smiled sympathetically, laid her hand upon the old man's cheek.

"I think I know how this story ends," Spurr said, lifting his head to peer carefully over the lip of the ledge and down the slope, where the outlaws had gone eerily quiet.

"How?" Greta asked, frowning.

"He robbed the parson's daughter's young husband's bank."

Greta gasped and turned to Drago, who was snickering like a schoolboy with a frog in his pocket.

"Boomer, you didn't!"

Laughing, squeezing his eye closed, Drago shook his head. "Spurr, you know me too damn well!"

Greta's lower jaw sagged as she regarded the old man, aghast. But then, despite herself, she started laughing, as well. And then Spurr began laughing, and they were all three cutting up when a shadow leapt up from below the lip of the cave — a Stetson-hatted shadow with a rifle in his hands.

The outlaw grinned as he leveled the carbine in his hands a half second before Spurr's own Winchester thundered loudly inside the cave. Flames lapped from the barrel.

The outlaw screamed as the slug tore through his brisket, pluming dust from his ankle-length rat hair coat, and punched him back down beneath the lip of the ledge and out of sight. His big body thudded and caused a small rockslide as it rolled.

Gritting his teeth, Spurr ejected the spent brass from the Winchester's breech, heard it clink onto the cave floor beside him, and then rammed a fresh cartridge into the chamber.

"Don't worry," Spurr growled. "I seen him comin' all along."

TWENTY-SIX

From the downslope, silence like that in boneyard at midnight on Halloween.

A few more rocks clanked as they slid down the slope in the dead outlaw's wake. Dust tinted copper by the sun rose like smoke.

Spurr stared through his own gun smoke out the cave opening, but all he could see from his angle was the other side of the canyon. The outlaws were well below, apparently quietly pondering their amigo's demise. To Spurr's right, Drago snickered and said, "Did you really know that hombre was comin'?"

"Of course I did," Spurr lied. He was tired and his senses had dulled. He'd just been fortunate to have looked toward the opening when the killer had lifted his head. "You don't think I'd let my guard down like what you done in Idaville, do you?"

Keneally's voice called from down the hill,

"Nice shootin' up there!"

Spurr shouted, "Thanks but a shaver could've made that shot!"

"You two old wolves are better than I figured!"

"Why don't you come on up, Keneally, and me an' Boomer here can give you a few pointers!"

Another silence, a brief one.

And then another outlaw said in a sneering tone, "Why don't you come down here and we can give that whore a few pointers? A few more o' what she got last time!"

Several of the outlaws chuckled.

Greta lurched forward, grabbing her rifle and racking a round into the chamber. Spurr grabbed her around the waist and hauled her back away from the opening. "Hold on there, girl. That's just what they want you to do — don't you know that?"

She tried to wriggle out of the old lawman's arms. "Let me go, Spurr!" Her voice was hard but then he heard her sob. Spurr held her tight against him, gritting her teeth as she continued to struggle. Boomer lifted his head, snapped his Winchester to his shoulder, and triggered a shot down the slope.

One of the outlaws gave a surprised yell.

Drago lowered his rifle and shouted, "You

sons o' bitches got no honor! The boys I rode with before you never woulda done that to a girl. We mighta been outlaws, but that was a line we never crossed, an' I'm damn ashamed to have ever ridden the coulees with you yellow-livered pecker-woods!"

He jerked his head back behind the ledge as two rifles popped on the downslope. One slug tore up sand from the ledge while the other hammered the roof of the cave opening. Sand sifted down from the roof. Dust wafted.

Drago lifted his head slightly above the floor and shouted, "You hear me, Keneally! You're a copper-riveted tinhorn, and I'm gonna kill you deader'n hell if that's the last goddamn thing I do!"

Keneally shouted, "Come down here an' try it, old man!"

Drago snarled, took hasty aim, and triggered a shot down the slope. The bullet gave a witch's screech as it ricocheted off a rock.

Keneally and several other outlaws laughed.

Spurr released Greta, who slumped, dejected, toward the cave floor. "Stop wasting ammo, you damn fool," he snapped at Drago.

The old outlaw whipped his head toward

him, lone eye blazing. "You're the damn fool! We wouldn't be in this mess if you'd have listened to reason."

"Reason? You mean your lies!"

"You see now I wasn't lyin'!"

"If you wouldn't tell so many long, windy ones, maybe a man could figure out which ones was true!"

Greta lifted her head and shook her hair back. As she slid back against the cave's west wall, she said with a weary, depressed air, "Fellas, your arguin' ain't gonna save us."

Spurr looked at her. Then he looked at Drago. The fire had gone out of the old outlaw's eye as he dropped his gaze to the cave floor.

Spurr curled his legs beneath him, trying to get somewhat comfortable on the uneven stone floor that was nearly as cold as a marble slab, and grabbed the bottle. He popped the cork, extended the bottle to Drago, and said, "Why don't we all have a drink?"

Drago looked at the bottle. He stared at it thoughtfully, appearing as depressed as Greta now, but finally grabbed it and threw back a couple of deep swallows. He extended the bottle to Greta, who shook her head, and then gave the bottle to Spurr, who finished it off.

"We got one more," he said, whipping the empty bottle past Drago and hearing it shatter on the downslope. "We're gonna need it tonight. Gonna get cold up here."

He set the bottle down against the wall near Greta, and scuttled onto his belly to Drago's left side. He crawled forward a little so that he could edge a cautious look down the slope. He drew his head back when a gun blasted, and sand flew up into his face.

Blinking the dust from his eyelashes, and spitting, he crawled back until he lay even with Drago, who gave him a wry look. "They got us bottled up purty good."

Spurr said with a vaguely chastising tone, "You realize our only chance of getting out of this is you telling them where the money is, don't you?"

Drago pursed his lips as he stared darkly straight out over the lip of the ledge. "They wouldn't believe me even if I did tell 'em."

"Couldn't hurt to give it a shot. If it was just me here, I'd say screw 'em — we'll shoot our way out of this crypt. Prob'ly get blown to our rewards, but at least Keneally wouldn't win. But we got Greta to think about, Boomer. She's young, got her whole life ahead of her."

"If you boys want to shoot your way out

of here, count me in," Greta said, setting her rifle across her knees and patting the forestock. Her blue eyes were resolute.

Spurr looked past Drago at her, wagged his head, and grinned. "If I were twenty years younger . . ."

"Thirty, more like," Boomer said.

Greta's eyes crossed in that pretty way she had as she curled her split upper lip. "If we ever get out of here, I'll marry both of you."

"You'd kill us both," Spurr told her.

"But what a way to go," she said, her eyes smoky.

Drago fingered his chin whiskers. "The only way Greta's got a chance is if I turn myself over to those boys. And that's just what I'm gonna do."

Boomer had no sooner started to rise to all fours, than Greta said, "No!" She threw herself onto the old outlaw's back, and he collapsed belly down against the cave floor with a sharp grunt.

Greta wrapped her arms around his neck and pressed her cheek against his fur coat, between his shoulder blades. "We're in this together for the long haul, Boomer!"

"Crazy girl — it's your only chance!"

"Ah, shit — they're not gonna leave us alive, Boomer." Spurr stared at the old outlaw. "You'd be throwin' yourself to them lobos for nothin'. Might as well stay here, help us shoot it out."

Boom glanced at him sidelong, narrowing his eye. "And when we're out of ammunition?"

"We'll start hurling rocks." Greta leaned forward and planted an affectionate kiss on the back of the old outlaw's nearly bald head.

The afternoon waned as shadows spilled down the ridges. Clouds slid into the sky over the canyon, making it even darker. Just after the sun went down, a fine snow began to fall.

Spurr could tell by the iron-sharp cold pressing into his bones from the cave floor and the increasing sting in his cheeks and nose, not to mention his gloved fingers and moccasined toes, that the temperature was dropping rapidly. There'd been no shooting since Drago's last shot, but, as though to taunt them, Keneally's men built a large bonfire about seventy yards down the slope, at the edge of the large boulder field.

Light from the fire danced across the rocks. Sparks columned upward.

Occasionally, one of the outlaws would shout up at the cave, "Sure is warm down here. Must be right chilly up there. You folks sure you don't wanna come down here and warm up, maybe have some beans and bacon? Got some rabbit to go with it. Plenty of hot coffee! Come on down, we'll make it a fandango!"

"We'll take turns dancin' with the whore!" another man shouted in a higher-pitched voice.

Several men cackled, and one yelled, "And then we'll draw straws for her — see who goes first!"

Spurr, sitting with his back to the cave's west wall, glanced at Greta, who sat beside him, resting her head on his shoulder. She did not react to the men's jeers. He could see her blinking, so she wasn't asleep, but she seemed deeply fatigued and on the edge of not caring about anything anymore.

Drago appeared the same way. The old outlaw sat against the opposite wall, staring blankly at the wall over Spurr's head, his rifle across his outstretched legs. Spurr probably looked as depressed as his cohorts. His shoulders were heavy, his chest tight, his heart beating feebly.

This was likely the end of his trail. He didn't care so much for himself, but he was damned sick about getting another girl killed. That's how he saw it, despite her following him and Drago of her own accord out from Diamond Fire. He could have turned her away, but he hadn't.

Always a sucker for a pretty blonde.

Well, now he'd more than likely gotten another one killed. He wasn't sure why — it made no sense whatever, as long as he'd been after the old outlaw — but part of him regretted Boomer Drago's imminent demise, as well. Maybe only because it would mean that his men had won. Or maybe it meant more to the old lawman than that. He couldn't be sure. His brain was as tired and as cold as the rest of him, and he couldn't trust his thinking anymore.

He dozed for a time with his eyes and ears open, but then, staring out past the cave's eastern wall, toward the solid stone ridge that trailed off beyond it, he came awake with a small fire kindling inside him.

The weird castings of the light beyond the cave — the blue of the twilight stitched with the white of the falling snow which in turn shimmered softly with the light of the outlaws' fire — revealed something that Spurr had not seen before in the ridge wall beyond the opening.

Sitting across from him but slightly left, Boomer said, "What is it?"

Greta lifted her head from where she'd leaned it forward against her rifle barrel.

Spurr glanced to his right, not wanting to get too close to the ledge, making himself visible to the men on the slope and get a hole drilled in his head for his carelessness. He slid a little closer to the ledge but leaned down low against the floor, looking up and out the cave opening on his left.

He narrowed his eyes, straining his vision, to get a better look at the ridge wall.

Sure enough, about six feet to the left of the cave there was a long, perpendicular cavity in what had previously looked like a flawless stretch of stone. It was like a tooth with a crack in it, and one side of the tooth had shoved out farther than the rest. The crack was now partly concealed by the outermost part of the tooth.

Spurr couldn't be sure from this far away, but the crack seemed to angle up the ridge. Rocks appeared to have fallen down from the crack to pile up on the ledge beneath the crack, which meant there might be ledges and cavities where someone climbing the crack could find foot- and handholds.

When Spurr did not respond to Drago's question because he was too intent on inspecting the crack, the old outlaw stretched his head out from the opening, craning his neck to follow Spurr's gaze. Someone from below caught a glimpse of the movement. A rifle belched loudly, echoing.

The slug missed Drago's head by inches and hammered into the ridge wall to his left with a tooth-gnashing screech. Rock shards ticked onto the stony ledge. Bits of gravel rattled down the slope.

The echo of the slug's crash chased the rifle's echo up and down the canyon, both echoes diminishing gradually to silence.

Drago had jerked his head back into the cave and was poking a finger in his ear as though to relieve the ringing from the slug's hammering.

"Damn near got a whole lot more pleasant in here," Spurr told Greta.

Angrily, Drago said, "What the hell you see out there?"

Spurr told him. Greta crawled toward the opening, keeping her head down and away from the lip of the ridge. Drago did the same, and together they inspected the crack, tipping their heads this way and that.

"You think we can make it up that?" Drago asked Spurr, incredulous.

"I think we got a rat's chance in a hole full of rattlesnakes some kid teased with a stick, but it's better than no chance at all. Because that's exactly what we have otherwise."

"Shit, even if the crack goes all the way up to the top of the ridge, and it's climbable — what makes you think us old men could climb it?"

"Nothin' does." Spurr was sitting back against the west cave wall, slowly, thoughtfully rolling a cigarette from his makings pouch. "Does that mean we don't try?"

"Ah, hell," carped the old outlaw. "I'm as droopy as a wrung-neck rooster. Even if I could make it out there to the crack without gettin' shot, I couldn't climb it. Not without wide marble steps and a bannister and someone pushin' from behind."

"Maybe we can't climb it, you old scudder, but that don't mean Greta can't. Later, much later, long after good dark, I'm gonna crab on out there and take a better look at it. If it looks like the crack might go all the way up, and someone beside our old selves *might* be able to climb it, I say we try it."

Greta and Drago shared a look. Greta turned back to Spurr, hiked a shoulder. "Why the hell not?"

Boomer shrugged, then, too. "Might as well die out there than in here, I reckon."

Twenty-Seven

The night got colder and darker. The snow continued to fall. It was not a hard, fast snowfall but a steady dusting that accumulated like feathers on the ledge outside the cave.

Spurr and Boomer took turns hunkering as close as they dared to the ledge, looking around in the darkness and listening for more outlaws intent on stealing up to the cave.

By the time midnight had rolled around, no one had tried. Keneally's men all seemed content on letting Spurr, Drago, and Greta endure a miserable night in the cold cave without further harassment. Even if they'd had wood to burn, Spurr would not have built a fire. A fire would have made him and his trail partners easy targets and made it impossible for them to watch for anyone stealing up out of the dark night.

The outlaws kept the fire built up after

midnight. Likely, they'd keep it going all night long. Spurr figured they'd have at least two men — maybe only one — watching the cave while the others slept. The way the outlaws would see it, there was little need for all of them to watch. After all, they were after only two old men and a girl.

One or two watchers, with the watch changing every couple of hours, would do.

At least, Spurr was banking on only that many keeping watch.

He was also banking on the notion that sometime after midnight, the watcher or watchers would nod off. Or at least get so tired that their senses would become dull enough that Spurr, Greta, and Drago could crab over to the cleft and climb without being heard or seen.

The three hunted ones waited restlessly, nervously, until after three A.M. Then Spurr took a drink of water, grabbed his rifle, slung his canteen over his shoulder, and kept his voice low as he told Drago and Greta, "Cover me. If I think that crack looks climbable, I'll give a soft whistle. Very soft, so be listening for it. Then Greta, you come. Crawl real slow and quiet-like. Then you, Boomer."

They were all three huddled together in the middle of the cave.

Spurr worried over it some more, tugging on his beard, and then he said, "And for godsakes, don't make any noise to draw their attention. I'm hoping whoever they got watchin' the cave fell asleep or is busy playin' with himself."

"Don't count on it," Drago said. "Just stay low an' quiet, Spurr."

Spurr curled his upper lip at the old outlaw. "Kiss me for luck, Boomer?"

"I will." Greta hugged him, pecked his cheek. "Good luck. I hope we can climb up out of here, but" — she shook her head — "I'm not counting on it."

"That's prob'ly wise."

Spurr took a final pull from their last bottle, handed the whiskey to Drago. He left his saddlebags, which would be too unwieldy to climb with in the event the cavity was climbable, and then crawled, belly down to the cave opening and beyond. He'd removed his hat so he'd make a smaller shadow, and now he cast a quick glance into the darkness of the downslope.

The fire shimmered orange between the black velvet silhouettes of boulders. He had no idea where a possible watcher would be lurking. If the man or men were close and keeping a sharp eye on the cave mouth, Spurr would likely find out soon enough.

Holding his rifle in his one hand, keeping his canteen slung straight down his back and away from the ground, he crawled around the left wall of the cave and, with painstaking slowness, gritting his teeth, continued to crawl along the base of the ridge. There was a slight breeze swirling the fallen snow — the snow had stopped falling around midnight — and he hoped it would obscure his silhouette.

Still, he held to a snail's pace, moving one elbow and one knee, and then the other elbow and the other knee, keeping his rifle above the slight ledge he was on so it wouldn't make any noise. Once, he dragged the butt, and he froze and whipped a look down the slope.

Nothing moved or stirred. The fire continued to shimmer but he could see less of it from his current vantage.

He continued crawling. When he'd covered the last few feet to the cleft, he was happy to see that it was even deeper than it had appeared from the cave. It was damn deep as a closet, and it was angled so that, facing the cleft, Spurr's shoulder was almost but not quite perpendicular to the canyon.

The cavity's angle to the canyon should keep Spurr and the others out of view of the outlaws. Now, to see if they could climb it . . .

Ah, to be a few years younger. Make that thirty years younger . . .

He leaned forward, squinted at the long fissure and followed it up with his gaze, pleased to see that it appeared to run to the crest of the ridge fifty or so feet away. He leaned his rifle against the ridge, set a moccasin on a little cleft about a foot up from the ledge floor, and reached up with his left hand, finding another hold — a pocket in the crenelated rock.

There was some gravel and shards in the pocket. He dug them out and started climbing, his heart beating faster when he found that the fissure seemed to have plenty of places to put his feet and his hands. At least it did within ten feet of the bottom.

He had to assume it would have plenty all the way to the top. He had no choice. The problem was, his heart was beating fast because of his excitement at having possibly found a way out of the cave and out of the canyon, but it was also beating fast from exertion. And his chest ached.

Sweat was cold beneath the band of his hat. He could feel the perspiration dripping like melting snow down his back.

Could he make it all the way to the top?

He eased himself back down to the floor and glanced at the rifle. He wouldn't be able to climb with it. Have to leave it here. He turned to peer back along the ridge to the cave mouth. He saw two silhouetted heads poking out of the cave's darkness, and made a brief, soft whistling sound.

One of the silhouettes slid out away from the cave mouth and dropped low to the ground. Spurr hunkered on his haunches, wincing nervously as he watched Greta inch her way toward him. It took her over five minutes to reach him, moving slowly and staying low, and when she did, Spurr helped her up and gently pulled her back inside the notch, out of sight from the canyon.

"You think we can climb it?" she asked in his ear.

Spurr nodded as he turned to watch Boomer crawl toward him. The old lawman stretched a glance out around the wall of the notch and saw the orange shimmer of the outlaws' fire.

A few granular snowflakes blew in the breeze. The night was eerily quiet. He wondered where the watcher or watchers were. If they were staring this way, he hoped like hell they didn't pick out the moving shadow that was Boomer Drago.

If they did, he and his partners were dead.

Drago took only a little longer to traverse the ten feet between the cave mouth and the cleft where Spurr and Greta waited, holding their breaths. When he did, Spurr saw that the old outlaw had brought his rifle, too.

"Gonna have to leave it," Spurr said in his ear. "Gonna need both hands."

Drago glanced out toward the gauzy-dark canyon, then turned back to Spurr and nodded.

"Who wants to go first?" Spurr whispered above the breeze rasping across the hollow.

"Greta should go," Boomer said.

She turned to look up at the crack running nearly straight down from the top of the brow-like mantle of rock. She leaned against the crack and started climbing. Spurr held his hands out in case she fell. When she was six feet above him, she stopped and looked down.

."All right?" Spurr asked her.

She nodded, looked up, and continued climbing, loosing chunks of rock in her wake. Some of the chunks pelted Spurr's hat brim and landed on the ledge floor around his moccasins with light clinking sounds.

Spurr turned to Boomer standing directly behind him, nearly brushing against him.

"You go next."

The outlaw shook his head. "You go. I'll cover your bony ass."

"I may not make it. Don't wanna block the way."

"You got as good a chance as I do."

Spurr was getting riled. He hardened his jaws as he put his face within four inches of Boomer's, and said in a raspy bark, "I ain't gonna stand here an' chin with you all night, Drago! Now, one of us has to go, an' I'm playin' the fiddle. Dance!"

As Drago gave a haughty chuff and stepped around him toward the cleft, Spurr gave his gaze to the canyon. Apprehension dropped like a stone in his belly when he saw a shadow pass in front of the fire, angling up the slope toward the cave.

He didn't see the shadow for long, but something told him it was not a good sign.

Someone was stirring. It might be one of the gang members heading up the hill to relieve one of the watchers, but it might also mean one or more was making a move on the cave. It would be a good time of the night to do it, when it was as dark as it was going to get and when the two old men and girl might have fallen asleep or at least let their guards down.

Drago bumped into him from behind.

341

"Shit!" the outlaw rasped.

Spurr turned to him, his heart thudding wildly now, anxiously. "What the hell is it?"

"Skinned my knee!"

"Get the hell up there, you old coot — I think your boys are movin' around!"

"Shit!"

Drago lifted a foot to a small cleft inside the cavity. When he put weight on that foot, it slid off the cleft, and he fell forward, cursing again.

Spurr sighed, shook his head. Oh, well, it had been worth a try.

"I don't think this is gonna work," Drago said in Spurr's ear.

Spurr looked up. Greta was about fifteen feet above him and Boomer, holding her position and looking above her as though for a place to put her hand. Spurr turned to Drago. "Give it one more try. If you can't make it, your boys'll be more than happy to entertain you for the rest of the evening."

Drago chuffed heavily and then turned back to the cavity. He fished around for some holds, managed to maintain them, and started climbing. He climbed clumsily, looking like he could fall out away from the notch at any time, but Spurr would be damned if the old outlaw didn't keep crabbing his way up the crack behind Greta.

Spurr glanced out at the canyon once more. Several shadows were moving along the slope. They appeared to be moving *up* the hill, toward the cave. In the quiet night, he heard the snick of a boot scuffing gravel. A man said, *"Shhh!"*

The shadows stopped moving. Spurr counted at least four. If he could see that many in the darkness cloaking the slope, there must have been more. The entire gang — which was probably down to six, more or less — must be closing on the cave, hoping to surprise their quarry with a lead bath.

Spurr looked up the cavity before him. Drago was moving slowly, carefully picking his hand- and footholds. Greta was so far up now that Spurr could only see her vague shadow against the darker background of the ridge.

Spurr thrust his left hand into the cavity, grabbed ahold of that pocket he'd grabbed before, and lifted his right foot onto a slight shelf about a foot above the ledge. He heaved himself up, feeling with his right hand and his left foot for another hold higher up.

He found them, pushed off his foot, and pulled with his hand. His heart fluttered. He was breathing hard, dizzy, his chest feeling like a bird was pecking away at his ticker. Behind and below, he sensed more than heard or saw movement on the slope beneath the cave.

He kept the brunt of his concentration on the cavity before him, picking out handholds by sight as well as by feel, probing each foothold carefully before setting his weight on it. One misstep and he'd fall to the ledge. If the fall itself didn't kill him, Keneally's men would have the honor, but they'd no doubt take their time acquiring it . . .

Spurr was about a third of the way to the ridge, feeling like a bug on a wall, moving slowly and deliberately but steadily, sweat dribbling down his forehead and his cheeks and down his back beneath his shirt. He set his right moccasin into the same crack in which he'd placed his right hand a moment ago.

The crack broke under his foot. Gravel went clattering off down the cavity. Spurr dug both hands into separate holds and syphoned all his strength to his arms while he ground his right foot deeper into the crack, until he'd regained purchase.

Cursing, he listened to the clattering of the gravel on the floor of the ledge now about thirty feet below.

A voice rose on the downslope — not loud

but loud enough for Spurr to hear from his lofty perch over the canyon. He heard foot thuds, the rake of gravel along the slope.

He cursed and continued climbing, gritting his teeth and grinding his jaws with every push and heave. He looked up to see Drago about fifteen feet away. The old outlaw had stopped. Spurr could see his face, firelight reflecting wanly off his cheeks above his beard, as Boomer looked down at him.

"Keep . . . g-goin'!" Spurr raked out as he pushed and pulled himself up the crack, Boomer's sweat dribbling cold against his face.

"Was that you?"

"J-just keep movin'!"

Boomer lifted his head and continued climbing. Spurr continued climbing, as well, but each push and pull was becoming a monumental effort. His knees ached. His calves felt like stone. He felt like he could throw up. His hands were so numb that he was having trouble finding holds much less using those holds to hoist himself up higher along the cavity.

He wondered what Keneally's men were up to. He got his answer a second later when gunshots sounding like near thunder erupted below and to his left. The din was so sudden that he jerked with a start, nearly losing his hold and tumbling down the defile. He pressed up tight against the crack, stretching his lips back from his teeth, expecting the bullets to rip into him at any second.

But none hammered the wall around him. And then he realized that Keneally's men were firing into the cave, not up at the cavity. They would soon, though, when they realized they were shooting at nothing but rocks and air.

He was right though he'd have sooner been wrong.

Less than a minute after Keneally's men had silenced their guns, realizing the cave was empty, one of them discovered the notch. Spurr could hear them yelling below him, hear their boots raking on the stone ledge.

Keneally's voice vaulted above the general, incredulous hubbub below the cavity: "Hey, you old men up there?"

"Ah, shit!" Spurr heard Drago say above him.

Spurr stopped climbing, pressed his right shoulder against the cavity wall, and, with both feet ground into toeholds, slid his Starr from its holster. He groaned against the pain of his taut tendons and muscles, his feet shaking like leaves in the wind. Still, he managed to snake the pistol across his belly, ratcheting the hammer back, and squeeze the trigger.

The gun thundered and flashed just off his left hip. Peppery powder smoke basted his face. He flicked the hammer back, popped off another shot, then two more, hearing the men below diving for cover. Knowing that they would now home in on his gun flash, Spurr slid the pistol back into its holster and, inspired by the thought of certain death if he lingered, continued to push and pull himself up the cavity.

Below, men shouted.

Guns began flashing and popping. Spurr could see the flashes in the corner of his left eye. He kept climbing. He looked up to see Drago crawl over the crest of the ridge and roll aside, revealing Greta's oval-shaped face staring down at him, her blond hair blowing wildly in the wind up there.

"Hurry, Spurr!"

Bullets crashed off the ridge wall around Spurr, some skidding along past him and continuing up toward the velvet sky speckled with stars. One bullet hammered the cleft six inches left of his left hand. Spurr thrust his right hand up and another hand closed around his wrist.

Boomer grunted and fell back on his butt as he ground his heels into the stone floor of the ridge and hauled Spurr up onto the crest. Drago cursed and cajoled Spurr as, grinding his heel into the rock, he scuttled back on his butt, dragging Spurr along with him. Greta reached down and grabbed Spurr's arm, and she grunted and groaned as she joined the effort.

Finally, Spurr was lying half on top of Boomer Drago, half on top of Greta while the muffled pops of angry gunfire continued below, the outlaws' lead screeching benignly skyward.

When Spurr finally caught his breath, lying flat on his back and staring at the stars, he said, "Well, now that we're up here, how you reckon we get down?"

"Shouldn't be too hard if a bear can do it."

Spurr and Greta both turned to Drago.

The old outlaw worked his nose, sniffing. "Yep, that's bear shit, all right — pardon my French, Miss Greta."

TWENTY-EIGHT

Greta climbed to her knees. "You mean a bear's been up here? Recently?"

Keneally's men had stopped shooting but Spurr could still hear his men yelling. They were madder than wet hens about having let their quarry slip away from them. For now, at least.

"Smells fresh to me," Boomer said.

Spurr climbed heavily to his knees. He ached all over and the crab in his chest still had a vicious hold on his heart, but he was amazed to be alive. He followed Drago's gaze to a large, dark mound about six feet away from Boomer. Spurr pushed to his feet, stumbled over his own feet — christ, he was dizzy! — and stared down at the black pile of goo liberally lumped with berry seeds.

"Nice big one."

"Griz, you think?" Boomer asked him.

"Never seen a black bear shit that big."

Spurr straightened, wincing and planting his fists on his hips as he leaned back, stretching. He was dizzy but the crab seemed to be easing up on his old ticker. "Must be an easier way down than the one we took up. A bear wouldn't climb that crack or anything like it."

Greta was still on her knees, looking around dubiously. "Fellas, what about the bear himself? That pile of shit does smell awfully ripe even to my untrained sniffer."

Spurr looked around. He didn't see anything of the bruin — probably a lone male laying in a good supply of tallow and padding its belly out thoroughly before forting up for the winter. Which meant it was hungry. Bears this time of the year would eat anything — flora, fauna, or human. A grizzly the size of the one that had dropped the shovel-sized, smelly load wouldn't bat an eye at running down a human, though the way Spurr currently felt, the bear wouldn't have to run very hard to catch him.

Boomer looked little better off. The old outlaw lay on his side, propped on an elbow, his chest rising and falling sharply. He looked around. "Well, shit. I hope we didn't crawl out of the frying pan to die in the fire."

"All we can do," Spurr said, "is to find a way down from here, get our bearings, and start walking."

"Where?" Greta said.

"Starting off, the path of least resistance."

Spurr stood near the top of the fissure they'd just climbed, staring down toward where Keneally's men had fallen suddenly, ominously quiet. He'd unsheathed his Starr because he thought maybe one or two had decided to climb the crack, but it didn't look like any had been than stupid.

Their fire was no larger than a pinprick of orange light from here. He couldn't see any shadows moving around it.

"Sounds like we done confounded 'em —"

Spurr stopped when a voice shouted up from the bottom of the canyon. The words were garbled, muffled by the wind and distance.

"What the hell was that?" Boomer said, pushing off a knee and gaining his feet.

The shout came again, louder but only a little clearer this time, so that Spurr could make out what sounded like, "Father." The voice echoed strange. It sounded as though it were being shouted from the bottom of a deep well.

"What'd he say?" Greta asked, moving up to stand beside Spurr, the cold wind blowing against them.

Again, Keneally shouted, "Something or

351

other father, Boomer!" He laughed bizarrely. The echoes of the laughter vaulted around the canyon for some time, sounding more and more hollow as they dwindled. And then there was only the sound of the wind.

"What the hell's he mean by that?" Spurr said, glancing at Drago standing to his left.

Drago shrugged, shook his head. "How the hell should I know? Probably drunk. And two parts loco. Here, I only thought he was one-part." The old outlaw crossed his arms on his chest, and shivered. "Brrrr! Cold up here!"

"I say we head for lower ground," Greta suggested.

Spurr turned to stare off across the caprock they were on. Most of the snow had been swept clean by the breeze. In the darkness, it was impossible to tell how far the slab extended to the north. He assumed it ran for quite a ways to the east and west, capping the ridge on the north end of the canyon they'd climbed out of. Likely, the only way to lower ground was to the north.

He hoped they wouldn't have to descend as steep a ridge as the one they'd climbed up. He doubted his old knees would take it.

Spurr started walking slowly northward along the caprock that was a massive, northward-sloping chunk of uneven granite from which, here and there, a wind-gnarled cedar fingered up out of small cracks. There were even a couple of junipers and wild current shrubs.

The wind pushed against Spurr from behind. He had to stiffen his back against it. No telling where the caprock ended and another canyon dropped away. Mostly, what he could see ahead of him was velvety darkness with the occasional humped shapes of granite outcroppings and stunted trees.

He moved through the widely spaced shrubs and cedars and occasional mushroom shapes of rock that had pushed up eons ago from the granite base. He was glad that the caprock continued to angle gradually downward. Maybe that meant there would be no sharp drop off.

After nearly a half hour of slow walking, the granite caprock stopped abruptly. Beyond lay only darkness, masking the northern terrain.

"Shit," Spurr said.

"What is it?" Greta asked, walking a few yards behind him.

Spurr thought he'd come to a deep canyon and would have to look for a way down, but no. He dropped to a knee at the edge of the caprock and stared down to where brown dirt and pine needles sloped away from the massive stove slab only four or five feet below. Beyond were more closely spaced pine and firs and the pale shapes of occasional boulders. On the wind was the tang of pinesap.

The old lawman cursed again, chuckling this time. He sat down, dropped his legs over the edge of the rock, and then dropped to the ground. "There!" he said, turning and smiling up at Greta standing at the edge of the caprock. "How'd you like that little piece of luck?"

He'd just extended his hand to the girl, when a guttural bugling sounded, echoing eerily. Greta gasped. Spurr looked around, groaning, caution rippling along his spine.

The sound came again — a deep, bellowing cry of feral anger. Because of the echo, it was impossible to tell where the sound had originated. It seemed to rise up out of the earth itself and resonate beneath the stars as it gradually dwindled to silence.

Only the wind sifting down over the caprock and nudging the branches of the pines and firs dropping down the gradual slope behind Spurr.

"There he is." Drago stood several yards behind Greta, a little higher on the granite slab. He was staring eastward, his thin hair blowing around the top of his bald-pated head. The strap of his eye patch angled blackly down the side of his head and across his earlobe.

"Oh, don't tell me," Greta said just loudly enough for Spurr to hear.

"Griz," Spurr said.

"An angry bruin," Drago elaborated. "Might have scented us. Maybe we're in his territory, and he don't appreciate strangers competin' for his precious deer vittles."

The bugling sounded again, starting low but then rising in pitch until it cracked at its apex. Gooseflesh rose along Spurr's back as that high, chortling squeal echoed loudly, savagely.

Spurr glanced at Drago once more. "Can you get a read on him, Boomer?"

Drago pointed. "I'd say he's somewhere off to the east, below the caprock somewhere. Must be a valley down that way."

Spurr extended his hand to Greta, and helped her down the shelf and onto the dirt-covered slope beside the old lawman. "We'd best head northwest, then. Come on, Miss Greta. Hope you still got some juice in your stewpot — sounds like you're gonna need it."

"I'll manage," the girl said, as she followed Spurr on down the slope, Drago dropping tenderly off the shelf behind them. "How 'bout you, Spurr? You still got some grain in your feed bin?"

"No, I sure don't. But it's just amazing how the hunting cry of one of those beasts will put some spring in an old man's step!"

Drago was breathing hard as he followed about ten yards behind, stumbling over fallen branches and low hummocks of ground as he looked cautiously off to their right. "Sure enough," muttered the old outlaw under his labored breathing. "Out of the frying pan and into the fire. Bad luck is what this old badge toter is. Spurr, I declare — I knew twenty years ago I was gonna rue the day I met you!"

Spurr only snorted at that and kept moving.

They continued winding their way down the gradual slope through the dark night, shivering against the steely, mid-autumn chill. Snow blowing off the branches peppered their faces. Not much lay on the ground but that which glowed in the starlight.

They heard the bear's savage cry only once more, and then, save for the occasional yammering of a coyote, the night grew quiet.

The slope seemed endless. But since the

trio's energy was not, they holed up in a nook of a stony outcrop, concealed by brush and junipers. Sitting side by side for warmth, Greta sandwiched between the two men, they shared water from their two canteens, and slept.

Spurr slumbered like a dead man. When he woke, he thought for a moment that he *was* dead and that he'd gone to heaven of all places. Imagine that!

Sunlight angled down through the branches of the pine to his right, bathing him in its warm, buttery glow. For a moment he sat staring straight ahead at a chickadee hopping about on the branch of a naked aspen just ahead of him and down the slope a few yards. The little black and white bird, too, was limned in the sun's golden glow. The chickadee gave its familiar "chick-a-dee-dee" song in a simple celebration of the sunny mountain morning, and then continued to pick at the branch for seeds, grubs, and larvae.

Peace poured through the old man's bones like warm syrup.

He meditated on the bird for a long time, feeling Greta's head on his right shoulder, her warm breath caressing his neck, and he thought how nice it would be for death to come now.

Something gave a deep, menacing snort up the slope behind him and right. There was the echoing crack of a branch beneath a heavy tread. The savage bugling that he and the others had heard last night rose again, causing Spurr's heart, which had been ticking so slowly and sweetly, to begin chuffing and hiccupping.

He snapped his head around to see a large, ginger-brown beast crashing through the forest behind and east of him and his trail mates, maybe a couple of hundred yards away, on the far side of a little ravine running down the slope to their right.

Spurr was about to call the others, but then Boomer, who'd been sleeping with his head bowed toward his chest and his crossed arms, jerked his head up. He gave a painful cry as his neck crackled like a dry branch, and he clapped a gloved hand to the back of it as he turned to see the demon coming down the slope at a slant.

The beast's fur was painted cinnamon by the morning sun filtering through the pine boughs.

The bruin gave a raucous snarl and continued lumbering down through the trees, trampling a juniper shrub in its wake. The shrub crunched and crackled loudly in the morning's quiet air.

Spurr placed his hand on Greta's arm and squeezed gently. The girl lifted her head with a groan and opened her eyes, squinting and blinking sleepily.

"Sorry, girl," the old lawman said. "Trouble."

Spurr pushed off the rock they'd all slept against and found that his legs had no feeling in them. His feet were stiff. He dropped to his knees with a grunt, stretching his lips back from his teeth as pain rocketed through every joint in his old sack of bones.

"Oh my god!" he heard Greta say. She dropped to a knee beside him, wrapped an arm around his waist. "Spurr, can you get up?"

She didn't wait for his reply but, holding his right hand down taut against her breasts, rose, sort of hoisting him with her. He straightened, gritting his teeth.

"Damn, that ground was cold!" Spurr looked past Greta toward the bear still tearing down the mountain.

"Things are about to get a whole lot colder," Boomer said. "It smells us."

"Yeah."

Spurr raked a hand down his face and tugged on his beard. He stepped away from Greta and slid his Starr .44 from its holster. "You two head off to the west. Run and keep on runnin'."

Greta jerked a worried look at him. "What're you gonna do?"

"I'm gonna distract him."

"There ain't no distractin' a bruin on the kill scent, Spurr!" Drago stared at him gravely. "There's only feedin' one."

"Then I'll feed him. Shit, I came to the end of the line yesterday. Last night 'bout done me in."

Spurr looked at Greta, jerked his head to indicate down the hill on his left. "Go, girl! Boomer, take her and haul your freight like you never hauled it before!" He tossed his canteen to Drago. "You might as well take that. I won't be needin' it."

He walked past them both, angling down the slope through the trees on his right.

"Spurr!" Greta lunged toward him.

Drago grabbed her as Spurr wheeled toward them, scowling. "You two get movin'!"

Drago swallowed, glanced toward the bear that had disappeared into the ravine though the bruin could still be heard, cracking brush and groaning savagely, hungrily. Leaves and pine needles rose in his wake.

The outlaw turned back to Spurr. "We're all three in this together, partner."

"How many times I gotta tell you, old

360

man? We ain't partners!" Spurr lunged threateningly toward Drago, who had ahold of Greta's arm, both of them staring worriedly at the old lawman, who threw his gun hand out angrily. "Get movin'. *Now* — before it's too damn *late*!"

Twenty-Nine

Spurr wheeled and began running down the slope slantwise through the pines and scattered, gray, moss-rimmed boulders. He clicked the Starr's hammer back and triggered a shot toward the bruin as he ran.

The bear was just then loping up the near side of the ravine, its hump bulging savagely atop its shoulders. Its cinnamon coat glistened in the sunshine. Just Spurr's luck to run into a rogue bull with a chip on its shoulders.

It was about a hundred yards away and moving down the slope toward Spurr's old position, but the bullet that plumed dust and dead leaves near its front feet gave it pause. Slowing slightly, it looked down the slope toward Spurr, both ears pricking, dark eyes seemingly moving a little closer together.

"Oh, boy," Spurr said, breathing hard as he increased his pace, his sore feet crying out with every step. "Here we go! *Bear bait!*"

He triggered another shot in the direction of the bruin, knowing a .44 slug could never penetrate a hide as tough and as thick as a grizzly's but only piss the beast off more. "Come and get it, you big, ugly, smelly son of a bitch! My meat might be a little chewy but it'll fill the gullet just fine!"

Spurr bounded around a stout, fragrant juniper and continued running down the hill. Behind him, Greta screamed and shouted but a glance over his left shoulder told Spurr that Boomer was leading her off to the northwest.

Spurr paused to lean a shoulder against a birch tree and catch his breath. He glanced up the slope behind him.

The bear was running toward him, looking like a billowy brown rug thrown over a fat horse. The copper in its fur flashed like the sun off a high-mountain lake. The bear's eyes glistened savagely. It shook its head as it ran, lifting its black lips high above the long, yellow, savagely curved fangs.

A glimpse of those fangs made Spurr's loins tingle.

He squeezed off another shot at the bear to keep him coming, and then he pushed off the tree and continued running straight down the slope. His right foot hooked a downed branch, and he flew forward, slamming against the ground on his belly and chest, dropping his pistol.

"Shit!" he bellowed, ignoring the pain shooting through him and reaching for his pistol that was partly covered by bits of pinecones and needles.

As he did, he glanced behind. The bear was now sixty yards away and barreling toward him, coat buffeting in the wind and glistening in the breeze.

Spurr hauled himself to his feet and, despite the agony in every limb, kept running. He had to buy Drago and Greta more time. He had to get as low on the mountain as he could before the bruin overtook him.

When he did, he just hoped the bear made it fast. He'd heard of men being eaten slowly while half-alive and able to watch the big, smelly beast dipping its bloody snout in and out of its quarry's private parts . . .

The thought made Spurr run faster — so fast, in fact, that he was afraid he'd outrun his balance and take a header down the slope and into a boulder. Easy pickings . . .

He could feel the ground bouncing as the beast bounded closer and closer, straight behind him now and closing fast.

He moved out of the trees and into an open area bathed in sunshine. The valley spread out below him, broad and vast. The bear was so close now that Spurr could hear the bruin's heavy panting, the air raking in and out of its lungs with the squawking sounds of dried leather.

Spurr slowed. His heart hammered, but a strange peace fell over him. He stopped and stared out over the tan and lime-green valley opening below him, beneath the spruce-green of the sun-hazed, pine-carpeted opposite slope. The sun was hot on the left side of his face.

He turned toward the bear lunging toward him, so intent on him that it would have taken a deadheading locomotive to cause the bear to swerve from the old lawman's path. But then, its eyes meeting Spurr's, the huge beast skidded to a halt, kicking up dirt and grass and pine needles before it. It slid several feet toward Spurr on its butt before it finally got itself stopped about twenty feet away.

It eyed its prey cautiously, shook its massive head, rippling the thick fur around its neck to which pine needles, dirt and bits of dead leaves clung. The bear's eyes were flat and molasses-colored, speckled with copper. They owned not the slightest hint of mercy, only a depthless, wanton savagery.

It pawed the ground, whipping up a thick

dust cloud speckled with pine needles.

The beast smelled like old piss, the tang of grapefruit and pine. The fetor was so strong that it made the old lawman's eyes water.

Spurr threw his arms up straight above his head, aiming the Starr at the sky. "Come on, you smelly bastard. I'm all yours, an' I hope you choke on me!"

The beast lifted up off its front paws that were easily the size of supper plates, and waddled toward Spurr on its back legs. It lifted its long, black snout toward the sky and loosed its bugling cry, which was so loud that Spurr thought his head would explode. The old man involuntarily backed away from it, squeezing his eyes closed.

The bear's bellow broke off sharply, on the heels of what sounded like a thunder-clap.

Spurr opened his eyes. As the thunderclap echoed, growing shrill as it dwindled, the bear staggered toward Spurr almost drunk-enly, its head wobbling on its massive shoulders. Spurr stumbled backward and fell on his butt at the same time that the bruin fell toward him, piling up on the ground and throwing several shovelfuls of dirt and gravel over Spurr's legs.

Dust wafted around the old lawman, who

sat squeezing his eyes closed and shaking his head against it.

When he opened his eyes again, the bear gave a low groan, turned its head back and forth. Spurr stared down at it. Blood matted the back of its head. It was oozing out around the bruin's head to pool on the short, brown grass, dirt, and red gravel beneath it.

"What in tarnation?" the old lawman said, looking up past the bear to see a short, stocky gent in a long bear coat standing on a flat rock about forty yards behind the beast.

The man was dark-haired, distinctly Indian featured. As he slowly lowered the massive rifle in his hands — a Sharps Big Fifty buffalo gun, if Spurr made his guess — he stretched his lips back from his teeth in a grin.

"Spurr!"

The old lawman turned to see Greta running toward him from upslope on his right. Boomer half ran, half stumbled along behind her, sort of dragging his right ankle as though he'd twisted it. The two canteens flopped against his sides.

"Spurr, you crazy fool!" Greta dropped down before him and threw her arms around his neck, hugging him so tightly he thought she'd crack his ribs, sobbing into his neck.

"Now, now," Spurr said, eyeing the bear lying still behind her and continuing to bleed out on the ground. "There, there."

Greta drew her head away from him. "Are you all right?"

"Fine as frog hair," the old lawman said. "Couldn't be better."

He stared at the Indian standing on the flat rock upslope from him. He spied movement to the Indian's right and turned to see a woman dressed similarly to the man pulling a two-wheeled cart down the slope toward the bear. In the back of the cart, a large wooden bucket rattled with its cargo of a half-dozen knives.

The Indian woman was even shorter than the man, and she was as round as a rain barrel. Straight, coal-black hair hung to her shoulders.

"Who're they?" Spurr asked Greta.

"Your guess is as good as mine," Drago said, limping up, chuckling, as he inspected the bear.

"That man ran past us when we were running down the hill," Greta told Spurr, glancing at the Indian now walking toward them. He wore knee-high, lace-up moccasins and he was still grinning, dark eyes flashing in his copper-skinned face. "The woman was pulling the wagon behind him."

"You good bear bait, white man!" the Indian said, stopping near the bear's outstretched back legs.

He pointed at the bear as he said, "I been huntin' him for couple weeks now. Been killin' folks down in the town." He ran a hand around on his belly covered by the bear fur coat. "Very hungry! Deer, rabbits not enough for him. Human blood taste good to him. Killed the schoolteacher last week — Master Embry, the white folks called him. Dragged him up high on the ridge there, had his meal. They heard big shaggy one there moanin' and groanin' all night long, breakin' bones. Master Embry musta taste very good!"

Greta regarded the grinning Indian distastefully. The Indian woman, sober as a parson's wife and taking no part in the conversation, stopped the cart near the bear and began stropping one of her knives.

Spurr held his hand out to the Indian. "Spurr."

The Indian shook Spurr's hand. "Lincoln."

Spurr was not surprised by the name. It had become the Ute way to name their sons and daughters after prominent people, even prominent white people. "Lincoln, I'd like to thank you for savin' my stringy hide."

"Ah, hell," the Indian said, flushing now as he looked down at the bear. "That's what I do, that's all. Hunt meat for the town yonder, the villages farther out in the mountains. Me an' Opin." He glanced at the Indian woman who'd set one knife down on the cart to begin sharpening another. "She's my woman."

"Market hunter," Drago said, nodding. "But what town are you talkin' about, son?"

"The one there. Green Valley."

Spurr followed Lincoln's glance down the long slope and into the valley. On a flat bench along the side of the opposite ridge, at least a mile, maybe two miles away, there indeed sat a small town.

It was too far away for Spurr to tell much about it except that there were maybe only twelve cabins, a few white tent shacks, and two or three false-fronted frame buildings straddling a wagon trail that curved in from the east and ran on out of the town to the west, climbing farther up the valley.

The town looked little larger than a tobacco sack from this distance, dwarfed as it was by the broad valley and the high, gradual slope on the other side of it.

A great deal of smoke rose from the

town's brick chimneys and tin stove pipes, roiling around the roofs and touched with the gold of the climbing morning sun. As Spurr stared, however, he saw that it wasn't only smoke hovering over the town but steam, as well. The steam seemed to be rising from a rocky slope on the town's far side, near a broad, wood-frame tent.

"Mulligan."

Spurr turned to frown curiously at Lincoln, who stepped up beside Spurr, pointing toward where the steam rose from the rocks near the tent. "Irishman. Mulligan. Steam baths. The water — it boils out of ground. Very healthy, the white folks think." He chuckled as he tapped Spurr's belly with the back of his hand. "Good for an old man's bones, huh, Mr. Spurr?"

" 'Specially for one nearly ate up whole by a bear," said Drago, shaking his head and regarding the old lawman incredulously.

"You got that right," Spurr said. "I could use a smoke and a shot of whiskey, too."

Greta looked warily toward the east, around the far side of the ridge they'd climbed over. "What about our . . . friends?"

THIRTY

"They'll be comin' — that's for damn sure," Drago said as he, Spurr, and Greta made their slow, weary way down the slope toward the little trail town of Green Valley. They'd left Lincoln and Opin dressing out the bear in a businesslike fashion.

Obviously, the husband and wife hunting team had killed their share of game.

"Maybe there's a lawman in the town," Greta said, walking between the two old men. "Someone who can help."

"Doubt it." Spurr was surveying the little town growing before them. "Not much there. What is there is fairly new because I never heard of it before. My guess is it's a little supply camp for the boomtowns deeper in the mountains — the Laramies, the Mummys, and the Medicine Bows. Not enough folks around to support a lawman. Oh, maybe a constable, but even that's doubtful. Certainly no one with the gun savvy to stand against Drago's bunch."

"They ain't my bunch," Boomer said testily.

"Well, they were."

"Well, they ain't no more!"

"Please, you two." Greta looked weary. "I'm too exhausted and hungry and thirsty to listen to anymore of your consarned jawboning. That steam sure looks good, but I'll fall asleep in such hot water and drown. I need a nap."

They were at the bottom of the valley now, a shallow stream trickling over rocks along a line of aspens whose bright yellow leaves littered the ground and the edges of the creek. As Spurr and the others crossed the creek, he looked up the hill toward the town and the steam from the natural hot springs rising on the other side of it.

Although the sun was a lemon drop in the clear, faultless blue sky, the air was cool. It had been bone-splintering cold all night, and Spurr could still feel that cold through every inch of him, as though his very marrow had turned to ice.

"Yeah," was all he said, staring up at the steam rising with the smoke of breakfast fires. He gave a shudder as he thought about stepping into a hot bath with a bottle of whiskey in one hand, a cigar in the other.

As they followed a path up the hill toward the town, a cacophony rose on the hill above them. The sounds resembled buzzards or pigeons fighting over carrion. Spurr lifted his head to see five or six young boys in all manner of rough garb run down the hill toward him, Greta, and Drago. The boys were jostling and yelling, trying to get ahead of each other, obviously excited about something.

A tow-headed, freckle-faced boy of around ten stopped in front of Spurr, and the other six boys ran up behind him, crowding close and regarding the strangers eagerly.

"Did Lincoln get the bear that ate Master Embry?" the towhead asked. "We heard a shot, and one shot's all it usually takes Lincoln. Did he get it? Did he get it?"

"He did at that," Spurr said.

"Oh, boy!" the freckle-faced lad intoned as he ran around Spurr and splashed into the creek, heading for the slope where Lincoln and Opin were dressing the bear. "I wonder if Master Embry'll fall out when they cut the nasty critter open!"

"Nah," said the tallest of the six boys, long arms and legs scissoring as he ran after the towhead. "I'm sure Ole Satan chomped him up good before he swallowed him."

"Yuck!" yelled one of the other lads

splashing wildly across the creek. One of the boys slipped and fell in the stream with an oath but gained his feet quickly, casting a sheepish look back toward Spurr, Greta, and Drago, and then went running through the aspens behind the others.

"Ah, to be young and full of vinegar," Spurr said, and continued up the trail.

He and Greta and Boomer gained the relatively flat area the town had been built on, and entered the village from its east end. They stopped and stared ahead of them, where the dozen or so buildings and a few shabby tents sat on either side of the rutted wagon trail, awash in the high-country sun.

There were two saloons housed in low log shacks, sitting almost straight across the street from each other, but what caught the brunt of Spurr's attention was a two-story, pink brick affair standing in the middle of the town, on the street's left side. The simple, elegant little building was the town's crown jewel.

A diamond in the rough, it was pretentious as hell yet it bespoke a civic optimism in the little supply camp's future. The shingle extending into the street before the place announced the Albuquerque Hotel and Restaurant. The tight, elegant little flophouse, trimmed in Victorian gingerbread and boasting a whitewashed front veranda with two colorful planters hanging beneath the rafters, connoted cotton sheets, thick quilts, and goose-down pillows. The stout but neatly attired and aproned middle-aged lady just now sweeping off the veranda while a black-and-white cat lounged on a near rail in the sun looked like she'd cook a juicy steak, as well. And she likely kept the premises free of bedbugs.

Spurr's old bones cried out for all those comforts.

First thing first, however. A general store was the first building on the right, and Spurr pointed his hat in that direction, bending his tired legs. Greta and Drago followed him up the porch steps, and they all sat down together on the steps, facing the street and leaning back, resting and letting the sun leech into their cold, exhausted bodies.

When Spurr had caught his breath, he pulled off each of his calf-high moccasins in turn and let his swollen stocking feet extend out over the edge of the next step down. Around the toes, the socks were bloody. The feet ached and burned. Blisters had opened, the ooze soaking the bottoms of his socks. He felt as though he'd walked miles over glowing coals.

Greta sat beside him, leaning back against Boomer's knees. She tipped her head back and closed her eyes. She lifted her face abruptly. "Spurr, what about Cochise?"

"Yeah, I know," the old lawman grumbled, staring off toward the ridge cloaked in pines and on the other side of which he'd left his prize roan stallion. "He'll stay where I left him, unless they took him. Either way, I'll find him."

He nibbled his lower lip as he considered the matter of Keneally's gang.

The mercantile's front door opened, and a short, bespectacled man stepped out, clad in a long green apron. "Did he get the bear? Lincoln — did he get the bear?" He stood against the railing, staring up the ridge. "I heard the rifle shot that could have been made by only the Indian's cannon."

"He did at that, sir," Boomer said.

"Oh, there'll be a party in the ole town tonight!" The man whom Spurr assumed was the mercantiler did a little two-step shuffle in his brown brogans and snapped his red armbands. "That bruin has caused all manner of misery around Green Valley over the past several weeks. Ole Satan dragged the schoolmaster out of his wood-shed last Saturday, ate him up on the ridge yonder."

"We heard," Greta said, giving a shudder.

"Lincoln wasn't around, and no one in town felt up to the task of going to Embry's aid, not against a bear as cunning and ferocious as Satan."

The mercantiler danced another shuffling two- or three-step, tapping his soles on the rough pine boards. "But we'll be celebratin' in Green Valley tonight. Mark my words. Miss, I hope you brought your dancin' shoes!" He chuckled and frowned at the hitchrack fronting his place. "Say, where are your horses, anyway?" He glanced at Spurr's bloody feet. "Don't tell me you three *walked* to our fair town!"

Drago groaned as he massaged his own right, bare foot, that ankle resting on his other knee. "We needed a walk to clear our noggins. You got any whiskey in there, mister?"

"And cigars?" Spurr added.

"Why, of course I have both . . . for . . . payin' customers." The mercantiler added that last with a halting, tentative air. The three strangers before him no doubt looked a little raggedy-heeled, trailworn, and empty-pocketed.

Spurr flipped the man a cartwheel. "Bring us three bottles of your best whiskey and a handful of your best cigars. And, tell me,

378

would you recommend the hotel yonder — the Albuquerque?"

"The finest flophouse in northern Colorado, don't ya know." The mercantile chomped down on Spurr's coin and winced, nearly cracking a tooth.

Then he contentedly flipped the coin in the air. "Why, the owner, Fred and Abigail Bertram, who came out West for poor Fred's ailing lungs, built the place after the fashion of their hotel in Memphis. We're all expecting Green Valley to grow considerably once the narrow-gauge railroad is laid through here, serving the mining camps farther up in the Laramies, the Medicine Bows, and the Never Summers."

"Where've I heard that before?" Spurr grumbled.

When the mercantiler had fetched the whiskey and cigars, Spurr uncorked one of the bottles and passed it around to his compatriots before he himself drank. "Not bad," he said, accepting his change from the mercantiler. "Much obliged, friend."

"Where you folks headed?" the man asked, fists on his hips as he stared down at the unlikely threesome.

Spurr gritted his teeth as he pulled on his left moccasin. "Right now, we're headed for a bath in that healthy hot water we seen steamin' up yonder."

"Not me." Greta pushed off the steps and started into the street. "I'm gonna settle for a sponge bath, and then I'm gonna take a long, deep nap. Wake me if we have any visitors — will you, fellas?"

"Sleep well, girl," Spurr said, "and here. Might need that."

He extended one of the bottles to Greta, which she took and hefted in her hand, narrowing an appreciative eye at the old lawman. "Thanks."

Spurr winked. "Don't mention it."

When she'd drifted off, Spurr and Drago finished pulling on their boots and walked around the side of the mercantile, the mercantiler staring after them curiously. The two oldsters found a path that climbed the slope to the tent that housed three large, deep, corrugated tin washtubs.

The man who ran the bathhouse, which, judging by several copper pots and a small maze of clotheslines strung between fir trees, doubled as a laundry, was a lanky, freckled Irishman whom Spurr and Drago found asleep in a Windsor chair parked in the cool sunshine before the tent.

A yellow-covered "dime" novel lay open on his lap; a cold cigar drooped from between his turkey lips. A scruffy-looking little poodle slept in a tight wooly ball beneath his chair until, hearing the strangers approach, he came out to bark and nip at the pilgrims' ankles.

The bathhouse manager woke, ambled over to scoop the feisty critter up in his arms, and said, "What's your pleasure, buckos? You both look like a couple of ore drays ran over you and then backed over ya to squeeze the rest of your oozin's out!" He laughed and extended a suntanned, freckled hand. "Jeff Mulligan at your service! I usually gotta couple girls around the place to spice things up, but Margie and Hannah done hightailed it out of the mountains in fear of the winter's first snow. So I reckon all I can offer is a bath — but the best, hottest, healthiest bath in the whole Front Range, and that ain't blarney!"

"That's the water down there, eh?" Spurr looked over to where salty-smelling steam slithered up out of the near rocks, past a sleepy-looking burro that stood hangheaded in the shade of a gnarled cedar. Four empty wooden buckets hung from the wooden pack frame strapped to the beast's back.

"Elixir of the Gods of the Mountains, my friend!" Mulligan laughed and led the bucket-laden burro down toward the steam, calling behind him, "Go ahead and make yourselves comfortable in the tent, gentlemen. Me an' my sweet Rosy will be back in two jangles of a whore's bell!"

The Irishman continued down the path toward the springs, the little poodle trotting along beside the burro, stopping occasionally to sniff and to lift one of his hind legs on a shrub or a rock.

Spurr set the bottles down on a bench and then sat on the bench himself and began stripping off his clothes, starting with the mackinaw. Boomer did the same. When they were down to their stiff, sweat-crusted balbriggans, socks, neckerchiefs, and hats, Spurr gave the outlaw a cigar.

"There you go — don't tell me I never done nothin' for you, Boomer. Whiskey and a cigar from the man who's been hopin' you was dead for nigh on the past fifteen years."

Spurr scratched a match to life on the seat of his canvas trousers lumped beside him on the bench, and extended it so Boomer could light his cigar. Puffing smoke, the old outlaw chuckled and leaned back against a post.

While Spurr lit his own cigar, Boomer said, "You saved my life, Spurr. I mean, of course, you almost got me killed initially, by not letting me go, but you just saved my life up there on that ridge."

"Nope." Spurr blew smoke in the cool air around his head and tossed the match in the dirt. "I saved Greta's life. Just so happens I saved yours in the bargain, but them's were the cards I was dealt. St. Pete'll find it in his heart to forgive me that one transgression."

"Shit, you know what, Spurr?"

Spurr popped the cork on the bottle. "What?"

Drago was watching Mulligan fill his wooden buckets at the springs. The old Irishman and the burro looked like ghosts inside the billowing, sunlit steam. The little poodle was a ways off, digging for a gopher.

"I think you an' me ain't all that different. That's why we was friends once. I think you might have gone my way under similar circumstances."

"What circumstances is that?"

"The right offer."

"You mean the right offer to join a band of cold-blooded killers and train robbers?" Spurr shook his head and took a deep pull from the whiskey bottle. "No, I don't think so, Boomer. It takes a special kind of weak man to do that. Me, I'd prefer to make an honest livin' as opposed to a *dis*honest one."

Boomer looked at him, scratching at a

mole at a corner of his mouth, and arching the brow over his good eye. "How can you be so sure what you'd do if the right offer came along?"

"I know," Spurr said, handing Boomer the bottle. "I just know, Boomer. Don't try to take that away from me, 'cause you can't. I just know. It ain't that I didn't have my own offers and opportunities. Where I traveled, lawdoggin', a man could do what he wanted. I chose to do what my badge and my own good conscience bid me to do."

He shook his head and watched Mulligan leading the burro and the splashing, steaming buckets back toward the tent. "I'm no saint. But I was a good lawman, by god. And I got that to take to the grave with me."

Drago took a deep pull from the bottle, glaring at Spurr. He pulled the bottle down, swallowed, blinked his good eye, and said in a sharp, caustic tone, "Well, good for you!" He rose and began skinning angrily out of his underwear. "Come on, Paddy. I'm freezin' my ass off out here!"

THIRTY-ONE

When Mulligan had filled his and Drago's tubs in the tent, which sat about six feet apart, Spurr skinned out of his balbriggans and asked the Irishman to haul a load of water down to the Albuquerque Hotel.

"Fill a tub for a pretty young blonde named Greta." Spurr winked and tossed the man two silver dollars.

"A pretty girl named Greta. You got it, bucko!"

The Irishman, the poodle and the burro ambled back toward the springs, Mulligan whistling happily for the unexpected business. Spurr stepped into the soothingly hot water, sucking a sharp breath.

He continued sucking that breath as he slowly lowered himself into the murky-gray, salty liquid that sent steam snakes slithering into the chill air of the tent. The tent was open so that the bathers could sit and soak and stare out over the roofs of the little trail town. Spurr sat down and drew his knees up, leaning back and curling his toes at the bottom of the tub.

They stung luxuriously as the hot, salty water cleaned out the scrapes and blisters.

Spurr glanced up to see that he was still wearing his hat. He chuckled as he tossed the hat onto the bench sitting to his right and on which the rest of his clothes were piled, and sat back once more, puffing the cigar in his teeth. Drago splashed around in his own tub for a time, and then the old outlaw grabbed his cigar off the bench to his left and looked at the coal.

Reluctantly, still miffed after the previous turn of their conversation, he asked for a light. Spurr chuckled and gave the man his cigar, and when Boomer had his own cigar going once more, he sat back in the tub and blew the smoke out over the sun-washed town.

"I expect we'll be forkin' trails here," the old outlaw said, cutting his cautious eye over to Spurr as though to see how the old lawman took the statement.

"I 'spect."

"What's that?" Drago said, skeptical. "I couldn't hear ya. My ears is still ringin' from all the gunfire."

Spurr rolled the stogie from one corner of

his mouth to the other, watching a small wagon pulled by a lean mule and driven by a bearded gent in buckskins roll along the main street of Green Valley. The wagon was just visible over the rooftops.

Several shopkeepers and saloon customers had drifted out of their stores and watering holes to chin on the boardwalks lining the street. They gestured and seemed generally excited. Something told Spurr that the news about the dead bear had blown through Green Valley, causing a mild uproar. He thought he could hear piano music emanating from one of the saloons.

Spurr turned to Drago, who sat back in his tub, scowling at the old lawman. "I said you can do whatever the hell you damn well please, Drago." Spurr picked up the bottle sitting on the ground between them, took a drink, and set the bottle back down.

"That's it, then? You ain't gonna try to bring me in?"

"I wouldn't need to *try,* Boomer. If I wanted to bring you in, I *would.* But the plain truth of it is, you're no longer worth my time. As far as I and the U.S. government is concerned, you died back in the canyon where Greta was savaged, and I done turned in my badge. I got bigger fish to fry."

387

"You ain't still plannin' on goin' after Keneally, are ya?"

Spurr flicked ashes from his cigar; they sizzled in the water, which was cooling rapidly. "I do indeed."

"Well, you're even dumber than you look, then. Dumb men don't learn from their mistakes. Or did you forget what we just been through — climbin' over a ridge to wriggle away from them boys and almost got ate up by ole Satan!"

"I'm gonna rent a horse, if there's one to be rented here in Green Valley. If not, I'll *borrow* one. Then I'll be goin' after Keneally." Spurr glanced at Boomer. "You do what you have to do to keep Greta from comin' after me. Take her out of the mountains, get her put up safe somewhere. After you do that, I don't care what you do or where you go."

"You can't possibly think that you alone can bring that gang to heel, Spurr!"

"No, but I can cut off the beast's head. By that I mean drill Keneally right between his eyes." Spurr glared at Boomer and tapped his index finger against the bridge of his nose. "And then I'll drill as many more o' them sons o' bitches as I can before we all go dancin' off to hell together."

Boomer slowly shook his head. "You got a

388

silly sense of things. And that's against the law, you know? That sounds like vigilantism to me, Marshal Spurr!"

Sitting back in his tub, Spurr puffed on his stogie and said, "Well, I'm due. And so is Greta." He heaved and hoisted and cursed himself to a standing position, the lukewarm water rolling off his pale, sinewy frame. "In the meantime, I'm gonna go fetch me a steak and get some sleep. I'm gonna need it."

"Well, hell — I'm comin' with ya, since we're all made up an' all!" Boomer rose from his own soapy water, grinning. "I'll even buy . . . if'n you're not too good to accept a gift from a notorious outlaw, that is . . ."

Spurr narrowed a serious eye at Boomer. "You just get Greta out of these mountains to safety, you hear?"

Boomer had just stepped out of his tub and was drying himself with a towel provided by the Irishman. He held Spurr's gaze for several beats, and then he grinned again. "Say, I think you're gone for that girl." A pensive cast stole over his eye. A longing sadness shaped his lips inside his grizzled black beard.

He said, "Oh, to be young again, eh, partner?"

■ ■ ■ ■

Spurr and Drago ate steaks with all the trimmings in the Albuquerque's dining room. Spurr ordered the persnickety and disapproving Mrs. Bertram to deliver a steak to Greta's room, as well, and the woman did so with a caustic chuff.

The middle-aged, full-hipped woman who ran the place with her husband, who rattled around in the kitchen, was candidly disapproving of her two raggedy, unshaven, old customers. In spite of their baths, they no doubt had the smell of the owlhoot trail about them, Spurr surmised.

Mrs. Bertram disapproved of the whiskey and tobacco they partook of liberally in her white-clothed dining parlor appointed with polished silver, an ancient grandfather clock, brocade drapes, and potted flowers hanging from the ceiling. Doubtless, she also suspected something amiss about the circumstances of the pretty girl she was housing upstairs and who'd not only had a bath delivered to her, but now a meal, as well.

After their meal, Spurr and Drago rented rooms from Mrs. Bertram, who kept her lips pursed as each man signed his name in the guestbook. When she'd dropped their coins in a box under the varnished oak desk, Spurr said, "What about the keys?"

"No keys on any of the doors," the old woman said with a haughty air, in a thick Southern accent, spreading her pudgy hands and smiling superciliously. "I find that men are more apt to behave themselves if the doors remain *unlocked* at all times."

Drago gave a caustic chuff. "Well, ain't you just —"

"Come on, Boomer," Spurr said, turning the man by an arm and nudging him toward the stairs. "Time for your beauty rest."

When Spurr and Drago parted ways on the second floor, Spurr went into the room the old woman had assigned him, room eight, and stripped as quickly as he could all the way down to his birthday suit. He left his clothes and his guns piled on the floor at the foot of the double bed. He'd no sooner crawled under the soft sheets and quilts and rested his head back on the deep feather pillow than his eyelids drooped down over his eyes and he was out like a blown lamp.

He doubted he'd ever slept so deeply, dreamlessly. It was like being wrapped in warm feathers, a cool breeze spiced with peppermint cat-footing across his aching brain.

When he woke and lifted his head in response to some unidentified sound — or was it his lawman's sense of imminent danger? — it took him several seconds to remember where he was and how he'd gotten there. The windows flanking the bed were both dark.

Noise of raucous revelry — men yelling, women laughing, pianos pattering, and fiddles fiddling — rose from the street outside. He could also tell from the sounds that people were dancing in the street. Smells emanating from that direction were of roasting bear. Spurr knew the smell.

The villagers were having a fest to celebrate the demise of Satan!

Spurr smacked his lips and ran a hand down his face. He'd just flopped back down against his pillow, intending to go on sleeping until morning, when there was a light tap on his door. He realized then that it had been a similar tap, not the din from the street, that had awakened him.

It took him a moment to find his voice. He wished he'd hauled his guns up closer to the bed. Ready to throw the covers back and leap for both pistols resting amongst his clothes, he said, "Who's there?"

"You awake?" Greta asked softly on the other side of the door.

Before Spurr could respond, the door latch clicked. The door came open, hinges squeaking quietly.

Spurr saw her slender figure silhouetted against the lamplight in the hall. Her hair spilled across her shoulders, flashing golden in the light just before she closed the door. Spurr also saw that she was holding a blanket around her shoulders. But as the door closed, he saw in the light from the villagers' cook fire pushing through the windows behind him, the blanket drop to the floor. It made a sibilant sound as it piled up at her feet.

Naked, Greta walked around the side of the bed, and threw the covers back. He could smell the intoxicating smell of woman about her, scrubbed of the smoke and horse smells and all the other trail smells, as she slid in beside him and drew the covers up to her bare shoulders.

She turned toward him, tenting the covers across her shoulders. Her hair hung down over her breasts, which sloped toward the sheets as she snuggled against him.

"Hold on, girl," Spurr said, finally finding his shock-pinched voice again. "One of us must be dreamin', and if it's you, I do believe you're sleepwalkin', honey!"

Greta laughed. He felt her warm lips part as she nuzzled his shoulder. "I got lonely, Spurr."

"You did?"

"Mm-hmm."

She wrapped an arm across his belly as she let her head sink down against his pillow, her face only an inch from his. He could smell her warm breath on his cheek. Her arm was warm and yielding across his waist. He knew that what felt like a tender flower petal pressed up against his ribs was one of her nipples. He tried to steel himself against the sensation of her, but he'd be damned if he didn't feel an erection coming on — hard and fast.

It was damned uncomfortable.

"Greta, I'm old."

"Older than the damn hills," she said with a humorous snort against his neck, squirming against him.

"You get the idea, then."

"What idea's that, Spurr?"

"That I'm old enough to be your father. Possibly even old enough to be your *grandfather . . .* though that's a liberal estimation." He chuckled.

"Oh, shut up about that, Spurr. I just got to missing you, that's all. No one knows how to take care of a girl like you do. And I don't think there's any man half your age any better or tougher than you are, neither."

"Be that as it may . . ."

She drew her arm tighter around him. She groaned as she snuggled harder against him, sliding one of her long, cool legs over his left one. "I didn't come in here to make love. I was just lonesome and wanted to be near you and to snuggle up against you" — he felt her lips part in a sexy smile against his neck as she whispered into his ear — "but I can see it's gonna happen."

She lowered her hand to his half erection. Her touch was light, gently probing, fondling.

Spurr opened his mouth to draw a heavy breath.

"Greta, did you forget what happened to you?"

"No, I didn't forget. And I don't intend to let you stick this ax handle in me, neither." She wagged his dong and smiled. She was whispering in his ear so that he thought he could feel her warm breath sweeping all through his head, straightening out and soothing the kinks and aches in his brain. "But I can do other things."

She gave a husky laugh as she rolled on top of him, straddling him, wrapped her arms around his neck and lowered her face very slowly to his. That one eye crossed as she very gently pecked his swollen nose.

"I'm not hurting you, am I?" she asked.

"Oh, no."

She pressed her lips to his. She moved her lips around on his mouth and then she pressed them more firmly against his, kissing him passionately. Of course, there could be no real passion in it — not for a girl her age kissing a man his age. But she knew her business — Spurr would give her that.

If it weren't for all his aches and pains, including the iron crab in his chest, he'd swear he was thirty, thirty-five years younger, taking a tumble with a girl his own age. He ran his hands down her arms and across her back and up and down her sides. He brushed his thumbs against the sides of her breasts that bulged out between them as she mashed them against his chest.

God, what smooth, supple, tender skin.

She pulled her head away from his. Her eyes had a coy, smoky cast. The corners of her mouth rose as she scuttled down his body slightly, lowered her head to his chest, and kissed him, rolling her face around in the tangle of hair along his breastbone.

Spurr's breath came raspier. He grew warmer. His pecker grew harder.

She continued to drop lower and lower on him until he felt her hair raking like satin across his nether region, and then he felt the warm moistness of her mouth closing over him. He groaned as he drew another breath deep into his lungs, felt his heart quicken. He chuckled at the thought that this girl might finally drive him over the edge, kill him.

What the hell. What she was doing to him down there — oh, so excruciatingly slowly and gently, using her tongue as much as her lips — caused him not to care about one other damn thing in the world. For the first time in a long time, he didn't feel the darkness of an open coffin resting at the edge of a coal-black grave staring him in the face.

She finished him and cleaned him with a sponge and then they slept curled together like a pair of cats in the sun, oblivious of the cacophony rising from the street outside the hotel.

Someone hammered Spurr's door twice loudly.

Spurr sat bolt upright in bed, reaching for his Starr .44 until he remembered that he foolishly hadn't wrapped the cartridge belt and holster around the bedpost on the bed's right side, like he usually did. Greta gasped and sat back against the headboard, holding the bedcovers over her breasts.

Boomer's voice thundered on the other side of the door. "You two awake in there?"

He didn't wait for a response. He threw the door open and entered the room, a large shadow standing at the foot of the bed, bending his head slightly toward Spurr and Greta. "I just figured out what ole Keneally was sayin'. He was sayin', 'Sins of the father.' "

"Sins of the father?" Spurr and Greta both said at nearly the same time.

"Last night, from down in the canyon — that's what he was yellin'," Boomer said, his voice quaking with emotion. "That dung beetle's goin' after my daughter!"

THIRTY-TWO

Spurr tossed his covers aside, leaving Greta covered beside him, and dropped his feet to the floor.

While Boomer stood at the foot of the bed, cursing under his breath and wringing his hands together, the old lawman lit the lamp on the dresser. He splashed whiskey into a water glass and handed the glass to Boomer.

"There you go — drink that. Settle you down. You been havin' a nightmare, Boomer."

Aware of his nakedness, Spurr looked around for his longhandles. Boomer threw half the drink back. "Ain't no nightmare. I been layin' there next door, hearin' you two carryin' on, and then for some reason I got to thinkin' about that last thing Keneally yelled up the ridge at us. Sins of the father."

"What's this about a daughter?" Spurr said as he stepped into his balbriggans.

Boomer looked around, closed the door, and sat in a chair in a corner near the foot of the bed. The chair squawked beneath his weight. He leaned forward, scrubbing a hand through his thin, tangled hair. He wore only his balbriggans, socks, and knotted neckerchief.

"Didn't know I had one, neither," he said, "till a few years ago. Her mother sent me a letter before she died of a cancer back in Missouri, told me about Sonja. Said I sowed the seed before I lit out buffalo huntin' an' we first met up, Spurr. Before we headed to Texas and the Brasada country. *Before* the banker."

"What the hell are you — a Brahman seed bull?"

"Anyways, the girl — Sonja — was married and had a family in a little mining camp called Longmont."

"That's just south of Camp Collins," Spurr said. "Been through there many times."

"I was through there once, a few months after Mayleene sent me the letter about her dyin' and about the daughter I had and didn't know about. I met her — Sonja. She's got a good man, a good family, but they're dirt poor an' her boy, Irvin — their only child — has some sort o' bone defect, can't walk too good."

"I don't understand," Greta said, holding her covers to her breasts with one hand and throwing her hair straight back over her head with the other hand. "What does . . . ?"

"Sonja's got the money. I sent it to her after that last holdup and then I headed into the Medicine Bows to try to throw Keneally and the others off my trail."

Spurr ran a skeptical hand down his patch-bearded face, blinking uncertainly as he studied the one-eyed man before him.

Greta said, "How does Keneally know about Sonja?"

"When I visited her, I told Keneally and the rest of the gang about her. About havin' a daughter I never knew about. Shit, that ain't something a man wants to keep under his hat. I had to tell someone, and them fellas was *my* fellas then. My gang. I told 'em about it."

Boomer bounded up from his chair, eye wild. "And Keneally figured out I sent her the money! At least, he guessed right, goddamnit!" Boomer tossed the last of his drink back and threw the glass against the red-and-gold-papered wall behind Spurr. The glass struck the wall with a ringing boom and shattered and rained to the floor.

"Boomer!" Spurr said, glancing back at

the mess. "You're gonna get that Bertram bat on our asses!"

Boomer looked at Spurr, his lone eye dark and grave. "We gotta get to Longmont, Spurr. We gotta leave right now. Tonight. They got a day's head start, and it's only a three-, four-day ride. They'll kill Sonja. They'll kill her whole family!"

Spurr leaned back against the dresser, thinking about all that Boomer had told him.

He shook his head. "We won't be able to rent horses tonight, Boomer. Even if we could, it's too damn dark to ride this broken country. We'd likely injure one of the horses and cook our gooses worse than they already been cooked." Again, he shook his head. "No, we gotta wait for morning. We'll stock up on supplies then, too."

The old outlaw stood stoop-shouldered before Spurr, glaring at the old lawman. "Sonja — she don't care for me. But she's all I got. I'll find a horse tonight if I have to steal one. I'll be pullin' out. You do what you have to do, Spurr."

With that, Drago opened the door and strode into the hall, leaving the door half open behind him.

"Goddamnit, Boomer," Spurr said when he was gone. He ran a hand over his face, blinking his eyes in frustration. "Shit!"

"I reckon we don't have no choice," Greta said, throwing the covers back and dropping her feet to the floor.

"I reckon I don't have no choice." Spurr stood holding his britches in one hand, pointing at the girl with the other. "You, young lady, are staying here. No more trailin' for you!"

Doing nothing to cover herself, she whipped an exasperated look at him. "Bullshit! I started this trail, and I aim to ride to the end of it!"

Haughtily, she picked up the blanket she'd dropped earlier, wrapped it around her shoulders, and stomped across the hall to her own room, the door of which she slammed behind her.

Knowing he'd lost another battle, Spurr merely cursed again and continued dressing.

"How much for that one there?" Spurr asked the mercantiler, whose name was Lloyd Gault. "That Winchester on the rack yonder."

"That one's twenty dollars," Gault said crisply.

Spurr had found the man in one of the saloons with a whore on his knee, and he wasn't happy about having to open his shop this late at night, nearly midnight and in the middle of the town's still-rollicking celebration of Satan's demise.

Not only was Gault grumpy, he was bleary-eyed from drink. It had appeared he'd been about to take the whore upstairs when Spurr had found him, so he was chewing that frustration, as well.

"Haul it down here an' let me take a look at it."

"You sure you can afford that weapon?" Gault asked with a weary, impatient air, looking Spurr up and down. "It's the latest model, and I won't come down on it!"

"Haul it down here!"

When Gault had climbed from a stool onto the back counter lit by two hanging lanterns, and plucked the Winchester from its rack mounted beside a buffalo bull's head, he climbed down off the stool and set the gun on the counter. Spurr didn't bother to inspect the weapon, nor the slightly older model already lying on the counter beside it and the two gunnysacks he'd ordered the mercantiler to stuff with trail supplies, including a cook pan and a coffeepot.

"All right, I'll take a hundred rounds of .44 shells, and then you can tally me up," Spurr said.

Gault rested his fists on the counter and

eyed Spurr skeptically. Outside, the raucous celebration could still be heard. Umber light from the bonfire over which the bear had been cooked danced in the dark street.

"You must be headed for the high country, eh? For the winter? Gets mighty cold up there, an' you . . . well, frankly, you look like you might be better off down here where the snow don't get so deep an' the fires burn a little warmer."

Spurr glanced out the window at the front of the store. Drago and Greta were fetching the three of them horses from a livery barn and, probably, another peeved businessman. They'd be here soon to load up the trail supplies. Spurr looked at Gault and scrunched up his eyes that were still discolored from his broken, swollen nose. "Mister, will you just tally up the damages for me, so I can get out of your hair and you can get the hell out of mine?"

Gault sighed and reached for his notepad.

"You got the whiskey, didn't you?"

"Yes, I got the whiskey," Gault said, resting his hand on a bundle sitting near a jar of cinnamon sticks while he began penciling the figures on a notepad.

Spurr rummaged around in his pockets until he found a government pay voucher. Gault wasn't happy about the voucher.

Most businessmen weren't, and Spurr didn't blame them, because they had to go to the work of paying for postage to send the voucher to Denver for reimbursement, which usually took months. Nevertheless, by the time Drago and Greta clomped up to the mercantile from the west, trailing a saddled livery mount for Spurr, the old lawman and Gault had hauled the gear he'd purchased out onto the mercantile's front porch.

"You get rifles?" Drago asked, swinging down from his saddle.

"Yes, I got rifles. One for each of you. I'll stick with the Starr. I don't understand how Winchester has remained in business, grinding out the crap he has!"

"Plenty of ammo?"

"Plenty of ammo. Now, will ya shut up and help me get this stuff on the horses before I change my mind and go back to bed an' sleep till morning?"

"Good lord," Gault said from the porch as Spurr and Drago began tying the gunnysacks to their rented saddles on their rented horses, "are you taking that poor girl out on the trail this late at night?"

"It's all right," Greta said, strapping one of the gunnysacks over the bedroll behind her saddle. "I'm here by choice. I wouldn't trust these two fellas on the trail by themselves. No tellin' what kind of trouble they'd get into."

"Say, don't I know you?" Gault said. "I thought I recognized you before. Didn't you work up at Diamond Fire for Reymont an' Chaney?"

Greta shut the man up with a look. "That was a long time ago, mister. I'm done with that awful place." She slid the new Winchester into her saddle boot, hardening her jaws as she added, "I'll be powderin' a fresh trail soon, just as soon as I take care of some unfinished *business.*"

Thirty-Three

Cliff Merriam worked the action on the brand-new Winchester repeater, holding it up close to his ear, almost tranquilized by how smoothly the hammer and the trigger and the springs in the housing between them worked together. The impressive piece had a stimulating smell — at least stimulating to a man like Cliff Merriam, who had never owned a new gun in his life.

That smell was newly forged iron, gun oil, and the varnish coating the walnut stock.

Cliff eased the hammer back down to the firing pin and held the gun flat side up in front of him, gazing admirably at the brass-chased receiver and the scrolled factory engraving.

"Nice gun — eh, Cliff?" said the owner of the Longmont Mercantile and Feed Company, George Canfield, who was dusting off the tops of the flour, meal, and candy barrels running along beneath the big windows at the front of the store.

Merriam's eight-year-old son, Irvin, stood near Canfield, leaning against one of the barrels, taking his weight off his game right leg over which he was forced to wear a steel brace. The boy was eyeing the rock and chocolate candy in the barrels before him.

"Dang nice," Merriam said, studying the gun, feeling his heart quicken. His hand wrapped around the gun grew warm.

"Winchester continues to produce the best rifles on the market." Canfield continued running his feather duster across the barrels. "Shall I wrap it up for you?" He chuckled. "Sorry, can't take credit for it. Not on one of the new Winchesters!"

Canfield laughed again.

Cliff felt his face heat up, peeved by the mercantiler's snide demeanor. He knew Canfield wasn't trying to be a smart aleck. With good reason, Canfield didn't think that Cliff Merriam — a poor shotgun rancher with a small spread northwest of town, in the shadow of Longs Peak, could afford such a prized weapon. Few men except for the half-dozen larger ranchers in the county could afford the new Winchester. Certainly not those of Cliff's ilk. Not one with a boy who'd been born with a bone disease and needed to see a doctor in

Denver every few months and would probably require surgery on his leg soon.

"Wrap it up for me."

Canfield continued dusting, his back to Cliff.

"Wrap it up for me," Cliff repeated. "And I'll take a box of shells for it."

Canfield looked over his shoulder at Cliff, his dark brows forming a bull's horns of surprise. His lips quirked up and down, as though he wasn't sure if he was being toyed with. "You're not serious."

"Sure, I am." Cliff looked at Irvin, who had turned around to stare down the mercantile's center aisle in wide-eyed shock at his father. "Son, what kind of candy would you like?"

The boy just stared at him, lips parted, looking especially frail in the wool coat that was a hand-me-down from the neighbors, and which was still a size-and-a-half too large for his slender frame. The thick red scarf his mother, Cliff's wife, Sonja, had wrapped around his neck didn't help matters. He wore a rabbit fur cap with ear flaps, and that and the scarf nearly hid his pale, rosy-lipped face. The boy looked like he'd topple under all that weight at any moment.

"Canfield, give Irvin a sack. Boy, you fill it half full, all right? That oughta get you through a week or two of candy-chewin', as long as you go easy." Cliff winked at his beloved son and pressed a finger to his mustached lips. "Let's make this our secret — all right? No tellin' Mom. She'd likely take the strap to both of us."

"You mean it, Pa?" Irvin said.

"I wouldn't tease about such an important thing as candy. And pick yourself out a new pair of gloves. That right one of yours there has a hole in the finger. You can't spend the winter with a hole in your glove, or you're liable to freeze that finger plumb off!"

When Canfield had given the boy a paper sack and a scoop, he walked down the center aisle and around behind the counter, looking at Cliff as though the rancher had grown an extra head. "What's happening here, Cliff? I told you I couldn't extend credit on the Winchester. Mighty expensive gun. You already owe nearly as much as what it's worth. I understand these have been tough years."

The tall, dark, clean-shaven mercantiler glanced at another gun rack along the cluttered mercantile's east wall. "Why don't you pick out one of the older rifles. There's a Spencer repeater over there that Galvin Davis had —"

"I don't need credit, Cliff. In fact, I'd like

to pay off what I owe you. Tally the rifle and the boy's gloves and candy and a box of .44 shells around the same snubbin' post as the rest of this stuff, and we'll take this green bronc to church." He chuckled at the age-old expression. "That's one of my pa's own sayin's."

Cliff set the new rifle on the zinc-covered plank counter, between a jar of pickled eggs to the left and cigar rack on the right. He took a handful of cigars out of a box marked Old Havana *Imperiales,* and set them amongst the bundles of coffee, sugar, and flour that he'd set out earlier and which had originally brought him to the store.

Canfield knit his dark brows over his skeptical brown eyes as he glanced at the cigars. "Those are twenty-five cents apiece, Cliff. I only sell 'em because Ben Walker buys a handful every time he comes to town."

Ben Walker was one of the richest ranchers east of the northern Front Range, and he had controlling interests in nearly half the businesses in Longmont. Walker walked tall and cast a long shadow in these parts.

"Add four *Imperiales* to the tally, George."

"My gosh, Cliff, what'd you do — rob a bank?" Canfield chuckled and shook his head as he grabbed a pencil to begin figuring up the bill.

"No, I haven't stooped to that level yet. Another hard winter and I'm liable to, though."

Cliff pulled a thick wad of folded greenbacks out of the pocket of his deerskin, wool-lined coat, which Sonja had sewn for him after they were first married and had recently moved out to this high, cold winter country from where they'd both grown up in Missouri. He saw Canfield eyeing the roll of bills. That made him flush with pride despite his natural inclination to self-effacement.

It was just that he'd never had a roll that size, and it made him, for the first time in his life, feel special and important and like he was worth something. He knew that money shouldn't make him feel that way, but he'd be damned if it didn't, just the same. His had been a hard life. That glint in Irvin's eyes as the boy limped down the center aisle toward the counter, the bulging paper sack in his hand, only made Cliff glow all the brighter.

"You got half a sack there, boy?"

Irvin held the bag up, his blue eyes round as saucers, a tentative smile on his lips, as though he wasn't quite sure his father wasn't funning with him, though he knew that Cliff would never have done something so cruel.

Irvin shook the sack and grinned delightedly. "Half a sack, Pa."

"Put it up here and we'll have Mr. Canfield weigh it."

Irvin dragged his stiff right leg along the aisle. The metal cage shone in the sunshine angling through the front and side windows. The sight of the contraption that was supposed to keep the knee from shifting and giving the boy's leg some strength, never failed to break Cliff's heart. The boy tossed the bag onto the counter beside the Winchester, and ran his glove with the hole in it down the frame, caressing the varnished forestock with the finger exposed by the hole.

"Wow — she's a beauty! Ain't it awful expensive, Pa?"

"Oh, it's not so bad." Turning to Canfield, he said, glancing down at the cash in his hand, "Sold a few more cows than I figured this fall. That mining camp up the Big Thompson needed beef to get its miners through the winter."

The lie took away some of Cliff's pride he felt at having this much money to spend on himself and his son, but he felt compelled to explain where it had come from, even if his explanation hadn't been the truth. Word of the thick greenback roll would likely spread, he realized with a rake of trepidation across the back of his neck. He hoped it wouldn't get back to Sonja. That was doubtful. Their ranch was pretty remote, and Sonja was so busy around the ranch that she didn't make it to town very often.

Besides, he'd soon tell her about the money. He'd have to. He was just biding his time, enjoying the extra load while he could.

Canfield scribbled a figure at the bottom of the notepad. "Well, if you're going to pay off your account, Cliff, the total comes to fifty-three dollars and twenty-five cents."

"Wow!" Irvin said, shifting his gaze from the wad of green in his father's hand to the bag of candy, seeming certain that the candy was about to be put right back in the barrels it had come from.

Cliff counted out the cash, separated it from the rest, stuffed the rest back into his coat pocket, and then counted each of the other bills as he laid them onto Canfield's open ledger book. He snapped down the last bill, dug into his pocket, and propped a quarter down on top of the bills, giving it a celebratory spin.

"There you go, George! Free an' clear!"

"Yes, sir, free an' clear, Cliff," Canfield said, shuttling his startled gaze from the cash to Cliff's smiling face. "Yes, sir, free an' clear. You fellas need any help out to your wagon?"

"Nah, we got it. Irvin, there's your new gloves, and there's your candy. You only get two, three pieces at the most on the ride home, so don't go sneakin' any extra!"

"I won't, Pa!" the boy said, glowing at the sack of candy that his father handed down to him, and dipping a hand through the top.

"And don't eat your quota before we even get back on the trail!"

"I won't, Pa!" the boy said around the chunk of cinnamon stick he'd just bitten off.

Cliff and Canfield laughed as Cliff hauled his gear off the counter, liking the feel of the Winchester in his hand, and crossed to the front of the store, the boy dragging his bad leg along behind him.

Cliff called, "Thanks, George. Probably won't see you till after Thanksgivin'!"

"Have a safe trip home, fellas. Hope you like that Winchester, Cliff. Tell your ma howdy for me — will you, Irvin!"

"You got it, Mr. Canfield!" the boy said, hobbling out the front door that his father held open for him and out onto the mercantile's broad loading dock.

Their orange-painted buckboard farm wagon sat in the street below the dock, a beefy paint horse whom Irvin had named Jabber in the traces. The horse shook its head in eager anticipation of getting back on the trail to their ranch as Cliff walked down the loading dock steps.

The rancher set the foodstuffs in the buckboard's box with the wheel he'd had repaired, along with a bolt of muslin for Sonja. He wrapped the rifle in a blanket and stowed it beneath the wagon's spring seat, with his hide-wrapped canteen and the old Spencer repeater he always carried in an ancient, cracked sheepskin scabbard that was worn clean through in places.

Cliff helped Irvin down the last few loading dock steps and lifted the boy up over the wagon's right front wheel into the seat padded with a heavy striped saddle blanket. Cliff inspected Jabber's driving bridle and harness, making sure all the straps were secure, and he climbed into the driver's seat beside the boy, and released the brake.

"Here we go, Jabber. Let's go home, ole son!"

The horse leaned into its hame, and the wagon rattled off down the broad main street of Longmont. At the west end of town, Cliff turned the horse onto the northern trail, pinching his hat brim to the jehu of the Golden–Camp Collins stage just entering town from the west, and put Jabber into a spanking trot.

It was a cool, clear day, the blue sky absolutely faultless. It had been a good morning for the two-hour ride to town, and it looked like the afternoon would be just as nice for the two-hour ride back to the Merriam Circle Slash M. Cliff settled back in his seat, both boots on the dashboard, and held the ribbons lightly in his gloved hands.

Irvin sat beside him, slowly chewing his candy and watching the prairie with its stirrup-high buffalo grass slide past. Out here on the prairie, with the Front Range jutting tall and dramatic and already limned with bright fields of fresh white snow jouncing around to their left, Cliff spotted several clumps of Ben Walker's copper-colored, glossy-coated cattle, driven down out of the mountains for the winter.

Cliff couldn't help eyeing the blooded stock with envy. Maybe someday he'd be able to afford such Durham bulls as the ones Ben Walker imported from Scotland to inject higher quality, shorthorn beef blood into Cliff's own stock that was still mostly of Texas longhorn origin and less able than the Durhams to weather the harsh winters of these high, northern climes.

A half hour after leaving Longmont, Cliff turned the wagon onto the left tine of the fork in the trail, avoiding the right tine that swung north and east toward Camp Collins, and headed west into the foothills. Here the trail grew steeper and more rugged, with pine-stippled buttes, red stone dikes, and cedar-studded mesas rising all around. The cone-shaped sierra of Longs Peak lofted like a statue from a massive stone base, straight ahead in the west. The crown jewel of the northern Front Range, Longs poked its stony, snow-mantled thumb straight up to tickle the underbelly of the arching, cobalt sky.

Higher and higher the wagon rocked and rattled beside the flashing stream of Arapaho Creek, through autumn-yellow forests alive with birds, squirrels, chipmunks, and infrequent clumps of grazing mule deer. They were almost home, Irvin sleeping with his head resting against his father's side, when Cliff spied movement up the steep mountain slope ahead and left.

Cliff eased back on the reins. "Hoah, Jabber — hoahhh!"

As Irvin stirred beside him, Cliff frowned at the horseback riders filing down the side of the slope. One by one, they came — tall-riding men in fur coats or long dusters, horses outfitted with bedrolls and rifle scabbards. They galloped out of the yellow aspens crowning the ridge, plunging nearly straight down the mountain and into the valley in which the Circle Slash M Ranch lay.

There must have been nearly a half a dozen riders in all, heading somewhere in an awful damn hurry.

What on earth . . . ?

THIRTY-FOUR

Irvin sat up in the seat and fisted sleep from his eyes, yawning. "What is it, Pa?"

"Not sure, boy." Cliff stared off beyond the bluff straight ahead and behind which the last of the riders had just disappeared as they'd descended the mountain. They were now in the valley in which his own spread lay and at the head of which sat his own humble headquarters.

They had to be headed to his place. There was no other ranch or farm in this canyon, and no other settler at all since Old Man Crawford had closed up his silver mine and aimed his mule and his wagon for Montrose nearly a year ago.

Suddenly a sick feeling came over Cliff. His hands inside his wool-lined leather gloves grew spongy. The crew he'd just seen descend that slope had been a good half mile away from him, but they'd a hard-bitten air about them. And they'd all been carrying rifles in their saddle scabbards. Cliff had seen a good bit of steel flashing beneath a few of the men's coats as well.

Gunmen. Outlaws, possibly.

Absently, he lowered his right hand to his coat pocket. He shoved the pocket against his side, felt the lump of bills residing there . . .

"Hold on, Irvin!" Cliff shook the reins over Jabber's back. "Gidyup, Jabber — let's go, boy!"

The paint lunged up the trail, pulling the wagon around the left side of the bluff and then up and over a low hill. As the wagon lurched down the hill's opposite side, Cliff saw the prints where the riders had entered the trail and began following the trail in the direction of his ranch headquarters.

Sonja was likely cooking supper. Cliff had cut loose both his cowhands after the fall gather. Sonja would be in the house alone.

Anxiety caused Cliff's chest to heave as he again flipped the reins over the paint's back, urging more speed. The riders' dust hung in the air, churning ominously. As the wagon thundered along the trail, Cliff felt Irvin's anxious gaze on him. He turned and placed a calming hand on the boy's knee. "It's all right, son. Everything's going to be okay."

His voice must have betrayed his hammering fear of what was happening at the ranch, for the boy's brows beetled, a fearful cast entering his puzzled gaze, as he continued to stare up at his father.

The wagon continued to pound the trail for another mile. When they'd bounded over the second to last hill in the trail before reaching the ranch, Cliff slowed the wagon in the crease between that hill and the next. At the hill's bottom, he swung off the trail's right side and into the rocky dry wash that threaded the crease.

He pulled the wagon around a slight bulge in the forward hill, near some small, dead cottonwoods, and stopped and set the brake. He reached under the seat for the Winchester, set it in his lap, and peeled the blanket away.

"Irvin, I want you to stay here with the wagon, okay?"

"What's wrong, Pa?" Irvin's voice sounded wooden as he watched his father reach under the seat for the box of .44 shells. "Ma's all right, isn't she?"

"I'm sure she is, Son. I just want to make sure of it. I'm going to do that by walking into the ranch real slow-like. You know — like an Apache?"

"Like an Apache?"

Cliff was stuffing the cartridges through the Winchester's loading gate. "That's right. I'm probably being foolish, but I just want to check something out. You stay here with the wagon, understand?"

The boy's voice trembled. Tears shone in his eyes. "I wanna come with you, Pa!"

Cliff stopped loading the gun and squeezed his son's arm. "Irvin, you're my top hand now with Luke and Thomas gone. Top hands do what the boss tells them. If I need your help, I'll call for you later, understand?"

"Should I get out the old Spencer?"

"No, not yet," Cliff said, continuing to punch shells through the Winchester's receiver. "For now, you leave the Spencer under the seat. I'll let you know if I need you and the Spencer's help, all right?"

He looked at the boy, who was staring fearfully up the side of the gravel-strewn western bluff toward the ranch where he knew his mother was working alone.

"Understand, Irvin?" Cliff said, urgency in his voice.

Irvin nodded as he sleeved tears from his pale cheeks. "I understand, Pa."

"Go ahead and have some extra candy," Cliff told the boy as he leapt down from the wagon, landing with a grunt. "Remember, the canteen's under the seat, if you get thirsty."

Quickly, he worked the smooth cocking mechanism, seating a fresh shell in the Winchester's chamber. He off-cocked the hammer, glanced once more at his son sitting the wagon and squinting his eyes at him, cheeks bleached with fear.

"Don't worry — I'll be back soon!"

Cliff turned and crossed the trail and continued along the wash on the trail's opposite side, angling around the headquarters' southern perimeter. He knew every rock and prickly pear lining the wash, because he and Irvin often took target practice with rifles and pistols out here, and they often hunted the wash for rabbits and sage hens. He knew without having to see the house where it would be in relation to the wash. When he reached the place he'd been heading for, where a juniper stood on the wash's south side, he climbed the low, steep slope on his right.

Near the top, he slowed his pace until he was within two feet of the crest. He stopped, doffed his hat, and stretched a look over the brow of the slope.

The sun had gone down about a half hour ago, and blue shadows filled the yard though the sky was still filled with a slowly darkening green light. The barn and corral were straight out in front of Cliff, the rear of the barn facing him. The bunkhouse and two more corrals including the breaking corral lay to the right. To the left of the barn, on the yard's westernmost side, fronting Thunder Creek, stood the long, low-shake-shingled log cabin that Cliff had built when he and Sonja had moved out here nearly twelve years ago.

From this angle, Cliff could see the front and south side of the cabin. Smoke unfurled from the large stone chimney on the cabin's near side. But what Cliff was staring at as his heart tattooed a frantic rhythm in his ears were the half-dozen or more horses just now being led away from the cabin, toward a corral about fifty yards in front of Cliff.

The man leading the horses was tall, broad, and lumbering. Indian featured, he wore a bullet-crowned black hat and thigh-length fur coat with a brace of pistols and a large knife holstered on the outside. The cuffs of his black pants were shoved down into his knee-high Indian moccasins. Another knife handle jutted from the man's left moccasin top.

A man on the cabin's front veranda called, "Hey, Quiet Ed — bring the whiskey out of my saddlebags. Appears the woman might need her tongue loosened a little!"

Cliff dropped his head down beneath the brow of the slope. He pressed his cheek against the dirt and finely ground gravel, gritting his teeth. Fear threatened to overwhelm him. He looked at the rifle in his hands. It was shaking.

The canyon was so quiet that Cliff could hear each footfall of the horses being led to the corral. And he could hear with horrifying clarity the sharp crack of a hand meeting flesh that vaulted out from the cabin's open front door.

Sonja screamed shrilly. From inside the cabin rose the thump of what could only have been Cliff's wife hitting the floor.

Cliff drew a sharp, terrified breath.

He couldn't just lie here, his heart beating fast. He had to get to the cabin and help Sonja.

Cliff glanced over the brow of the slope. The Indian was leading the horses into the corral and beginning to unsaddle them, cursing and shaking his head, apparently not too happy with the task he'd been assigned.

Cliff pulled his head back down behind the hill, donned his hat, and quickly thought through his options. He didn't have many. All he could do was try to sneak up behind the cabin without being seen, and . . . then what?

He'd cross that bridge when he came to it.

Cliff dropped back down into the dry wash. He continued following it west. When the wash curved off to the left, where it met the stream farther south, he climbed out of it and crawled through the sagebrush, staying low, until he'd gained the pines along the stream. Now he was about fifty yards from the cabin's rear southwest corner.

He dropped to a knee, mopped his brow with a handkerchief. It was cool and getting colder as the sun continued to drop behind Longs Peak behind him now. He worried about Irvin. The boy was frail and didn't do well in the cold. But mostly Cliff's thoughts were with Sonja. There was no more noise issuing from the cabin, and that had him especially worried.

What were they doing to her? She was six months pregnant, for godsakes . . .

A couple of the windows facing him were dimly lit, and he could see occasional shadows passing in front of the lamps. He had to get to one of those windows and try to get a handle on how many, and what kind of men exactly, he was dealing with. Then, somehow, he and the Winchester would try to get the upper hand and get rid of them, hopefully without shooting.

Cliff surveyed the cabin once more. Then he snugged his hat down low on his forehead, wrapped both hands around the Winchester, and took off running through the brush, shrubs, and small trees that grew back here behind the house.

He ran to the privy and from there he cast another furtive look at the cabin. Seeing no one looking out the windows, he ran ahead and left to the back of the red-painted, peak-roofed woodshed that was about the size of a rich man's buggy shed.

When Cliff had caught his breath again, he sprinted the last thirty feet to the cabin's rear wall, between the back door and the window nearest the south wall. There were several corrugated tin washtubs out here that Sonja used for washing clothes, and he was careful not to kick one.

Cliff swallowed, drew a deep breath, trying to calm his nerves, and walked forward, ducking under the window. At the house's southwest corner, he paused again, looked around the corner toward the front. None of the hard cases appeared to be outside — at least not on this side of the cabin. The Indian was no longer inside the corral. The horses had gathered on the corral's east end, facing the yard, and were contentedly eating the hay in Cliff's crib. Their saddles were resting over the corral's top slap, near where the corral abutted the barn.

Cliff could hear voices behind the stout cabin wall. He could not hear Sonja's, however.

He quickly slipped around the cabin's rear corner and moved slowly along the wall. He ducked under the first window he came to. It was the window of Cliff's study and a curtain was drawn across it. He could hear no voices behind it, so he continued moving to the next window. He stopped, crouching at the edge of the window, and dropped his hat on the ground.

Staying low, he slid his head across the edge of the window frame until he could see past the curtain. A candle burned on the little table beside Cliff's rocking chair. A man sat in his chair — a rangy, blond-bearded man in a black opera hat and a long, black leather duster. He was rocking in the chair, hands on the scrolled mountain lion arms, as though it were his chair. As though it were his cabin. As though the pregnant woman working in the kitchen were his, too.

Sonja, her belly bulging behind her green-and-white-checked dress and apron, was chopping meat at the table on the other side of the cabin, beneath the light of the two lanterns hanging over the table from a stout log beam into which Cliff had scrolled his and Sonja's name after they were married, and then scrolled Irvin's name after the child was born here in the cabin, where the next one would be, as well. Two men sat at the near end of the same table that Sonja was working at, pots bubbling on the stove behind her. The two were playing two-handed poker. Another man sat in a chair beside the door. Sonja's cat, Lester, stood on the man's left thigh. Lester arched its back and curled its tail as the man patted the cat affectionately, grinning at it.

There were at least three other men scattered about the room, on the couch angled before the fireplace abutting the wall to Cliff's right, and in chairs — all lounging about, enjoying the fire and having a woman cooking for them, as though they owned the place.

Cliff had glanced over the inside of the cabin in less than five seconds, placing everyone, and now he jerked his head back and down beneath the sill. Through the wall, he could hear Sonja saying inside, ". . . Don't know where you got such a notion in the first place."

Cliff thought it was the man rocking in the chair who said, "Who else would he send it to?"

"I saw my father only once in my life, and like I told you before, we didn't get along. He knew how I felt about him and just to prove it, I sent that old outlaw packing. Never saw him again. So why would he send such a gift, as you call it, to his daughter who wanted nothing to with him?"

Cliff's heart beat faster. Shame and dread was a heavy weight in him. Again, his hands shook. He pressed his left shoulder against the cabin wall and tried hard not to throw his guts up.

What was he going to do? He was not a fighter. He was a rancher. He couldn't very well storm into the cabin and start shooting. Even if he had that kind of sand in him, he'd probably hit Sonja and the baby.

But then the dilemma was suddenly solved.

The round, cold steel maw of a pistol pressed against the back of his neck, and Cliff heard the ratcheting click of the hammering being drawn back.

An impossibly deep, guttural voice behind him said, "What you doin' out here? Your wife — she in there."

THIRTY-FIVE

Cliff turned his head slowly to look behind him.

The Indian stood there, tall as a barn door, keeping the pistol pressed up against the back of Cliff's neck. The Indian's face was like chiseled, black granite.

It suddenly cracked. The lips spread to reveal large, yellow teeth as the big man grinned wolfishly and held out his gloved right hand. Cliff looked at the new Winchester. Reluctantly, he handed it over to the tall Indian, who then pulled the pistol away from Cliff's neck and backed up a step.

He aimed the pistol at Cliff's face.

Cliff turned and walked slowly forward. Too slow for the Indian who gave him a savage shove that sent him into a stumbling run. He almost tripped over his own feet and fell, but he caught himself against the side of the cabin. He glanced back at the Indian, anger burning in him. But then the

Indian grinned again, and Cliff knew he was in trouble.

Deep trouble. And there was nothing he could do about it.

He walked around the cabin and onto the front veranda. He stopped in front of the door, hesitating, feeling like a Christian about to be thrown to the lions. The Indian gave him another shove that sent him flying against the door so hard that if it were not made of halved timbers he would have broken it down. He fumbled with the string latch, opened the door, and half fell inside until he got his feet under him.

The man sitting to the left of the door bounded to his feet and swung toward Cliff, reaching for the rifle that had been leaning against the wall behind him. The man loudly cocked the carbine as the others in the room all jerked to their feet or snapped their heads toward the open door.

The man in the chair right of the snapping hearth merely stopped rocking and turned his sober gaze toward Cliff as the Indian walked in behind him.

"Seen him from the barn," was all the Indian said in his low, rumbling voice.

"Cliff!" Sonja ran toward him from around the table, her brown eyes bright with beseeching. She stopped before him, clutching

434

at the front of his coat, tears glistening in her eyes as she said in a pinched voice, "These men think my father sent us money. Stolen money! I can't convince them he did no such *thing!*"

Cliff looked at the tall, blond-bearded man in the opera hat sitting in his, Cliff's, rocking chair. He looked at the others including the Indian standing behind him. "What's this?" Cliff said, manufacturing as much of a shocked expression as he could muster. "What . . . money . . . ?"

The tall, lanky man in the rocking chair crossed his long legs. "Boomer done told us about his family. The only one he had. Didn't know he had one till a year ago. Came for a visit. Told us about the place, almost braggin' like. He had him a good daughter married to a *good* man who had a ranch though he wasn't much good at it — ranchin'. They had 'em a boy. A *crippled* boy. Boomer's eyes done clouded up when he told about the boy."

Cliff's chest rose and fell sharply. He had an arm around Sonja's shoulders. He licked his dry lips and said over her head, "What makes you think he sent the money here?"

"What else would he do with it? Didn't have it on him. He probably took enough out for himself — an old man like that

435

wouldn't need much — and decided to lose the men he double-crossed in the mountains." The tall man rose slowly from the rocking chair. "Oh, I could be wrong." He walked toward Cliff, his brown eyes searing holes in Cliff's face. "You tell me I am truthful-like, an' I'll believe you. You tell me a lie, an' I'll see it. That's the way I am."

One of the other men — they were all standing now — snickered. "Keneally — he's got him a special way —"

Keneally turned his head sharply. "Shut up, Dayton!"

Sonja turned and looked up at Cliff. "Cliff, where's Irvin?"

It took a few seconds for the question to sink in. She'd seemed to ask it from a long ways away. Cliff said, "He's . . . I left him with the wagon . . ."

"It's cold outside." Sonja turned to the man called Keneally. "I have to fetch my boy. He's not well . . ."

Keneally looked at the big Indian standing statue-still in front of the door. "You fetch him, Ed."

"Make Bill go," the Indian said tonelessly. "I tend the horses." He jerked his chin toward the corral.

Keneally was still staring at Cliff with those wide, brown eyes. "Bill . . ."

"Shit," Bill said, walking out away from the table at which he and the other man had been playing two-handed poker. Bill glared at the Indian as he moved to the door.

As he opened the door, Keneally said, "Don't hurt him. We don't know if these people are lyin' . . . yet."

Bill chuckled, then opened the door and went out and drew the door closed behind him. Sonja sucked a sharp breath and glared at the tall, blond-bearded man in the opera hat. "We are not lying, and you leave my boy alone!"

"Shut up," Keneally said.

"Look," Cliff said, feeling cold sweat dribbling down the sides of his face. "You got it all wrong. You figured it wrong. This is a question you'd best leave up to Boomer Drago."

"Sit down. You, Mrs. Merriam, you keep makin' supper. The boys is hungry."

Sonja looked up at Cliff. Her eyes were sharp with worry. Slowly, she turned away from him and walked back into the kitchen where a stewpot was bubbling on the range, filling the tense air with the pepper-and-onion smell of beef stew.

Keneally continued holding his gaze on Cliff. "Sit down."

Cliff sat down in the chair at the table opposite the door. The chair squawked slightly beneath him. He looked up at Keneally, his mind racing. His mind was a stubborn thing that seemed almost apart from the rest of him. It had wrapped itself so tightly around the money that it would not let go. Heavenly Jesus — forty thousand dollars. He hadn't told Sonja, because she would not have let him keep it. She would have had him take it to the sheriff in Longmont.

Forty thousand dollars!

That much money could get them through two years, help Cliff build up his herd with blooded stock, pay for the surgery that Irvin needed . . .

Why wouldn't these men just accept his lie and go?

Cliff's mind screamed its frustration between his ears. Why did everything have to be so hard?

"Where is it?" Keneally said, standing over him, clenching his fists at his sides.

Cliff looked up at the tall man, cleared his throat. His tongue felt swollen. He shook his head. "I haven't seen no money. You got it wrong. Please, won't you just go and let my family be?" He almost sobbed that last.

Keneally drew a deep breath. "You're lyin' to me, Mr. Merriam."

His right hand closed over the handle of one of the three Colts he wore on his waist. His thumb clicked the keeper thong free from the hammer. He lifted the pistol from its holster with a snicking sound of steel against leather. Holding the pistol near his waist, he turned the barrel toward Sonja's pregnant belly and clicked the hammer back.

Sonja gasped and stepped from the table, pressing her flour-caked hands to her belly.

"Once more," Keneally said, "where is the money, Mr. Merriam?"

Cliff stared in horror at the cocked gun aimed at his wife's belly. The fist of his mind opened. He dropped his gaze to the floor and said in a hollow voice rife with shame, "The barn."

Cliff felt Sonja turned her stricken gaze to him. It was like a hot branding iron pressed against his cheek.

Outside, a gun blasted.

Sonja screamed and pressed her fists to her temples, staring in horror at the door.

"No!" The shout exploded from Cliff's lips as he bounded up out of the chair and rammed his head and shoulders into the tall man's belly. As Keneally flew backward off his heels, the outlaw's Colt exploded, stabbing smoke and flames over the table.

Sonja screamed again. It was a strangled, agonized cry. The cry died in Cliff's ears as the gun butt was smashed down hard against the back of his head, and darkness engulfed him.

Sitting in the wagon, holding a blanket around his shoulders, Irvin looked toward the brow of the hill rising above the wash on his left. The night was quiet. It had gotten dark, stars kindling in the sky that had only a little lilac left in it.

Coyotes yammered in the canyon behind Irvin. From the direction of the ranch yard, boots were crunching gravel. The crunching sounds grew gradually louder. The man was heading toward Irvin.

Irvin widened his eyes. Was his father, having taken care of whatever trouble he'd thought was occurring at the cabin, coming toward him?

Irvin called tentatively, "Pa?"

The only response was the continued, rhythmic crunching of the boots and the faint jangle of spurs.

Irvin called a little louder, "Pa?"

But he closed his mouth suddenly when he remembered that his father had not been wearing spurs. He'd had no use for spurs today, because he'd been driving a wagon not riding a horse.

Irvin's heart quickened as he listened to the footsteps growing louder. They were coming from the direction of the trail off behind the wagon and on down the canyon. The man who was not his father would come down the trail and see Irvin in the wagon.

The boy lurched into motion, pushing up out of his seat, and then turned and lowered the foot of his good leg to the small iron step bolted to the side of the wagon, beside the top of the iron-shod wheel. Irvin put all his weight on that foot and then slid his bad leg that would not bend because of the steel cage over his knee off and down over the side of the wagon. He let it hang there for a second before he released his hold on the spring seat and dropped straight down to the ground.

He landed with a thump and a grunt and fell on his butt.

The footsteps were growing even louder as was the jangling of the man's spurs. Then a man's voice overlaid the other sounds: "Kid?"

Irvin gasped.

"Kid, you out here? Your pa sent me to fetch you." The man chuckled. "Him an' your ma are in real hot water, and that means you are, too."

The man laughed again.

Irvin looked at the blanket-wrapped Spencer repeater beneath the wagon seat. As the footsteps continued growing louder, until Irvin could tell that the man was at the top of the slope and starting down into the wash, he pushed himself to his feet, threw himself forward against the side of the wagon, and reached up to grab the rifle.

He slid the blanketed bundle out from beneath the seat, quickly shed the blanket, shuffled backward a step, and half fell to a sitting position on a rock. Quickly, he set the rifle across his lap and used the trigger guard cocking mechanism to slide a cartridge into the old rifle's chamber.

He hauled the heavy hammer back, and raised the rifle to his shoulder. It was a heavy weapon but Irvin had held and fired it before countless times because, while he was a cripple, his father never treated him like one. A boy his age should know how to shoot, and his father had taught him well.

Seated on the rock and aiming the gun along the wash that was a wide, pale line in the growing darkness, toward the trail, he drew a slow, deep breath to steady his nerves. A shadow was coming down the trail, dropping toward the wash. There was still enough light that Irvin could see the man had his head turned toward him.

"Kid? Say, kid, get your ass over here!"

The man slanted away from the trail into the wash. He was carrying a rifle down low by his side. He hadn't seen Irvin sitting on the rock beside the wagon, but he must have seen him now, aiming the rifle at him.

He stopped with a start. "Why, you little . . .!"

The Spencer leapt and roared in Irvin's hands.

The man-shaped silhouette sort of crouched with a grunt and stumbled two steps back, slapping a hand to his side.

Got him!

"Why . . . you little devil!" the man shouted hoarsely five seconds later, when he realized he'd been shot. He bolted into a run toward Irvin.

The boy screamed and dropped the rifle, slid down off the rock, and tried to run, but of course he couldn't run. Not with the six pounds of steel encasing his right leg. All he could do was sob and drag the leg past the paint that was nickering and prancing in its traces, and head off down the wash as fast as he could, which was maddeningly slow. He could hear the man closing on him fast, running full out, boots pounding the short grass and gravel, spurs jingling.

The man closing on him shouted, "I'm gonna cut your tongue out and wear it around my neck, you little devil!"

The man was so close on Irvin now that the boy could smell the man's horse and sweat fetor. In the corner of his eye, he saw the man reach for his collar, and Irvin screamed and ducked away from the man, and fell.

"Gotcha!" the man bellowed through clenched teeth a half second before a gun thundered along the draw's east bank.

Irvin had seen the flash. The echo of the blast rocketed skyward, the echo growing quieter and quieter until the stars seemed to suck it up and swallow it. Irvin saw his attacker stumble away from him — a tall shadow in the darkness. The man dragged his boot toes, clutching the side of his neck with one hand, until he dropped to his knees with a groan and fell on his face.

Irvin looked toward the opposite bank. Three silhouetted figures sat three horses there, one of the riders still aiming a pistol propped on his opposite forearm. There was enough light in the sky behind the shooter that Irvin could see smoke curling from the gun barrel.

"Damn, that's some awful nice pistol

work, Spurr!" said one of the other riders, who slapped his horse's rump with his rein ends and rode down the slope and into the wash.

Irvin stared, dumbfounded, as the man climbed with the heaviness and grunting of an old man down from his saddle and dropped to a knee beside him, muttering, "Oh, god — what have I done?"

He placed his hand around the boy's arm. "Irvin, is that you, boy? I'm your grandfather, and everything's gonna be just fine!"

THIRTY-SIX

Spurr swung down from the back of his rented horse. Greta did the same, and they both scrambled down the side of the slope and into the draw.

"Where's your, Pa, Irvin?" Drago asked the boy, who stared incredulously, still a little fearful, at his grandfather, shifting his gaze to Spurr and Greta.

"It's okay, son," Greta said, dropping to a knee beside Boomer and placing a hand on the boy's right knee. "We're here to help."

"Who . . . who are they?" Irvin asked, flicking his gaze between Boomer and the strangers.

"Bad men," Greta said. "Very bad men. But we're going to . . . settle things . . ."

Again, Boomer asked his grandson where his father was.

"He went around that way," Irvin said, nodding in the direction of the trail.

"He followed the wash around the ranch

yard?" Drago asked.

Irvin nodded.

"How long ago?" Spurr asked the boy.

Irvin hiked a shoulder. "Half hour ago, maybe."

Spurr turned to Greta. "Will you stay with the boy?"

"Only if you . . ." She glanced at Irvin, who was watching her closely, obviously surprised to find a girl out here — especially one so pretty.

Dropping her voice, Greta slid a breeze-blown lock of hair away from her cheek, and said, ". . . Give me a shot at him. I want one last shot at him. You know who."

Spurr smiled grimly. "If we can, you got it."

Drago said, "Irvin, this nice lady is Greta. She's gonna stay with you while me an' Spurr go lend your ma and pa a helpin' hand. You stay here with Greta, all right? This should all be over soon. When it is, we'll come and fetch you back to the cabin where you belong. All right?"

The boy swallowed, his eyes worried as he stared at his grandfather. "All right. I reckon."

Spurr straightened, as did Boomer. The old outlaw picked up the dead man's rifle, worked the cocking lever, and then looked at Spurr, who glanced down at Greta and then at Drago and nodded. He walked off down the draw toward the trail, and Boomer followed, holding the rifle down low by his side.

When they reached the trail, Spurr paused and stared at where the trail climbed the rise into the ranch yard. From here he couldn't see over the brow of the hill and into the yard. The cabin was out of sight.

"The men in the cabin probably heard them shots," Spurr said, running the sleeve of his coat across his mouth. "We'd best assume Keneally sent someone to check it out."

"Oh, he will."

"How far back's the cabin?"

"About a hundred yards."

"How much cover between the top of the hill and the cabin?"

"There's a barn and corral on the left, some small shrubs. On the right there's a pole barn for hay and a little shack that Cliff uses for a blacksmith shop though he ain't much of a blacksmith." Boomer gave a wry chuckle.

"All right. I'll keep to the left. You keep to the right." Spurr started walking up the hill, half crouching, holding his Starr in one hand, the Schofield in his other hand. "We'll approach the cabin slow . . ."

"And then what?"

"We'll cross that bridge when we come to it."

Boomer walked beside Spurr also crouching, chin held up to get a look over the brow of the hill. Keeping his voice low, just above a whisper, Drago said, "If I got my daughter killed because I sent that loot, I'm gonna want you to drill a bullet through my fuckin' head, Spurr."

"No problem at all, amigo."

Spurr kept walking until he could see up into the ranch yard, and then he stopped. Two men were moving toward him and Drago — two slightly jostling shadows against the cabin's lit windows behind them.

Spurr whistled under his breath, jerked his chin toward the cabin on the far side of the yard. At the same time, he and Drago bounded to opposite sides of the trail. They hunkered down in the brush at nearly the same place the trail dropped down over the side of the hill toward the wash.

Spurr doffed his hat as he crouched behind a small boulder sheathed in buffalo grass and a spindly sage plant. The two shadows were moving between the barn on the left and the blacksmith shop on the right, the windmill a little behind them and right.

Spurr looked toward where he'd last seen Drago. He couldn't see the outlaw now, which was good. The man was hunkered down as low as Spurr, who slid his gaze back toward the two men sauntering toward them. Starlight winked off the rifles in their hands and off the silver trimmings that the man on the right wore on his cartridge belt and holsters.

Behind them, the cabin hunched long and low, gray smoke rising from the stone chimney on the cabin's left side.

One of the men stopped in the yard, and Spurr dropped his head even farther, until he could no longer see the pair through the grass. "Hey, Avrial — you out here?"

The outlaw's call echoed briefly around the yard.

Spurr inched his head up until he could see the two shadows stopped in the yard about halfway between Spurr and the cabin. One was a little ahead of the other. Both cradled rifles in their arms as they looked around.

"Avrial?" the other man called. His voice was a little higher pitched than the other's. "Hey, Avrial!" he said again, pitching his voice with impatience.

On Spurr's right, a low, rasping voice said, "Pssst! Over here, fellas!"

Spurr stared at the two in the yard. They looked at each other and then they started walking again, moving toward where the trail started dropping down the hill but angling slightly toward Boomer.

Spurr opened his mouth to breathe as quietly as possible. He squeezed the handles of the pistols in his hands, gloved thumbs caressing the hammers. He could hear the footsteps of the approaching men, the faint trilling of their spurs. One kicked a rock. It thumped as it rolled.

"What you got there, Avrial?" one of the two called as they drew within twenty feet of where Spurr assumed Boomer was.

They each took two more steps and then they stopped. At the same time, they began taking their rifles in their hands.

The one with the silver trimming said, "Avrial, what in the hell . . . ?"

Spurr raised his Starr above the weeds. Starlight must have glinted off the barrel, because the man on the left jerked his head toward him, yelling, "Hey!"

Spurr's Starr flashed and roared.

A half a wink later, Drago's rifle blasted.

Through his own wafting powder smoke, Spurr watched both men stumble backward and away from each other. The man with the silver trimmings dropped his rifle. The other man was trying to regain his balance and swing his rifle toward Spurr, who popped off three more shots and watched the man stumble backward and dance in two quick circles before falling in a heap. As Drago's rifle crashed twice, lapping flames about thirty feet off to Spurr's right, the man with the silver trimmings was blown up off his heels and straight back to hit the ground with a hard smack.

He gave a ragged groan. He lifted his hatless head and then let it fall back to the ground. Spurr could see both men jerking on the ground as they died. A rifle lay against the left boot of the man he'd killed. He needed a long gun bad . . .

Before Spurr realized what he was doing, he took off running toward the dead men, Drago rasping behind him, "Get back here, you crazy coon!"

Almost simultaneously, there was a blast in each of the two front cabin windows, one on each side of the door. Then the door opened, and Spurr saw a murky shadow standing there, and then the doorway filled with the bright orange flash of the rifle in the man's hands.

The slugs tore up the ground around

Spurr as he headed for the brush where Drago was crouched, because it was closer than his own original perch. The rifles yammered behind him. The slugs spanged off rocks around him, pluming dust and rustling the brush. When Spurr saw Drago crouched behind a low pile of weathered lumber, he dove forward and rolled twice down the slope behind the old outlaw.

"Christ!" Drago raked out over his right shoulder, his lone eye bright in the starlight.

Several yards behind Drago, Spurr grunted and sat up. He'd dropped the rifle but now he picked it up and rested it across his thighs. "I'll be damned!" he said in amazement. "It's my old '66!"

"Shut up, fool!" Drago shouted, ducking low behind the lumber and looking down the slope at Spurr. "You gone loco?"

"I reckon so. Ow!" Spurr winced and released the rifle to clutch his left shoulder, which he'd set to yapping during his impersonation of a much younger man.

"Serves ya right!"

Spurr sucked back the pain in his shoulder, noticing that his knees and ribs were barking now, too, and crawled back up to where Drago hunkered behind the three-foot-high pile of lumber. The shooting from the cabin had stopped. A menacing silence had replaced it.

Spurr wondered how many of Drago's old gang were left. If he'd counted right, probably four. Those were better odds than seven against two, but Keneally's men had a definite advantage, forted up as they were with Drago's daughter.

As if to corroborate his estimation of the predicament, a woman's sharp, brief cry sounded from the cabin. The outlaws had blown out the lamps; the cabin was dark except for starlight reflecting off the shake-shingled roof. The only movement was the smoke rising from the chimney.

The woman groaned inside the cabin. Nerves pinched the skin along Spurr's spine. Drago sucked a sharp breath and shouted angrily, "You better not hurt her, Keneally! You lay one hand on her —"

"That you, Boomer?" Keneally called from the dark cabin. The outlaw laughed. "Had a feelin' it was you. I reckon you know who we got in here."

Boomer looked at Spurr. Sweat shone on him. Several beads rolled down from beneath the band of his eye patch. He anxiously drummed his fingers against the forestock of the rifle in his hands.

The woman groaned again, and Boomer jerked his fiery-eyed gaze toward the cabin, gritting his teeth. He rested his rifle over the top of the lumber pile.

"I s'pose you know she's got a bun in the oven, Boomer!" Keneally's jeering voice echoed. He hadn't shouted it, but the night was so quiet, the air so light, that it had carried like a shout. "She's in a very delicate condition. So easily harmed — her *and* the child!"

The woman groaned again, louder. Spurr saw a shadow in the doorway atop the veranda. Two shadows. Keneally was just outside the open front door, holding the woman before him. A whole head shorter than the outlaw leader, she appeared to have her arms pinned behind her back. Keneally held a rifle in his free hand, straight up in the air.

"I'll exchange her for you, Boomer. Come on in!"

The girl said through a hard sob, "Don't do it, Boomer! Don't do it!" She squealed and stumbled sideways, and then Keneally slapped the side of her head, and she dropped to the porch floor with a thump.

Boomer jerked his head up, grinding his teeth. "I'm comin'."

Spurr shook his head slowly. Dread was a living, writhing snake in his belly. "He'll kill you both, Boomer."

"Hurry up, Boomer!" Keneally shouted. "I'm gettin' so frustrated I'm liable to kick this poor woman in her belly!"

Boomer jerked another look at Spurr. "I don't think he knows you're out here. He thinks I came alone."

Spurr had been getting the same impression. He nodded slowly, holding the rear stock of his prized Winchester taut against his side. He was hunkered as low as he could get without pressing his face flat to the ground.

"All right," Spurr said, working out a plan. "All right, you go on ahead. I'll work around."

"Be careful," Boomer whispered, staring toward the cabin again. "Be damn careful. I don't care if he kills me, but he kills my girl . . ."

"You're a damn fool, Boomer." Spurr looked at him. "But we'll get them sons o' bitches if it kills us both. Now, haul your raggedy ass!"

THIRTY-SEVEN

"I'm comin'!" Drago shouted at the cabin.

Spurr stayed low as Boomer rose from behind the lumber pile and began making his way through the brush and into the yard.

"Throw the rifle down!" Keneally called.

Boomer tossed the rifle away and kept walking toward the cabin. As his figure diminished and became a shadow in the cool, starry night, Spurr back-scuttled lower on the slope and then, when he was sure he was out of sight from the cabin, began running along the side of the slope toward the north.

He aimed to skirt around the yard's north side, using the pines and scattered buildings and the windmill for cover, until he could swing back toward the cabin and take Keneally and the three other remaining gang members by surprise.

When he'd reached the blacksmith cabin, he edged a look around the front corner.

Drago was within twenty feet of the house, walking slowly, hands held chest high, palms out. Keneally remained on the porch, three steps up from the yard, Drago's daughter crumpled at his feet.

Spurr pulled his head back behind the blacksmith cabin and then jogged, breathing hard, down the side of the log building and around it. In the darkness, he didn't see an empty barrel sitting snug against the building's back wall, and rammed into it, knocking it over and falling on top of it. He snapped out a curse as he rolled off the barrel to the ground.

Wheezing, he gained his knees and sucked a sharp breath. He pricked his ears, listening for any indication from the cabin that the outlaws had heard him.

"Damn fool." Spurr reached through his coat and into his shirt pocket for his pouch of nitro tablets. He shook one into his hand, popped it into his mouth, and rolled it beneath his tongue. "Should have gotten out of this work five years ago, when you still had enough health left to enjoy yourself with the senoritas down in Mexico. Shit, them girls get one look at your old sack of bones now, they're liable to die laughin'!"

He returned the pouch to his shirt pocket, heaved himself to his feet, his knees and ankles popping like an old wooden chair, and set off once more, heading in the general direction of the cabin.

He didn't have much time. Keneally was likely to start pumping Drago full of lead at any second. Spurr didn't know why that mattered to him, but it did.

At the far side of the smithy shop, he cast another glance toward the cabin. No one was outside. The front door was closed. Lamps had been lit. The glow washed through the front windows.

Shouting rose from inside. Spurr could hear Keneally's voice drowning out Drago's.

Spurr ran out from behind the privy. He covered the twenty feet at a crouch, breaths rasping in and out of his lungs, cold sweat drenching him. He ducked down behind the windmill's stone stock tank, surveyed the cabin once more, and then ran from the stock tank to the cabin's north wall.

"Please, don't hurt him!" Drago's daughter said inside. "He did a foolish thing but he only did it to help me an' my family!" She sobbed that last, her voice breaking and quaking.

There was a grunt and a thump as a body hit the floor.

Spurr's old heart chugged. Cold sweat

dribbled down his cheeks, drenching his beard. Strands of his grizzled hair hung in his face. He raked it away from his eyes and sidled up to a window. A curtain had been pulled over the glass, but it was thin enough that Spurr could see inside.

Drago was on his knees. Keneally and the other three men stood around him. One was just then drawing his leg back from a kick. Seeing that bit into Spurr like a war hatchet, fueling his rage.

They were going to kick the old man to death in front of his daughter, who sat on the floor near the kitchen table, hands on her swollen stomach, her back against a ceiling post. Her lips were bleeding. Another man whom Spurr assumed was Sonja's husband lay beside her on the floor. He lay on his side, unmoving. Blood shone brightly behind his left ear, matting the hair at the back of his head.

"Well, that'll be enough o' that," Spurr groused as he ducked under the window and ran toward the back of the cabin. He hoped there was a back door. The outlaws were so close to the front that they'd likely hear him if he mounted the porch.

"Think you can steal from us and get away with it?" one of the tough nuts was shouting furiously.

There was another sharp grunt and a groan as a boot hit its mark.

The woman screamed, *"Stop!"*

Spurr turned the cabin's rear corner and was relieved to see that there was a back door. Now, if only it wasn't locked. He stopped in the bald depression fronting the door, where a slender trail led off to both a privy and a woodshed. The door had a string latch, and the string was on the outside, thank god.

Spurr gently tripped it. The latching bolt sprung free and the door hiccupped as it jerked toward Spurr, scraping lightly against the jamb. Slowly, biting his lower lip, Spurr swung the door half open. Ahead lay a dim hall that stretched for fifteen feet between curtained doorways before opening into what must have been the main part of the cabin, because there was light in it. Spurr could hear sharp, loud voices and the woman's sobs.

Drago was groaning. He sounded like a heifer in labor. They were beating him up pretty good.

Spurr squeezed the old Winchester in both hands and gently clicked the hammer back as he moved quietly through the dim hall toward the lighted main room.

"He's done," said one of the hard cases

461

ahead of Spurr. They were still gathered around Drago, in front of the front door and to the right, Drago's daughter and unconscious son-in-law slumped toward the left. "I do believe it's time to finish him and fetch the loot."

Keneally, standing over Boomer in front of the door, aimed a pistol at the old outlaw sprawled before him.

The other two men surrounding Drago were passing a bottle.

Spurr stopped at the mouth of the hall, dread tickling his insides.

He could see only three outlaws. Through the window, he'd seen four men standing around Boomer. A gun clicked to his right. He turned his head slightly to see a cocked revolver sliding out through a curtained doorway.

The curtain was jerked back to reveal the grinning, rough-hewn features of the big Indian, Quiet Ed, who stood half a head taller than Spurr. His long, greasy black hair hung to his shoulders.

In the main room, the other outlaws laughed.

Keneally said, "You think we didn't see you in the window, old man?" The blond-bearded man in the black opera hat slid his smiling, green-eyed gaze to Quiet Ed standing in the doorway behind Spurr and to the old lawman's right. "Drill him."

A fierce bellow rose from the main room. Spurr bounded straight back as Quiet Ed's pistol exploded. The slug carved a burning line across Spurr's forehead. Pivoting, Spurr rammed the butt of his rifle into the big man's belly.

Quiet Ed grumbled as he bent forward at the waist. Hearing commotion in the main room and seeing wild movement in the corner of his left eye, Spurr rammed his Winchester butt against the top of Quiet Ed's head and then as the big Indian stumbled back into the room behind him, Spurr shot him twice in the chest.

Quiet Ed's pistol had already set up a loud ringing in Spurr's right ear. His own loud blasts had deafened him as well as peppered his nose with the rotten-egg smell of gunpowder.

It had also wrapped him in a haze of gray smoke through which he could see Drago standing with Keneally against the cabin's front wall, knocking pictures off their nails.

Boomer was hammering the big, lantern-jawed outlaw with both fists and raging like a wounded grizzly while his daughter screamed and the other two outlaws bounded toward Boomer. One was just then about to ram the butt of his raised pistol across Drago's head.

Seeing the frenzied movements ahead of him but hearing nothing but the high-pitched screaming in his head, Spurr aimed quickly and drilled a round through the side of Avrial Farmer. The bullet whipped the man around, pressing him back against the wall made bloody by the exiting slug, right of where Drago struggled with Keneally.

As Farmer dropped straight down to his knees, head wobbling and eyes already dead, Spurr stepped instinctively to his right, near the popping hearth. The movement saved his life, because the bullet fired by the other outlaw, Harry McClerk, screeched past Spurr to thump into the doorframe of the room in which Quiet Ed was dying.

Careful not to hit Sonja, Spurr pumped two rounds into McClerk's chest and belly, and while that outlaw fell over a kitchen chair, bellowing loudly, Spurr turned to Drago just as Keneally rammed the butt of his pistol across the old outlaw's jaw.

Boomer yelped and flew back into the cabin's sitting area, hitting the floor loudly.

Keneally turned toward Spurr, swinging his revolver toward the old lawman, who dropped to a knee and fired. The rifle's thunder rocked the cabin. The slug punched Keneally back into the door with a shrill curse.

As Spurr pumped another round into the Winchester's breech and prepared to drill Keneally once more, Boomer bounded off his heels and into the blond outlaw leader, and they rolled down the wall toward the kitchen, Boomer slugging the man with both fists.

Spurr shouted, "Goddamnit, Boomer, get the hell out of the way!"

By now, Sonja lay over her husband, who appeared to be conscious and trying to push up off the floor. She shoved him back down, sticking her fingers in her ears against the gun blasts.

Spurr ran around them to get them out of the line of fire, and as he did, Keneally punched Boomer in the jaw. Drago stumbled backward, tripped over the dead man, and fell into the table.

Cupping a hand to his wounded shoulder, Keneally swung toward the door. Spurr triggered the Winchester, but his slug struck the edge of the door as Keneally jerked it open and then ran outside.

Spurr bolted forward, slipped in a thick pool of blood, and dropped to his left knee with a curse. He pushed up off that knee, threw the door wide, and ran out onto the porch, aiming the Winchester straight out from his right hip.

"Hold it!" he shouted.

He eased the tension on his trigger finger. Keneally stood only a few feet out from the bottom of the porch steps, facing the night. He was a tall, broad shadow in the darkness.

In the sudden silence and beneath the ringing in his ears, Spurr heard the outlaw say, "Ah, shit — it's you."

He appeared to be looking down at something or someone in front of him.

Keneally's voice was brittle as he raised his hands and, backing toward the porch, said, "Wait, now, you little bitch — just you *wait!*"

Pop!

Keneally jerked his shoulders.

There was another pop, and Keneally jerked his shoulders again. As he stumbled backward and piled up on his back on the porch's three steps, Spurr saw Greta standing in the yard, holding the new, smoking Winchester straight out from her waist.

Keneally lay writhing on the steps, kicking his feet and making his spurs ring. Greta walked toward him, lowering the carbine slightly to keep it aimed at the outlaw.

Keneally stopped writhing and looked up at her. He convulsed, sobbed, and screamed, "You two-peso whore!"

Greta smiled as she aimed the pistol at the man's head. "Nope. Considerably more than that, and I'm about to extract it from your hide, you ugly bastard."

The Winchester popped, stabbing flames at Keneally's head, which jerked back sharply and bounced off the edge of the porch's top step before the man swung sideways and rolled down to the yard.

Greta lowered the rifle and stood staring at the dead man before her.

Behind Spurr, footsteps sounded beneath the slow-dying ringing in his ears. He turned to see Boomer walk slowly through the doorway, a revolver in his hand. The old outlaw, beaten and bloody but with a stalwart light in his eye, stopped beside Spurr and looked down at Keneally.

He sighed. "Well, hell."

He smiled at Greta, winked. Then he turned and walked back into the cabin where Sonja was helping her husband to his feet.

Spurr walked into the yard, stepped over Keneally's inert body, and took Greta into his arms. She pressed her face to his chest and cried.

EPILOGUE

A week later, Spurr reined Cochise to a halt on a low bluff overlooking his cabin on the slopes of Mount Rosalie. He reached forward and patted the horse's sleek neck, glad to be astraddle his old friend and trail partner again.

He'd been thrilled when, after the dustup at the Merriam place near Longmont, he'd found Cochise fit as a fiddle in the Merriam's corral. Apparently one of the outlaws, probably Keneally himself, had appropriated the fine roan stallion.

Keneally might have been a no-good scoundrel, but he'd known good horseflesh when he'd seen it — Spurr would give him that.

Spurr had left Boomer Drago with the old outlaw's daughter and son-in-law. Sonja and Cliff Merriam had agreed to take him in and provide a home for the old wolf. Despite the trouble he'd caused by sending them the stolen bank loot, they'd realized he'd only done it to help their family and to provide for their crippled boy, Irvin.

Spurr had ridden away with the loot — or what had been left of it after Cliff Merriam had spent some of it, which, under the circumstances, no one could blame him for.

But Spurr had left the family with Drago and that, Spurr thought now, chuckling, wasn't much of an exchange for them. But when Spurr and Greta had ridden out of the yard the next day following the shoot-out, Drago had been sitting on the porch with his grandson, filling the kid's ears with the start of what would likely be one of many long windies to come.

So Irvin had gotten a grandfather out of the deal, and by the wide-eyed, admiring look on the child's face, he'd thought that was a fine exchange, indeed . . .

Now Spurr sat Cochise atop the bluff and stared down at his old, weather-silvered log cabin and the stable and privy flanking the humble place. Mount Rosalie was a vast cone rising atop a broad evergreen plateau behind the cabin, to the west, draped in the ermine of the recent snowfall.

Several feet had fallen on those higher slopes. Down here, a foot now mantled the slopes with here and there a patch of sage spiking through. The snow drooped down over the roof of Spurr's cabin. Icicles that had been nurtured by the sun earlier in the day now hung from the eaves, frozen up solid again in the wake of the sun's recent colorful plunge down the backside of Rosalie.

Spurr's breath steamed the air around him. It was a cold, gray world out here, growing darker by the second. It would get colder and grayer the farther he tumbled into winter, living out here alone with only his dog though he couldn't see the mutt anywhere around.

Maybe Dawg had run off to warmer climes.

Spurr had turned in his badge earlier that day. And he and Henry Brackett had had a glass of brandy and a cigar together. And that had been it.

A lonely ache spiked through Spurr now as he stared down at the quiet cabin. All the crazy, wild, colorful years had come to this — a withered old man sitting out here in the cold winter twilight staring at a weathered old mountain cabin little larger than a whore's crib, dark and quiet as the grave.

"Should have gone to Mexico."

Too late for that now. Too late in the year. Too cold to make the trip. He'd live up here for the winter. If he was alive come spring, he'd figure out something else.

Most likely, he wouldn't have to worry about that, he thought now, noting the iron crab in his chest that each day seemed to be chomping a little harder on his ticker.

He looked at Mount Rosalie, quickly losing the last of the thin salmon rays cast by the dying sun, and then shuttled his gaze down those lonely slopes to his cabin once more. Faint lines dug into the dark brown bridge of his nose as he gazed at what appeared to be thin gray tendrils rising from his stone chimney to unfurl against the darkening sky.

Smoke? How could that be? He'd headed for Denver early that morning to turn in his badge and the stolen money. By now, his morning fire should have burned down to cold gray ashes.

An umber light flickered to life in the cabin's front windows, setting a muscle to twitching in Spurr's right cheek.

Someone was inside.

He reached over and slid his Winchester '66 from his saddle boot, cocking the rifle one-handed. The cabin door opened with a squawk, and he looked down at the hovel to see a slender female figure in a form-fitting cream dress step outside, holding a lantern.

"Spurr?" Greta called, canting her head to one side, staring up the slope. A dog yodeled inside the cabin and then came running out into the yard, barking. Dawg looked toward Spurr and then gave a yip and bolted up the side of the bluff, sprinting full out, whimpering happily, in Spurr's direction.

Spurr slid the rifle back into its boot and gigged the horse on down the slope. Dawg ran up to meet the old lawman, barking a delighted greeting and wildly wagging his tail. The mutt swung around to run along beside Spurr and Cochise as they dropped down into the yard.

Spurr reined up in front of the porch and stared down at the girl staring up at him, smiling and holding the lantern. She looked clean and fresh. She'd piled her hair atop her head, leaving a few delicate curls to dangle down along her smooth cheeks.

Spurr was incredulous. Two days ago, he'd put her on the train to Cheyenne, where she'd intended to look for work. What most folks would call "decent" work.

"What on earth," Spurr said, his tone belying the rapid, delighted skipping of his heart.

Greta hiked a shoulder and looked around. "I don't know, Spurr. I got to Cheyenne and I was so damn lonesome without you, all I could do was cry. So I bought a ticket and came back." She looked up at him again. "You don't mind, do you?"

Spurr just stared down at her, puzzled.

"I figured you're alone . . . and I'm alone. The least we could do was keep each other company over the winter." Greta smiled down at Dawg who sat near her, staring up at her and wagging his tail. "Your dog likes me. At least, he liked the stew bones I just fed him."

Spurr swung heavily out of the saddle, dropped the reins, walked up to Greta, and placed his hands on her shoulders. "Girl, you got better things to do than spend a winter up here in this godforsaken place with a tired old man with a run-down ticker."

She sucked her lips in and shook her head. "Not really, no."

"I'm three times your age."

"You're younger than you think you are. And I'm older than you think I am."

"I may not make it through the winter."

She nodded, blinked. "Me, neither."

Spurr looked at the open door. Inside, flames danced in the hearth. "God, somethin' smells good."

"I got beef stew cookin'. You tend Cochise, and we'll have a whiskey together in front of the fire, and then we'll eat and curl each other's toes." She smiled up at him devilishly from beneath her brows. "What do you say?"

Spurr took Greta in his arms and kissed her long and hard. He gave her rump a playful swat as she strode back into the cabin to pour the whiskey. She winked at him before she closed the door.

And the man who walked his horse around the cabin to the stable, his dog barking after him, was about thirty years younger than the one who'd ridden into the yard only a few minutes earlier.

"Fellas, here's all I got to say about the recent turn of events," Spurr said to his horse and Dawg as he approached the stable, moccasins crunching the new-fallen snow. "To hell with Mexico."

ABOUT THE AUTHOR

Peter Brandvold has penned over seventy fast-action western novels under his own name and his pen name, **Frank Leslie**. He is the author of the ever-popular .45-Caliber books featuring Cuno Massey as well as the Ben Stillman, Rogue Lawman, Lou Prophet, and Yakima Henry novels. He wrote the horror-western novel, *Dust of the Damned,* featuring ghoul hunter Uriah Zane. Head honcho at Mean Pete Press, publisher of harrowing western and horror ebooks, novellas, and stories, he lives in Colorado with his dogs. Visit his website at www.peterbrandvold.com. Follow his blog at www.peterbrandvold.blogspot.com.

The employees of Thorndike Press hope you have enjoyed this Large Print book. All our Thorndike, Wheeler, and Kennebec Large Print titles are designed for easy reading, and all our books are made to last. Other Thorndike Press Large Print books are available at your library, through selected bookstores, or directly from us.

For information about titles, please call:
(800) 223-1244

or visit our Web site at:
http://gale.cengage.com/thorndike

To share your comments, please write:
Publisher
Thorndike Press
10 Water St., Suite 310
Waterville, ME 04901